SCAPEGOATED

JEFF OLIVER

Aggadah Try It
2006 Idlewilde Run Dr.
Austin, Texas 78744

Cover by Liz Blazer

Interior Layout by Lori Michelle
www.TheAuthorsAlley.com

For more information, address:
john@madnessheart.press

www.madnessheart.press

To my grandparents, who instilled in me a love of stories and kugel.

CHAPTER 1

NEW JERSEY HAS the best garage sales. In the same pile as you might find a stained Baby Shark onesie and a Ziplock bag full of 1,000 Ikea Allen wrenches, you may discover a garter belt worn by Marie Antoinette or another garter belt worn by Baby Shark. So, perhaps it shouldn't have surprised me to happen upon a goat pee stained box that housed a series of old diaries, hard drives, and email printouts that changed the way I view world history.

I like to think of myself as fairly well educated and not just because I co-created the popular Tik Tok trend "TED Talk Lip Syncs." But still, I remained naïve on the subject of The Schtinklers, a family who did more for Jewish history than Mel Brooks and the inventor of babka combined. Theirs is the story of Sara, a mother whose scientific research nearly saved the world. Of Reuven, a father whose newfound machismo almost destroyed it. And of Joshua, a son who finally found his place in the world in the most unlikely of settings. It's also the story of how Scarlett Johansson's face ended up on all world currency, but we'll get to that.

Of course, my garage sale box and its contents belonged to The Schtinklers, gaining me access to a unique glimpse of history, not to mention a sweet two-book deal.

So I begin my account in simpler times—almost twelve years ago—before the human spread of "Fainting Goat Syndrome," before non-Jews were mandated to wear

“Gentile helmets,” before global upheaval and mass relocations, and, of course, before this book won a Jewish Book Award for “Excellence in Depicting the Truth Behind the One Time All That Crazy Stuff Happened With the Goats.” I start the day prior, in fact, to when everyone in the world started fainting when they experienced the slightest bit of anxiety. Fainting like goats in a Tennessee field. Stunned. Frozen. Useless. Everyone . . .

Except for the Jews.

CHAPTER 2

FIRST, I GIVE you the mother, Sara. Her bulbous, curly hair has been likened to Barbara Streisand *and* Barry Gibb's on the cover of the 1980 disco album "Guilty." If for some reason you're not familiar with that album cover, let's just say her hair was a tremendous round mess of brassy orange curls that her co-workers at the lab joked covered her enormous brain. Sara had small eyes, but with glasses so thick that she looked like an anime character; a small pursed mouth that seemed to hold secrets; and a loose hippie style of dress featuring Birkenstock sandals and brown cardigans that always smelled of goats.

Sara Schtinkler, along with her co-workers, spent her days at The Center for Animal Oddities. It was previously The Weird Wildlife Foundation until they were sued multiple times by the World Wildlife Foundation. There was a team analyzing why cows all faced the same way when they eat, why dogs dragged their butts on the ground even after you yelled at them, "Nigel! Stop dragging your butt on the carpet!", why parrots repeated phrases like "Shit-Twizzler," and "Cheese-dick-breath" as opposed to saying useful things like "There's a fire," "Call 911," or "This marriage was a sham from day one!"

Sara was in charge of fainting goats. Why they fainted, could anything be done about it, and should humans take it personally. Her assignment wasn't by chance. Sara Schtinkler loved goats. Goats, goats, goats, goats—oh those silly little creatures! She had a baby goat tattooed on her calf, which she thought was funny because of course a baby goat is called a 'kid' not a 'calf,' but some people *still* don't even know that! Sara dedicated her last ten years to researching, writing about, and boring people at dinner parties on the subject of fainting goats.

"The crazy thing is that they don't even really faint at all!" she marveled, as her guests' wondered if they could will themselves dead. "Fainting involves losing consciousness due to a lack of oxygen to the brain. When a myotonic goat falls over, it's because of problems with their muscles not their brain, and they remain completely conscious for the whole episode, isn't that absolutely fascinating?" Ignoring the uncomfortable side glances and even blatant eye rolls of her guests, Sara persisted, "The Myotonic or Tennessee Fainting Goat, it's also known as the *Falling, Stiff-legged* or *Nervous goat*, or as the *Tennessee Wooden Leg*, is a small domestic goat breed that first appeared in Tennessee in the 1880s. Myotonia congenita is caused by an inherited disorder of the chloride channel in the muscles of the skeleton (CLCN1), an autosomal dominant trait with incomplete penetrance or a recessive trait, resulting in the varying severity of the condition . . . "

Some more polite guests would just go to that special Zen place in their mind like a beach in the Bahamas or a jacuzzi full of acid. Others might politely excuse themselves and go stand in the bathroom, hoping it would soon end. One or two just held out their hands and pleaded, "Stop!"

Sara's own teenage son, Joshua had cried out more than once. "You love those fainting goats more than you love me!" Was it true? Of course not. She adored her only son Joshua, regardless of his snarky teenage quips and mercurial moods. But how she did love those clever, versatile, and naturally comedic little goats. She had goat-themed clocks, socks, and fridge magnets that always made her smile. If you still don't believe me, maybe her vanity license plate will convince you: *GOATLOVR*.

Now in the lab, reading glasses pinched over her nose, Sara typed in her most recent data about the behavior of her in-house goats, including tracking their "FPD" or Faints Per Day. She made sure to also log the letters she received from her farmer friends Burt and Molly, who lived up in the wilderness of northeast Tennessee and sent her regular updates on their local fainting goats. Once Sara was done entering the new data, she removed her lab coat, changed from Birkenstocks into sneakers, and walked out to the barn directly behind the lab.

Three goats leaped off a row of tires and ran over. They wagged their little goat tails and waggled their little goat heads, bleated in high tones as if to say, "Oh, look, Barbara Streisand is back." There was Spencer, the dumbest of the goats, who threw some hay in celebration, which covered his eyes and momentarily blinded him; Lilia, who was vain, licked around her lips to make them look fuller and poutier; and Chewy who was secretly in love with Sara, did a pit check to make sure he wasn't kickin'. Sara gave each goat a good tickle under the ears, then she fed them each one fresh pear, which they gobbled up greedily, and followed it up with two teaspoons of organic pumpkin seeds straight from the Summit Farmer's Market. The goats watched with great anticipation as Sara took out her gym bag, put on sports goggles, a headband, and sweatbands for her wrists.

"Ready to get your butts kicked again?"

As stated in Sara's Ted Talk, "Goats are amazing at tetherball," goats are *amazing* at tetherball. Sara was no slouch at tetherball either. She swaggered onto the court where a yellow ball hung from a rope tied to a pole and cracked her knuckles loudly. The goats leaped and butted the ball with their heads, more than once flipping their entire bodies in the air in an effort to push the yellow ball in their direction. But Sara's graceful form, not to mention her "having hands," bested the goats over and over. In three-on-ones, one-on-ones, and then tournament style, Sara defeated the goats at their own game, exhausting them thoroughly.

"Nice try." Sara huffed, drenched in sweat. "Better luck tomorrow?"

The goats bleated, as if to say, "This defeat is our personal Goat Alamo, and we will avenge it. But in the meantime, any more snacks?" Sara sat on a tire and put her goggles and sweatbands back into her gym bag. Then came her least favorite part of her day. She removed a gruesome Freddy Kruger Halloween mask from the same bag and pulled it over her head. Then she leaped into the air with her fingers outstretched like claws and yelled at the goats at the top of her lungs. "Kraaaagg!"

The goats all reeled back in shock and then fainted, or scientifically speaking their muscles stiffened in a myotonic spell. Regardless, they went flat as boards and then keeled over to their sides and onto the ground where they lay lightly twitching. Sara took off her gruesome Halloween mask, then leaned down and took each of the goats' vitals. She wrote down the data in a little red journal, including how long each faint lasted. It usually averaged about two minutes. Then she caressed each goat softly under the ears as they regained control of their muscles and kissed them goodbye. This gave Chewy, who was in love with Sara a boner. Please don't Google goat boners. It's for your own good.

Back in the lab, Sara typed in the new vitals from her red journal, sighting that the changes in diet and exercise had done nothing to cure the goats of the severity of their myotonia: *One pear each, two tsp organic pumpkin seeds,*

twenty-two minutes exercise. No change in myotonic reaction. Note: Tomorrow try pomegranate seeds, add three minutes to tetherball play, and pretend you don't notice Chewy's erection but instead compliment his strong sense of social justice.

Just as Sara finished typing, Kent, the Manager of the lab, entered. As usual, he wore his lab coat and a silk turquoise tie. His silver hair was cut to resemble his idol Anderson Cooper. Kent even puckered his lips like Anderson Cooper, and Sara had caught him practicing in his office mirror more than once. But right now, Kent abandoned his pucker to crinkle his nose like he was smelling something unsavory.

"Did you have goats in here again?" he asked.

"No. Why?" Sara sniffed her cardigan but didn't smell anything.

"Never mind." Kent rubbed his eyes and sighed. He pulled an envelope from his lab coat and held it in the air. "Might as well rip off the bandage. Funding's been cut for goat research, Sara. They want to use the resources in, and I quote, 'Ways that will have any benefit for humanity'."

Sara gasped. "What could be more beneficial to humanity than fainting goats?"

Kent checked his binder and read, "Why sloths are such great swimmers."

Sara was aghast. She threw her hands in the air. "Ugh, sloths. So trendy."

"We knew this day might come, Sara. Honestly, it's a tribute to your work that you've lasted this long on the goat study without a major breakthrough. Of course, I've recommended strongly that you stay on for the sloth research."

Sara pretended not to hear that. "What will happen to Lillia, Spencer, and Chewy?"

"Who?"

"Our goats!"

"Oh, uh, I'd send Spencer and Lilly to a petting zoo, but

not Chewy. He seems to get aroused around humans." Kent put a consoling hand on Sara's shoulder but then pulled away, seeing all of the goat hair there.

"I'm sorry about this, Sara." Kent went on, "They've given us until Friday. After that this lab is full-time sloths. You might actually really like them. They smell as bad as goats and they always seem like they just fainted. Please think about staying. I'd hate to lose you from the team, Sara."

"Have you told Bruce yet?" Sara asked.

"I was hoping you would. You know I can't handle crying, and he's so sensitive."

"Leave it to me."

Kent smiled sadly and walked out of the lab. Right as he left Bruce stumbled in. He was Vietnamese, with an amazing mop of black hair for which both The Beatles and The Bieber would be envious. His eyes were already wet, his short, stocky frame crooked into a question mark. As usual, he was wearing an empty BabyBjörn across his chest even though his newborn was at home with his wife Jackie.

"Tell me it's not true, Sara!" Bruce's face was wet with tears. "Jackie's going to make me work at her dad's Kosher Pickle kiosk in the mall. What do I know about kosher pickles? Or kiosks? And you don't know how mean my father-in-law is."

"He can't be that bad..." Sara forced a grin.

Bruce was so confused his face appeared broken. "When I suggested converting to Judaism for Jackie he offered to perform the circumcision himself. And my father-in-law has severe hand tremors!"

Sara hugged him, and Bruce's tears puddled on her shoulder, mingling with the goat hair. "Don't give up," she whispered in his ear. "Your day will come. I just know it." Those words were as much for him as for herself.

"The Pickle kiosk is terrible," Bruce sobbed. "He throws gherkins at my head to make his cat laugh."

SCAPEGOATED

Sara drove home slowly, thinking about the disaster that had just transpired at work and the sad prospect of losing her goats. She arrived at home and parked across the street for twelve minutes before finally pulling into the driveway. Based on journal entries, she had walked in the door at precisely 5:15 p.m. every working day for years. And knowing Joshua, any deviation from that would immediately set off a line of questioning that Sara wasn't sure she was ready to answer. Joshua was a stickler for consistency.

"What happened?" Joshua asked as soon as she walked in the door.

"Why? It's 5:15."

"5:14. You lose your job?" Joshua looked up from his book. "You aren't wearing your badge."

Sara reached for where her badge always was and realized she'd left it at work. "Fuck."

Joshua shut his book, Frank Herbert's classic, *Dune*. His concerns were confirmed that his mother had just hurled an F-bomb—he grinned. "Nice one. I'm only fifteen."

"Sorry," Sara said. "And no, I did not lose my job. There've just been some . . . funding diversions."

"It's the dog butt draggers, isn't it?"

Sara hung her head. "Sloths."

"Ugh, so trendy."

"Exactly what I said!"

"And that, Mom, is why you're the G.O.A.T.," Joshua said. "Greatest of All Time."

Sara smiled despite herself. "No, you're the G.O.A.T.," she replied with a wink.

Regardless of which one of them truly was the G.O.A.T., they both undoubtedly smelled like goat, especially after Joshua got up and hugged his mother. He was short for his fifteen years, and still carried a prepubescent layer of baby fat that made him snuggly. Sara knew that it was one of the reasons why school was so hard for her son. In a grade full of zitty six-footers with armpit hair and boners, Joshua looked more like a middle-schooler who'd wandered onto the dancefloor at Senior Prom, and the height of his voluminous copper Jewfro did nothing to help. Joshua had transferred from a small Hebrew school mid-year to one with hardly any Jews at all. It made it hard for him to make new friends, but easier to meet new bullies. Maybe with her new free time Sara could get more involved in the school? Join the PTA?

"You're not going to become one of those meddling PTA moms now, are you?" Joshua asked, reading her mind.

"Didn't occur to me," Sara lied. "Why? Did something happen today?"

Joshua averted her gaze. "They drew an Israeli flag on my locker."

"Was it accurately drawn?"

"Yeah, six-point star and everything."

"Well-researched anti-Semites are the worst. Did you tell Principal Davies?"

"Yeah, he complimented them on getting the star right and suggested I try to be proud of that flag, then everyone wins."

"He didn't actually say that?"

"Then he bragged about how he's going to the West Bank this summer to volunteer for human rights. Made me look through a brochure. He said given the oppression by the Israelis, there's a need for conscientious objectors like him."

"That's it. I'm joining Moms Against Anti-Semitism," Sara said.

"You despise those women, Mom. You said Julie Kramer's mom is a pathological narcissist who makes celebrity deaths all about her on Facebook."

"Someone needs to hear what's going on. Maybe they have resources. Maybe if we walk into the Principals' office together, he'll . . . "

"No one's going to believe Principal Davies hates Jews," Joshua said. "He was married to a Canter from Beth Shalom. And no one wants to hear about a Hebrew School kid getting bullied about Israel. Things will only get worse for me."

Sara hugged him. What else could she do? According to a framed photo that I found in the box, Sara's grandmother, a Holocaust survivor, had bright orange hair like Lucille Ball, and wore tasseled suede vests and turtlenecks until she died at ninety-six. As a child, Sara's grandmother had warned her of what she called the double standard of anti-Semitism. "When we're poor they call us dirty ethnic vermin to be exterminated. When we succeed, we're greedy white bankers who need to be overthrown. So, which is it?" And her grandmother had very strong opinions about those who had strong opinions about Israel. "And Israel, well, that's the anti-Semites' greatest gift. It allows them to rebrand their hatred of Jews as anti-Zionism. People who've never shown the slightest interest in world politics, who couldn't find Egypt on a map of Egypt suddenly obsessed with Palestine? Spare me. They just love to push around the Jews and finally found a politically correct way to do it. Listen to me, Sara, and don't you ever forget: anti-Semitism is a monster hiding in the closet ready to attack at any moment." Sara, just a little girl then, listened attentively and then spent her adolescence prepared to be terrorized for her heritage. And yet in her adolescence and adult life Sara had only experienced fleeting cases, none of them particularly scary. But now her own son, sweet innocent Joshua, was getting it firsthand, and in that exact can't-put-your-finger-on-it way that her grandmother had described.

"Maybe there's a way to scare them off..." Sara wondered aloud.

"What, you're gonna unleash the fainting goats?"

"Lilia is very brave in the face of injustice."

Sara gave Joshua a long squeeze. The two of them went to the kitchen and cooked vegetable ramen side by side. Then they sat on the couch in the den and ate on vintage TV dinner trays while watching old episodes of Master Chef Junior.

"Ooh, that kid's totally over-salting her jus. It's going to be a sob-fest when she's eliminated," Joshua observed.

"I've got five bucks the kid with the braces is going home for under-spicing that Cornish hen jambalaya."

"You're on."

"I'm ho-ome!" Reuven's nasal voice called out, as it did every night when he stepped through the door from work at 7:43 p.m. He was tall and wiry with dark wavy hair, small ears, and a square head too big for his body. Friends generously compared him to Anthony Bourdain, adding, "if his head was shaped like a microwave." Reuven peeked his massive head into the den where Sara and Joshua were perched with their TV dinners. "Joy Reid on yet?" he asked.

"As usual, *The ReidOut* is live on MSNBC in seventeen minutes—just enough time for you to heat up what's in the fridge."

As Sara spoke, Reuven was already looking down at his cellphone and shaking his head. "It's Claire. She needs something. Be right back."

"Like clockwork," Sara said.

"Yeah, tell her to leave you alone for once, dad," Joshua said.

But Reuven was already waving Joshua off, having dialed his boss' number. "Where am I? Home . . . well, there's no Wi-Fi on the train so it cut off . . . Now? But . . . Yeah, sure . . . Um, okay . . . Yup. I got it." He hung up. Looked at his family sadly. "I'll be done before Joy starts."

"That's what you always say," Sara said.

SCAPEGOATED

Reuven retreated into his basement office. On the wall were cue cards that plotted the screenplay he'd been planning to write since 2003 but just hasn't had a chance to. Reuven had been the Breakout Writer of his senior class at UBC Film School, a lock for big things. And then right when he finally got an agent there was a Writer's Guild strike, Sara got pregnant, and he'd taken a job in reality TV to fill in the time.

"This is beneath me," he used to say, but over the years that changed to: "Oh, God, please don't let me lose this job that's beneath me."

Indeed, there was security in being staff at Lowbrau Productions, an international production company that did hundreds of episodes of *Celebrity Cabin Hunter*. Reuven initially pitched the format as a gameshow where contestants get to hunt celebrities in a row of cabins but that was dumbed down to celebrities buying luxury cabins. That put him in golden handcuffs. He'd earned a steady paycheck and dependable family health insurance, but in the process his youthful swagger and cavalier confidence had been replaced by a nagging worry that even this career in reality TV might go away.

So, at 7:53 p.m. after a full day in the city, he did what was asked of him. He booted up his laptop, took a deep breath all in his chest, and pounded out a pitch deck about summer camp for adults who like to dress up like *My Little Pony* tentatively titled *Wet, Hot, American Bronies*, and sent it off to his boss, Claire.

Before he could stand up to get back to his family, Claire responded with a text. "Send it as a PDF as well as a Word doc. We've discussed this numerous times, Reuven."

Reuven winced, resaved the document as a PDF, and sent off both as instructed. He then slumped out of the room and up to the den to finally join in his family's nightly ritual.

"He has risen!" Sara said, patting the seat next to her on the couch. "Hurry, Joy is wearing her purple velvet jacket, which means she's really going to go off on one."

"Probably going to link immigration policy to the Byzantine Empire," Joshua said.

"Boris Markinoff was an 19th century Russian Oligarch and spy who may have changed the way you eat breakfast cereal. And I'll get to that," Joy Reid said on TV. "But first, breaking news."

"Called it!" Sara bragged.

The Breaking News was from Los Angeles, where the Democratic Primary votes were taking place. But the news wasn't immediately about the polls—it was that a significant delay in voting had occurred due to a series of traffic accidents that brought the 405 Freeway to a halt. Many of the drivers, who were stuck in gridlock under intense heat, reported suffering fainting spells as the reason for the accidents.

"Weird!" Joy Reid arched an eyebrow. "Many of the, uh, fainters were unable to control the wheel and just rolled into the cars in front of them causing more accidents and injuries. No deaths have been reported however, thank heavens. Oh wait, my producer tells me we have a clip of one of these occurrences, let's roll that."

The iPhone footage that appeared onscreen showed a frustrated blonde woman in a tennis visor in the throes of road rage, slapping her dashboard and repeatedly honking at the cars in front of her. Then, all at once, she stiffened like a board in her seat and then keeled over to one side as her car rolled forward and slammed into the SUV in front of her. Joy looked thoughtfully at camera. "She passed out faster than a Republican Senator passing out ear marks to Fossil Fuel Corporations."

"Looks like that woman had a seizure," Joshua remarked.

"That's no seizure," Sara replied. She'd placed her dinner tray to the side and stood face-to-face with the TV, her heart thumping. "That's myotonia congenita."

Sara got a text from Bruce. "Are you seeing this??"

Joy Reid went on, "The car crashes that took place were perhaps only equal-to-worse than the full-on train wreck that the McCord campaign faced as Joyce Johnson swept the polls across Southern California and Arizona . . . "

And Joy returned to covering politics. Only using the episode of mass fainting as a way to frame the big news of the Democratic Primary election. But Sara, Bruce, and possibly Kent, too, all knew what had just happened.

"But how?" Sara yelled at the TV screen. "How could she not see that myotonia congenita is caused by an inherited disorder of the chloride channel in the muscles of the skeleton (CLCN1), an autosomal dominant trait with incomplete penetrance or a recessive trait, resulting in the varying severity of the condition?"

"Well, when you say it that way I have absolutely no idea," said Joshua.

CHAPTER 3

THE NEXT MORNING, Joshua rode his bike to school using the same route he did every day. Along Ridgewood Road, where cars could see if he got circled by bullies, and then across Crestwood Park to where it would be impossible for them to corner him. Per his diary, Joshua had been thinking a lot about his mom on the ride. "*I hate that she's losing her job,*" he wrote. "*When she talks about her work with the goats there's a light in her eyes that I love seeing. Not like Dad, who always looks miserable when he talks about his pitches and the ratings and whether or not there will be a fifth season of Surgery Pranks: Penile Implant Farm. His work seems terrible. But Mom's work with fainting goats is special.*"

Joshua fantasized about making goat-centered Tik Tok videos that feature his mom's scientific research, and he was so excited about his idea that he didn't even notice what was waiting for him at the mouth of the park, at the one place on his route that was covered and dangerous, the one place he routinely sped past at top speed.

"Late for your *bat mitzvah*, fucktard?" Joshua barely registered William's voice. He didn't have a chance to possibly correct him that *bat mitzvahs* are for girls not boys before a stick lodged between the spokes of his front wheel, and Joshua went flying over his handlebars and onto the rocky pavement. His palms hit first, scraping the skin off there, then his knees hit, tearing the fabric of his jeans. He rolled on the ground and stayed down, feeling fire where his skin used to be, seeing William, Chin, and Zed circling him through a haze.

"Aw, you got a boo-boo, Joshua? Want me to call your mommy?" William said, picking at the cystic acne on his chin.

"If you want her number it's in my phone under Blowjobs," Zed said, who was big as a linebacker but with a tiny, pointed head.

Joshua fought back tears. "Why are you so obsessed with me?" His voice cracked despite himself.

"Whoa, William," Chin said, slapping his massive forehead. "I think he just called you gay."

"Did this ugly Israeli kid just call me gay? I'm going to take my time on this."

William climbed on top of Joshua and pinned his arms under his knees. He then coughed up a phlegm ball in his mouth, and while the other two cheered him on, let it ooze in a thick viscous string towards Joshua's face. Right before it landed, he slurped it up back into his mouth. "That was a test run. Next time it hits."

Joshua struggled under William's weight. He maneuvered his legs out for a second and kicked, landing a soft knee on William's back. This rebellion awakened a fury in William. His eyes grew wide and ghoulish, his acne glowed red like little puss-filled sirens. Joshua winced, ready to get pummeled. William held his meaty fist above Joshua, but then just froze in place as if he was gathering up strength to hit harder. Seconds passed. Zed and Chin laughed. This was some next level sadism even for William. But Joshua knew that something wasn't right. William appeared to be paralyzed in place rather than just messing with him. His body had gone completely still, and his hand took on more of a curve than a fist. Then slowly, almost comically, William keeled over to the side and fell cheek-first onto the pavement next to Joshua. He twitched lightly.

Zed looked down, baffled. "What kind of Jew magic?! You better not have circumcised him! William, you okay, bro?"

"I think he's having some kind of se-se-seizure," Joshua stuttered.

"Oh, you're gonna pay for this shit!" Zed stepped forward to tackle Joshua, finish him off, but then he too stiffened, freezing mid-stride and then keeling over to the pavement like he was playing some strange improv game. Chin looked at his two friends in horror and just ran away.

Joshua got up from the ground and wiped blood from his hands onto his jeans. Then he picked up his bag from the ground. He looked down at William and Zed, who were still frozen in place, eye wide open.

"*Bat mitzvahs* are for girls. Get your anti-Semitism right, assholes!" Joshua said, tears streaming down his face. Then he jumped on his bike and pedaled off.

Reuven was feeling especially uneasy that morning as he took New Jersey Transit to the city. The 8:05 a.m. train was late again and then cramped, and then seats were taken up by feet even though the conductor said not to put your feet up, and that threw him off even more. He listened to a meditation playlist in which an Australian woman said to think about inhaling ocean air, and that always made him feel calmer, but his mind whirled with the list of things he should be worrying about: Sara losing her job and what will happen with the goats, (Oh fuck, is he going to end up with a dining room full of goats?). Also his son getting bullied at school by those racist assholes and Principal Davies doing nothing all about it, etc. But Reuven knew the real reason for why he felt nervous, and that filled him with self-loathing: The PDF. That he had forgotten to attach a PDF as well as Word document to the email to Claire last night shook him. He had the moral high ground after all, he worked past 8 p.m. again, put in the extra effort, and no one could write up a deck like him. Surely he deserved a break and even a promotion after nine years at the company. Still, that PDF . . . one stupid move might have cost him everything. How could he forget a PDF? What sort of fuck up forgets the PDF? Holy shit, the letters PDF spell out Please Don't Forget. Or maybe for him they should spell PDF: Pretty Dumb Fuck!

When Reuven finally arrived at the office he got his morning coffee, checked social media leisurely. People were posting about the Primary election and also that weird fainting video. That's when he spotted Claire walking through the hall with Jake Morgan. Jake was Reuven's equal in the corporate hierarchy but his absolute nemesis in work, life, and the battle for who had better hair. Basically, all things. Jake, who was even taller than Reuven and had bright blue eyes and lush, sandy hair, was Claire's favorite. She'd taken him under her wing, and Reuven heard from his Coordinator that she was planning to bring him to the Senior Meeting that morning, which meant he was being shown off to the higher-ups as promotion material. Reuven tried to look busy as the two of them walked straight to his office. Claire opened Reuven's office door, not even bothering to knock on the glass.

"Join us," she said.

"For what?"

"The Senior Meeting. Jake's going to talk us through creative strategy for the third-quarter, but I was hoping you could give a quick summary of the Brony Camp pitch you sent last night."

"Like right now?" Reuven barely got that out, his breath had so completely left him.

"Unless you have something more pressing that the Senior Meeting?" Claire chuckled.

The thing that was more pressing was digging a hole in the ground and never coming out from it, but Reuven said nothing. A flood of panic made his heart pound and his brain completely scramble. But when he saw Jake's arrogant smirk, perhaps a reaction to seeing Reuven's blanched and sweaty face, he looked down and said, "The hole digging can wait."

"Great. Come, come." Claire turned and walked off.

Reuven grabbed his work bag. He had Xanax in there and was hoping he'd have a chance to drop a pen into his bag and then grab a pill while he was fishing it out. It took about twenty minutes for the drug to work. Still, maybe there'd be a whole bunch of other agenda topics before he had to speak in front of a roomful of people who could determine his career, up against a guy who spoke to a room full of executives as directly as if he were explaining to a toddler why the game of squash is different to racquetball. Reuven followed Claire and Jake down the hall, and then peeled off artfully to the bathroom.

"Be right there," Reuven said.

"Don't take too long," Claire replied.

Reuven entered the bathroom and relieved himself, then quickly washed his hands. There was no one in any of the stalls, so he dug into his bag and retrieved a tiny white pill and popped it. He tried to swallow but the pill got caught, so he waved under the sink and had his face under the faucet when Jake walked in.

"Thirsty much?" Jake said, and the smugness in his voice made Reuven wince.

"Forgot my water bottle," Reuven said, gulping down the Xanax pill.

"Well, I hope you didn't forget your balls. Brigit is in there. Flew in from London last night. Claire said your presentation should be two minutes max."

The mention of Brigit, the President of the entire production company, sent chills down Reuven's spine. He felt his fight-or-flight mechanism kick in, and his reaction was definitely flight.

"Relax, it'll all be over quick. I've been given five minutes." Jake looked in the mirror, brushed his sandy hair over his tanned forehead, and smiled. "Showtime."

The conference room was impossibly bright and packed with SVPs, EVPs and BMOCs whose BMWs were no LOLs. The video conference from London showed a packed house of higher-ups as well. Serious, successful faces—leaders with eyes a bit more focused and clothes a little more British than the rest. Reuven followed Jake inside like a man condemned to the gallows. He took a seat across from Claire, who gave him a look that said, "Better not fuck this up." Reuven thought about how many minutes had passed since he'd popped the Xanax. If he was down a bit on the agenda, maybe he'd survive.

"Perhaps we should get started," Brigit, a tall, thin woman in her mid-fifties, said cheerily. "We have two special guests on the list today . . . Jake Morgan, hi Jake, nice to see you on this side of the pond. And uh, Reuven, um . . . Stop, I know it, how foolish . . . no, I . . . Claire?"

"Schtinkler."

"Right. Didn't want to mess that up. Jake will run down programming strategy for three-Q, and Reuven, you have a pitch you'd like to discuss with us?"

Brigit turned to Reuven as did the entire room, and all the air escaped his lungs, as if even the air wanted nothing to do with him.

"Me first?" Reuven replied with a slight wheeze.

"The room is yours," Brigit said, waving around the table, and to Reuven the entire universe. At once, sound became a vacuum. All Reuven could hear was the impossibly loud thumping of his own heart, which tapped S.O.S. repeatedly.

"Right, um . . . the show is, uh, about adult summer camp for people who dress up like My Little Pony. Heh, heh, the children's show. So adults go to this camp . . . really in uh, Delaware . . . and they do uh, campy things—well, not 'campy'—not drag, but like uh, canoeing, and uh . . . what's that thing with the ball on the rope? Tetherball, yeah. And uh . . . that's sort of the meat of it, so yeah . . . uh, camp for Bronies as a show . . . "

Reuven managed all that on a single mouthful of air, and when it was over he stopped more from lack of oxygen than a nasty glare from Claire. There was the kind of silence in the room reserved for a child's funeral.

Brigit tilted her head. "So, this is about the counselors?" she asked, revealing that she hadn't grasped even the fundamentals of Reuven's "pitch."

"No, the uh . . . the kids . . . but it's now adults, and they love My Little Pony from their childhoods. Adults going to camp like when they were kids."

"Who are the counselors then?"

"Also adults."

"Why would adults want to be taken care of by other adults?"

Sensing doom, Claire cut in, "It's a world that genuinely exists, Brigit, believe it or not. Not as kinky as BDSM, but close I think. Peter Pan syndrome is a big Millennial affliction. And these folks just hate being adults and loved summer camp and My Little Pony growing up. So they yearn for a return to their childhood with no guilt attached to reconnect with nature and be a community and frankly to hook up and let loose in pony costumes. The counselors are more curators of their time there, rather than traditional counselors." Claire had quoted Reuven's write-up to the word, which made him feel both proud and ashamed, which was a frequent emotional combination when you worked in reality TV.

"Sounds like a swingers club to me," Brigit said with a grin, and the room erupted in laughter. "A naughty key party in the woods, is it?"

"We could pitch it that way!" Chaz Merk, SVP of Communication, said. "Or depending on what's in the ether a more wholesome and good-natured comedy about adults who never wanted to grow up. A Peter Pan angle."

Brigit looked straight at Reuven and he felt his entire body recede under the pressure of her gaze. "I don't hate it. Not sure if it will work for the Networks. Sounds a tad niche. Research, can you do a soft focus on this?"

"Right away, Brigit."

Reuven coughed. "Uh, thanks. I'll uh . . . "

"We'll send an update as soon as it's in," Claire interjected, taking back control.

Reuven could tell that Claire was not pleased with his performance. It hadn't been a total disaster, but it wasn't good. The pitch should have been an easy sell to get money to produce a 20-minute presentation reel, but now it was stuck in Research, who loved to shit on new ideas.

"Okay, Jake, you're up," Brigit said. "Give us that strategy update."

While Reuven reshuffled his papers and tried to avoid direct eye line with everyone in the room, he noticed Jake smile confidently next to him.

"Absolutely," Jake said. "Prepare to be blown away." Jake stood up from his chair, opened his mouth to speak again and then his body stiffened like a rod. For a moment Reuven thought it was part of his presentation like some Big D Energy power pose. But then as he froze entirely, Jake's six-foot-four inches of towering Alpha male keeled over, first teetering forward and then falling straight back like a great oak tree who had suddenly realized the burden of being a tree was just a bit more than it could handle. Reuven thought fast. He leaned back in his chair and managed to wedge his hand under Jake's head, which was barreling towards a sharp window sill. Reuven felt a crunch on his knuckles and a deep pain, but he caught Jake's stiff body with the other hand and eased his rival onto the conference room floor. The entire room got up, and people started racing in an out with water and ice. Jake stayed frozen and twitching lightly, like some kind of bizarre spell had taken him. He gazed up in shock at Reuven, who continued to cradle his head.

"Don't worry, I got you, Bud," Reuven assured him.

When the EMT arrived and Reuven stood up he felt a hand pat him on the back.

"Quick thinking, Reuven. You might have just saved him from getting terribly hurt." Reuven turned to see that it was Brigit who was speaking and had her hand resting on his shoulder. She gave him a squeeze, then looked down at Jake, pitifully. "Poor guy. How embarrassing," she added.

The medics came and tended to Jake, who eventually gained consciousness and said he felt fine, but the meeting was rescheduled for later. Reuven walked out confused by what had just happened but sensing that the strange turn of events had worked in his favor, almost like a person who wins a free haircut after the barber draws blood on their ear.

At the Center for Animal Oddities, Sara wasn't certain what exactly she was looking for under her microscope. She'd peered down at those same samples countless times and analyzed them down to their smallest molecules. But if those cases of road rage she'd seen on TV the night prior weren't human myotonia congenita, then what was the use of spending your career studying goats? Per Sara's writings in Volume 1 of *The Journal of Fainting Goat Studies*—the only surviving copy of which was caked in goat urine at the bottom of Sara's box—there'd only been fourteen known cases of myotonia congenita in humans that could be categorized as "severe" over the past twenty years, meaning full-on fainting-like spells that could last up to five minutes. The less severe cases experienced something akin to muscle clamping, which could be dulled and even cured with muscle relaxants and an anti-inflammatory diet. But the severe cases, much like for goats, seemed to have no cure, at least none that Sara had been able to find despite her relentless work. Sara had secured living tissue samples from three of the known "severe" human cases, and she was currently observing them, one by one, under her microscope.

What Sara saw didn't strike her as out of the ordinary. According to her notes it was just a constantly moving mass of purplish specs (the myotonia congenita), which bounced around between the cells and then latched in the chloride channels, causing muscle fiber membrane to become hyper-excitable, and triggering a contraction that weakened the nearby cells, before peeling off. The way she described it in one of the journal's few comprehensible lines, " . . . myotonia was like a leach that shot adrenaline into its prey until said prey's energy was naturally sucked away by their own hyperactivity."

Sara was about to pack it up when she noticed an irregularity in the third sample that was in none of her previous notes. The myotonia tried to latch onto one particular mass of mutated cells, and it pinged it off. In fact, that strange cell mutation seemed to drain the myotonia of its size and strength, as if reversing the effects. The myotonia, now sluggish, tried again to latch but was once again depleted, so it veered away and continued down the path to rebuild its strength on other less punishing prey. Sara triple and quadruple checked to be sure, but this mutated mass that seemed to combat the myotonia was familiar to her on a personal level. In her early thirties, Sara had tested positive for the BRCA 2 gene, a cancer-promoting mutation that she learned was especially prevalent in Ashkenazi Jews. Sara was diagnosed after what the first doctor called, "a bad mammogram." Then the second doctor said, "saying this a bad mammogram is like calling the Titanic a disappointing boat ride." She opted for a double mastectomy and to have her ovaries removed rather than risk cancer. And though the whole experience had been traumatic and painful, she'd become fascinated by the bizarre make-up of the BRCA mutation, and then spent much of her recovery time reading about other diseases that seemed to affect Jewish people most prevalently, including a dog-earned edition of *Soy Gavult: How Veganism (and an Asian lover) Saved my Tatas*. Sara gained extensive knowledge on Tay-Sachs Disease, Familial Mediterranean Fever, Fragile X Syndrome, Smith-Lemli-Opitz Syndrome, Bloom Syndrome, Canavan Disease, Gaucher Disease, Joubert Syndrome, Nemaline Myopathy, and Wilson Disease, etc. All disorders that were common to all Jewish groups, regardless of where the Jewish people may be from in the world. Even Connecticut. What Sara observed under her microscope recalled many of the gene formations of those "Jewish" diseases she's spent time studying, and this mass, if her eyes could be believed, seemed to be a grouping of them all in one. Sara had to blink away her incredulity and even take a deep exhalation to make sure she wasn't imagining it, but the visual transformation of the mass was sharp-edged in two equilateral triangles, shaped almost like a Star of David.

"Can't be," Sara muttered to herself, peering back in.

It wasn't exactly BRCA 2, or Tay Sacks, or Smith-Lemli-Opitz, or any of them at once, but sort of a pumped-up version of the group of them, cartoonishly muscular, as if they'd locked arms in solidarity. Sara opened the file on the sample and found the name of her third human "severe" myotonia case: Hannah Goldenfarb, 1955-2020.

"Well, if that's not a fellow Jewess, I don't know who is."

"Back in business!" Kent bounded into the lab, a printout flapping in his hands, making Sara flinch. "The Gods have been kind to us Sara. The sloths will have to wait, which is kind of perfect, because they're very good at waiting. They're like nature's buffering website. You got two more months of funding on fainting goats. Two more!"

"That's great news, Kent," Sara said absently.

"Are you even listening to me? The incident in Los Angeles heightened the board's interest in your work. They want to see if there's any correlation with the fainting goats." Kent peeked at the human samples laid out before her microscope. "I see you're way ahead of me on this. See anything new? You look a little spooked."

Sara wasn't sure why she shook her head no. She wasn't a good liar. But something told her not to share what she'd just seen under the microscope. A mutated Jewish gene acting like a superhero against human myotonia congenita? Sara's grandmother, with her fiery red hair and tasseled vests popped into her mind—a knowing glare, a crooked finger, warning of the monster in the closet, always the monster in the closet. Sara decided to stay silent until she could do more research.

"Is it true, Sara? Tell me we're back! Oh, hi, Kent." Bruce burst through the door. His four-month-old baby was asleep in his BabyBjörn.

"We're back in business," Kent confirmed.

Bruce kissed his baby's head softly in celebration.

"Not only that," Kent said. "But if this fainting thing spreads, goats may be a permanent fixture around here!" Kent danced towards the door, his silver hair shining under the florescent lights. "Now back to work. I've got to go let the sloth breeders down gently."

That night the Schtinkler family came together as they always did to watch Joy Reid on MSNBC. Retro TV diner trays across their laps, they chomped and joked and shook their heads at the news. Each of the Schtinklers had had an eventful day. Joshua's hands were in bandages after being thrown off his bike that morning. He'd decided to leave it as an unlikely bike crash with his parents and not worry them with the story of William, Zed and Chin; their ambush and their sudden fainting spells. Reuven, wore a large Ace bandage wrapped around his left hand, and regaled his family endlessly about the "miracle" that had occurred, marveling at how his quick reflexes had saved the day and possibly positioned him for the promotion he'd been waiting for. Sara, though not physically battered, suffered from a twisted brain after her discovery that a mass mutation of Jewish diseases seemed to fight off human myotonia congenita like some kind of superhero force-field. She kept that info to herself but did share that she was granted two more months of goat funding at the lab, and when she saw how happy that made Joshua and Reuven, she felt happy too.

"To goats!" They toasted, raising their burrito bowls.

The Schtinklers were all a bit happier that night. Reuven marveled at how delicious the ground beef in his burrito bowl tasted, richer in flavor than usual. When Joy Reid appeared on screen with a new hairdo and her purple velvet jacket, Joshua said, "Uh-oh." They all burst out laughing, and Sara was in tears, cackling at her son's comic timing.

"Javier Chatipo-Marquez, a political dissident jailed for peacefully protesting the oppressive lavender candle monopoly in Cartagena, Columbia has a story that is breathtaking in its injustice. And I'll get to that," Joy Reid said. "But first we have breaking news,"

"No shit you do!" Reuven joked, and they all laughed again, though Sara slapped her husband's knee for swearing.

"Last night we showed you footage of a driver on the 405 Freeway in Los Angeles seeming to faint from road rage," Joy said, a grave look on her face. "Well, today, more cases of these fainting spells have spread in different parts of the country—Portland, Seattle, and now New York. Reports state that people who experience even the slightest jolt of anxiety or anger are having their bodies commandeered by a stiffness in their muscles that makes then keel over like in a fainting spell, for sometimes up to five minutes. I apparently am not immune." Joy Reid lifted her arm, which was in a black sling that had been previously hidden by the camera. "I got mad at my printer. Next thing I know I froze up."

Sara watched spellbound as Joy introduced an expert from the CDC who she knew from conferences, Dr. Greg Harley. He was a serious scientist with thinning gray hair and weary eyes under wireless glasses. "What can you tell us about this, Dr. Harley? Should we be worried?"

"Well, Joy, it does seem like people are suffering from spells similar to severe myotonia congenita, a condition that stiffens the muscles to the point of freezing the whole body momentarily. Like a faint, but you stay conscious. Until now it has mainly been found in certain goat breeds, and there have only been a handful of cases I can recall of it existing in humans this severe. Fortunately, I know of at least one lab in New Jersey that has been studying myotonia congenita for years."

"He's talking about you, Mom!" Joshua nudged Sara, proudly.

"In terms of the spread," Joy went on. "What's going on here?"

"Well, Joy, it seems to be acting like it's a flu strain, spreading fast in certain communities, globally. That is, certain types of people seem to be most susceptible, while others, or one community in particular, we've seen zero cases in."

"Can you elaborate?"

"Not yet, but here in New York for instance we've seen rampant cases spread across the Brooklyn area, and yet the religious community in Crown Heights haven't seen a single case."

"The religious . . . Jewish community?" Joy asked.

Sara leaned in. Joy didn't even have to say it out loud.

"Did she just say that Jews aren't affected by this thing?" Reuven asked.

Joshua put on a Yiddish accent. "Vould it be the vorst thing in the vorld for us to catch a break for vonce?"

Reuven laughed, but Sara shushed them, absolutely

transfixed by what she was hearing. She flashed back to what she'd seen at the lab—how a mutation of Jewish diseases seemed to fight the myotonic cells. But just as quickly, her grandmother appeared in her mind. That flaming red hair, the wagging finger, reminding Sara to never, ever forget of the monster hiding in the closet.

CHAPTER 4

MYOTONIA CONGENITA SWEPT the globe in a matter of weeks, with only Alaska and certain isolated islands in the Pacific holding out about a month before mass fainting afflicted the planet. Were there injuries? Millions. Deaths? Tens of thousands. Hospitals filled up worldwide with cases of broken limbs and concussions. There was a plaster shortage from too many casts. And it only got worse once the stress of the operating room made the doctors faint as well.

The War Measures Act was instituted, forcing global manufacturers to create soft helmets for people to wear, as well as knee and elbow pads. The soft helmets with chin straps became quickly mandatory for all fainters. The world began to resemble a 1930s football team or a high school wrestling club. Glofit, a well-known yoga app, became not only free but mandatory for daily use, with emergency yogic breathing session alerts going out twice daily. India and the Upper East Side of New York City were ahead of the curve in yogic practice, but soon the entire world became experts in Vinyasa Flow Yoga. Celebrities did what they could of course, encouraging fans with heartfelt online messages that trended on Twitter more to point out how out of touch the stars were with regular people than to laud them. Project Runway did a special episode where designers competed to create soft helmets and padding that was fashionable as well as accessible in the modern era.

For Jewish people things were a bit different. At first, many tried to blend in, as was their natural inclination. They wore soft helmets and padding in public and led free yoga workshops in solidarity with their Gentile brothers and sisters. But it quickly became apparent that they were different, and some resented their attempts at fellowship as cruelly patronizing. TMZ and other online gossip sites exploded when certain non-Jewish celebrities were revealed to be non-fainters, and DNA tests proved deep Jewish roots. Some wore it proudly. Actors Tom Holland and Laura Linney, and musicians like Lady Gaga were of note though not too surprising. Prince Harry of the Royal Family—to everyone's amazement—was mostly Sephardic, bringing up new theories about the love life of Princess Diana. RuPaul and Jackie Chan, both 31% Jewish, were equally surprising but enthusiastically welcomed into the tribe. Others, including the leader of a prominent chapter of the Klu Klux Klan in Alabama, feigned fainting for a while until his own members frightened him in a prank that saw him react not-at-all. A DNA test revealed that not only was he 93% European Jew but that his great-grandfather had been a lauded Hassidic Rabbi in Austria and had once famously told a young Adolf Hitler to "go eat a gefilte-shit sandwich." Memes began as humorous but as was their fashion turned quickly anti-Semitic: *First, they control the media and now consciousness!* The Left veered from old school anti-Semitism to more modern forms of online shaming: *Jewish folks better check their non-fainting privilege! #freepalestine.*

The Jews did their best to help the world financially, donating millions to infrastructure and hospitals, and also through volunteering. When it became clear that most firefighters stiffened up when confronted by a dangerous blaze, scores of bespectacled Noahs and Rebeccas came in to take shifts. When there was concern that pilots might faint during commercial air travel, schedules were changed to accommodate "Pilots of The Book," some of whom only knew how to fly passenger planes for hobby, but they were quickly trained up. Fortunately, the medical industry was packed with Jewish surgeons, but when their schedules filled, medical schools opened the gates to Jewish students and fast-tracked them to become full MDs. Was that a bit unfair to the other medical students? Yes, but this was an international emergency, and what had to be done was done and fast.

Some more awkward hires took place as the world scrambled to employ every available non-fainter for all kinds of work. To a degree, it became the reverse of the *Shabbos Goy*: everyone wanted to hire a Jew for their house. Hassan Rouhani, the President of Iran, hired a Brooklyn Jew named Schlomo Moskowitz to be his personal bodyguard. Russian President Vladimir Putin's Defense Minister was a former kosher butcher whose family had been persecuted during the pogroms of the early 1900s. Mel Gibson brought on the great-grandson of New York gangster Meyer Lansky to be his driver at a salary of $3 million a year, but rumor had it, Lansky liked to stop abruptly when Mel got racist just to see him pass out.

Perhaps most awkwardly, sports changed, and most agreed not for the better. Turned out that the aggression and stress of a televised sports competition was too much for the athletes, and dangerous fainting spells caused a full-on halt to games. The NBA season, deep in the march to the Playoffs, utilized the luxury tax to sign on entire teams of Jewish athletes, and the league quickly became a kind of a Maccabean Games, with the new average height of players at 5'8, short-sighted and doughy. The "new Lebron James," a *nebbishy* HR executive named Avi Meyerhoff, could dunk with semi-consistency and was showered with endorsement deals.

Among those non-fainting Jews, of course, were the Schtinklers, and their lives had also changed immeasurable. Sara's lab had become the epicenter of research on fainting goat syndrome, and how the myotonia congenita that existed in goats could help the world understand the disorder in its human form. Lillia, Spencer, and Chewy quickly became internet celebrities. Sara's daily tetherball games with the three goats were livestreamed on Twitch. Kent represented the work in the media and appeared daily on cable news shows (more than once with his idol Anderson Cooper). When Kent was double booked Sara did a couple of radio interviews, and producers were both charmed and bored by her excited, esoteric way of speaking about myotonia. Funding had been extended indefinitely for Sara's work, and Bruce was spared from working at his father-in-law's Kosher pickle kiosk. The sloths just hung out, as was their proclivity, waiting to be called up and enjoying their lazy days.

As for Reuven, his Ace bandage had been upgraded to a small cast for his sprained left hand, and as a reward for his heroic save of Jake's head during the Senior Meeting it was signed by none other than the Brigit, the President of the Company, "Nice catch!" The Brony Summer Camp project he'd pitched had been greenlit to full-length presentation tape for a Network pitch, and Reuven was given sole control over creative. Since there were now more eyes on him, Reuven bought nicer clothes on nordstromrack.com, paid for an expensive haircut at The Art of Shaving, and even wore the gold neck chain with a Star of David that he'd been gifted at his *bar mitzvah* by a distant aunt thirty-two years prior. Previously ignored-to-tolerated by Claire's twenty-five-year-old assistant, Pamela, she now openly flirted with Reuven, going so far as saying he'd be "The King of JSwipe," if only he weren't married. Reuven tried to focus on his job but found himself getting more social by joining in for after-work drinks and enjoying that his co-workers laughed more freely at his jokes. Reuven's boss Claire had started referring to Reuven as "My Jew," but it had gone from chiding to light flirtation with alarming speed, and Reuven would be damned if he was going to put a stop to that.

As for Joshua, previously bullied and lectured by his school Principal about Israeli occupation of Palestinian land, he'd also experienced a change in tide since the pandemic began. Being one of the only Jews in the school and the only one to have attended Hebrew Day School had been a huge knock against him socially, but now he couldn't walk the halls without getting fist-bumped by jocks or patted on the back by those who had previously ignored or even bullied him. Even William, Chin, and Zed paid their respects. "You kicked our ass, Bro. Respect," they'd said.

But unlike for his father, who enjoyed the new treatment, and his mother, whose work benefitted from it, Joshua saw through it all as hypocrisy and he despised it. These phonies who'd considered him a waste of space at best and punch-able at most only months before suddenly lionized him, and all because of a genetic fluke? It was the same kind of chance that had warded off puberty for Joshua, making his armpits hairless, his cheeks still chubby, and his stature a foot shorter than many in his grade. And now they were willing to overlook that to focus on his newfound Hebraic superpower of not keeling over when he got nervous? It made him ill. Joshua was keenly aware that his improved treatment would all go back to normal when the pandemic ended. The fist pumps would disappear, the bullies would resume their work of making his life miserable; he would be invisible-to-punch-able again. When Principal Davies called Joshua into his office only to urge him to consider running for Student Council, Joshua held himself back from telling him where to stick it, and instead ran out to the back of the school to let off some steam.

"Frauds!" Joshua yelled and kicked a trashcan. He felt a rage within him that he'd rarely felt before. An urge to violence. He kicked the trashcan again. "Stupid two-faced phonies!"

"That'll teach 'em," a voice from above said, stopping

Joshua mid-kick. He looked up to see a girl with heavy black eyeliner, a black hoodie, and skulls on her soft helmet. She sat up on the fire escape casually smoking a vape pen and swinging her legs down. "Poor garbage can's just doing its job. Have mercy, 'kay?"

Joshua recognized the girl as Brie Sandler, an art freak who was rumored to have bit William's tongue at a party in fifth grade and had been publicly shamed for it ever since. Also, there was word that her mother was an alcoholic who crashed her Nissan Sentra into the local pizzeria. Long story short, Brie was someone to avoid at school, someone so low on the social totem pole that even lowly Joshua should shirk her.

"Sorry," Joshua said, reflexively. "Just needed to . . . "

"Release some anger? Yeah, must be frustrating having your ass kissed all day for being a non-fainter."

"You wouldn't understand."

"Lemme guess," Brie said. "You realize that you're just a genetic freak and when this thing reverses you'll go back to being the school's punching bag?"

Joshua squinted at her. It was exactly what he was thinking, but it felt weird hearing from someone else. He looked up at her, fixated on the vape.

"It's just CBD. I'm not stupid. Want a hit?" She held it out for him, but he shook his head. "Suit yourself. This strain makes you feel like the popular kids do for a little while. Total stupid confidence. Helps in gym class."

"Why do you want to feel like them?" Joshua asked, sincerely.

"Why should I have to feel like shit all the time?"

Joshua saw her point. Something about Brie filled him with daring. He walked towards her, took the vape from her hand and inhaled. He suffered an immediate coughing fit and then in seconds little stars danced around his vision. Joshua wobbled a bit.

"The ultimate irony would be if this stuff made you faint. You good?" Brie asked.

Joshua nodded.

"There are worse things than a fainting spell," Joshua said, and it sounded philosophical to him.

"True," Brie nodded. "You know Jenn Caldwell, Prom Queen? She has like three eating disorders, has to sleep at a clinic on weekends. Blake Travis, the baseball douchebag? He walked in on his mom screwing his math tutor. Now he lives with his dad who's a manic depressive addicted to online poker. So, you're right about worse things."

"How do you know all that?"

"I hack their social media, read their DMs."

"You hack mine?"

"Way too boring."

Joshua laughed. Just then Principal Davies stepped into the alleyway looking miffed. Joshua braced himself.

"Brie. Come here right now, young lady," he said.

"Ugh, coming," Brie called out.

"He's your . . . dad?" Joshua asked flabbergasted.

"Uncle. I live with him. Didn't you hear that my mom drove drunk into the pizzeria?" Joshua shrugged as Brie jumped off the ledge. "He's not so bad. Except you have to listen to his heroic luxury trips to the Middle East all the time. He literally just does it to get back at his ex-wife who ran off with some Israeli guy named Isnot."

"Wow."

"Enjoy feeling like a superhero, Joshua. Who knows when they're going to develop kryptonite, and all this will be a dream."

Joshua watched in wonder as Brie sauntered off down the alley towards Davies. He wasn't sure if it was the effects of the vape, but he swore that she sparkled.

That night Joshua lay in bed thinking about Brie and how she read his mind and how she smelled like grape bubblegum and how she was probably magical in some way. He sniffed his armpit and smelled something off and noticed that some hair had sprouted there. He checked the other pit too and there were a few scraggly hairs there as well. "When the hell?" He went to the bathroom and opened the sealed Axe deodorant that his mom had bought him years ago, anticipating this day. It smelled like a leather saddle doused in whiskey that had been spilled in a bar fight between two feuding libertarian bike gangs but at least it covered his B.O. Was this puberty? Had Brie just triggered it? He looked down in his pants and confirmed it. Joshua made a note to buy some different deodorant the next day like a real teenager. Then he went back to bed and opened his Instagram, on which he only had his old Hebrew School classmates and two cousins as followers, and he saw that Brie had sent a follow request. He waited an entire nine seconds before accepting.

Sara lay on the couch downstairs trying to piece together the facts of a global pandemic that had landed directly in her lap. The connection between the human fainting spells that had spread across the globe and myotonia congenita had been proven beyond any doubt, but why it was occurring in humans, how it spread, and why not in the Jewish populace were big open-ended questions that needed immediate solving. Sara had quickly taken herself out of the debate about ethnicity, thank heavens. Geneticists around the globe as well as religious zealots of all stripes were debating that daily, and it had gotten dumb and clumsily anti-Semitic almost immediately. But Sara's discovery about the BRCA 2/Tay-Sachs/Gaucher mutation weighed heavily on her mind. She had managed to keep that quiet all this time, needing to collect more human samples and do more substantive research before she went public, but eventually it was information that she would need to share. *And then what?* Sara closed her eyes to think but every time she did her grandmother, with her red hair and wagging finger, emerged in her mind. "Don't forget the monster in the closet."

"Yeah, yeah, how can I forget. It's all you ever talk about!" she replied.

Upstairs, Reuven showered luxuriously, letting hot steam fill his nostrils and fog up the bathroom mirrors. He had spent the day fantasizing about Claire's assistant, Pamela. She had complimented his hairy forearms, and he pleasured himself to the thought of her, but made sure not to finish as he was hoping for a more Biblical completion with the spouse. But when he climbed into bed next to Sara that night she rolled onto her side and turned off the light.

"I'm already asleep," Sara said when Reuven grinded up against her.

"But you're still on your phone," Reuven said.

"Trying to sleep. I'm almost there."

"How about some fun-a-lingus?" asked Reuven with a devilish grin.

"Gross. I have an irregular period."

"Don't care."

"Exactly."

Sara inched away further and put down her phone, still thinking about her grandmother. How could Reuven possibly think about sex at a time like this?

Reuven rolled onto his back and sighed. Hadn't he earned some affection? The way he was excelling at work? The way he was being complimented for his physique, and the hair on his arms and his thick neck. He wondered if he'd been younger, unattached, and this whole fainting pandemic had hit what kind of woman would sleep with him then? Maybe Pamela? Ah, it's just fantasy. Okay to fantasize. Something to put out of his head later, but for now it felt nice for Reuven to savor Pamela and her perfect behind as he faded into sleep.

CHAPTER 5

THE SHOWER REUVEN enjoyed that morning was long and luxurious. He went straight blade and even used the brush and that expensive tub of Vaughn shaving cream he'd gotten for Father's Day years before. He applied peelable eye treatment from Kiehl's, and then brushed his teeth with this new charcoal toothpaste, which didn't seem to take away the yellow. He considered getting them professionally whitened? Pricey, but probably worth it. He wrapped himself up to his waist in a towel and looked at his reflection in the mirror. Not bad for forty-five. He still had round shoulders and nice arms, left over from the years of weight training that his father had pressured him to do even past college. Sure, he could lose a few pounds, but he'd kept things up with twice-a-week gym visits. What had he been training for all these years? He thought it was just in case he bumped into his Ex from college who had moved to the next town over, and he wanted to make her feel at least a bit remorseful. But maybe it had been for this moment all along?

To say that Reuven had grown cocksure since the pandemic began would be like saying peacocks "sort of" like to show off their plumage. He waited for his 8:05 a.m. train out of Chatham Station, face freshly moisturized, shirt unbuttoned to reveal chest hair and his Star of David *bar mitzvah* necklace. Reuven sized up the men waiting alongside him on the platform like they were his playthings. He marveled that with one "Boo!" he could easily hurl them onto the tracks to their deaths. Surely, they feared him? He stole glances at the working women standing alongside him and fantasized that one (or more) might pull him into the bathroom during the commute for a brief sexual encounter. Surely, they desired him? How could they not. He was a Jew. Reuven hid a hard-on behind his workbag as the train arrived, the real possibility of a dalliance between stops tingling in his mind.

As he rode the train, Reuven's mind wandered to Junior High, where he'd spent three miserable years at a Waspy private school in the suburbs of Toronto called Shield Academy. The uniform had been a barfy green blazer and striped tie, there were no girls, and the teachers had free reign to terrorize the students in the military-style. On his first day there, scrawny twelve-year-old Reuven had been thrown up against a locker by his neck by a teacher for not having his tie knotted correctly. Reuven had been stunned by the violence but when the teacher stalked off, Dale Stevens, a popular kid in his grade shot him a grin and said, "You've got to learn the ropes." During Reuven's second week at Shield, his History teacher covered WWII and told the class that Nazism was so popular in Germany in the late 1930s that everyone in the class would have been a Nazi back then. Reuven, who'd attended Hebrew school since he was three years old, raised his hand and said obviously not *everybody* would be Nazi, some would be persecuted. The other kids in the class laughed at him, and the one kid who he thought would have his back, Dale Stevens, told him flat-out that he was embarrassed in him. Courage fled young Reuven and did not return for the duration of his time at Shield. When kids started drawing swastikas on their backpacks (for reasons that probably had something to do with British punk music), he did nothing. Reuven winced thinking about the one time he'd confronted anyone about it, cornering his nemesis Robert Winthrop III in a bathroom for drawing a swastika in his geography textbook. But he'd only punched him in the arm. The arm! He was teased about that too. Reuven fantasized zillions of times about ramming the kid's teeth into the urinal and then walking out of that shitty school forever, middle fingers raised high in the air. But he hadn't. He'd been a coward and feared that he had remained that way far beyond escaping Shield Academy. Well, no more. He wasn't saying God favored him in particular, but he did feel that he'd been granted a chance to make up for that terrible time in his life. An opportunity to prove that he'd grown up to be a strong Jew, one who wouldn't be fucked with. Reuven tensed up his biceps as he walked off the train. Not bad, he smirked. This is my moment—take it.

When he got to work and sat with his morning coffee an alert came onto his calendar for a one-on-one meeting with Claire. Reuven's pulse quickened by instinct—the hell was that for? He grabbed for his bag, pulled out his little wooden box with the Xanax, but then paused. "No, Reuven. That was the old you." He dumped the pills in the trash, took a deep nasal breath, and decided to depend on his newfound Hebraic testicular fortitude to stave off an anxiety attack.

"You ready for Claire, sweetie?" Claire's assistant, Pamela, came to his office. Her silk blouse was unbuttoned to reveal cleavage, and her lipstick was extra red as if the official name of the color was "Oops, We Put in Too Much Red."

Reuven stood up from his chair, measuring his breath.

"No, she'll come for you. Or come to you. Come on you? Sorry, ha . . . She's on her way." Pamela smiled again at her off-color joke, giving Reuven extra eye-contact.

Reuven sat back down. This had to be serious. Maybe he was getting fired? He tried to focus on his breath. He really wished he'd taken that Xanax. Was it too late to fish it out of the trash? Claire rounded the corner, knocked lightly, and then entered, shyly almost, as she took a seat across from Reuven.

"I have something rather important to talk to you about, Reuven," she said. "Well, two things."

"Shoot and double shoot," Reuven replied, trying to say the most confident gentile thing he could think of.

"Reuven, you've been an exemplary part of the team. Hard-working. Smart. I don't need to tell you that you're the best writer on the floor. I wouldn't trust anyone else to type out an important pitch. And I know I've been hard on you at times. The PDF thing—I regret being bitchy like that."

Reuven was taken aback. Had his boss, EVP of Production Claire Nichols, just referred to herself as "bitchy"? He didn't know what to say.

"Uh, don't worry about that. You're a great boss, Claire. And I should always attach the PDF—"

"What I'm saying is," Claire cut him off. "Things should be easier for you around here than they are. You should enjoy more autonomy. Don't want to stress out those swimmers, right?" Claire said, then her eyes went crazy. "Whoa, uh, Freudian slip."

Reuven forced a smile. Had his boss who had just called herself bitchy now referred to his sperm count, Freudian slip or not? Was he still asleep, tossing and turning in bed and dreaming all this?

"This is delicate, Reuven, so I would appreciate if what I'm about to say stayed between us."

"Of course. Discretion."

"Yes, great word. You always have the best words." She smiled, then took the kind of deep nervous breath that Reuven recognized from his own behavior. She stared at her hands. "Ugh, this is hard. But I'll just say it. It's no secret that I've had no luck with men. They confuse me. And the apps, well, they've been no help. So now I find myself an old spinster, forty-four years old with no children. My ovaries have spider webs. My gynecologist says it's not probable but before menopause it's possible to uh, conceive. To finally have a baby of my own."

"Oh, that's great, Claire. I'm so happy for you," Reuven said, relieved as all hell. "When are you due?"

"No, you don't understand." She squinted at Reuven, a bit annoyed by his thickness. "See, in order to try to have a baby, I need a donor." Reuven just stared blankly. "A sperm donor, Reuven. I need good swimmers." She tilted her head, exasperated. "You've conceived successfully. You have a son. A handsome one, I saw on Facebook. So your swimmers . . . they work, and, well . . . I'd like to request some."

"Request what exactly?"

"I want you to father my child, Reuven."

Reuven thought he couldn't be any more stunned than he had been, but his eyes nearly popped out of his head.

"I know, I know, it's crazy!" Claire said, waving her arms and grinning at how, well, whimsical she was. "An HR nightmare to begin with. Feel free to report me right away. And I know that you're married. I assume . . . happily?" Reuven nodded, and she looked disappointed. "Good. Well, then you would need to discuss this with your wife. But before you both say no . . . I would make sure that you have time to deal with the stress of this situation. Some extra vacation time with your family would be necessary. A work-at-home day moving forward. Maybe Fridays, as you've requested for I-don't-know-how-long?"

Reuven thought about it. "Why me?" he asked. But as soon as those words left his mouth and Claire looked at him almost confused by how dumb he was, Reuven finally understood. He was surprised he hadn't seen it right away. For a second, Reuven actually imagined that Claire admired him, that she saw him as a good specimen, had always seen him that way, had been thinking of this maybe since hiring him. *No, no, Silly... I'm just a Jew at an unusually Waspy production company*. Her Jew. At this strange time Jewish people have a genetic advantage, but before, not so much. This was just like Shield Academy but in reverse. Claire was Robert Winthrop III in drag caught drawing a swastika in his geography textbook but instead they were little hearts. This time he wouldn't miss his opportunity. This time he would administer something harder than a punch in the arm. Over Claire's shoulder, Reuven noticed Pamela leaning over her cube, poking out her pouty twenty-five-year-old behind and chewing on the end of a highlighter. She flashed him a smile, arched an eyebrow. How he'd love to get a run at that.

Reuven refocused. "Claire, this is an honor, really."

"Then, you'll do it! Because Ray in Accounting has a family history of psoriasis . . . "

"I am flattered that you would think of me. And that you would consider the feelings of my family, and how this all might be made easier."

"What a relief," Claire said, unable to suppress a smile. "I'm so glad you said that. So, scheduling—"

"But," Reuven cut in, and a strange smile came over his face. "If you want what this Jew has it's going to cost a lot more than Summer Fridays to get it."

Then he just stared at her. Claire reddened.

"Oh. Uh, okay, hardball, huh?" she asked. "Well, what do you have in mind?"

"The Senior Vice President role."

"Well, I can't just—"

"With a healthy salary bump, of course. Fifteen percent? And I want Jake's office. It should always have been mine. And no more calls after seven o'clock, Claire. I have a family. You'll soon understand what that can mean in terms of demands on your time."

Claire blanched. "Yes, of course."

Reuven gave her a look that he'd received many times when meeting with a superior in their office. It was, "Well if there isn't anything else please leave now." Claire seemed to understand the role reversal. She bowed her head.

"Okay, well, thank you for your, uh, kind consideration and your time. And discretion. Thank you, Reuven."

Reuven smiled tightly. Claire bowed again as she walked out of his office. Behind her, Pamela straightened up and put back on her glasses like she'd been waiting for

Claire the whole time. Reuven sat back and exhaled. He was back in the bathroom at Shield Academy with Robert Winthrop III in 7th Grade. But this time he'd taken that Nazi's head and rammed it into the ceramic toilet until his teeth scattered like Chicklets and he did it all with his sperm! *Who's the coward now?*

Sara drove Joshua to school that morning and it took a fraction of the time it used to. Some drivers were so susceptible to myotonia congenita that a simple yellow light would cause enough stress to send them into a faint, and after a few weeks of wild car crashes and thousands of deaths, the government enforced that only "essential drivers" should take the road for the time being along with, of course, non-fainting Jewish people. Sara felt odd driving the empty streets, getting nodded at by the other smug Jewish drivers who were free to speed or have road rage or whatever. She swore that she spotted others who were less fortunate sneer at her from the sidewalks. Those with soft helmets and elbow pads, legging it with their grocery bags and dragging their children along, stopping periodically to open breathing apps and center themselves. Sara would give them all lifts if she could, but the lab beckoned as always.

Joshua was silent for most of the ride but not mopey-silent like he usually was on the way to school, and that pleased Sara. Not one mention of skipping class to come to the lab as she let him do periodically when things got especially tough for him. In fact, when they pulled into the parking lot Joshua almost jumped out of his seat while they were still moving instead of pleading to not have to go in.

"Hugs?" Sara asked as Joshua left the car.

"No offense, but I don't want to smell like goats today."

"Of course," Sara said.

It was then, out the window, that Sara noticed the girl

dressed all in black with skulls on her soft helmet and too much eye makeup for her taste. She didn't seem to be waiting for Joshua in particular but did clearly "wave" two fingers his way when she saw him. Some woman's intuition told Sara precisely what was going on. Joshua walked off towards the girl and Sara watched as they both looked down at their phones and then walked off together. But there was something odd about how the girl walked alongside her son, glancing behind her back to see if people were watching. Single hyenas did that when they appeared before prey, knowing that there were about twenty other hyenas hidden in the bushes ready to attack. Sarah leaned out the window at this teenage goth hyena.

"Joshua!" she called out, far too loudly. "You're the G.O.A.T.!"

Joshua turned around, half-waved, and walked off again with the girl, shaking his head slightly. Sara had the urge to park the car and follow her son and that girl into school, but she fought it. Had Joshua not heard the concern in her voice when she told him that he was the goat? Did he care? Sara was slightly mortified that she was so suspicious of a girl just because she seemed to be interested in hanging out with her son. Joshua could make friends, girls even. He was smart and funny. "A real *mensch*," her grandmother would have said, but then might have waggled that finger in warning at what happens to *mensches*. "*Menches* get stitches."

"Oh zip it, Gran," Sara said. She pulled out of the parking lot and headed to the lab, trying to shake it off. Her plan for that day was to follow a wild hunch she'd had about molecular distancing, and she was hoping for a slow exploratory morning in front of her microscope. But when she arrived onto the lab's dead-end street and pulled into the parking lot what she experienced put all that in flux: a mob of reporters ran towards her car, cameras snapping through her windshield like paparazzi. Sara rolled down her window.

"You must have the wrong parking lot," she said. As more reporters swarmed, Sara put her car in park and got out, thinking that her emergence would clear up this case of mistaken identity. "See?"

"Dr. Schtinkler, is it true you've discovered a mutation of Jewish diseases that blocks fainting goat syndrome?" one reporter asked.

"Who told you that?"

"Is that why NBA players can barely touch the rim now, Sara?"

"Is it true you're planning to experiment with molecular distancing today to see if that will help? Will it?"

"No comment," Sara muttered, totally flabbergasted.

"Don't you think it's a conflict of interest for a Jewish person like you to be at the helm of looking for a cure to a pandemic that basically benefits you?"

Sara stopped in her tracks, stunned by the question. "I'm a scientist. This is my life's work."

She kept walking and squeezed through the scrum of reporters into the front entrance like a rock star heading backstage after a show. A security guard blocked the reporters from following her in. Sara saw Kent waiting for her in the hall. He was wearing his paisley tie and a plaid soft helmet combo that he usually wore for big TV interviews. His silver hair poked out in the way Anderson Cooper styled it.

"What was all that about?" Sara asked.

"They love you." Kent smiled. "And you're finally getting the recognition you deserve. Isn't it fabulous?"

"They know about the Jewish cell mutation. That was in my computer files, locked up. But it was speculation. I needed more time to research before sharing even the basics."

"About that," Kent said, now wincing.

Sara was shocked. "You shared my notes?"

"I had to give them something." Kent held up his hands and spread his fingers to show he was unarmed and harmless. "An order from the top, from the funders. The press needed a taste or else they'd give up on us. Frankly, I was upset that you hadn't shared it with me already."

"It was just a hypothesis." Sara stared at him like he was crazy. "Nowhere near enough research went into that. You hate unproven hypotheses, remember?"

"I gave a vague overview," Kent said, ignoring her question. "They were going to report that we're wasting time and donor money. And now your work is all they're going to talk about for days. This might be a major breakthrough. And the fact that you have the BRCA 2 gene yourself, what a story."

"How do you know that?"

"Uh, part of your notes."

"You look at my mastectomy photos too, Kent?"

Kent reddened, then just sighed. "I'm sorry. I crossed the line. Honestly, the stress of it made me faint multiple times. But you have every right to be mad at me. I buckled."

Sara gave Kent a stern look, but she'd been with him too long to stay mad. "I'm back to gene manipulation today," she said. "Tell them I have a new theory about isolation, and it's promising."

"Great!" Kent said, and his mood changed immediately back to elated. "Back to work. What are we paying you for, Rockstar?" Kent checked his watch. "Oh, I'm late for that CNN thing. And again, sorry. But, yunno, gun-to-head and all."

"Good luck with Anderson, Rockstar."

Kent skipped out, thumbs up. Sara sighed deeply as she walked into her lab. She opened her computer and clicked on the file that Kent had plundered for public consumption. Under that day's date, she typed, "*Ongoing data.*" Then she closed her computer and opened up her red journal. From now on all scientific research would be handwritten and she would have to guard that red journal with her life. If she couldn't trust Kent, who could she trust?

CHAPTER 6

PER THE DIGITAL LOGS that I found on a dusty flash drive labeled, "Reuven's Stuff," that evening Reuven received a text message from Sara saying that she'd be home late for "some interview," this time for local TV. Then he got another text from Joshua. He was going out to a movie with "a friend." Neither would be back until well past 10 p.m. Normally, Reuven would take this rare opportunity to head home and sneak in some porn on his laptop and then smoke one of the stale cigarettes he had hidden in a box in the basement. A solo night of self-care. But he felt too good to waste himself on his himself. He was too well-groomed. So, he did something he'd never done in all of his years commuting to the city; he went to a swanky bar alone.

It was on 28th at 3rd Ave. He'd overheard the interns say that's where celebs hang out sometimes. He strolled up to the bouncer, who nodded him in, impressed when he saw Reuven's very Jewish name on his ID and his hairy arms. "Awfully Hebraic, my man." The club was dimly lit with plush leather couches, dark wood, and pops of neon pink and gold. It had perfected that masculine/feminine sexy vampire vibe. Reuven took a seat at the bar and waved at the bartender, who had pale skin and slicked back hair. "Double Jameson on the rocks and a ginger ale on the side."

"Now that's a real man's order," the bartender said.

Reuven hadn't read a novel in years, but when the

bartender winked as he laid down his drinks, he felt like Charles Bukowski or John Fante or some other beloved misogynistic writer. He took a sip of whiskey and winced, quickly chasing it with the sweet soda. Reuven deserved a drink, even two tonight. He was a man with a lot to think about. He had a lot to celebrate. And all thanks to his super Jewish sperm. If he impregnated his boss then he'd get the promotion he'd long-deserved, some time off, and even summer Fridays. He'd be a hero to Joshua, and everyone who had doubted him along the way could kiss his hairy Jewish ass. And surely, he'd be rewarded by Sara with some long-awaited sex. It stung when Sara turned away from his sexual advances, but maybe it was partly him? He was always so whiney about work, which wasn't exactly sexy. With a promotion he'd have swagger, and no woman can resist swagger, even his darling wife, Sara. Honestly, he just needed to have more swagger than a goat.

Reuven took a long swig of his whiskey. He looked at the attractive young people holding drinks. Their bodies looked amazing. So confident. So thin. A group of them were gyrating against each other like they were trying to scratch off lottery tickets with their groins. Reuven was wondering what it would feel like to be among them, when in the scrum of gyrators he saw a striking image of swollen curves. She was, well, wiggling, and her tight burgundy dress showed all the peaks and valleys of a Playboy centerfold. It took a while to realize that he was staring open-mouthed at Pamela, Claire's twenty-five-year-old assistant from the office. Her eyes caught his and she giggled, played with the long silky hair falling out her soft helmet. When she waved, Reuven felt a shot of embarrassment up his spine.

"Enjoying the view?" A man's voice from behind Reuven asked.

Reuven whipped around. Next to him was a bald guy with a thick neck and a mouth that seemed to only grin, as if he'd been in on an inside joke for years and was dying to share. Reuven's blush turned to a knowing grin when he saw a Star of David neck chain mingling in his chest hair. Another non-fainter like him. "And what if I was?" he asked.

"Ha, exactly what I hoped you'd say!" The man slapped Reuven's shoulder. "No one could stop you except some other Jew, and I ain't about to get in your way. Big guy like you might swing and the wind would bowl me over."

The compliment wasn't true at all. This guy was thick, looked solid to the ground, probably a wrestler back in high school. Still, Reuven liked being referred to as a big guy.

Reuven flexed his bicep. "Mostly free weights," he said and they both laughed.

"I figured. And what are you six-two, six-three? They don't build Jews like you around here. Where you from?"

"Toronto, originally," Reuven said.

"A Canadian Jew! You've got to be shitting me."

"We have to be tall in Canada. It's cold and the sun is way up there."

The bald guy whooped it up like it was the funniest damn thing he's ever heard. Reuven had told that joke dozens of times and gotten precisely zero response.

"Sam Kanter," the man said, sticking out a surprisingly large hand. His watch was also big and manly, a TAG Heuer, one of those watches you see in GQ worn by Harrison Ford in a pick-up truck. It made Reuven think that this was the kind of bald guy who was bald from too much testosterone.

"Reuven," he replied.

"Nice to meet you, Reuven." The man lifted his drink and waved it around the bar. "This is the life, right? We've got our pick of the litter; the bouncers bow at our feet. What choice do they have, right? I bet you're killing it at work?"

"As a matter of fact, I may have gotten a promotion today."

"*Mazel Tov*!" He clinked glasses with Reuven. "Get it while you can, right?"

“I was due for it,” Reuven said.

“Sure, you were,” the guy said with a wink, and Reuven winced. “It’s gonna end, Reuven.” His demeanor changed suddenly from convivial to darkly serious. “And when it does these anti-Semitic fucks are going try to smack us down like whack-a-mole. I know it and I know a smart guy like you knows it too.”

“Well, I . . . ” Reuven hadn’t even considered it.

“Of course, you do. You’ve got eyes. You can see through all the bullshit. These hypocrites kissing our ass, offering us crumbs to bide their time while a few months ago they were openly slamming Israel on social media! Not to mention the actual neo-Nazis out there who’d prefer us dead. Last year they were out there in the streets chanting, ‘Jews will not replace us.’ Now? ‘Jews, can you replace a lightbulb for us?’ They’re just lying in wait, Reuven. The minute there’s a vaccine for this thing—the second—expect pogroms. Eh, I wish there was something we could do about it . . . ”

“There’s got to be something,” Reuven said because he knew by the way his neck hair was standing on end that the guy was speaking truths.

“Yeah, yeah, there’s got be. Or else we’re toast. Literally not figuratively because they’ll have us in the ovens again. Me and the boys were just talking about it. You should come around back and meet ‘em. They’re like-minded, Hamish types.”

“There’s a back to this place?”

Sam Kanter slid off his barstool and motioned with a tilt of his bald head. Reuven followed, eager to meet more men like Sam. More tough Jews who seemed to mistake him for a tough Jew, too. He walked past the dance floor. Pamela caught eyes with Reuven again and this time blew a kiss, which made Reuven have to press down a stiffy.

Sam and Reuven walked beyond a velvet curtain where a Neanderthal-sized bouncer waved them through, and Reuven found himself in a dull but spacious backroom where they kept the mops and cleaning supplies. A roomful of men sat at round tables playing cards, not a single one wearing a soft helmet. Some smoked cigars, others nursed glasses of whiskey. Reuven had always wanted to visit a secret back room like he'd seen in movies. He never thought he'd be in such a situation but had always assumed it would be less guys who looked like they would throw their backs out from holding chairs during the hora. On the far wall was a row of pinned-up photos, some of men's faces, and some black and white surveillance-type shots. Reuven noticed an image of a skinhead saluting the Nazi flag, a man in an Arab headdress burning the Israeli flag, and group of black men in bowties holding up copies of The Protocols of The Elders of Zion. At the top of the board was a framed photo of slain Jewish journalist Daniel Pearl, like he was a biblical hero looking down and demanding revenge.

"This is Reuven," Sam told the room. "He's *mishpacha.* Got a promotion today."

"*L'chaim,*" several of them said with a chuckle. They raised their glasses. "Me too!"

Reuven got the sense that he was being teased a bit and that made him feel uneasy. But it was nice to be in a roomful of Jewish men, and he felt pride at seeing so many different kinds. Most were Ashkenazi types like him with broad foreheads and Eastern European noses, but there were also darker-skinned men with bushy black eyebrows who Reuven assumed to be Persian or Yemenite. He thought they were called "*Mizrahi*" Jews, but he wasn't sure if that was considered racist or not. There were also several black men, and even an Asian guy. Reuven recalled from his Sunday school education that there was once a prominent community of Jews in China called Kaifeng Jews who he thought were functionally extinct, but maybe they were just biding their time for this moment? Or maybe he just had an Asian mom? The Asian man, along with a few others, wore *kippahs* and *tallit* tucked under their shirts. Reuven instinctively averted his gaze from them, since his only experience with religious Jews was when he dodged their attempts to lure him into their "*Mitzvah* Tank" in front of Penn Station. He always felt worried that they were going to quiz him on something he should have learned in Hebrew school. A test he never studied for.

Sam walked to the front of the room, the wall of photos behind him. "All right, let's get this party started," he said. "Thanks to Eli's handy work we found the IP address to four different enclaves just beyond the Pennsylvania border. Doesn't hurt to have a computer genius amongst us." Eli, a short doughy man wearing a vest with a tech company logo on it, bowed and grinned. "Biggest one he found is in Kunkletown. If you can believe it, it's only three miles from my kid's Jewish summer camp. Who knows what these motherfuckers were planning before the Blessing, maybe on my own kids!"

"*Baruch Hashem*," a couple of the men said.

"We all know there isn't much time. If we're going to get these sons of bitches, we need to get them now and where they live. Any questions about the plan?"

Reuven had a million questions starting with what plan and ending with, seriously, what plan? Sam saw it painted on his face. "The plan, new-guy Reuven, is direct, immediate action. Raid their base, scare 'em a bit and leave 'em with bruises. Then burn down their place of Nazi worship so they can't meet there again. Any other questions?"

"What about the police?" Reuven asked.

Now the whole room of men snickered, and Reuven reddened. A minute ago these guys had all been buddying up to him, and now he'd revealed himself as a noob.

"Sorry, I—"

"Relax, relax. You're new," Sam smiled. "Cops come, we leave them alone, right fellas? Maybe buy 'em a round of cronuts for their troubles. We leave all innocents and children unharmed. No one gets hurt that isn't a goddamned neo-Nazi fuckwit. Now, if there's nothing else, Kadima, let's get going."

And just like that the entire room of men stood up from their chairs and headed for the back exit. Reuven followed. He'd be damned if he was going to call it quits now and risk being labeled a quitter by his religious brethren. In the back alley were four black vans, and the men, including Reuven, all climbed into one. In Reuven's van was the religious Asian man named Shane, Eli the computer hacker, and a few other guys who looked like Persian brothers. Sam drove. Eli broke out a cooler and handed out cold turkey sandwiches from Zabar's (the best) and of course there was cream soda for everyone, except for Eli who revealed he was trying to cut calories, so he could lose enough weight to get rid of his sleep apnea machine. As the van drove off a chorus of munching and slurping and burping began, so loud it could be heard over the engine. A few of them started rapping "Paul Revere" by the Beastie Boys a cappella and the whole van joined in.

"Mike D was in my Hebrew School class," Shane said to Reuven. "I turned him onto the whole Adidas tracksuit thing."

"No kidding?"

When that was done, they talked about the Knicks being crap but glad it's all Jews again like it used to be at the beginning. But they missed dunking. Thank God for Avi Meyerhoff. MVP! MVP! Reuven had a pit in his stomach the entire ride. He looked around at the men in the van. They seemed so at ease, like this was normal. Internally, Reuven was a wreck. What did they think this was? What did they think of him? Sam leaned back from the front seat and passed everyone handguns like they were passes to Six Flags. Reuven did deep nasal breathing to stave off an anxiety attack.

"I was like you the first time," Shane said to Reuven, seeing him blanch. "But the guns are mainly a prop, like a *mezuzah* without the scroll inside. We don't use them or anything."

“Are they loaded . . . with scrolls?” Reuven asked.

“Just make sure your safety’s on,” one of the Persian guys said. “I saw a guy accidentally shoot himself in the *schvantz*. His wife didn’t mind but his girlfriend was pissed, heheh!”

Reuven held the gun tightly by his side. He watched the others wave theirs around carelessly as they made a point about sports or politics. Sam put on some Grateful Dead, Reuven’s favorite, and he tried to calm down by singing “Box Of Rain,” and it did pass some time. He had heard that song hundreds of times, but this was the first time while holding a gun. He wondered what Bruce Springsteen’s “Nebraska” would sound like while holding a gun? After an hour or so they entered the country, it got darker, and the vans came to a stop on a dirt road shielded by sloping trees. There was a penetrating silence that Reuven and the other city dwellers weren’t used to, and as Reuven climbed out of the van, his nostrils inhaled something totally unfamiliar. After a moment Reuven realized it was fresh air. Sam gathered the boys around a flashlight.

“They’re right through that gate,” he said, pointing. “The barn has a red light on, which means the neo-Nazis fucks are meeting right now. What do you say we go interrupt said meeting?”

“I see the red light!” one of the men said excitedly, and was shushed by all.

“Good. Let’s show these Jew-haters what The Maccabees are all about,” Sam said.

“We’re called The Maccabees?” Reuven asked Shane.

“Can you think of something better?”

“Macca-bros? Cha-Bad Boys? Mazel-Toughs?”

“Shush!”

And they went. Ducked low through the darkness along a dirt path, flashlights turned off. Sam led. The gate had a chain link and a lock, so one of the men used bolt cutters and snapped through it. A guard dog barked in the distance, as if to say, "Hey, watch out for approaching Jews." It ran towards them and Reuven's pulse quickened. He watched Sam remove a juicy brisket from wax paper and toss it in the dog's direction.

"You're gonna waste a whole brisket on a mutt?" Eli said. "Couldn't you find something trief?"

The dog stopped on a dime ten feet from them and began to chomp at the tasty meat as the men walked past. Reuven couldn't believe his eyes. Of course, it was a German Sheppard, the most anti-Semitic of dogs. Sam had the balls to pet the dog's head. "Nighty night when the sleeping pills hit, little doggy," he said, and the men snickered.

The barn was off in the distance. The single red light above the door reminded Reuven of the Eternal Flame that was set over the arc in the synagogue where he had his *bar mitzvah*. Same deep hew of red. He probably would have been more confident at his *bar mitzvah* had he been armed. Still, Reuven's heart pounded and sweat poured down his back and into his butt crack. He started regretting that he didn't just stay home and jerk off.

As they neared the barn, voices could be heard from inside. Someone was sermonizing while others cheered:

"Do you want these evil Jew rats to take our land?"

"*Hell, No!*"

"Our wives?"

"*Hell, No!*"

"Steal our money like that wasn't always their way?"

"*Oh, hell no!*"

The Jewish men, "The Maccabees," as Sam called them, huddled outside the barn eavesdropping on the screed. Through a crack in the wood Reuven and the others were able to peek inside. A white power flag with the German Cross was hoisted above a pulpit on which a fat guy with a shaved head and suspenders spoke.

"Are we going to let these slimy rat Jews push us around? Tell us what to do? The Elders of Zion prepared us for this. We've gotta take 'em by surprise. All at once."

Reuven felt the urge to flee this danger, leave this situation at once, when Sam suddenly pushed past him and swung open the big barn doors.

"How about right now, you pathetic Nazi fucks?" Sam asked the room of men. "Did The Elders of Zion prepare you for right goddamned now?"

What the neo-Nazis saw framed in their barn door—a gang of middle-aged Jewish men of all colors—might have caused some vague concern a few months before. Maybe even amusement. The lambs had wandered into the lion's den. Certainly Reuven, who winced in fear like he'd just made a terrible mistake and may not live long enough to regret it would not have inspired much in the way of fear. But now that "The Blessing" had occurred the collective emotion in the room of seething anti-Semites could only be described as terror. Their eyes widened in panic, color flushed from their already pale faces, and they froze in place as if hit by a magical beam of ice.

"Didn't think so," Sam said, and the men laughed.

The neo-Nazis were immobile as statues. Most keeled over onto the dirt floor and then lay there in odd positions, twitching. Reuven noticed several were laid out in the shape of a swastika. They even faint in an anti-Semitic way. Others fell up against a wall of the barn and held there, awkwardly immobile. Sam and the rest of The Maccabees ambled forward with total disregard, inspecting the frozen Nazis as if looking over the details of rejected wax dummies in storage at Madame Tussauds.

"Aw, cute. This one pissed himself," Sam said.

He removed a knife from one of the frozen men's hands and casually tossed it onto the ground. He then pushed his middle finger into the man's forehead, causing him to crash to the ground like a vase off a buffet table. Sam, his bald head shining with sweat, looked to his men and grinned. "Have at 'em, boys," he said.

The men of The Maccabees rushed forward and unleashed brutal violence on the room of the afflicted.

Each attacked the Nazis in their own way. The one guy who took Krav Maga during his year abroad in Israel, went to town, kicking their testicles. The guy who did capoeira in college did impressive dancey flips around a Nazi until the wind of his movement knocked him down. Two others simply took a neo-Nazi by the feet and arms and threw him up against a wall, and they howled with laughter when a hook caught the back of the man's suspenders and held him up. Sam ripped down the White Power flag and tossed it on the ground.

Reuven watched, worried there'd start shooting soon. But not a gun was brandished. Instead, more Jewish methods of violence materialized: One man, an accountant named Larry, sat with a stiffened Nazi and explained how to write off entertainment on his tax forms. "This entire barn could all be considered a home office," he said, waving around the place. Another Jew sat with a frozen Nazi and complained that his favorite deli was shutting down. "Where am I going to find that brand of sour pickle? And the pastrami, from heaven, you know what I mean?" Eli complained endlessly about his marriage to one of the frozen neo-Nazis, "When we were dating, every night, like rabbits. The minute we're married I can barely get a birthday blowjob, and that's after showering. It hurts, I tell you. It's a kind of abuse."

It was sadism by extreme Jewish culture, and Reuven didn't know what to think. Sam noticed Reuven's reaction and pulled him aside.

"C'mon Reuven, have some fun. These guys would rather see you dead and all because you're circumcised. You heard 'em yourself, didn't you?" Sam motioned to two of his men. "Glatt, Remi, hold up that fat one. Reuven needs to pop his Nazi-punching cherry." The two men lifted up the leader, who'd been calling Jews rats previously. "Don't you want to know what it feels like?" Sam asked.

Reuven shook as he walked towards the frozen man.

With his shaved head, suspenders, and black boots, he looked almost *too* Nazi, like he was in a Halloween costume. There was something sad and childlike about him like a big chunky baby all grown up. “C’mon, Reuven! I can’t hold him for long. He’s one heavy Nazi!” Remi complained, straining under the weight. Reuven understood that this man wasn’t Robert Thurston III, and he wasn’t in 7th grade at Shield Academy anymore and that this wasn’t fair, but fuck it; it hadn’t been fair then either. He’d had to deal with a school full of Jew-haters all by himself and was expected to stand up to them? This asshole had it coming even if he did look like a big, fat drooling baby. Reuven set his feet wide. He remembered from a cardio boxing class he’d taken at Lifetime Fitness that a good punch needed weight behind it, was all in the hips, like swinging a baseball bat. Reuven made sure to clench his fist tightly as well, it would be embarrassing if he just slapped the guy in the face. He pulled back and let a punch fly, quite solidly, it turned out. When Reuven’s fist met the neo-Nazi’s face there was a satisfying thwack, and the man twirled before falling to the ground. As Sam and the men cheered, Reuven waved his sore right hand just like in the movies.

“Atta boy, Reuven! Or should we call you, One-Punch Schtinkler?” Sam said, and they all hooted at “One-Punch! One-Punch!”

Reuven couldn’t suppress his smile. This was even better than the first time he had sex. And this time he wasn’t even crying.

“That felt fucking amazing. Can I do it again?” he asked to no one in particular. As the others walked off, Reuven approached another frozen man who was stuck leaning up against a wall. Reuven mustered the balls to look him square in the eyes, which were cold and blue and twitchy. “Robert Thurston III, this one’s for you, bitch!” He pulled back and punched the man in the nose, sending him spinning and then collapsing to the ground. Reuven picked the man back up from the floor and leaned him up against the wall again, then hit him in the ribs then directly under the nose like he'd seen Mike Tyson do. Blood sprayed from the man's nostrils as he hit the floor again. "Yeah, ya stupid Nazi bitch!"

"Whoa, looks like One-Punch caught the bug, ha-ha!" Shane said, and Reuven had to smile.

The Maccabees of New York City ransacked the barn. Sam took from the pulpit the copies of Mein Kampf, The Protocols of The Elders Of Zion and the complete works of Roald Dahl (sorry to ruin your childhood, but *major* anti-Semite). He tossed them in a pile on top of the White Power flag. Eli poured gasoline on top and did a good old fashioned book burning. The pages crackled in flames, and as the fire took hold, the Jews warmed their hands on the heat. Reuven got a big laugh when he turned around to warm his ass on the fire. Then one by one The Maccabees lifted all of the stiff Nazi bodies out of the burning barn and into the open field. Some were so big it took three of them to carry one. Others were smaller, and the bigger Jews threw them over their shoulders like sacks of wet laundry and dumped them onto the dirt. Sam made sure that all of the Nazis were laid on their side, positioned so that they would be watching their own barn burn to the ground. Sam then stepped in front of their view.

"Any word of this to the authorities and we'll be back. Blink twice if you understand," he said. The Nazis all blinked twice. "Good. Now, you even think about having another one of these little get-togethers, we'll find you and rest assured that this gang of hairy, crooked-nosed kikes won't be so nice next time, you hear me? Blink." They blinked. "Heil Hitler," he said.

Sam, Reuven and the rest of the men swaggered off, leaving the neo-Nazis to watch the destruction of their headquarters. It was all so heroic and unsettling that Reuven's whole body tingled. This feeling, this feeling he'd never fully experience but had seen in Brigit and some other British higher-ups at work was somehow unmistakable to him: Power. The men ambled off to the gate and past the German Shephard, who slept next to a half-eaten brisket. They climbed into their vans, which slowly rolled out of the darkness and onto the country road. There was silence in Reuven's van for a while as each man tended to their sore knuckles and presumably reveled in their feelings internally. But Reuven couldn't control himself. He was in a state of total exhilaration. He let out a "Woot!" like he was celebrating a winning touchdown. The other guys smiled and shook their head at the rookie, but then Eli "wooted" too, and they all joined in, until the whole van sounded like a bunch of frat boys at a tailgate.

"This calls for 'Paul's Boutique.'" Sam cued up the classic Beasties' album. Reuven and all the guys rapped along word for word.

When the vans got back to the club in New York City there was beer, cigars, and girls waiting. The Maccabees celebrated and laughed and gave high fives.

"Did you see how that Nazi with the big ears was crying? Snot running down his face like a little baby!" Sam walked up to the board and drew a big red X on the photo marked 'Kunkletown,' and the men raised their drinks and hooted wildly. "You kicked some serious Nazi tuchus tonight, boys!" He was answered with roars.

Reuven was euphoric. This was by far the single greatest night of his life, and he never wanted it to end. He finally felt like one of the boys, and this time the boys were all Jewish like him. And what made it even sweeter was the knowledge that this wasn't even about him and his little prep school neurosis. Fuck Robert Thurston III. He was small fries compared to this. This was about good versus evil on a grand scale. And maybe, Reuven thought, just maybe he hadn't been such a coward back then after all. Maybe he'd just been gathering his strength for this glorious moment to finally arrive. Boy, oh boy, was he ready for it.

CHAPTER 7

SARA HAD NEVER done live TV before, but Kent was so overloaded with requests that this one fell on her. It was a local piece, low stakes, a pop culture reporter who mainly covered red carpet entertainment and celebrity fashion but wanted something a touch serious for tonight's show. Should be a breeze, Kent assured her. A car picked Sara up at the lab and in the backseat Sara read through her notes, trying to put together a straightforward narrative of her life's work that would be easy for an entertainment audience to digest. She wasn't nervous per se, more eager for it to be over with. Kind of the way a goat must feel at the annual "Namaste Goat Yoga" event in South Orange, New Jersey. Who wants that kind of attention?

In the lobby of the studio, a short, chubby man in a too-tight-t-shirt, sparkles on his moustache and glittering pink stones on his soft helmet introduced himself as Mitch The Makeup Maven. "Magical earth goddess hair!" Mitch marveled at Sara's copper curls. "Thank heaven itself you don't have to wear one of these tragic helmets. Though mine is fierce as all get up."

Mitch led Sara to a small mirrored room packed with powder and hairspray, and got to work. "Girl, your skin is dry as the Sahara. Ever hear of moisturizer?" He applied some, and Sara's skin drank it in.

"I don't have much time for self-care," Sara attempted as an excuse.

"There's always time to look fabulous, darling. Now let's unleash these magic locks." Mitch fluffed out Sara's hair, adding to the already massive volume. "Trust me, with hair like this you don't even have to sound smart on this show—he'll be mesmerized just the same."

Mitch powdered around Sara's cheekbones, removed some strands of goat hair from her cardigan, then looked her up and down. "She ready," he exclaimed with a snap and a twirl.

A Producer with a clipboard led Sara to a cold, dark studio where a desk was set up in front of a fake backdrop that appeared as though it was looking out into the city streets. Sara sat across from a man in a purple sequin suit with shiny hair poking from a silk-sheathed helmet, bronzed skin, and teeth bleached so white that she was sure he looked ridiculous. But when she glanced at him in the monitor she saw that he looked like a movie star.

"This is going to be bliss!" the Host, who called himself 'The Rules,' said. And then they were counted in and The Rules turned to camera flashing those blinding white teeth. "Welcome to Fab Hour on City TV. I'm The Rules. Bliss! Bliss! We are fortunate enough to have a deadly serious guest tonight. Just kidding, she's fabulous. Look at her hair! The scientist Sara Schtinkler. Three S's in a row—alliterations! I feel like a soft slithery snake! Welcome, Dr. Sara Schtinkler."

"Thank you for having me."

"She's a Senior Lab Researcher at the Center for Animal Oddities—my ex did something odd with an animal once—and she is going to talk to us about this trés tragique fainting pandemic that is ruining my dating life, and maybe talk about how to accessorize for it. Welcome, Sara."

"Thank you for having me."

"You are America's preeminent expert on, oh, I'm going to say this wrong, on myotonia candy."

"Congenita, yes. Or as it is more popularly known, fainting goat syndrome."

"Yes, that! Give us a dumbed-down version. Fainting Goat 101 for The Rules."

Sara explained what she had countless times in obscure scientific journals and dinner parties gone awry. About how myotonia congenita is caused by a disorder of a chloride channel in the muscles of the skeleton (skeletal muscle chloride channel 1, CLCN1), inherited as an autosomal dominant trait (with incomplete penetrance) or a recessive trait, resulting in the varying severity of the condition. She was used to seeing that glazed look on the people she spoke to on the subject, but The Rules appeared captivated. He turned to the camera, jaw unhinged. "I'm not sure I understood a word of that, but I am just fascinating over your curls! What's your secret to the volume?"

"Of my hair?" Sara asked. "Born this way, I guess?"

"Lady Gag reference—snap-snap! A woman after my own heart. Let me smell?"

"Um . . . "

The Rules leaned over and took an epic huff of Sara's mane. "Oooh, it's earthy, almost smells like Yves St. Laurent V mixed with a campfire, not that I've ever been camping."

"It could be the goats in the lab."

The Rules tittered at that thinking she was kidding. "So, everyone wants to know: how close are you to a vaccine? This fainting thing is bringing me to my knees and not in a good way."

"Research is an ongoing process. We're working with an array of variables but our feeling is optimistic about—"

"She's feeling good about it, ladies and gentlemen!" The Rules cut in. "We love to hear that. Thank you and your fabulous hair for enlightening us today. Dr. Sara Schtinkler, everybody. Bliss! Bliss!" The host turned to a different camera and said, "After a quick break we'll spill the tea on yesterday's red carpet disasters." After a cut, he excitedly turned back to Sara. "Listen, Dr. Schtinkler, would you be so kind as to stick around for the next segment? No more science-y questions, but I've gotten a note that our Twitter is blowing up. People find you to be a truly authoritative voice. Would you stay, pretty-pretty please?"

Sara didn't know how to say no. She sat through the rest of the segments and smiled as the host talked about a former movie star who had opened a sex toy shop in Queens, the finale of a TV show about Indonesian drag queens, and of course how to accessorize your soft helmet for the Fall. "The Fall collection, ha! Double entendre alert. Bliss!" When it was done the Host thanked Sara profusely, and she was led out to the car as if the whole thing was a dream. Her phone rang as soon as she turned it back on.

"A star is born!" Bruce said.

"Oh, please, the whole thing was silly."

"Sara, your hair is trending on Twitter. People are obsessed. I'll send you screenshots."

A flurry of texts arrived from Bruce:

"@unrealhousewife—Drooling over Dr. Sara Schtinkler's curls. #jewishhairgoals," and "@cougarchaser5—Hebrew Goddess giving wifey vibes on the news right now. #marrymesaraschtinkler!"

Sara was not a vain person. She saw beauty in purely scientific terms: necessary to attract the opposite sex for procreation and therefore vital to the survival of the species. She kept her hair so big because the goats liked it, not to attract strangers on Twitter. (The one time she trimmed it they wouldn't play tetherball for a week). Even when she'd been diagnosed with BRCA 2 and had the preventative double mastectomy it hadn't occurred to her to do reconstruction—her breasts had already fulfilled their duty, which was feeding Joshua. She knew that Reuven would prefer breasts, but when the doctor told her that she would probably not have sensation there anyway—it would have just been awkward watching Reuven caress them or get aroused by dead tissue. So she kept herself flat. She'd understood it meant that her days of being hit on at the grocery store might be over, but she never liked that attention anyway.

"You are a straight-up sex symbol, Dr. Schtinkler!" Bruce's wife, Jackie, screamed out from the background and then grabbed the phone. "I know you don't love this, but for all us moms who still have an extra thirty pounds of baby weight and couldn't get whistled at by a bus full of convicts, enjoy it a little."

"Thanks, Jackie. Kiss the baby for me."

"Kisses to you, fellow Hebrew Goddess," Jackie replied.

It was all inane fun—a few people sexualizing a TV scientist and her voluminous hair. Sara picked up her car from the lab parking lot and drove home in silence. By the time she got to the house it was dark and she was already late for Joy Reid, so she'd have to watch it on DVR. Joshua was out for a movie with Brie, and Reuven had "stayed late for drinks," something he'd only started doing recently. Reuven had been acting different lately—he'd become, well, a bit vain, she thought. With his new shaving products and tighter shirts and that ridiculous gold neck chain with the Star of David? In all of their years together Reuven had never once visited a synagogue willingly and even whined about attending High Holidays services, and now suddenly he's religious? Please. Sara entered the quiet house, poured herself a tall glass of red wine and walked up to her bedroom with the bottle. She took a shower, cued up Joy, and then finally (finally!) lay down in bed. It had been a long day, and she didn't even feel bad skipping the family ritual to watch her favorite newscaster alone. Sara had just pressed play on the DVR when she heard the sound of men's voices out her window.

"Time for this Zionist bitch to learn what's what," one said.

"Ugh, what now?" Sara said aloud.

It took all she had to put her wine aside, get out of bed and look out the window. What Sara saw made her rub her eyes in disbelief. A red pick-up truck was parked in her driveway. Three men wearing white Klu Klux Klan robes and hoods hammered a big wooden cross right on her front lawn. They fastened it down with ropes and then one grabbed a gas can from the back of the truck. Sara thought for a moment that this was some kind of silly art performance, but these guys looked too big and clumsy to be artists. She watched as the biggest of the three lifted the gas can and doused the base of the cross. Another threw a match on it. Flames leaped up the base of the cross, fully engulfing it, and it was so startling that Sara flinched, and her hand hit the window with a clank. The three men looked up in surprise and saw Sara watching them. This seemed to really freak them out because just like that all three men in hoods froze and keeled over like dominos right on her front lawn. The biggest one fell close enough to the burning cross that his robe caught on fire. The flames spread across him and then reached the other two men as well, and soon all three Klansmen were in flames.

"Oh, for crying out loud," Sara sighed.

She quickly retrieved the fire extinguisher from her bathroom, ran down the stairs and out onto her the front lawn. The cross was now fully engulfed, and the fainted men were on fire as well, just twitching and sizzling. Sara opened the pin and pointed the extinguisher at the men. It expelled a stream of white foam onto the Klansmen's robes, and eventually she put them out one by one. Sara then pointed the extinguisher at the cross but there wasn't enough foam left to extinguish that. Sara's neighbor Nancy walked out on her deck in a nightgown, a phone in her hand having already called 911. Sara just stood there hoping the fire from the cross wouldn't set the whole neighborhood ablaze. When the fire department and ambulance arrived, the blaze was put out quickly, and the men in robes were taken away in stretchers.

"You sure you don't want to press charges, Dr.

Schtinkler?" The police officer asked after reading her report.

Sara declined. "It was just some art project gone wrong," she said.

The cop shook his head before tipping his hat and driving off. Minutes later, Sara lay back in bed with her red wine and her soft pillow and Joy Reid on DVR.

"Finally, some peace," she said and pressed play at last.

CHAPTER 8

JOSHUA AND BRIE sat in the back row of a movie theatre watching *Bloodbath 3: Blood Sauna.* Most theatres had long stopped screening horror movies since frequent audience fainting made them too dangerous. But a couple of independent theatres still risked late-night showings, though they insisted that audiences sign waivers and wear soft helmets, regardless of whether they are fainters or not. Brie had suggested the movie, and Joshua was impressed that even through the pulse-pounding violence of a spa weekend gone terribly wrong, Brie kept conscious. She even giggled when a Wellness Coach's arm was cut off and dragged like a rake through a Zen garden.

Joshua's heart thumped loudly the entire time but not because of the movie. He'd never spent this much time so close to a girl before. Brie's smell of grape bubble gum and vanilla was an elixir that proved dizzying to him. When their hands accidentally touched as they both reached for the Twizzlers, Joshua's entire body tingled, and an uninvited boner strained against his jeans as if it too were reaching out for a piece of candy.

Brie leaned in to whisper, and he felt her hot breath. "So, how's this going to end, do you think?"

Joshua thought about it and said, "The tantric masseur's going to kill the intuitive astrologer with a blunt crystal, then the breathwork guru will save the day with some organic soap chemical that will blow the place up."

Brie giggled. "Not the movie, silly. With us."

Joshua turned to Brie, who gazed at him hungrily. She leaned in and kissed him, and Joshua experienced the softness of her lips, the taste of buttery salt from the popcorn and sweet saliva. His head nearly exploded, and he felt years of stunted puberty rush towards his groin in a roaring tidal wave. More than anything, Joshua tried his best to kiss right. His mother had once complained that his father kissed like a Golden Retriever and used too much tongue, so he kissed with his lips, but when Brie stuck her long cold tongue into his mouth he reciprocated, and their tongues intermingled. He felt her panting, and when she touched his chest, he touched hers, and he could feel her heart pounding like an urgent knock at the door. Onscreen, a chainsaw sounded over screeches, but Joshua and Brie kissed until his neck was sore, and his tongue was tired, and his pants almost burst from the pressure.

"I love this part," Brie said.

"You've seen this before?"

"Not the movie, silly."

And then she fainted. Stiffened in her seat like a board. Joshua looked around concerned about making a scene, but he saw that others in the audience had fainted too. He held his hand behind Brie's neck to make sure that she wouldn't keel over and hurt herself. But once he got her steady, he just gazed at her adoringly. Brie's face was flushed and smiling, and she bit her lower lip softly in a way that Joshua had seen movie actors do when they've achieved sexual bliss.

After the movie, they hopped in Brie's Mitsubishi Mirage and she dropped Joshua off at home. "Text me, stud," she said with a wink, then drove off.

Joshua walked towards his house. His lips still tingled

from Brie's kisses and his groin ached from being trapped in his pants. All of the sensations were heightened. He took a deep inhale to savor Brie's aroma but was confused when he smelled burnt grass and gasoline. He walked up his driveway and saw police tape cordoning off a big patch of blackened grass. He looked up and saw that the TV was on in his parents' bedroom. He would ask his mom what that was all about, but maybe later since right now all he wanted to do is go journaling and maybe Google how masturbation worked. But then his dad's Uber drove in right behind him, blinding him with the lights and evaporating the erotic tingle he'd felt. Joshua waited for his dad to emerge, and when he did, Joshua saw that his father now had bandages on both hands, one tied to an ice pack.

"Is that blood on your shirt?" Joshua asked.

"It is," Reuven replied, a proud glint in his eyes. "I'm afraid Dad had to punch some Nazis tonight."

"Okay . . . "

"How was your night?"

"Didn't punch any Nazis."

"Is that hickey on your neck?" Reuven asked. When Joshua blushed, his dad said, "Atta boy."

"Don't tell mom, okay?" Joshua said. "I don't think she can handle much more stress right now."

Reuven patted his son on the back. It would be their manly secret, but Reuven was overcome with pride. He's out kicking Nazi ass and his son is out slaying shiksas. Living the dream. They walked into the house together. Reuven tossed his bloodied shirt in the washing machine. He wondered which stain remover was best for Nazi blood? He headed towards his bedroom while Joshua tiptoed into his room. When Reuven entered the bedroom, Sara lay in bed pouring more red wine into her glass.

"How was the interview?" Reuven asked.

"Rather not talk about it. How was drinks?"

"Same."

"Did I hear Joshua come in?"

"Yeah, he's beat. Just wanted to hit the hay," then he whispered, "He had a hickey on his neck!"

In response, Sara gulped down a big swig of wine and poured the rest. "You want to watch the rest of Joy with me?"

"I'm going to shower," Reuven said. "Go on without me."

And so, for the first time in a long time the Schtinkler family skipped their ritual of watching Joy Reid together. Reuven stood in the shower fantasizing about Nazis, Joshua lay in bed jerking off to a masturbation tutorial on Masterclass from Jeff Goldblum, and Sara closed her eyes and thought about the goats.

They'd all had quite a day.

CHAPTER 9

THE CENTER FOR Animal Oddities had become such a hotspot for reporters that it was near-impossible for Sara to get any real work done. Journalists came by in throngs asking even the janitor about how close Sara might be to finding a vaccine to human myotonia congenita. "Closer than dust mites to a Swiffer," he was quoted as saying, confusing everyone. Others simply wanted information about Sara's hair, and how she kept it so voluminous. Admirers held up signs like "Marry Me, Dr. Schtinkler!" One morning, a reality TV producer snuck into the lab and waited in a bathroom stall to ask Sara if she was interested in being the new *Bachelorette*.

"I'm married with a teenage son," Sara replied, baffled.

"We can message that. There's always a creative work-around," the Producer said before Sara shooed her away.

Sara cordoned herself off in the barn with Lillia, Spencer, and Chewy, and was about to decimate them in another game of tetherball when she got a text from Burt, her farmer friend in Tennessee, "Don't suppose you would consider moving up your annual trip down to see us?"

"What is it?" Sara replied immediately.

"Something you should see with your own eyes."

"I'll be on the next flight."

"Molly will bake a fruit pie," Burt replied.

Air travel to Tennessee from Newark Airport was surprisingly easy. Sara got lucky and found a cheap return flight to Nashville, then, per her receipts, was upgraded to a midsized sedan for her four-hour drive to Gatlinburg. She told Reuven and Joshua that she'd have to stay the night but would be back the next day by noon since the last flight out of Nashville was 4 p.m. They could call in Chinese food.

Sara drove along the remote areas of Tennessee, listening to country radio and marveling at the ever-changing view out her window. Near the Great Smoky Mountains, a series of verdant low ridges became swampy lowlands, which became gorgeous rocky hills along rushing rivers. At the edge of a thick forest next to the road she spotted a family of red-tailed foxes and even a bobcat. The beauty of Tennessee was undoubtedly underrated, but Sara loved it even more because she knew that she was nearing Mecca for Fainting Goats.

At the base of a high green mountain, Sara arrived at a dirt road that led straight uphill. And indeed, thirty minutes in the other wildlife became scarce, and soon there were only goats: small, adorable fainting goats, true native Tennessee Stiff-Legs! Sara quivered with joy as she watched the little hoppers scatter and lay around and play as she drove past. This mountain was their own little paradise, where fainting goats reigned supreme. She was so happy gazing out at them that she almost drove off the path several times, so she tried to focus. When Sara finally arrived at a small gravel clearing in the woods about an hour up, there Burt stood waiting for her in front of a red barn and a small farmhouse. Burt wore a soft helmet made of denim along with denim overalls tucked into rain boots. His eyes were so bright blue they twinkled over his scraggly white beard.

"Where's Daisy Dukes?" Sara asked out the window. "She's usually right by your side."

"Unfortunately, Daisy Dukes has gone to goat heaven."

"Oh, Burt. I'm so sorry."

Burt got a little teary-eyed. "I loved that damn goat."

"Is that Dr. Sara?" Molly, Burt's cherubic wife, walked out of their home holding a pie covered in cloth. Sara could smell the buttery crust from her car and her mouth watered. "You must be tired after such a long trip," Molly said. "Come in. Take a load off already."

"Wouldn't mind a slice myself," said Burt.

"Oh, you greedy so-and-so you'll get some when it's good and ready for you."

Sara parked and followed the adorable couple into their cozy farmhouse. Handmade quilts lay on worn furniture, and cast-iron pans hung from the walls. They sat together at the kitchen table and Molly set a hot slice of blueberry pie and homemade vanilla ice cream in front of Sara. It was so sweet and delicious that she almost cried.

"I reckon life's been pretty busy for you since things started with the fainting spells," Molly said. "At least you don't have to bother yourself with it. You people were chosen for a reason."

Sara was still emotional about the pie, but managed to say, "My hair's trending on Twitter."

"What's Twitter?" Burt asked.

"God I missed you two," Sara said, shaking her head.

"Okay, okay, enough of the love-fest. We've got business to discuss." Burt pulled out his ancient laptop and plunked it down on the table. It turned on with a great roar, and Burt put on his reading glasses as he cued a video. "I did just like I do every week. Went up to the hills, snuck up on the goats and gave them a good scare just like always. Every time, well, you know, same thing—myotonic spell—a faint. Like clockwork. Then a couple of weeks ago this started to happen." Burt pressed play on a video. There was a long shot of a goat chomping grass on a hill, then Burt tiptoed into frame carrying a shovel. He raised the shovel above his head and smashed it down on a rock, causing a loud clang. The goat looked up at Burt startled, but then instead of freezing and collapsing the goat just scrambled away, leaving Burt there scratching his head, confused.

"That was the first time from a few weeks ago," Burt said. "Been like that every day since, if you want to see the rest of the videos? Not a single faint. And I scared every goat in the hills. Tried everything but jumping out of a bush wearing a clown suit."

"Are you sure that was the same breed?" Sara asked.

"Exactly what I said to Molly. So, the next day I found that spotted goat, Dilly, I've come to call him. Now he's a fainter. So much as a stiff breeze will send that goat to the ground. I tracked him down. And here's a video of Dilly."

And then another video, and again the same thing. Burt came up from behind with a shovel. Slammed it down. Nothing. The goat scuttled away, scared but not fainting.

"I almost thought I'd lost my mind. So, I went down to my own barn - those goats are worse than Dilly. If I so much as put down a book too fast they stiffen like a board. I lit a whole pack of firecrackers. Might scare the bejesus out of a ghost. No reaction. Not a single fainting episode. Been like that a few weeks now."

"Did you take samples?" Sara asked.

"Fecal and blood like always. Right in the barn freezer."

"Let's go visit the barn," Sara said.

They put away the empty plates and headed out to the barn. Sara recognized the goats from her last few visits. She had rarely seen such nervous goats. Sara actually named one of the goats Rodney, after Rodney Dangerfield, since it had bulged out eyes and similar levels of anxiety.

"Do your worst," Burt said to Sara.

Sara pulled out her Freddy Kruger Halloween mask and rushed forward and screamed at the three goats, an easy way to make myotonic goats faint. And faint they did. All three of them. Stiffened and then keeled over like three-legged chairs. Burt was aghast. His mouth dropped open. He rubbed the side of his head.

"I swear to you Dr. Sara, this is the first time in weeks. I certainly wouldn't have made you come all this way if—"

"Let's check the ones in the hills," Sara said.

They hiked up through the forest and up into the rocky

hills. In the distance, there was a small myotonic goat drinking from a pond.

"There's Chilly," Burt said. "Called her that because she gets the chills even seeing her own shadow. Hasn't had a spell in weeks, and I even shot off a rifle near her."

"Do it again."

Burt pulled out his rifle. Shot it in the air. The goat's head cocked up like it was looking up to the sky. Then it froze and keeled over.

"Well, I'll be damned," Burt said.

Back at the barn, Burt retrieved the samples he'd taken from the goats during what he called their "non-fainting period" and handed them to Sara, who was in deep thought.

"When did you say Daisy Dukes passed away?" she asked.

"That would have been January 25th, so a few weeks ago now. Gee, Sara, I sure am sorry for the false alarm."

"Are there any other non-fainting goats around here?" Sara said. "Or was Daisy Dukes the only one?"

"Not for a good fifty miles, at least. I feel confident in saying that. All fainters for many miles up in these hills. Daisy Dukes was our sole non-fainter all this time."

"Any predators come around this season? Invasive species?"

"We had raccoons last winter. Round this time of year these goats are pretty isolated, though. Not a predator in sight save for the odd snake, but they don't pay them too much attention. Gee, I sure am sorry to have troubled you all this much. I am just beside myself for crying wolf when there wasn't a damn wolf in sight. But I swear to you . . . "

Sara packed Burt's samples into her medical cooler, hugged Burt and Molly goodbye, and got back into her car. "I believe what you're telling me, Burt. And I thank you as usual for helping me. Let me get these samples back to the lab and I'll give you a call if I see something unusual," said Sara and then turned to Molly. "And thank you for your hospitality and the heavenly blueberry pie."

"Safe trip back!" Molly waved.

Sara pulled out of the driveway and drove the hour down through the forest and then four more hours to Nashville before checking into a roadside motel called Tranquil Travels. In her room that night, Sara pulled out her microscope, opened the cooler, and looked over the blood and fecal samples that Burt had given her. Burt was not one for delusion and certainly not one for calling attention to himself when it wasn't necessary. If Burt said those goats had stopped fainting, they had. And indeed, when Sara observed the samples from the last three weeks, the myotonic cells seemed to have receded almost to dormancy. Next, Sara examined the samples taken from the goats that had fainted that day. The myotonia had come alive again, active and moving. *But why?* The only change in the weeks had been the death of Daisy Dukes the goat. Could it have been Daisy's presence, a kind of alpha goat in comparison, that had kept the other goats on edge and prone to fainting? Might the myotonic goats, in fact, have considered Daisy Dukes a kind of predatory species that put their fight-or-flight mechanism on high alert, triggering myotonia congenita? And if that was the case then why had they started fainting again now? And that's when it dawned on her. Sara was embarrassed at how long it took to remind herself that she was an animal just like the goats, and that it was her silly human pride that made her so blind. A new non-fainting Alpha predator *had* in fact been re-introduced into the myotonic goat's stratosphere despite what Bruce said; and it was her. Sara pricked her finger and let the blood drop onto a glass slide. She placed it under the microscope and studied it alongside the goats' samples. It was like a scene out of CSI, but with goat poop.

"Can't be," she said, stunned by what she saw.

Sara opened her red journal and began scribbling furiously. That night she harkened obscure chemical formulas she'd studied in college, mathematical equations she hadn't used in decades, readings she'd poured over from her Masters' thesis, and of course all of the years of research into diet, exercise and gene manipulation at the lab. In the darkest hours of a Tennessee night it all coalesced into one thought, a thousand tiny light bulbs becoming a single blinding beacon. In that cheap goat-feces-lenient Nashville motel room Sara came to a kind of conclusion, a formula that when written out appeared so utterly bulletproof that even the nit-picky scientific community would agree that while this may not be the cure exactly, it provided a path.

Sara lay in bed as the morning sun rose out the window, red journal held close to her chest and staring at the stained ceiling in wonder. It would take months to prove and maybe years of clinical trials before it was accepted, but goddamned it if she hadn't found the answer at last.

CHAPTER 10

AND WHAT WAS Reuven off doing while his wife was busy trying to save humanity with fecal samples? It started innocently enough, but spun out of control from there, kind of like when you browse Amazon with no intention of buying anything but end up with a prefabricated home in a shipping container and 1,500 live ladybugs.

Reuven was closing up at his office in New York when a text came in from Joshua saying he was staying out "with a friend" again. It was disappointing to Reuven. With Sara in Tennessee overnight he was looking forward to some father-son one-on-one bonding time with the boy to talk about sports and girls and how one day ear hair "just magically appears," often years after co-workers have already noticed it.

A wince of regret made Reuven realize that he'd never really given Joshua "the birds and the bees" talk. It hadn't seemed like a remote possibility he'd needed it before. Even at fifteen his son was basically pre-pubescent. But now signs of puberty had emerged like the first daffodil in Spring, and then that hickey appeared on his neck, which was a sure sign he was getting some, whatever "some" was these days.

Since he had time to burn, Reuven decided to check in on The Maccabees to see if anything was on for the night. His first venture had been scary but exhilarating. He still wondered if it was a dream, and he longed for more. So,

Reuven walked to the club and breezed past the bouncer with a knowing wink. But when he got to the back room there was only Larry the Accountant sitting at a table scrolling his laptop.

"We're dark on Fridays for Shabbat. You didn't get the memo?" Larry smirked.

Reuven didn't want to let on that he wasn't on any official memo chain, and as Larry got back to work he decided not to confirm what a noob he was. "Of course. Just checking in to see if you got the memo, which I see now that you have received. Shabbat Shalom, Larry."

"Shabbat Shalom."

Reuven walked back into the club, took a seat by the bar and was about to order a lemon martini but then he realized that a lemon martini is not very masculine, so he ordered a Whiskey Sour, adding, "Extra sour." He'd sent Sara a text but received no reply, and when he called her number it went straight to voicemail but then said her mailbox was full. A flush of marital "I told you so" came over him, an annoyance that he had pleaded with her to erase some messages before her trip to Tennessee. Some were likely important given her research. Reuven was making a mental note to scold Sara about it when a hand landed gently on his shoulder and a cloud of peachy perfume wafted into his nostrils. It was at that moment that his mental note taker took the weekend off.

"Thought I'd get to you first before the other the girls do," a woman's voice said.

Reuven turned and found himself inches from Pamela, Claire's 25-year-old assistant. She was wearing a silky blue blouse with a burgundy bra poking out, and her cleavage seemed to strain to get out, like a barn full of wild horses. Pamela's face was more dressed up than at the office. She had glittery green eyeliner and her lips looked poutier, redder, and moister than usual. Everything about Pamela was poutier and moister, Reuven noticed.

"Oh, uh, Pamela . . . do you go here?" Reuven managed to ask.

"You know I do, Reuven. I live upstairs. Just a quick elevator ride away, so . . . "

Reuven decided to be playful. "You could use a fireman's pole to slide down," he replied.

"Why, are you a fireman?" Pamela said and then exploded with naughty laughter. She slapped Reuven's knee and then held it there. "Ha, listen to me! You make me think dirty thoughts." Their eyes met for a second too long. "I'm bored of this place anyway," Pamela went on. "Want to come upstairs for tea?"

Tea sounded so civilized. "I just went up for tea," one might imagine themselves explaining if it ever came up, which it *totally* never would. "A mentoring thing." But as Pamela took Reuven's hand and led him out of the club, he felt his heart pound and his palms get clammy, as if they were trying to explain to Reuven that the only brand of tea Pamela was serving was English Bareback. Reuven looked around the club to see if anyone noticed the middle-aged man leaving with a girl almost half his age, but none of The Maccabees were there and the bouncer was engaged in taking a bribe from a group of under-aged Instagram influencers for a video called, "You won't believe what happened when we offered a Bouncer a hundred grand in Supreme Gear to get into a club. WATCH TO THE END!" So, Reuven followed Pamela's trail of peachy perfume like Pacman following dots, out of the club and into the apartment building next door. Perhaps Reuven's Spidey-Sense tingled as they entered the elevator together, or maybe the tiny voice that was his conscience spoke up because when Pamela's manicured finger pressed the button to the eighth floor, he hesitated.

"Maybe this isn't such a good idea?"

Pamela moved her body up against Reuven's, her hand now on his thigh. "We're long past good ideas, Reuven. Bad ideas—that's what's trending. And so much more fun." She pressed her lips against his and gave a little bite as the elevator dinged. Pamela took Reuven's hand and lead him down the hallway until they arrived at her apartment door. She pulled out her key, which still had a Boston University decal on it, and that alone might have sent off warning signals, but Reuven was too far gone. He was just a regular dumb guy with a woody like back in college.

Pamela's bedroom was a mess of pink glitter and faux fur in pastel colors, as if an arts and crafts store had impregnated a Forever 21. A large pillow on her unmade bed had the face of Lady Gaga in the Andy Warhol style, and a RuPaul poster above her bed read, "Basic Betches Unite!"

Pamela scrolled her phone and put on some awful mumble rap, and then checked her texts. "Bathroom's back there if you need to freshen up."

Reuven went in there and a basket of makeup and hair irons and creams were piled messily next to the sink. There was toothpaste on the mirror and her toothbrush was shaped like a flamingo and had googly eyes—a child's toothbrush. Reuven looked at himself in the smudged mirror and frowned. He couldn't do this. He shouldn't even be here, not by any stretch. What he needed now was a quick and easy exit. Reuven turned on the faucets, splashed his face with water, and flushed the toilet. Then he walked out, ready to let this kid down easy and in a way where she wouldn't tell anyone. "Pamela, I—"

Pamela lay on her bed completely naked, waving a condom in her face like it was a small fan or tickets to a Cardi B concert. Even lying sideways her breasts remained high, like they were standing on their toes in a crowd trying to get someone's attention, "Yoo-hoo, I'm over here." Her pubic hair was shaved into a tiny exclamation mark. Reuven had only seen anything like it in porn, or a Cardi B video. He gasped but didn't look away. Reuven considered briefly whether he should go back into the bathroom and shape his pubic hair. Maybe into the Hebrew letters for "Adonai."

"Finally, a man who doesn't faint when I undress," Pamela tittered. Reuven kicked off his shoes, unbuttoned his shirt. "Keep the *bar mitzvah* necklace on," Pamela instructed. "So hunky."

When it was over, Pamela drew on a raspberry flavored vape and blew rings in the air. Reuven stood up and walked the condom to the bathroom, like a dog owner with a poop bag. He threw it in the toilet and watched to make sure that it flushed properly. He caught sight of himself in the mirror and saw an old hairy flabby man with a *bar mitzvah* necklace and felt disgusted.

He walked back to the bedroom, picked up his pants, and pulled out his cellphone. There was a text from Joshua seventeen minutes ago. "Pick me up outside the Chatham Cinema at 11 p.m., please?" Reuven looked at his watch. He could make it if he hurried.

He texted back. "See you there, bud."

"Gotta go," Reuven told Pamela.

"So soon? I was hoping for another round."

"Love to, but . . . " Reuven couldn't bear to say that he had to pick up his teenage son who was far closer to Pamela's age than his, so he let that sentence trail off. "I have somewhere to be."

"Ugh, just like a man." Pamela grinned. "A very sexy man who just made me come like a FedEx package. On time and with email notification."

Reuven wasn't exactly sure what this meant, but he knew it was good. His worst instincts wondered if Pamela would share news of his sexual prowess with her friends at the club. He'd like that.

"See you."

Reuven rushed out of the bedroom and exited the apartment. In the hall, he found himself leaving at the same time as an older woman wearing a soft helmet who lived next door. She was probably Reuven's age, and Reuven was acutely aware of how gross he might seem doing the walk of shame from Pamela's apartment next door. Reuven's eyes hit the floor as he walked to the elevator, praying she wouldn't follow, but of course she did, and the tension was thick as they stood waiting for the elevator to arrive. Reuven hid his wedding ring under his hand but was sure she'd noticed. In fact, as they entered the elevator Reuven could sense her judgmental eyes. He looked up and wasn't wrong. The woman sneered.

"Pathetic," she muttered under her breath. "A man of your age with that young girl?"

Reuven couldn't have agreed more, and at any other time in history would have begged for forgiveness. He was lower than a snake. But this wasn't any other time in history, this was now—Reuven's time. And in Reuven's time he wasn't about to be shamed by some old Waspy Karen who reminded him of his teachers at Shield Academy.

"You don't get to judge me, lady," he said.

"You're old enough to be her father. And all because you're, you're—"

"What? A lowly Jew?"

"I never said that," the woman replied.

"Didn't have to."

Filled with the adrenaline of disdain Reuven turned to the woman and swelled up like a bear and then roared at the top of his lungs. The woman froze, her body wobbling a bit before collapsing against the elevator wall. Reuven eased the woman onto the floor. As he did her purse fell open and a few pieces of gum fell out. Reuven popped one in his mouth.

"Refreshing, thanks."

He rode the rest of the way down, chewing loudly. As the woman watched in horror from the elevator floor, Reuven stepped out of the elevator and onto the wet New York streets before taking a left towards Penn Station.

Reuven caught the 9:57 to Chatham, jumped in his car and arrived at the movie theatre a few minutes past 11 p.m. It was drizzling slightly, not a full rain, still he was glad Joshua asked to be picked up. If Sara asked where he'd been that night, he could simply say that he'd worked late and then gone to pick up Joshua, which was basically true, as long as you didn't know what 'true' meant. Reuven spotted his son under a gazebo and watched as he hugged a girl wearing all black, who then slunk away.

"Who's the lady friend?" Reuven asked as soon as his son got in the car.

"Nobody."

"Didn't look like that. Is that the one who gave you the hickey?"

"Why does it smell like jailbait in here?" Joshua asked.

"Huh?"

"It's the peach-scented perfume all the Senior girls wear to attract college guys. They call it jailbait because the girls are underage but the guys aren't so they could go to jail for statutory rape."

Reuven sniffed his collar. He rolled down the windows.

"There's a rumor going around that one jailbait girl in my class slept with a guy who's thirty. Gross, right?"

"Um, yeah. Ew," Reuven winced.

"When's mom home?"

"Not 'til tomorrow afternoon. I was thinking you and me might hang out tomorrow. Some guy time—mano a mano?"

"Maybe."

"Like old times. We can do manly things." Reuven grinned. His mind flashed to The Maccabees, to the fun he'd had, and he wondered if Joshua was mature enough to have The Talk—*the Nazi-Hunting Talk*. "Let me ask you a hypothetical question," he said, dipping his toe in. "Say you knew there were Jew-haters nearby. Like real racist assholes with Nazi flags and they were gathering and spewing hatred all within driving distance. Would you, you know, want to go do something about it?"

"Like what, kill them?"

"No, no, nothing like that." Reuven chuckled, though he liked Joshua's spirit. "But you know, scare 'em a bit, rough 'em up. Show 'em you don't mess with our kind. Make sure they don't do it again, you know? What if you could be part of a group of guys who went and did that?"

"Hypothetically?"

"Yeah."

"Honestly, that's just weird, Dad," Joshua said. "Sounds vaguely homoerotic."

"Nothing like that."

"Are these racists actually hurting anyone now or just talking about it?"

"They might. I mean, they probably have, but—"

"So, in your scenario you don't have proof. But you're going after them anyway because you're suddenly more powerful than them because Jews don't faint. But you were too scared to do it before?"

"They could fight back before."

"Yeah, that's what's so lame about it. You're taking advantage of a genetic glitch. It's more about power than it is about fighting racists. It's actually kind of cowardly if you ask me."

"Cowardly?" Reuven asked, appalled. He decided to shift gears. "How do you propose making change then? If you don't fight the bad guys how do you heal the world?"

"By being a decent person. By not being a hypocrite," Joshua said, obvious enough to him. "Beating up Nazis when they're weak is just acting like them. It feeds evil."

"Well, I firmly disagree," Reuven said a bit too loudly. He was shaken by the turn in the conversation and really didn't like the ideas in his son's head. Maybe Joshua just misunderstood him? This concept was probably too intellectual. His son was only fifteen and surely wasn't aware of what the world was really like. If he did then he'd likely jump at the opportunity. Reuven decided to rephrase his proposition. "So if your dad wanted to take you with him to smash some Nazis in real life you wouldn't want to come with?"

"On a dick-measuring expedition with a bunch of old Jewish dudes? Hard pass, Dad. Maybe a movie instead?"

Reuven looked at his son like he didn't know where he'd gone wrong. It wasn't a dick measure expedition! This was a life lesson! If Joshua wasn't so stubborn he could show him that it's valuable to use your fists as well as your brains in life. That we're not made of glass. That Jews could be powerful and don't need to be scared weaklings. He could explain all of that and more if only Joshua would listen to his words.

Instead, his son took another big whiff of the smell inside the car and said, "Yup, that's definitely jailbait."

CHAPTER 11

THE STORY NOW flashes forward a couple of weeks because the pages of Sara's journal dating February 12th-26th were smeared in goat feces, making them illegible. On the evening in question, specifically February $27^{th,}$ Sara stood in front of a mirror adjusting a sequined, feathered mask over her eyes, also blissfully unaware of all that would transpire.

"Why do we have to dress up again?" she asked Reuven.

"I told you. It's a Purim party. Formal masquerade wear. No mask, no entry, like the invite said." Reuven was fixing his bow tie for the umpteenth time. "Trust me. It's the biggest party of the year."

"And how did you get invited to the party of the year again?"

"I take offense to that," Reuven replied. "I'm an SVP now. Basically means I'm a celebrity. They probably invited me first."

Reuven knew of course that the invite he'd received to "Purim-Palooza" had nothing to do with his promotion or his job but had been extended as a result of his less-than-loose affiliation to The Maccabees and their work smashing neo-Nazi skulls. But why tell Sara that and worry her? She looked so pretty in her rented gown and mask, and he was excited to parade her around as his own Queen Ester. Reuven had actually forgotten what a vision Sara was without a goat-hair covered cardigan and Birkenstocks.

Her long pale neck, wild hair and slender shoulders made her a sight to behold.

"This is going to be so cool," Reuven smiled.

As for Sara, the whole affair was a bit of an annoyance, but Reuven was so excited that she didn't have the heart to say no. She'd been unsettled ever since returning home from Tennessee two weeks prior. Though she'd never been prone to paranoia, she swore that a blue Honda SUV had been following her around town since she returned and had even been sitting idle in front of their house that morning when she left for work. If it was a paparazzi, hopefully they were just trying to find out what kind of hair product she used, information that she'd happily divulge under duress or not (Maui Moisture Curl Quench Shampoo and Frizz & Flyaway Fighter), but she feared it was something worse. To be safe she'd ripped out the notes she'd written in her red journal and hid them in the office safe. Based on the epiphany she'd had in her motel room in Nashville she may have cracked a cure to a global pandemic that affected billions. But it would take months of clinical testing to prove anything, and she'd be damned if some snooping journalist was going to share her work with the world before it was ready.

"Where's Joshua?" Sara asked, finally done fitting the mask.

"Probably showering again. I guess puberty finally showed up for him."

"He's not masturbating, Reuven."

Reuven arched an eyebrow. "If you say so, but he's going through tissue boxes like cell phone data."

"Joshua!" Sara called out down the hall. "We're leaving. Don't forget to close the lights when you go to sleep."

"Got it, mom. Just getting in the shower."

"Wankin' it." Reuven smiled as they walked out.

Sara couldn't help but laugh. It was true that puberty had hit Joshua hard and all at once. She'd had to donate piles of clothes and shoes that no longer fit him, buy him deodorant, shaving cream and acne medication. Though it pained Sara to the core, Joshua was a real teenager now, independent and capable of staying home alone, and she was just a regular mom heading out on a Thursday night date with her husband.

"Maybe I should stay home with him?" Sara asked Reuven.

"Now, you stop it."

To Sara's surprise a shiny Lincoln Town Car waited for them out front of their house, and there was a little Israeli flag on the back antennae. The driver, who wore a black tie and pressed shirt, welcomed them with a thick Russian accent.

"I love a *Purim Spiel*," he said, as Sara and Reuven climbed in. "You'll never see one like this, I promise you that." When Reuven replied that he hadn't been to one since he was a young boy, the driver took a second look at them in the rearview mirror. "You must be pretty important that they sent a car. Even the celebrities are being told to Uber."

Reuven welled up with pride and squeezed Sara's hand.

"He's just been promoted to Senior Vice President," Sara said, proudly.

"Mazel Tov," the driver said. "If I knew I was driving such a *macher* I would have worn a jacket!"

The car drove towards the Holland Tunnel and arrived at the Javitz Center just past 8 p.m. There were dozens of other limos pulling in, and out the window Reuven marveled at the elaborate red carpet and the crowds of journalists snapping photos.

"Whose party is this again?" Sara asked.

"I told you, it's an industry thing." Reuven leaned forward to pay the driver with a nice tip. "Thanks, you've been a *mensch*."

"No thanks, Mr. Schtinkler. It's been all taken care of by Mr. Rabinsky, plus some. He said to save your money."

Reuven shrugged, thanked him again, and he and Sara entered the fray.

"Who's Mr. Rabinsky?" Sara asked.

"Probably one of the marketing organizers," Reuven lied.

Reuven and Sara had their names checked by security and then walked the red carpet, a mass of photographers blasting them with flashes. One of them called out to Sara by name, "Your hair looks beautiful, Dr. Schtinkler!"

"How do they know me?" she whispered to Reuven.

"Your fabulous local TV appearances?" Reuven ventured.

The entrance to the event was decked out like the Golden Globes. Thirty-foot statues of biblical characters, a 360-degree slo-mo camera sponsored by Sabra Hummus. Sara took a whirl and her image lit up on a giant screen. Past a line of security guards Reuven and Sara walked inside the venue. What they witnessed was a display of Jewish opulence not seen since Neil Diamond's Oscar party in 1977. Bowtied waiters served Russ & Daughters caviar croquettes, seltzer stations poured from old-time glass jars, there was a Chagall sculpture made entirely of Nova Lox, and a disco dancefloor shaped like a *Torah* scroll. And Jews, Jews of every shape, color and hair problem schmoozing, *kvelling* and *noshing* like they didn't have a kvetch in the world. Reuven and Sara were dazzled by the spectacle and walked amongst the crowd as if they had stumbled into the dream of a Jewish sleep-away camp counselor. Up front was an enormous stage that seemed lit for a presidential debate. Red, white, and blue lights flashed above a fifty-foot screen where an American and Israeli flag waved together graphically. Round tables were dressed in white table cloths, and Reuven spotted their names on two hand-inscribed cards on a table near the front. Larry, the accountant, was already seated there.

"Table of honor for a brave Maccabee and his wife," Larry said, and Reuven gave him a head shake to imply that "yes, this was his wife, but no, she was not aware of their exploits." Larry seemed to get it.

"This is Sara. She's delighted to be at this TV industry event." Reuven winked.

"Right, right, Hi Sara. Larry Baum."

"Do you two work together?" Sara asked.

"Sometimes."

"Larry's in accounting and often complains how expensive my freelance producers are. Don't you, Larry?"

"Sure, sure."

The old Reuven would have had an anxiety attack lying so brazenly in front of his wife, but this was the new Reuven—a real man who could lie and scheme brazenly on command! He was secretly commending himself when the stage exploded in pyrotechnics, interrupting their conversation. A woman dressed as Queen Ester strut out under a gale of dramatic lights. She wore a bejeweled purple headdress, a white flowing robe, and a massive Star of David on her chest.

"Thank you," she said to the room, and there was a burst of applause. "Soon we will perform our *Purim Spiel* for you, followed by food, dancing, and an abundance of babka. But now it is my sincere pleasure to introduce the man of the hour, our patron, Dr. Jacob Rabinsky!"

There was a roar from the crowd as a tall man with wavy gray hair, an enormous bleached smile, and an expensive suit strut on stage.

Larry leaned into Reuven. "If we're The Maccabees, that's Judah Maccabee himself."

Rabinsky took his place at the podium with all the confidence of a movie star accepting a Lifetime Achievement Award. He gazed out at the crowd smiling widely, pointed at a few people in the political style, and then faced forward, seeming to look at everyone in the audience directly, simultaneously.

"Purim is a holiday that commemorates the Jewish people's defeat of Haman, an Achaemenid Persian Empire official who planned to kill all the Jews," he said. "It wouldn't be the last time someone tried that, and it wouldn't be the last time we won!" He threw his fist up in the air in victory and the crowd cheered. "Haman was a bad, bad man," Rabinsky continued. "And because he was so bad, I'm going to ask you for a little help in making him feel less-than welcome. Every time his name comes up, I want you to pick up those noisemakers on your tables and give it a little whirl to blot out his name. That's right, spin those graggers when I say Haman. I can't hear you! Haman!"

The audience, including Reuven, Sara, and the rest of the attendees, picked up the graggers and spun them vigorously, creating a deafening cacophony in the room. Rabinsky still wasn't satisfied. He cupped his ear and leaned out.

"I still can't hear you! Maybe this audiovisual will help?"

Behind him, the fifty-foot screen projected the words "Haman Sucks!" And then an animation of an eagle carrying both an American and Israeli flag swooped across the screen with a screech. The eagle descended on an image of Haman with his black robe and triangular hat, scooped him up in its talons, and then dropped him into an erupting volcano. The crowd went wild.

"Not exactly how the original story went," Sara complained to Reuven, who was entranced.

"And yet, I still can't hear you!" Rabinsky said. The graggers went even louder. "Maybe we need a little more help?"

And then a towering diesel-powered monster truck with wheels the size of boulders roared out onstage behind

Rabinsky. On the back of the truck was a gragger the size of a baby elephant that spun with a grinding thunder that could likely be heard for miles around. The crowd applauded under the deafening sound, as if witnessing a Jimi Hendrix solo of *Hava Nagilla*.

"That's more like it," Rabinsky said, finally satisfied. "And now to perform the *Purim Spiel*, the original Broadway cast of Hamilton and playing the role of Mordechai, our very own Canadian Jewish brother, Drake!"

Reuven lost his shit. No, it was more than that, it was as if Reuven lost all concept of what shit even was. He danced around the table and waved a napkin. Reuven loved Drake, always had. Sara, for her part, was indifferent to the rap star but she liked seeing Reuven so happy. Her husband seemed different tonight, more joyful and less stressed about work. And even though this event was a totally absurd and vulgar display, who could dampen the spirits of a man who looked so happy?

Back at home, Joshua lay in bed reading *Love In The Time Of Cholera* when a text came in from Brie, "Whatcha doing, sexy?"

Joshua sent a pic of his book.

Brie replied, "Nerd. Are your parents making sure you finish all your homework?"

"My parents are out partying. Rare sight."

"Can I come over? I want to take something from you."

"What? My Trig homework?"

"No, your V Card." Brie added a wink emoji.

"How do you know that I'm a virg—Forget it. When can you be here?"

"On my way."

Joshua's parents weren't wrong about their son's

sudden leap into full-blown puberty, nor his newfound enjoyment of masturbating in the shower. Brie had awoken a beast within him, and that beast excreted a lot of semen. Joshua was both enjoying his raging hormones and fearing that something was deeply wrong with him. Hair sprouted from places they'd never before, and when he looked in the mirror, his head was higher in placement. But full-on sex? Was he ready? Would he embarrass himself? Would she want him anymore once she saw him naked? Joshua jumped in the shower and soaped himself until he smelled like an Irish Spring factory. Then he went searching for condoms. He opened his dad's closet, riffled through his mom's underwear drawer. Did married people even use condoms? Who could he call? There was no one! He could only think of one other place where there might be some, and it was because he had the kind of mother who thought of everything before he did. He went to his mom's office and keyed in the digits for her safe. His mother had once given him the code just in case there was an intruder. She kept a pepper spray gun in there as a last resort. Joshua emptied the entire safe, including the pepper spray gun. There were mainly documents, birth certificates, etc. There was a small bag of diamonds and an antique wedding ring. But no condoms. Not one.

"What am I going to do?" Joshua asked himself in a panic. He read online that a guy had once used Saran Wrap as a makeshift prophylactic, and he wondered if that could work? And if they were out of Saran Wrap, could he use aluminum foil? As he re-packed the safe Joshua saw a few loose-leaf pages with his mother's handwriting. The pages had jagged edges and had clearly been ripped out of some journal. At the top of the first page it was dated just a couple of weeks before. There was a bunch of math and then this clearly legible note, "Goats stopped fainting when isolated from non-fainting breeds. Could confirm theory of isolation plus vaccine as a path to cure. Stool and blood samples reveal CV-Chlorine + S-100 could work. Is vaccine

+ isolation of Jewish people from non-fainters (at a certain distance for a specific time) the answer?"

Joshua sighed. His mother's scientific hunches were rarely wrong, and if isolation was part of the cure then he would have to be separated from Brie, and he was pretty sure that he loved her. But there wasn't time to think about that. He placed the notes back in the safe and locked it, then headed down to the kitchen to search for Saran Wrap. But on his way down there was a knock at the front door.

"Hi, Stud." It was Brie, and she was holding a box of Trojans. "I figured you could use a restock."

Back at the Purim party, Reuven waited in line with Sara to get Drake's signature.

"Don't say anything embarrassing when we get up there," he reminded Sara. "The signature has to be for Josh. It's too sad if Drake knows it's for me."

"Agreed."

But when Reuven finally got to the front of the line he couldn't contain himself. He gushed about what a fan he'd been since the mixtapes and then revealed that he had also graduated from Forest Hill Collegiate in Toronto, though years earlier than Drake. When Drake got up and hugged him, whispering into Reuven's ear, "Forest Hill Falcons for life, my Jewish brother," Reuven welled up with tears. Reuven and Sara walked around the party hand in hand, enjoying the free drinks and food. Reuven all but floated. He noticed several fellow Maccabees from his group, and though they gave each other knowing winks and nods it was understood that the whole thing was on the down-low. They were undercover agents playing for the good guys.

Across the room the man of the hour, Dr. Jacob Rabinsky, was swarmed by gushing guests. One of them literally bent over and kissed his pinky ring, leaving the logo of Brandeis University imprinted on their lips. But when Rabinsky spotted Reuven and Sara across the floor he escaped the crowd and walked over.

"One-Punch Schtinkler, so glad to finally meet you," Rabinsky said and shook Reuven's hand firmly.

Reuven was almost breathless. "Dr. Rabinsky. An honor. And uh, thank you so much for the ride over."

"It's nothing. And please, call me Jake. We're *mishpacha*, after all."

"I didn't realize you knew each other," Sara said.

"Oh, I know your husband by reputation. He's one badass Jew," Rabinsky said with a wink.

"Appreciate that," Reuven managed to say, shyly. He was so into Rabinsky's praise that he completely forgot to freak out that Sara might catch on to the truth of his double life as a smasher of Nazis. "This is my wife, Sara."

"Oh, I know Dr. Schtinkler too, from TV." He shook Sara's hand. "You're doing important work. Any closer to finding that cure?"

"Working on it."

"Take your time, would you? Not sure we could have gotten Drake without it." Rabinsky laughed, and Reuven joined, but not Sara.

"People are suffering," she said under her breath.

"He was just kidding Sara, relax," Reuven pleaded.

"No, I'm afraid she's right." Rabinsky smiled. "Myotonia congenita has been a tragedy for most people around the world. There's been injuries and death. I shouldn't make light of such a serious pandemic."

"Thank you—"

"Still," Rabinksy interrupted, "doesn't a little bit of you feel that, much like with the Passover plagues, God has bestowed this pandemic on the gentiles to help free the Jews from persecution?"

"Not even a little bit," Sara replied.

"Well, it seems you and your husband are at

loggerheads then. The work he has done proves that he's committed to the cause of Jewish survival."

"Reality TV development?" Sara asked.

Reuven tried to cut in, but Rabinsky was ahead of him. "He's a Maccabee," Rabinsky said, patting Reuven on the shoulder. "Surely, you told your wife? You should be proud. Who knows how many Jewish lives you've saved giving those neo-Nazis a taste of their own medicine?"

"What's he talking about?" Sara asked her husband.

"It's a project in development," Reuven said, averting his eyes, and Rabinsky laughed.

"Your husband is a soldier of The Maccabees, a lion unafraid to shed blood to hold off our enemies. He's one of the good guys. But the research you're doing? Imagine if one of the Jews in Egypt had found a cure to God's plagues against the Egyptians? The boils, the locusts, the death of their slave-master's firstborn? His own people would imprison that Jew, or worse."

"Is that supposed to be some sort of threat?" Sara said.

Reuven all but convulsed. "No, he's not—"

"I would never," Rabinsky said. "But I'm one of the nice ones. I'm afraid there's a contingent of people who are a little more insistent that we keep things as is. People who are prone to violence." Rabinsky winked at Reuven, who squirmed. "Well, lovely to meet you both. Enjoy the evening. After all it's a celebration. Have fun!"

With that Rabinsky turned and walked off into the crowd to greet others. Reuven was speechless, and the lasers that Sara shot into him made it even harder to speak.

"I want to leave now, Reuven," she said.

"But I heard Drake's going to do his version of Adam Sandler's Hanukkah Song."

"Now!"

Though he knew this would mean missing out on the after-party and swimming in the *hamantaschen* hot tub, Reuven shuffled after her.

At home, Joshua stood next to his bed with a glass of water in his hand and a look of deep concern on his face. Brie was frozen in a myotonic spell, sheets strewn over her body, a blissful look on her face. "You okay?" Joshua asked.

When Brie unfroze after a few minutes, slowly regaining control of her muscles, she sat up in bed and took the glass of water from Joshua. "That was amazing." She purred. "But how do you feel? I mean without your V-Card?"

"Good. I just worried when you froze up like that, though. I don't want you to get hurt."

"It's my favorite part." Brie put back on her bra. "Fainting for me is like the best orgasm ever. It's scary if I'm alone or with someone else who faints. But you don't faint, so . . . " Brie kissed Joshua and squeezed his butt. "I better go. Your mom's got eyes out for me. I worry she'll murder me if she knows I deflowered her baby. You were so sweet. But hey, next time you bring the condoms. You know how creepy it felt stealing condoms from the Principal's closet?"

In the Uber home from the Purim Party Reuven confessed everything to Sara. Well, not everything-everything—certainly not what he thought would mean instant divorce: his affair with Pamela, and of course his deal to impregnate Claire in exchange for a promotion. But he did spill everything about The Maccabees. From how he met them at the bar to the neo-Nazis they first beat up at the barn in Kunkletown and the other "missions" he'd recently made. He apologized for lying about where he'd been on those nights. He pleaded for forgiveness for sneaking around behind her back. And yet as he spoke, part of Reuven hoped that Sara might be impressed. Didn't all women secretly want a man who wasn't afraid to throw their fists around in the name of justice? She might be into it?

"I knew when I married you that you weren't exactly Einstein, Reuven. But I thought you had a kind heart," Sara said, staring at her hands. As the car pulled up to their home she all but jumped out.

"Sara, wait!" Reuven said, concluding that she definitely wasn't into it. He tried to stop her but was distracted by the sight of a girl in a black hoodie slipping out the side door of his house and rushing off down the street. By the time Reuven got out of the Uber, the girl was gone and Sara was struggling with her keys at the front door. She finally pushed the door open and bounded up the stairs. She grabbed her stack of books and her scented eye pillow from the bedroom and went to the guest room. Reuven stood at the bottom of the stairs watching.

"Sara don't be crazy." He sighed.

"Me be crazy?" Sara asked. "You're out there living some juvenile fantasy, and I'm crazy? You have a family, Reuven. You're an adult. Act like one." Then she slammed the guest room door shut.

From his room Joshua heard all the commotion and assumed the night had not gone well. But the last thing he wanted to do was come out of his room now lest his parents intuit that only minutes earlier he'd had sex for the first time. It was perhaps the first time any kid has ever been happy that their parents are arguing.

Reuven dragged himself up the stairs and entered the bedroom. He took off his clothes and lay in bed alone, feeling bloated from all the seltzer and *rugelach*. He was annoyed at Sara's reaction but actually felt relief that he'd gotten at least some of his lies off his chest. He was planning a second apology when his phone pinged, an email from Claire. "Will need another sample of your . . . writing. Let's schedule something for Monday morning?"

Reuven saw that Pamela was cc'd on the email, which made his brain spin and his stomach churn. His arrangement with Claire had been simple at first. He'd handed her a sample of his semen in a pill bottle and she'd gone to the executive bathroom to inseminate. Reuven wasn't quite sure how this worked, maybe there were stirrups in the executive bathroom, or perhaps next to the Dyson hand dryer they had some sort of Dyson impregnator? When that hadn't worked, they'd moved to more direct insemination, and had sex in the private bathrooms next to the Wellness Lounge. Claire's email meant that their most recent encounter hadn't done the job and she still wasn't pregnant. Maybe she was infertile? Maybe he'd gone sterile? Reuven wondered if she could take back his promotion? He hated to think that all of the sex he had with his boss was a total waste.

Reuven's phone pinged again, this time a text from Sam. "Need you tonight, Bud. Rabinsky asked for you by name. Can meet on the Jersey side. Let me know and I'll send coordinates."

Reuven took a deep breath, replied with a thumbs up, and put back on some clothes. Sara was right that he wasn't Einstein. He couldn't contribute to humanity with a microscope and clinical trials of formulas that looked like whirling numbers to him. But he was stronger than she gave him credit for. And he was kinder too in his own way. In Reuven's gut he knew that The Maccabees were doing some good, protecting the helpless and the weak. The Jews who were outnumbered and beaten down, as he had been at Shield Academy. And so maybe he was doing it for himself too, or at least that 7th grade version of himself facing down Robert Thurston III. Didn't he deserve a little redemption in this life? As if it were the universe's way of answering this question, he received one more text message from Sam with the directions to the meet-up spot in Hoboken. It was only a quick drive away.

CHAPTER 12

WHEN REUVEN ARRIVED at How You Brewin?, the Hoboken bar that was the headquarters for the New Jersey chapter of The Maccabees, it was almost empty. A few stragglers were leaving and the bartender was cleaning glasses. In the back there was only Sam, who was gazing up at a wall of photos just like the one in New York City. He had just finished X-ing out a photo of *The Masked Singer* host Nick Cannon in red when Reuven walked in.

"Am I early?" Reuven asked, looking around the empty room.

"Just you and me tonight, pal," Sam said. "You must have really impressed Rabinsky. Only a trusted soldier is asked to do a solo mission."

"Solo?" Reuven gasped.

"He called you a real Maccabee Lion," Sam said, and Reuven couldn't help but blush. "Don't worry. I'm coming with. I'll tell you all the details in the car. Should be an easy one actually. In and out."

"I like an easy one. I'm used to being with the gang, you know, so . . ."

Reuven's heart pounded as Sam led him out to the parking lot and into a black van. Sam went into it, explaining that the guy they were hitting was a real son of a bitch, an enemy of the Jews who had information that could hurt the cause and even lead to the loss of Jewish life.

"He's got stolen information we need to take back. It's all printed out in a green binder in his kitchen. Like this."

Sam waved a binder he had on the dashboard as he pulled out onto the freeway. Inside the binder was a photo of the guy Reuven needed to rob. He was a stocky Asian man with a BabyBjörn across his chest but no baby. Under other circumstances the guy didn't look like a threat at all. But when Reuven looked closer there did seem to be something wrong with the guy. Something ominous. Definitely something anti-Semitic.

"Just in an out. No one gets hurt. That's an order from Rabinsky," Sam said.

They pulled off the Garden State and into a quiet neighborhood near Irvington. There were rows of small houses and playgrounds, tricycles left out in driveways next to rusty cars. It looked like a nice place for working-class families, like where Reuven had grown up in the Greek area of Toronto. Sam turned off the van's headlights as they rolled onto a tree-lined street and then stopped in front of a small blue house with a quaint porch.

"That's the one." Sam pointed. "Get in, get the binder and get out. No questions. I want you wearing a mask for this one so there's no chance it gets back to you. No one needs to know you were even here."

"Do they have security? A dog?" Reuven asked, hoping to find a loophole to get out of this.

"No dog and their home security system's been broken for over year, confirmed. The back door is loose and will open with a firm push. Once you're in, get the binder from the kitchen counter on the far shelf above the toaster and walk on out. He puts the binder there every night. That's it. Easy." Sam handed Reuven a black ski mask and then a gun. "A precaution."

Reuven pocketed the gun and put the ski mask over his head. He had once supervised a true crime reality show about stand-up comedians who murder called, *They Kill!*, and he tried imagining that he was one of the actors just doing a recreation. The gun had the same heft as the prop one in wardrobe, and maybe he could just disassociate through this whole thing.

"I'm just an extra in a recreation," he said aloud.

"What?"

"Nothing," Reuven replied. He was sweating profusely, and the addition of the mask drenched his neck as if trying to create a surface slick enough for Reuven to slide out of the situation. "Keep the motor running," he told Sam, a likely next line in a show script.

Reuven took a deep breath, exited the car and ran low towards the house before sneaking along the side alley into the backyard. There was a children's playset on a patch of yellowing grass and a picnic table. There was also one of those charcoal grills he'd always wanted because they make the meat taste smoky. He wondered if they were really worth the money. If he weren't breaking into the house, he would ask the person in the house about it. He arrived at the flimsy back door, which was loose, as promised.

"In and out," Reuven told himself. "Like I wasn't even there." The door gave with a slight screech but not loud enough to wake anyone at this hour. Reuven stepped into a mudroom. He'd always wanted a house with a mudroom too, so he added that to his list of things he might discuss with the homeowner under other circumstances. He nudged away some boots and walked to the kitchen. It was outdated brown with beige Formica floors like from his childhood in the 80's. There was a baby chair and a jar of applesauce with a plastic spoon still sticking out of it, and Reuven winced realizing that the backyard playset wasn't a leftover from some grown-up college kid—there was an actual child in the house. At the far end of the kitchen Reuven saw the toaster and above it a shelf. He tiptoed over and next to a bowl with keys was a green binder, just as Sam had described it. "In and out, like I wasn't even here," Reuven muttered to himself like a mantra, and stepped forward to grab it.

"What are you doing in my house?" a voice asked.

A small, stocky man in a bathrobe stood in the living room, holding what looked like an enormous bowl of Mini-Wheats. Reuven tucked his hand in the pocket without the gun and pointed, but his mind flooded with totally irrelevant thoughts. Ohhh Mini-Wheats, I love Mini-Wheats. I wonder if he's tried the chocolate kind. What kind of Nazi eats Mini-Wheats? Shouldn't he be eating Nazi cereal? Is there a Nazi cereal? Swastik-Ohs? Start your day off Reich? . . .

"I have a gun," he said finally, his voice cracking.

"Take whatever you want just don't hurt my family," Bruce's startled voice said. He held up his hands and the bowl of cereal tipped, spilling milk onto his Yoda slippers.

Reuven stepped forward and picked up the green binder, then turned to leave.

"My work binder?" Bruce said, squinting. "Who are you?"

"Brucey?" a woman's voice came from down the hall. "What's going on, honey?"

And right then, Bruce fainted. His cereal bowl went flying and without his soft helmet on, his chin banged hard against the dining room table, and then the rest of him collapsed with a thump onto the floor. Reuven turned and saw a short woman with big hair and a sleeping baby in her arms. She looked at her husband lying on the ground and then at the masked man in her kitchen.

"Who the fuck are you and what the fuck do you want?" she asked.

"Sorry," Reuven couldn't help but say. "I, uh, like your mudroom. Where'd you get the shelving?"

The woman placed her baby in the highchair and grabbed a baseball bat that was leaning on the wall behind it.

"Get the fuck out!" she yelled, waving the bat.

Reuven didn't have much experience making Nazis faint on his own. Usually they just froze up when they saw a group of Maccabees racing towards them. So he tried what he had with the woman in the elevator at Pamela's apartment. He put his hands up in the air like a grizzly bear and roared. Far from fainting, the woman just rolled her eyes.

"I'm Jewish, you numbskull," she said. Then she swung her bat. Reuven ducked and tried to unzip his jacket pocket to get the gun, but the zipper was stuck. The woman swung the bat again and struck him hard on the shoulder.

"Ouch!"

"Get out, you son of a bitch! Out of my house!"

"I'm trying!" he replied. "I swear!"

Sweat fell into Reuven's eyes, blinding him and he stumbled back. His left foot stepped directly into an Elmo Training Potty and caught there. He tried to kick it off, but the plastic seat gripped his ankle. He staggered forward and fell headlong onto the counter and both of his hands landed directly in the slots of the toaster. As his eyes cleared of sweat, he worried that the woman might pull down the side lever to burn him. Then he'd literally be toast. Instead, the woman swung the bat again, but this time Reuven managed to grab hold of it. The Elmo Potty broke under the weight of his foot and he fell forward and accidentally threw an elbow that caught the woman on the side of the face and sent her to the ground. She started howling with rage, which woke the baby who started crying loudly too. Bruce, covered in Mini-Wheats on the ground, woke up from his faint but then fainted again from renewed fear.

"I'm so sorry," Reuven said. "I never wanted to do this. Or break your Elmo potty. Or get Mini-Wheats on your floor. Or covet your mudroom. Just let me take this, okay?"

"Go fuck yourself, coward!" the woman yelled, shielding her face.

Reuven agreed with her sentiment. He tucked the

green binder into his jacket and ran towards the back door. The woman and the child continued to cry, and Reuven just wanted to get away from it. "It was an accident!" Reuven cried as he stepped into the backyard and sprinted down the alley.

Sam started the engine as soon as he saw Reuven appear. "Go! Go!" said Reuven, jumping into the van. Sam screeched off down the street and took a sharp right towards the freeway. Reuven pulled off his mask, which was drenched in sweat, and huffed and puffed, tears still streaming down his face. Sam handed him a bottle, which Reuven chugged. Then Reuven spit it out. It was sanitizer.

"Why'd you drink that? It's sanitizer?" Sam said.

Reuven wretched, straining for breath. "I thought we were stealing from Nazis! What the hell was that, Sam?!"

"You get the binder?" Sam asked.

"There were Jews in there, Sam. A wife and a kid. I punched a Jewish mother! I broke a child's training toilet!"

"You took a shit in a child's toilet?"

"With my foot!"

Sam just looked over at the binder Reuven was holding. "They didn't identify you, did they?"

"No," Reuven said. "But that woman hit me with a baseball bat. My shoulder really hurts. I think it's dislocated."

Reuven put the green binder on the dashboard. At a stoplight Sam opened it and scanned the contents. Reuven caught a glimpse and almost lost his mind when he saw the logo for The Center for Animal Oddities at the top of a page. He knew the logo well—Sara's 'Employee of The Year' award, which sat over the fireplace, had it emblazoned over her name. Reuven pulled the van's emergency brake.

"What the hell are you doing?" Sam asked.

"Is that what this is about?" Reuven said, keeping his hand over the break. "My wife's research at the lab? Did I just rob my wife's co-worker for you?"

"You don't know what you're talking about."

"He could have known me, Sam. He could have seen photos of me and known!"

"Exactly why you wore a mask," Sam said.

"Fuck this. I'm turning myself in to the cops." Reuven seethed.

Sam took control of the emergency brake and pulled the van to the side of the road. He glared at Reuven. "The fuck you are," he said. Reuven tried to meet Sam's angry glare but wavered, instead looking out at the road ahead like he was pondering some philosophical questions. Am I bad person? Am I a violent person? Did their mudroom come with that shelving or did they have to buy it separately?

Sam filled the silence, "You did what you had to do in there for the cause. For Rabinsky. Your wife may think she knows this guy, but he's bad news, believe me."

"Well, you can tell Rabinsky this the last time," Reuven said. "She had a kid, Sam. A baby in there." Reuven began to cry again and didn't stop for a while. Sam handed him tissues. Then he pulled the van out and started the drive back to the Hoboken club.

"I know that was hard," Sam said once they arrived in the parking lot. "But you did good tonight, Reuven. You accomplished an important mission. More important than you can possibly know. And I promise you after this, just Nazis for a good while."

"Promise?" Reuven said, still wiping away tears.

"You betcha, bud."

Reuven left the van and walked back to his car. He used his left hand to drive home since his right shoulder hurt from being smashed by a baseball bat. He cried some more as he drove, and as he blew his nose into his last Kleenex it finally dawned on him what this "mission" was really about. Yes, Sam likely wanted to nab some research about a cure for myotonia congenita, almost certainly with the intention of blocking it, but the real reason he'd asked Reuven to do it had nothing to do with Rabinsky being impressed with him at the Purim Party, or that he was a so-called "Lion." It was to send him a message, "Your wife is next."

"Idiot!" Reuven said. "I'm such a fucking idiot!"

He slammed the dashboard and it really hurt his shoulder. The pain caused him to swerve off the road and onto the sidewalk where he hit a lawn sign for a manure delivery company. The sign stuck to his bumper, but Reuven decided to keep driving rather than get out of the car and possibly have his face caught on someone's Nest camera. Instead, he sped the rest of the way home and tried to avoid stop lights. He screeched into the driveway and jumped out of the car, ready to tell Sara everything this time, and to warn her what might happen if she wasn't careful. But he didn't want to wake up Joshua. So, he carefully creaked opened the front door and gently eased it closed behind him, then tip-toed into the house so as not to cause the floors to creak. It was the second time that night he would sneak into a house and also the second time that an ambush would be waiting for him.

"Jesus, Dad. Are you okay?" Joshua stood there in his pajamas staring at Reuven with his sweat-soaked shirt, his crooked arm, and the dried tears on his cheeks.

"I'm fine," Reuven said, startled. "Took a late-night walk. Fell into a racoon hole but the raccoons didn't bite me. I hurt my arm. Anyway. Go back to bed."

"Afraid that's not going to be possible," Joshua said. "She already woke me up. Threw pebbles at my window thinking it was you."

"Who?"

Joshua motioned to the dining room. And there, sitting at the table crying into a glass of water, was Pamela. She was wearing a Phi Beta Kappa Sorority sweatshirt, pajama pants, and glasses. She had a big red zit on her forehead and looked more like a homely college freshman than the sexy Assistant from the office. Tears streaked down her face as she looked up from her glass.

"Reuv, I think I'm pregnant. If Claire finds out she's going to fire me."

Reuven's mouth was sandpaper. He didn't know what to say, except to possibly accuse her of a poking hole in the condom, but then he thought that might not be wise.

Sara walked down the stairs yawning. She put her arm on Joshua. "It's three in the morning. What's going on down here?"

"Ask Dad," Joshua said, and motioned to the visitor in the dining room.

Sara took one look at the crying girl and then at Reuven's hangdog expression and knew it was going to be a long night.

Mother, father, and son sat silently around the dining room table. When Reuven tried to speak Sara shushed him and Joshua added, "Dad, this is one of these times you're going to have to zip it."

More awkward silence. Then the distant sound of a flushed toilet. Pamela, in her oversized sorority sweatshirt, walked into the dining room holding the pregnancy test Sara had given her. She handed it over and fell into Sara's arms like Sara was her mother, which she certainly could have been. Reuven strained to see the verdict of "Not Pregnant" written on the test.

"Oh, thank God!" he exclaimed, and Sara shot him a look of pure hatred.

"I'm going to go now," Pamela said, tearfully. "I'm so sorry for everything. You must hate me so much."

"None of this is your fault," Sara replied.

"Yeah, I guess you're right," Pamela said and glanced at Reuven, who turned away, so she turned back to Sara. "I love you, Mrs. Schtinkler. I wish you were my mom. And Joshua, you're such a nice kid. Follow me on Insta, 'kay?"

Joshua waved awkwardly. Pamela stood up and walked out the door to her waiting Uber.

"Joshua, give your father and me a moment," Sara said.

"Have at it." Joshua walked out, shaking his head.

And then Sara and Reuven were alone.

Sara looked at the ground, and when she spoke her voice was low and steady. "I want you out."

"You want me out?" Reuven repeated.

"Out!" Sara snapped, and her red eyes widened as she glared at him. In all of their years together Sara had rarely raised her voice. "RIGHT NOW!"

Reuven was stunned. He stood up fast like he'd sat on a thumb tack and tried to grasp for some authority. "This is my house too," he said, but Sara just squinted as if unable to grasp his full stupidity. So, he stomped off like a little boy sent to his room. Moments later he returned with a suitcase. "I'll, uh, leave the other keys. And I put my laundry in the machine. They're wet, but—"

"You want me to do your laundry?" Sara asked, not looking up.

"No, I just . . . they're dirty, so—"

"You don't get to tell me what to do, Reuven. You don't get to tell me anything anymore. Goodbye," Sara said, adding. "Oh, and my car's in the shop for a new transmission. So, you'll be taking an Uber to wherever you're going, I honestly don't care."

Reuven was about to protest and try to explain why there was a manure services sign attached to the bumper of the car, but Sara just lifted her hand. So, he turned and walked out. What else could he do? Just a man with a suitcase leaving his own home at three in the morning with no place to go, not even a car to sleep in. On the street he spotted a man sitting in a blue Honda SUV smoking a cigarette out the window. Maybe it was an Uber driver he could catch without waiting? That would be lucky. He waved and made a move to walk over, but when he did the driver revved his engine and screeched out of his spot and into the empty road, leaving Reuven scratching his head.

"Has everyone gone nuts?" It was at that moment when Reuven remembered why he'd raced home so fast earlier. He hadn't had the chance to tell Sara about what had taken place with Sam that night, nor had he been able to warn her about what might come her way if she's wasn't very careful. But if he told her now he'd also have to fess up about what he'd done to Sara's co-worker and his wife—burglary and assault. In her state Sara was liable to call the police. He was already in a world of shit. Reuven looked up at his home and made a promise that he'd keep a keen eye out for Sara and Joshua. If it took sitting outside on the lawn for the rest of eternity to keep them safe that's just what he'd do, at least metaphorically. A man's duty was to protect his family above all, and he would be diligent in his duties, even if it had to be from afar. But first he needed to find a place to sleep. It was late after all. He opened his Uber app and directed it to take him to the local Hyatt. A hot shower and a few hours' sleep would be just what he needed to get strong, and then he could try to make things right again.

CHAPTER 13

NEITHER SARA NOR JOSHUA slept much after the whole Pamela/Reuven pregnancy debacle. They tossed and turned in their beds. Sara tried relaxing by cutting Reuven out of the photos in their wedding album. But the adrenaline of the young girl's late-night visit, the revelation of Reuven's infidelities, and then his exit from the house with a suitcase kept things pumping. When Sara finally gave up and made coffee at six in the morning, Joshua joined her. They sat together watching *Morning Joe* on MSNBC until it was time for Joshua to shower and head to school.

"You sure you want to go today?" Sara asked. "I can call in and say you're sick."

"I have a science quiz," Joshua replied and picked up his backpack.

"You mean you want to see that girl?" Sara asked, to which Joshua just shrugged. "Her name's Brie, right? Like the cheese?"

"Did you hack my phone again?"

"No, I hacked the way sound waves move through the air."

Joshua stared at her not knowing what that meant.

She clarified, "You're very loud."

Sara drove Joshua to school, holding his hand as much of the way as he would let her. She felt so sorry for her son that she almost burst into tears many times. More than anything she just wanted to be with him today and assure him that everything would turn out all right, though at this point she wasn't quite sure what "everything" entailed or how to possibly measure "all right."

"Is it too late to teach you about the birds and the bees?" Sara asked.

"Afraid that ship has sailed, Mom."

Sara switched gears. "Look, Joshua, about your father and this situation—"

Joshua put up his hand. "I already know what you're going to say."

"You do?"

"You're angry that Dad chose this moment when I finally hit puberty and found a girlfriend to reveal the ugliness and cowardice that can emerge from a sexual life."

"How did you—"

"It was unforgivably selfish of him for many reasons. I've had a hard enough time at school, and now I have to live through the trauma of witnessing last night's clusterfuck. You wonder how this might manifest in my adult life."

"I wasn't going to swear, but yeah . . . "

"Don't worry about me so much, Mom. I know Dad's a screw-up and that most people don't act that way. If anything, this will teach me how stupid it is to cheat and that you have to be honest even if it's hard. And if you absolutely do need to cheat, don't pick someone who's going to show up crying at your family's house reeking of teenager perfume."

"How did you know I wanted to say all that?" asked Sara, a single tear rolling down her cheek.

"Because you're the G.O.A.T.. Greatest of all time."

"No, you're the G.O.A.T."

"No, you're the G.O.A.T."

When they pulled into the school parking lot Brie was waiting by a tree scrolling on her cellphone. Joshua leaned in and kissed his mother and then got out of the car. Sara sat there and watched her son walk up to Brie. If this were a nature film, the narrator would say something like, "The mating rituals of the North American teenager include approaching one other, laughing as they stare at the ground, checking their phones, and then holding hands and walking into school." Sara noticed that this time Brie didn't check behind her back to see if others were watching. She actually snuggled up to Joshua in a way that goats do with their mates.

"Afraid that ship has sailed," Sara repeated to herself and started crying again. "And is probably having sex with another ship."

She pulled out of the parking lot and was wiping away tears when she spotted that blue Honda SUV that had been trailing her lately parked across the road. She took a quick left to confront the driver and rolled down her window, but he tossed his cigarette on the road and quickly drove away.

"What do you fucking want from me!?" Sara yelled out into the street, and a crossing guard frowned at her. "And smoking is really bad for you!" She glanced at her blood-shot eyes in the mirror. "Reuven's right. I must be going crazy."

Sara's mood did not improve when she got to the lab. She booted up her computer and was going to type up something very basic in her log when she got an alert that she had tried too many passwords and was blocked for 24 hours.

"That's it. I've had it," she snapped. She stomped over to Kent's office as irritable as she'd ever been and with less sleep. "I know you're my boss, Kent, but if you want to look through my research you need to ask me. No more trying to break into my computer. That's off-limits."

Kent looked up at Sara with a weary expression. He could sense that Sara was frazzled because her eyes were bloodshot, and one half of her hair was matted to her face, while the other half was so stretched out that it looked like it was desperately trying to find another head to live on. She wouldn't take anything but the cold truth. "There was a break-in last night," he said. "Two men in masks came through the bathroom window, rummaged around. No one was hurt, thank God."

"Did they take anything?"

"A bunch of tranquilizers and some other random pills. The cops are saying it was low-level drug dealers."

"Why would drug dealers try to access my computer?"

"Looking for codes to the safe?" Kent shrugged. "I filled out a report and the police are launching a full investigation."

Through the window of Kent's office Sara saw Bruce walk in. He had a bandage on his chin tucked under the strap of his soft helmet, and his arm was in a sling.

"What happened to you?" Sara asked, walking out into the hall.

Bruce looked at the floor, unable to make eye contact. "I'm okay. Jackie and the baby are okay. But we had a burglary last night at the house. And it got violent."

"Jesus Christ."

"I fainted, but Jackie got beat up a bit. She's okay, just bruised, but it was scary. The baby's fine." Bruce started sobbing, and Sara hugged him close. Bruce sniffled on his own snot as he continued. "He didn't even take any money. My wallet was right there on the counter. All he took was my green binder."

"Your work log?" Sara said.

"I keep asking myself why? I mainly put receipts in there for coffee runs. I guess he thought it was some kind of top-secret research." Bruce looked at Sara seriously, eyes wet and red. "Please be careful, Sara. Something weird is going on and if anything happened to you, I might go off the deep end."

Sara hugged Bruce again. Over his shoulder she saw Kent on the phone in his office, looking stressed. "Low-level drug dealers my ass," she said.

Perhaps the only thing stronger that Joshua's desire to ace his science quiz was the sudden urgency of his pubescent libido, so when Brie suggested they skip class and go back to her house, which was Principal Davies' house, his boner pointed the way. The Principal's house was just as Joshua pictured it would be—exceptionally dull but with photos of the Principal's volunteer work in the Middle East and art from the region on every available surface.

"Is he smoking a hookah in this photo?" Joshua asked.

Brie pulled Joshua's arm away from the ridiculous photos and led him upstairs to her bedroom. It was painted entirely black and had posters of rock stars everywhere, a stark contrast to the soft colors elsewhere else in the house. Also, there was this really cool rack of Samurai swords over her bed. As soon as Brie closed the door, she had her shirt off and was kissing him.

"I'm starting to think you're only interested in me for my body." Joshua smiled.

"And what if I am?" she asked.

"I'm an old pro by now," Joshua said. "It's been what, twelve hours since I lost my V card? Let's level up."

"I love it when you compare love making to video games." Brie jumped in bed, grabbed a scarf and wound it around her wrists, then hooked the scarf over the bedpost. "Oh look, you tied me up, you mean video game villain. What are you going to do to me now?"

"Uh, is this like role-playing?" Joshua asked. "Because if so, you're in luck. I'm a World of Warcraft master." He cleared his throat, trying to summon a script in his head. "Um, yes I tied you up, Vixen! And it won't be the worst of it until you submit to my wizard power!"

"Yes, use your magic wand on me, Great Wizard," Brie said. Joshua got into bed and was on top of her.

"Are you thinking I'm more of Garrosh Hellscream or Ner'zhul in this role?" he asked.

"Put your hands around my neck," Brie instructed.

"Definitely Ner'zhul. But okay." Joshua lay his hands gently on her long pale neck. "How's that?"

"You're going to hurt me, aren't you?" Brie asked. "Tell me you're going to hurt me bad."

"I am going to cause you low-level pain. Like an itchy mosquito."

"Tighten your grip!" Brie shouted.

"Won't that be uncomfortable?"

"Shut up and do it!"

Joshua tried.

"Harder!"

Joshua applied pressure. Not enough to hurt her but enough to freak him out him, that was for sure. Brie began to moan and soon froze with that same blissful smile on her face that Joshua had seen before.

"All righty then." Joshua removed his hands from Brie's neck.

She'd be out for about four minutes, or at least that's what he'd observed. Was sex always like this, he wondered? How did sex work before people passed out? Was it always over as quickly? How does it work between two gentiles? He had so many questions, but Brie wasn't exactly in a position to answer them. So, he got out of bed and looked around Brie's room. He perused the really cool rack of Samurai swords and then looked at all the posters on her wall. Mainly old punk rockers: The Ramones. Lou Reed. Perry Farrell of Jane's Addiction. Adam Yauch of The Beastie Boys. She definitely had a type.

"What, no Itzhak Perlman?" he asked.

Joshua's mind flashed to the night prior with his father and the sorority girl with the zit cream and the pregnancy test. He wondered if she also had a gallery of *Jews Who Rock* on her bedroom wall? Probably. Using that math, the sorority girl was like Brie and he was just like his father?

So it was settled. It would be painful, but Joshua would have to cool it off with Brie for a while, the first girl he'd ever been intimate with. He would look her in the eyes and be brave, tell her the truth and extend his friendship as a consolation. Hope that she didn't grab for one of her Samurai swords. They would ease back on the sex stuff. For a while. A week at least. Okay three days. But that's final! He wouldn't be anyone's fetish. Joshua walked over to the bed to get the conversation started.

"Ready for another round?" Brie grinned, having finally unfrozen. "This time I want you to be one of the guys in *Seven Samurai*."

"Kikuchiyo or Kambei?" Joshua quickly replied.

Brie smiled. "Definitely Kikuchiyo!"

"Danger always strikes when everything seems fine," Joshua said in his best Toshiro Mifune. Brie squealed with delight.

Maybe being used wasn't so bad after all, depending on who's using you and what for, Joshua thought. The least he could do was find out. And if that took kicking the no-sex conversation down the road a bit, who would be the worse for wear? Besides, Brie looked so incredibly happy.

You know who didn't look so incredibly happy? Reuven, who at that moment lay restless on an army cot in the back of the club in New York City. He'd tried to check into the Hyatt in Jersey City the previous night but there was some kind of gaming conference that had the area booked solid. Eventually he just asked his driver to head over the bridge and ended up at the club, where the closing staff gave Reuven a knowing look. He wasn't the first Maccabee to show up with a suitcase and a tale of woe at 4 a.m. They led him to the little cot next to the fridge in the back.

When Reuven woke up mid-afternoon the next day with a Snickers wrapper stuck to his cheek and a nasty crick in his neck, Larry was there crunching numbers on a laptop.

"Troubles at home?" Larry said with a smirk, when Reuven sat up.

"Is it that obvious?" Reuven groaned, rubbing his neck.

"She'll take you back. They always do," Larry said. "It's not like there's a whole bunch of available Jewish men ready to step in your shoes and provide for her."

"That's the thing." Reuven felt all the guilt rush back. "She doesn't need providing for. She's a scientist with a decent job. And I'm an idiot."

"Eh, don't be so hard on yourself."

"I betrayed her, Larry. With a girl half my age. And the worst part is that my kid knows."

"That part is unfortunate," Larry conceded. "Still, on some level he's got to be proud that his old man can still bed a young broad. Means he's got virile genes. He'll benefit from that when his time comes."

"He does finally have a girlfriend." Reuven smirked.

"Then he's already benefitting!" Larry chuckled, earning a full, prideful laugh from Reuven. "Just lay low for a bit. Then go back groveling on your hands and knees and beg for forgiveness. Buy her some flowers and sparkly jewelry. I guarantee it will all work out."

"From your lips to God's ears."

Reuven opened the fridge and grabbed a seltzer. He took a long swig as he perused the board of photos that Sam was so fond of X-ing out. From his first neo-Nazi raid in Kunkletown to the other white power enclaves and racist bars they'd made a wreck of. Amongst the photos not yet X'd out, Reuven saw the house he'd raided the night before, and an image of the man he'd encountered in the kitchen. He felt a deep pang of regret at the violence that had occurred over a stupid green binder. He picked up the marker.

"I did this one myself," Reuven said, and was about to X it out.

"Wouldn't do that," Larry warned. "Sometimes, it's considered an ongoing mission."

Reuven put down the marker and continued to browse the photos when something familiar caught his eye. It was a blurry surveillance photo of an empty parking lot, nondescript, but at the edge of the shot was an oddly shaped tree. The tree appeared to be a Japanese Maple and had peculiar nobs and a dramatic windblown stance that made it look like a bonsai. Reuven gasped. In the dozen or so times he'd dropped Sara off at The Center for Animal Oddities over the years he'd always noted the strange beauty of that tree in such an odd location. Sirens went off in Reuven's mind, but he decided to play it cool.

"What's the plan with this parking lot?" he asked as casually as his pounding heart would allow. "Nazi meet-up location?"

"Beats me," Larry said. "But if it's up on the enemies' board you know there's a plan of action."

"It just looks like the parking lot of where a friend of mine works."

"Well, your friend might want to look for a new gig." Larry smirked.

"I got to take a leak," Reuven said.

He walked to the bathroom and once inside pulled out his phone and texted Sara, "We have to talk. It's important. Please, please call me now."

Reuven waited for a reply when he heard voices outside. Larry speaking with someone in low tones. When Reuven emerged from the bathroom, Sam was there along with two beefy guys with thick unibrows Reuven had never seen before. Don't get me wrong, he had seen unibrows before, just not these particular unibrows, on these particular beefy guys.

"Well, if it isn't Mr. Casanova?" Sam smiled. "I won't lie, I've logged a few nights on that cot myself."

"I think I smelled your cologne on the pillow," Reuven said, trying his best to sound affable.

"Gotta say it was worth it in retrospect. Though I did have to eat a pound of shit with the wife when she found out."

"I booked a hotel in Jersey City. I won't be staying here another night if someone needs it," Reuven said.

"Stay as long as you like, right, Larry?" Sam said, and Larry waved. Then he turned to his men. "Boys, this is Reuven. He may not look like it but he's as tough as nails."

The two men bounced their unibrows respectfully to Reuven. Still, they hadn't spoken a word, and that made Reuven uneasy. "Hey Sam, you got a minute?" Reuven asked. "It's sort of a private thing."

Sam nodded, and they walked to the far end of the room while the beefy men stood guard. "What's up, buddy?" Sam asked.

"Last night, I, uh, said some things, you know. I got emotional and I wanted to clear the air."

Sam waved him off. "I completely understand Reuven, and it's already forgotten. All I told Rabinsky is that you accomplished the mission beautifully, and he said he wasn't surprised."

"Good. That's good," Reuven said, relieved. "I wouldn't want to ruffle feathers. But about what I saw in the binder. It seemed to be from my wife's lab, which is okay, but now I'm seeing a photo of the parking lot to her lab up there on the board. I don't want to take too big a leap here, but we're not planning something there, are we? Because my wife works there, you know, and I need to protect my family."

"That photo up there?" Sam pointed. "We just needed a reference for where that guy worked. That's all. I just haven't X'd it off yet."

"Oh, thank God," Reuven said, finally exhaling.

"A leftover, nothing more. Here, I'll X it out right now for your pleasure."

"Appreciate that."

The two thugs walked over, frowning. "Everything okay there, boss?"

Sam smiled. "It's fine." He turned to Reuven. "My word is my bond, Reuv." He walked over to the board, lifted the red marker and crossed out the photo of Bruce and then the image of the parking lot for The Center for Animal Oddities. "Happy?" he asked Reuven, who nodded. "Fabulous. Now, what do you say we grab some late lunch? I know this place that serves the best shawarma around the corner."

"Love to," Reuven said. "But the hotel said I can check in already and I won't ask you to smell me, but I need a shower something awful. Raincheck?"

Sam nodded so Reuven grabbed his suitcase and headed to the exit. Sam stopped him before Reuven got to the door. "Hey, Reuv. We're good, right?"

"Absolutely," Reuven forced a smile. "Thanks again for the shelter and the cot. Let's hope I won't be needing it again. But then again, so many *shiksas*, right?"

Sam laughed, "You're not wrong about that!"

As soon as Reuven left the club he raced to hail a cab. "Chatham," he told the driver.

"Jersey side?" the driver said. "There's gonna be tolls." Reuven waved a stack of bills from his wallet and the cabbie nodded, "You got it, Boss."

There was traffic on the way to the tunnel, giving Reuven more than enough time to stew. He called Sara's cell a dozen of time. Texted her, but nothing back. He didn't want to type anything specific about the lab. God forbid what happened to her co-worker Bruce was traced back to him. He eventually called Joshua.

"What do you need, Dad?" Joshua said.

"Are you with your mother?"

"She doesn't want to talk to you."

"I know. And I deserve that, believe me. But something serious has come up and I must speak with her. I'm coming home now in a cab. But will you just ask her to call me, please?"

"I'll try."

The cab made it through the tunnel, and as they merged onto the 78 Freeway Reuven reflected on Sam's thinly veiled lie that he just hadn't crossed out the parking lot to Sara's lab yet. He'd said it in a way that reminded Reuven of the first night he'd met Sam, when he'd complimented Reuven for being such a big Canadian Jew, and how he encouraged him with the macho nickname "One-Punch" at their first outing in Kunkletown. Reuven now realized all of the manly Jewish camaraderie was never actually about him. All this time it was Sara that Sam wanted to get to. Her work on the cure for human myotonia congenita. Reuven was just a stepping-stone to get closer to her and the plan had worked beautifully. How could he have been so blind to think "big Canadian Jew" was a genuine compliment? He shook his head in disgrace.

When the cab finally arrived at his house Reuven grumbled about the $150 fee, but then paid it, because what the fuck was he going to do? He rushed to the front door and took out his house key, but it didn't fit in the hole. He kept struggling with it thinking he was going mad.

"Amazing how quick you can get locks changed under the circumstances," Sara said from above. She was leaning out the bedroom window, her hair wet from a shower. "Go away, Reuven."

"Sara, thank God! I have to talk to you. Please let me in. It's serious."

"Yeah, Josh told me you're in a real panic," Sara said.

"Yes!"

"So, say it from there."

Reuven looked around. His nosy neighbor, that wrinkled old bat Nancy was sitting out on her porch watching the whole thing.

"Yeah, say it from there, Reuven," she crowed. "I'd love to hear some fresh bullshit."

Reuven rolled his eyes at her, looked back up at Sara. "It's not for public consumption. Sara, you may be in danger."

"Want me to call the cops?" Nancy called up to Sara.

"Hold that thought, would you, Nancy?"

"Got my finger on speed dial for you, Hon."

"Sara, I'm begging you," Reuven said. "I'll do anything you say. I just need to speak to you about one thing for five minutes. Then I'll leave."

"My answer is a simple and final no, Reuven, and if you don't comply then I give all the power to Nancy. She loves to call 911."

"Sometimes they bring sexy firefighters." Nancy purred.

And with that, Sara shut the window.

Reuven kicked the banister. "Goddamnit!"

"Kick that rail again and I'll have you in for destruction of property," Nancy said.

Reuven bared his teeth but then just skulked away fuming. He threw his now-defunct house key over the fence into his backyard, cursing it to high heavens, then he pulled out his phone and keyed in an old contact.

"ZBT Brother Card," Reuven said into the phone when a man picked up. "Top secret."

"What do you need, Brother?" the man replied as if he'd been waiting.

"A spare car for one night. No questions asked."

It was his old frat brother Ollie, who he hadn't contacted in over a year even though he lived blocks away. Little known secret in the Greek system that everyone knows: Zeta Beta Tau Fraternity had a strict code, and the ZBT "Brother Card" was sacrosanct as a means of asking for a single, undeniable favor. Ollie had already used his up, hitting up Reuven for tickets to a live taping of *Celebrity Surgery Pranks*, Season 8.

"My daughter's Tercel is on the side driveway," whispered Ollie. "She's on a ski trip until Monday. I'll leave the keys under the front right tire."

"Thank You, Brother."

"ZBT for life."

Reuven legged it to Ollie's house and found the blindingly bright neon pink car and the keys tucked under the front tire. He pulled the car out of the driveway as inconspicuously as you could a car with multi-colored LED under-lights and a bumper sticker that says, "Jersey Girls Don't Pump Gas!" He took a left onto Orchid Avenue and headed towards The Center for Animal Oddities.

Sara finished drying her hair and was applying moisturizer that Mitch The Makeup Maven had recommended called, "Gizelle's Hydro Boost Yogurt Magic Cloud Cream Aqua Bomb." As she looked in the mirror Sara swore she heard her skin scream, "Oh, Jesus God of Mercy our day of moisture has finally arrived!" But their cries were interrupted when Joshua entered the bathroom.

"Sorry you had to see all that," Sara said to Joshua loudly, having to speak over her screaming skin.

"You sure he's okay?" Joshua replied. "I've never seen him so agitated before."

"I've known your father for more than twenty years. He's someone who can benefit from a cooling-off period. In this case I'm thinking five days until I sit down and talk to him. You think that's too harsh?"

"I just worry he won't act like an adult when you finally do sit down," Joshua said. Then he checked his watch. "Listen, I need to go out for a bit. Brie and I need to talk." Then Joshua said a sentence that six months earlier would have seemed like something out of science fiction, "She's only into me because I'm Jewish and it makes me feel like I'm taking advantage of her. I have to tell her to her face. Be back in an hour, hopefully."

"I'm proud of you for being so brave," Sara said. "Let her down easy, okay?"

Joshua kissed his mom on the cheek. "You're the G.O.A.T.," he said.

"No, you're the G.O.A.T."

Sara put away her moisturizer and went to the kitchen

to pour herself a glass of wine. She sat in the den and turned on Joy Reid, who now had a bandage over her left eyebrow. "As you can see, I was on hold with customer service for a frustratingly long time." She chuckled. Sara laughed at that and looked over on the couch as if to laugh along with Joshua and Reuven, but no dice. She missed the family ritual of TV dinner trays and ramen, but that all seemed like a million years ago somehow. Joshua was only a boy then and now he's a full-on teenager, off to break up with a girlfriend. He'd grown half a foot in a few months and was shaving, and Sara wondered where her baby had gone? But this was all right in its own way, being alone. Cozy, actually. Her son was a first-rate mensch, and though his father was a cheating disaster and dealing with him would be painful, Sara sensed in Joshua a strength that could handle any situation with honesty and class. Still, that Reuven . . . ugh. For the first time Sara wondered if it had been a mistake marrying a Jewish man. On some level she knew that she'd yielded to her grandmother's pressure to avoid marrying out of the religion, and there'd been a few nice non-Jewish men along the way that she'd considered. "If you marry a Jewish man and you get in a fight, he'll never be able to call you a dirty Jew," her grandmother warned her as if that explained everything.

"Well, Grandma, look where that logic got me!"

Sara would take mild anti-Semitism during a domestic dispute over cheating any day. She opened Facebook and spent a little time stalking old flames who definitely never had a *bar mitzvah.*

During Joy Reid's final segment, an interview with the Chairman of the Center for Disease Control, she heard the front door open. "How'd it go with Brie, Honey?" Sara asked. When there was no response, she paused the show. "Joshie? I'm in the den." When there was still yet no response but the sound of heavy feet in the hall, she shook her head. "Jesus Christ, Reuven. You have no right to be here." She shot up from the couch and stepped into the hall to confront her idiot husband and probably threaten to call the cops when she found herself standing feet away from a large man in a ski mask who was rifling through the pages of her red journal. Sara turned to run but the man dropped the book and rushed forward, tackling her to the ground. Sara shrieked and struggled under the man's weight until she felt a leather glove against her mouth and the hard metal of a gun push up against her head.

"Scream again and I'll shoot you," the man said, his voice low and gravely. "Nod if you understand."

Sara nodded.

"Good. There are pages ripped out of your notebook. Where are they?"

He lifted his gloved hand and Sara gasped for breath. "I threw them out," she said.

"Don't dare lie to me. One more goddamn lie and I kill you and then go after the people at your lab."

"Okay . . . "

"Where are the missing pages?"

Just then there was a knock on the front window and a woman's voice called out. "Sara? Everything okay in there? I heard a shriek." Sara's neighbor Nancy pressed her face against the glass, but she couldn't see through the curtains. "Sara?"

"Tell her it's nothing." The masked man growled. "Or she dies too."

Sara gathered herself. "All good, Nancy. Just burned my hand making tea is all. Holding it under cold water. I'll come out in a bit to chat."

"Oh, okay, dear. Holler if you need me."

The man put his hand back over Sara's mouth and waited for Nancy to leave. Then he lifted his glove again. "I'm going to ask you for the last time and then I won't be so nice. Where are the missing pages?" He grabbed Sara's wrist roughly, adding pressure. Sara was just about to tell him about the safe upstairs when she was interrupted by the sound of a rifle cocking.

"You don't drink tea, Sara." Nancy stood in the doorframe with a rifle pointed at the masked man. "Now what you going to do, tough guy? How about you take your dog and pony show and get the fuck out of my friend's house."

Then Nancy fainted. She froze, and her body folded into a heap on the floor. Her rifle slid across the floor and right under the masked man's knee as if choreographed. The man sighed, then tightened his grip on Sara's wrist, and she could feel it breaking. But then another voice entered the house.

"Mom, I'm home," Joshua called out. "I broke it off with Brie and she cried, but we're going to try to be friends. She gave me her favorite Samurai sword as a breakup gift. It's really sharp. Hi-YAH, ninja!"

"Jesus Christ, a fucking Samurai sword?" the masked man muttered to himself. He leaned into Sara and whispered. "I'll be back. And you better give me those pages, or I'll kill your son first." Then the man stood up and ran out the back door.

"Mom, are you home?" Joshua called out. "Oh, my God, Nancy, are you okay?"

Sara got up and staggered to the hallway where Joshua was cradling Nancy's head.

"Mom, what happened?"

"There was an intruder," Sara replied. "I'm going to call the police. But I need you to stay here and take care of Nancy until they arrive."

"Wait, where are you going?"

"The lab," Sara said. "I have to save it."

In one of the more obvious stakeouts in New Jersey's storied stakeout history Reuven sat in his frat brother Ollie's daughter's neon pink Tercel, watching Sara's lab building from the far corner of the parking lot. It was dark with only a few lights on in the building, presumably from the night janitor. Reuven settled in. If he had to sit there all night, he was going to make sure The Maccabees didn't mess with Sara's research any more than they already had. Robbing his wife's co-worker was one thing but messing with the place where Sara spent her days? That was a direct threat to his family. He didn't care what Sam or Rabinsky thought or how they might punish him, that shit was unacceptable.

Eventually, the night janitor did exit the building and locked up. He was an old guy probably in his late seventies, and Reuven thought he remembered that his name was Ernest, which was maybe the oldest-sounding name he'd ever heard. Ernest put away his keys and rolled a cart of boxes towards his old pick-up truck. Reuven watched the guy bend his creaky knees and strain to lift each box onto the back of his truck. Reuven had an instinct to get out and help him, and that instinct alone made him feel hopeful, like maybe he was meant to do good after all. When the janitor lifted a final box, he stumbled and dropped it on the ground with a crash. Reuven heard the man grumble and then watched as he clasped his chest and fell to his knees.

"Oh shit." Reuven went for his phone to call an ambulance, but it fell out of his hands and slipped into that tiny gap between the chair and the consul that seemed intentionally designed for phones to disappear forever. "Jesus Christ!" He opened his car door and stayed low as he ran across the parking lot. "Uh, Ernest, you okay?" Reuven whispered to the crouched man. "You need help?"

"I—I had a fall." Ernest looked up at Reuven confused and a bit frightened. "I think I'm okay. Just need to catch my breath."

"Okay, just rest, I'm here for you. I can call an ambulance if you want?"

Ernest didn't reply but then looked over Reuven's shoulder just as Reuven heard footsteps from behind. He didn't have a chance to fully turn around before something heavy hit him in the head with a clang. It's hard to get too much detail about what heavy object is hitting you in the head from behind, but as Reuven collapsed, he thought a lot about it. His best guess was a fire extinguisher, based off of the noise it made, but it could have also been one of those big police flashlights. A second after his face hit the pavement, pieces of the blunt object landed next to him. "Oh," Reuven thought, both surprised and amused as he saw that the object that hit him was a menorah. "That's funny," Reuven thought. Then he didn't think anything, because he passed out.

Sara raced full speed to the lab, rounding tight corners and zooming through yellow lights. If that masked intruder was telling the truth, the lab was in danger, and who knows who'd get hurt in the process. According to traffic light footage I obtained from the local Police Department, she fully ran a red light to get onto Longview Road and then sped along the dead-end street to the lab parking lot. Right away she saw an orange glow and smoke billowing from the barn behind the main building.

"Spencer, Lillia, and Chewy!" Sara shouted as her car screeched to a stop and she jumped out. Sara ran towards the main entrance fumbling for her security card and caught sight of a black van parked at the edge of the lot. The side door of the van slid open and a man came tumbling out onto the concrete, dumped there like garbage. Then the van screeched off in a hurry. On most days, a man being pushed out of a van would be a pretty high priority for investigation. Today, however, this barely measured in the top five of Sara's concerns. The barn was on fire and her goats were in danger. Sara waved her security card and rushed forward into the lab and through the dark halls towards the back exit. When she got back outside the heat was almost unbearable. Flames leaped out of the barn windows and a dark cloud of smoke enveloped her as she pulled the barn doors open.

"Spencer, Lillia, and Chewy!" she called out desperately, and then covered her mouth so as not to inhale the smoke.

Though her eyes singed and watered, she found the three goats lying on the dirt floor next to the tetherball court, frozen in fear. Spencer, who was only half conscious, seemed to be trying to still swat at the tetherball from the supine position, which was a testament to his commitment to training. Sara strained to lift Lilia off the ground and then just dragged her by the legs towards the door as fire raged around her. She got about ten feet out before going back into the barn, dodging flames to get Chewy and then Spencer out as well. Sara collapsed next to the goats and spat dark sludge from her lungs. The barn's roof was now fully engulfed and looked to be collapsing, so Sara dragged each goat further away so that they wouldn't be hit by falling debris. The fire alarm went off in the main lab building and Sara saw that the fire had spread in there as well, and smoke billowed from an open bathroom window. Amongst the dangerous chemicals and expensive medical machinery inside there were many helpless animals in there too—birds and monkeys and sloths in cages. None of this would have happened if she had just agreed to study sloths instead. In addition, amongst the samples in the fridge were the fecal and blood samples that Burt had given her in Tennessee. If those samples were a piece of the puzzle towards a cure to myotonia congenita, they could not be lost either. Sara touched Spencer's head for courage, and then rushed into the burning lab building.

Four miles away at the Livingston Fire Department sirens blared as vehicles rushed towards a fire they'd gotten an anonymous 911 call about. They made it to the road when a far-off explosion stopped them in their tracks. A bright orange flash lit the sky, followed by a thunderclap as loud as an F29 jet. Then an ominous white cloud billowed into the night sky.

"We've got a Code 10-41," the Fire Marshall said into his walkie. I'm not totally familiar with Fire codes, but I believe that a 10-41 is a goat-involved fire. "Looks like it's coming from Longview Road."

At the location of the explosion a mushroom cloud swelled above The Center for Animal Oddities. Flaming debris had flown in every direction, and glass and metal littered the parking lot where Reuven, who had come conscious to the sound of the explosion, refocused his eyes and watched in horror as Sara's lab burned to the ground. He struggled to free himself from the duct tape around his wrists and mouth but couldn't move or scream as he wanted to. Fire trucks raced in and firefighters unfurled their hoses and got to the work of putting out a blaze that had already done calamitous damage. An ambulance and several other cars screeched into the parking lot as well, and amongst them was Sara's neighbor Nancy who had Joshua in her passenger seat.

"Mom!" Joshua shouted, seeing the burning building. He pushed the car door open and ran towards the building but was held back by police. He fell to his knees and wept. On the grass patch next to the parking lot, the goats Lillia, Spencer, and Chewy lolled around, dazed. There were other animals in the field as well; cats, dogs, a macaque monkey, and several sloths, all finding their new freedom from the ravaged lab disorienting. The sloths made a run for it, or as much of a run for it that sloths can make. In the far corner of the parking lot, Joshua noticed a man lying on his stomach with his hands tied behind his back. As he ran over the man became more familiar to him.

"Dad?" Joshua said. "What are you doing here? What happened?"

Joshua removed the duct tape from his father's mouth and then untied his hands. Reuven choked and rubbed his sore wrists. His eyes welled with tears. "I didn't see them," Reuven said. "They hit me from behind. Tied me up. When I woke . . . When I woke up . . . "

"Where's Mom?"

"I tried to stop her. I saw her going in, but I couldn't move or speak. I tried, Joshua, you have to believe me. I kept screaming for her, but she couldn't hear me."

"You were here because you knew something was going to happen," Joshua said, his face darkening.

"It's not what you think."

"Liar!"

An EMT ran up to them. "Sir, do you need help?" Reuven tried to get up to prove he was okay but almost collapsed in the process. "Lie down. We'll get you help."

Another EMT brought over a stretcher, and they hefted Reuven on as Joshua glared disdainfully.

"I only wanted to protect her. I swear to God." Reuven sobbed.

Joshua turned away as the EMTs rolled Reuven towards the ambulance and loaded him in. They injected him with an IV for fluids. After a few minutes a police officer climbed in.

"Reuven Schtinkler?" the officer asked. "Husband of Dr. Sara Schtinkler?"

"Did you find her? Please tell me she's okay?"

The officer shook his head. "I'm afraid the heat of the explosion melted a lot in there. We found this inside." The officer held up a brown cardigan coated in goat hair and smeared with dark blood. There were burned bone fragments also stuck in the fabric.

"Oh no. God no!" Reuven wept.

All that time he thought he was being heroic. Slaying the monsters of his childhood, being the Alpha who could stand up for himself and his family against anti-Semitism. But now he could see that he was twice the coward he'd ever been, twice the idiot. Robert Thurston III hadn't been beaten by The Maccabees; he'd succeeded now more than ever. Sara was dead and Reuven had led them right to her.

"I surrender." Reuven lifted his wrists to the police officer, eager to be handcuffed and tossed in a cell where he could contemplate his gruesome crimes for the rest of his miserable life. But when the cop leaned over to handcuff him, he fainted.

"Are you fucking kidding?!" Reuven exclaimed.

CHAPTER 14

THE FUNERAL FOR the Mother, Sara Schtinkler, took place on a bright Sunday morning at a verdant cemetery only miles from The Center for Animal Oddities. From the sheer number of the attendees it was clear that Sara had been a beloved human being. She was admired by her co-workers who came in droves, and adored by family members, friends, neighbors, and Spencer, Lillia, and Chewy who arrived in crates, but now chewed grass by a tree. There were groupies in attendance too. "Schtinklers," they called themselves. They held signs and sang dirges from the back. Throngs of admirers of Sara's work, TV appearances, and her glorious hair showed up, including Mitch The Makeup Maven and The Rules. Even the Klu Klux Klansmen who'd burned a cross on Sara's lawn who were now out of the hospital from treatable burns attended, and they even wore yarmulkes out of respect for the woman who'd saved their lives.

Kent was there of course, and Bruce with his wife Jackie and baby. Bruce cried endlessly, and his baby cried too from the BabyBjörn across his chest. Bruce still wore a bandage on his chin from the fall he'd taken after being robbed of his green binder by Reuven, and he used the end of the dressing to dab at his tears and wipe away his snot, which wasn't how you're supposed to use bandages, but did it really matter anymore?

At the front, staring at the casket in disbelief was Reuven, and seated several chairs away, avoiding eye contact with him was Joshua. When Reuven tried to reach for Joshua's hand, his son pulled away. After Sara's death Reuven had gone to the police precinct and sat in a holding room ready to spill everything about his "work" with The Maccabees; from his break-in and assault of Bruce the lab assistant, to the photo of the parking lot at The Center for Animal Oddities up on the wall at the club in NYC. He was happy to name names, share details, and pay the consequences no matter how dire they were. Joshua could live with Sara's younger sister in Berkley, California, and there was money saved for college. Joshua would likely despise Reuven for the rest of his life once he heard the truth, but at least he'd have a life of his own. But when the police officer walked into the holding room without even a pad of paper to take down Reuven's confession, he knew something was off.

"You're here to report an assault," the police officer said to him. It sounded more like a demand than a question.

"That's just the start of it, Officer. I have a lot to say. I know who blew up the lab."

"Won't be necessary," the office said casually to Reuven's shock. "We have video evidence of the arson. A group of neo-Nazi skinheads from Pennsylvania. They assaulted you and tied you up. Then they lit the barn on fire and planted the explosives that killed your wife. We've already detained them, and they've confessed. I know this must be hard for you, Mr. Schtinkler. I saw your wife on TV, and she seemed to be quite a special person."

Reuven was stunned. "But how did they do all that without fainting?" Reuven asked, testing the veracity of the story.

"We're still trying to figure that one out. We found a lot of drugs in their system. Maybe they were so blitzed the myotonia didn't kick in? Anyway, I'm no scientist. Sorry, sore subject. They'll get their justice for what they've done, I can assure you of that." With that, the officer stood up.

"Oh, almost forgot to say, Dr. Rabinsky sends his thoughts and prayers. He's a patron of the precinct. Said you were very brave, and that your instinct to protect your family almost got you killed. He said that you are a great ally to the cause and that he hopes you remain that way. So please keep your story to yourself. You must be confused about it after getting walloped over the head with a menorah. You don't want anything like that to happen again, do you?"

Reuven felt a chill run down his spine as the officer gave him a hard look. "No, Sir," Reuven said.

"Good," the officer said. He opened the door to the holding room. "You're free to go, Mr. Schtinkler. Be safe."

When Reuven got home, Joshua had to let him in since the locks had been changed on the front door. And though Reuven tried to confess to his son as well, Joshua closed his door and blasted punk music so loud that he couldn't hear his father's voice, and it went that way ever since.

Now at the funeral, Joshua's snubbing was just a continuation of the punishment that he felt his father deserved. Reuven's eyes wandered to the crowd of people in attendance. Sam, Eli, Larry, and several other of The Maccabees were there, but when Reuven caught eyes with them, his gut told him that they were less there in sympathy than to monitor his behavior.

The Rabbi recited the Mourner's *Kaddish* and then the casket, which housed only Sara's brown and bloodied cardigan, was lowered into the ground. Reuven tearfully shoveled dirt onto the casket, followed by Joshua and Sara's immediate family. Then the Rabbi urged the invited to head to the synagogue around the corner where a reception was being held.

It was a brightly windowed room next to the main sanctuary with a long table packed with rugelach, tuna and egg sandwiches, and coffee for the mourners. There was an oversized photograph of Sara on an easel next to white flowers where the immediate family was asked to be received. In the photo Sara was wearing an "I Break 4

Goats" button, and it suddenly has a deeper meaning, as if she was now broken for goats. Relatives accosted Joshua, some he'd never met before, though all hugged him tightly as if they wanted to heal his pain. Older women left lipstick stains on his cheeks and sour floral perfume on his lapel. They all remarked how much he'd grown—seemingly in a flash—and told him what a handsome young man he'd become. The older men smirked as they told him to leave some ladies for them.

"Sara always depended on you to be the man of the house, even more than your own father," one Aunt said, looking over Joshua's shoulder and eyeing Reuven disdainfully.

Another, even less tactful, whispered in Joshua's ear, "Your father is a weak and flawed man, but you are strong. You have Sara inside you, I can sense it." And then she broke down in tears.

Brie showed up too in a black dress but also light makeup that brightened her look. She waited her turn to speak to Joshua.

"You were right to break up with me," she said, eyes to the ground. "I was selfish. But I'm wondering if I could take you up on your offer to still be friends?"

"I'd like that," Joshua replied, and they hugged.

Reuven's reception from family and friends was less heartfelt and had far less goodwill than it did for Joshua. Immediate family gave him sympathetic squeezes, and his old frat brothers, including Ollie, patted him on the back and gave him guy hugs, the carefully balanced hug which was designed to give the bare minimum amount of compassion/intimacy.

The attendees had all heard about the state of his marriage to Sara at the time of her death. "I hope you can find peace, Reuven," one mourner granted him. Others were not so generous. Sara's younger sister, a political activist who lived in Berkley, California, sobbed as she told Reuven, "You killed her soul years ago making her a housewife in the suburbs. And now your pathetic sneaking around finished her." Her voice was getting louder and people were starting to look over. "Shame on you, Reuven!" And then she hugged him but pinched his arm, hard. It was Sam that cut in on that scene.

"Sorry to interrupt. Reuven, I was hoping we could have a private word?" The sister looked up at Sam and frowned. "Men and their fucking secrets!" She hissed and stomped off.

"She's a firecracker." Sam arched his eyebrow.

"She's upset," Reuven said, sadly.

Sam looked both ways and then stepped close to Reuven. "Listen, Reuv, Dr. Rabinsky wanted to send his condolences. He tried to be here but had to be out of the country on business."

Reuven wanted to tell Sam where Rabinsky could shove his fake sympathy but instead said, "Thanks. That means a lot."

"Crazy to me that those Nazis would go to this extreme. Even scarier that they managed to do it without fainting."

"Yeah, it doesn't make a whole lot of sense," Reuven said.

Sam caught Reuven's eye. "Look, I know that you may suspect that they had some help from our side, but we had nothing to do with this, Reuv. I swear on the lives of my children we didn't. We were sneaking around, yeah, but we would never do this. I only wish we'd been sneaking around that night. Then we might have stopped those bastards."

"Or finished the job?" Reuven found himself asking.

"No," Sam said. He seemed almost hurt. "Look, you're in mourning. Me and the guys appreciate the sacrifices you've made for the cause. And we're here because we will always be your friend." Sam glanced over at Sara's sister, who was skulking around the perimeter ready to take another run at her beleaguered brother-in-law. "Seems like you could use some friends right now?"

Sam squeezed Reuven's shoulder and then walked off with the other Maccabees. Reuven turned to the photo of Sara on the easel, looked her right in the eyes, and had never felt so alone in his life. He caught sight of Joshua, who was surrounded by well-wishers, and wondered if maybe his son would talk to him now, but when he walked over Joshua slipped away, and Reuven was caught in a new scrum of mourners eager to offer condolences/insults.

Joshua snuck out the back door of the synagogue for a breather. Next to the parking lot was a playground set up on the grass, part of the religious school. Joshua was charmed to see a tetherball court next to the swing set, and that made him think of his mother. By the edge of the park, smoking a cigarette and staring in space was a red-headed guy in his early thirties with an ill-fitted suit and a spotty beard.

"Can I bum one?" Joshua asked him.

The guy looked Joshua up and down and smirked. "I don't want to be a bad influence on a minor, but on the day of your mother's funeral . . . here." The man handed Joshua a cigarette and a liter, and Joshua lit up. "Pretty shitty day, huh?" the guy asked.

"You could say that," Joshua replied, exhaling a puff of smoke.

"Wish I could tell you it gets easier from here," the guy said. "I lost my mom too when I was young. And all those people in there trying to tell you they know how you feel like it's your responsibility to reassure them instead of the other way around, it's twisted? Adults are so dumb."

"Did you know my mom?" Joshua asked.

"I interviewed her a couple of times about goats for a nature magazine. Never met anyone who talked about her work with such enthusiasm. Full disclosure, I'm a reporter on duty today for *The Daily*. They want me to write something about Dr. Schtinkler's funeral, so . . . "

"Well then . . . " Joshua started to walk away. "Thanks for the smoke."

"I don't think what happened to your mother was just some Nazi skinheads," the man said.

Joshua stopped in his tracks.

"My old man's a retired detective. When he saw the video of the guys who broke into the lab, he said it looks staged. Like the guys went out of their way to look up at the cameras and get caught. Even idiots would wear masks or smash the cameras. And giving the Nazi salute directly? There's too many holes."

"So, who did it?"

"I'm not one for conspiracy theories, but my old man said that there are a lot of people who could benefit from your mother not finding a cure."

"So, powerful Jews killed my mother?" Joshua smirked. "You sure you aren't a conspiracy theorist?"

"You're probably right," the reporter said with a grin. "Just a wild theory."

Just then next to the playground Spencer the goat wandered by. He walked up to the tetherball court and hit the ball listlessly, maybe wondering where his playmate was.

"Got to get back," Joshua said. "Thanks for the smoke."

"Nice to meet you, Joshua," the man said. "I'm Eric O'Malley, by the way. You ever want to talk, here's my contact. I'm best by text." The reporter handed over his card. "I didn't know your mother well, but I do know that she loved her work, and I suspect that she was onto a vaccine. Conspiracy or no conspiracy, I think she wanted an end to myotonia congenita, and her memory deserves to see that through."

Joshua stubbed out his cigarette. He looked down at the card, slid it into his pocket and walked off.

After the funeral was over, Joshua got in the car with his father, who immediately sniffed at his suit jacket.

"You smell like cigarettes," Reuven said. "Have you been smoking?"

"You smelled like jailbait perfume that night you picked me up from the movies," Joshua replied. "Had you been having an affair with a college girl?"

They rode the rest of the way home in silence. When they arrived, Joshua tried to jump out of the car before it even stopped but Reuven locked the doors.

"I lost her too, you know," Reuven said.

"You lost her way before she died, Dad," Joshua replied. He unlocked the car door manually and jumped out. Reuven just sat there, stunned.

Joshua entered the house and raced up the stairs to his mother's office. He keyed in the code for the safe and opened it, pushing aside the passports and jewelry to retrieve those loose-leaf pages of his mother's research he'd found on the night when he was searching for condoms. Seeing his mother's handwriting again almost made him break down, but he fought it. He held the pages out one-by-one and took screenshots with his phone. Then he pulled out the card that the reporter Eric O'Malley had handed him and keyed in the numbers.

"It's Joshua. I may have found what you're been looking for. I'll send it if you promise to tell the whole world."

"I will," came the quick reply.

Then Joshua attached the screenshots of Sara's pages to the text and pressed send. He heard the front door click open and his father enter the house. Joshua stuffed the pages back into the safe and closed it quietly, then rushed out of the office.

"Don't talk to me," he said to his father as he walked by, and Reuven obliged.

CHAPTER 15

IT BECAME KNOWN as "The Schtinkler Formula," or as Sean Hannity accidentally or probably not accidentally referred to it on Fox News, "The Schtinkler Solution." Eric O'Malley, the reporter Joshua met by chance in the parking lot at his mother's funeral, was true to his word, and he spread Sara's research as far and wide as he could, which as it turned out was pretty far and decently wide. It quickly became global news. An international tribune of scientists analyzed Sara's data and formulas, in particular her theories about social distancing between fainting and non-fainting breeds over a matter of months. They scrutinized her ideas on exercise and diet restrictions that had been scribbled on the loose-leaf pages released for public consumption and found them to be well-researched and scientifically sound. They even replayed some of the goat tetherball games Queen's Gambit style. All of her work, in fact, checked out, and soon there was a global consensus that Sara Schtinkler's formula pointed to the best and possibly the only cure to global human myotonia congenita.

In preparation for more significant changes based on the formula, the entire world (including me) began playing 1.3 hours of tetherball per day and eating a strictly vegan diet weighing heavily on cranberries, bulger grains, and other totally gross anti-inflammatories. That shift alone improved global pulmonary health, though I'm not sure eating the culinary abomination called "tempeh" was worth it. And while it did reduce the severity of human myotonia, it did nothing to cure it. The more controversial change, which would take longer to implement, had to do with social distancing. Based on Sara's research you couldn't just put the non-fainters 50 miles away from the fainters for a few days and expect a remedy. There was a gravitational pull based on population. That is, the fainting breeds could sense the threat of non-fainters based on distance but also numbers. So, five miles might work if there was only one predatory non-fainter around a fainter. But if there were two or ten or a hundred thousand within that distance, more distance would be required, and so on. A team of MIT scientists performed a slew of failed experiments using their own math, but eventually returned to Sara's mathematical formula based on space and time with an adjustment for humans versus goat breed. With that they confirmed that The Schtinkler Formula could work if all of the world's approximately 23 million non-fainters were separated from the global populace of 7.7 billion fainters by approximately 2,000 miles for approximately three months.

A UN Global Forum met in Kyoto, Japan, and a bi-partisan body of world leaders and prize-winning scientists know as the Kyoto Institute for Knowledge and Eradication (or K.I.K.E. for short) declared that the findings were worthy of next steps. What those next steps were precisely was the hard part. Namely, how to separate the entire global Jewish population from the rest of the inhabitants of the planet by two-thousand miles for three months, and who would they even ask? It took weeks of bickering and debate for the Jewish community to agree who would represent them at the negotiation table, and finally, ten influential Jews emerged. Amongst them, Dr. Jacob Rabinsky, The Governor of New York, The Prime Minister of Israel, the owner of Canter's Delicatessen in Los Angeles, and for a reason no was clear on but everyone was excited about, Winona Ryder. And if the arguing around who would represent the Jews in the negotiation was fraught, the deliberations to decide how to make The Schtinkler Formula work was a train wreck that took place inside of a dumpster fire. In the end, both sides felt they'd been cheated and left the table bitterly, only to celebrate in closed quarters.

The rules to implement The Schtinkler Formula were as follows:

All Jews would move to Israel for three months. All surrounding populations must be relocated outside the 2,000-mile radius, regardless of national borders.

The displaced would receive lodging, food, a cash stipend, and would be guaranteed their place back home just as they left it in exactly three months' time.

For their troubles, the Jews, who were upending their own lives for the sake to the planet, were offered:

Free return airfare on El Al Flights to Israel and back, plus food vouchers.

Paid "Executive" accommodation in Israel for the duration of their stay.

A fifty-dollar-a-day stipend for hummus, baba ganoush, and steam baths.

Sandals and sunscreen.

A pipeline of New York water would be built directly to Israel so that Jews living across the world could make decent bagels.

Unlimited Nova Lox.

All online retail would 50%-70% off, with free shipping and a 30-day "no questions asked" return policy.

Finally, certain permanent changes would be made as a reward to the Jewish people if the experiment worked and the world became free of human myotonia congenita:

Banks and Media agree to *actually* be controlled by Jews.

A computer system would finally settle what day it is in Israel, so Jews outside of Israel can stop accidentally observing holidays for extra days.

Israel would keep its current borders but would now include Miami Beach.

Scarlett Johansson on all world currency.

It was amazing how well the world could cooperate so long as it meant finally putting an end to fainting. Religious, political, and gender orientation was set aside, as well as the behavior of those people who just couldn't help being an asshole. The world simply got in step for once. All it took was an international agreement to isolate every Jew.

As for Reuven and Joshua Schtinkler it was a disorienting time, especially for Reuven as he transitioned to life as a single dad. Despite her full-time job as an unheard-of goat scientist and later a very-heard-of goat scientist, Sara had also managed to do the lion's share of the housework, all of the bookkeeping, and most of the parenting. For his part, Reuven had done the lion's share of fucking up. Reuven had to call over his neighbor Nancy, who hated his guts, to show him where Sara might have kept the car insurance documents, and how to work the laundry machine. Joshua, who'd only spoken in monosyllables to his father since the funeral was surprisingly helpful, showing flashes of Sara's natural competence and her understanding that if you want to accomplish things you need systems and that takes time, something that Reuven only ever understood in the abstract. Reuven faced the fact that he was only really comfortable working his job and doing that one thing medium-well, and though he thought that his steady paycheck and dependable health insurance had been a generous contribution to the family, he now saw that it barely scratched the surface of helping. Reuven yearned for the deadline to arrive when all of the Jews would need to pack up and head to their ancestral homeland mainly so that he could stop doing housework. Also, he'd always wanted to do a dead sea mud mask.

It was the day before "The Great Schlep" when Reuven took his final trip to his job in the city. In his office, an empty cardboard box had been placed on his desk, presumably to help him pack what he felt necessary to take with him to Israel. The scene felt eerily similar to the day he'd been fired by Pluto Network years back and had to fill a box with personal items before doing the walk of shame past his co-workers. They had all averted their eyes.

As Reuven began to fill the box with binders and note pads, Claire entered, smiling coyly. "I guess this is bye for now," she said, clasping her hands. "As your Supervisor I've been asked to say that we so appreciate your sacrifice, Reuven, and we look forward to having you back in the office when all is back to normal." Then a light sparkled in Claire's eyes, and she closed the door behind her. "But as your friend with certain benefits I want to announce . . . I'm late," she said to Reuven. Then she embraced him. "Thank you for putting this baby in my belly," she whispered in his ear. Reuven hugged Claire back, but it quickly got awkward, and Claire pulled away. When she did her eyes were wet. "Don't worry, by the way. When the baby is born, I won't ask for anything. You don't need to be part of this child's life. Or, uh, we could talk about how to if you want to, of course. I know that since Sara passed it's complicated. So, I leave it up to you."

"That's nice of you to say, Claire," Reuven replied. "You're going to be a great mom. Congratulations."

"I believe the term is *mazel tov*. After all, the child will be half Jewish." Claire winked. Then she bounded out of Reuven's office on clouds, muttering to herself, "I'm going to have a baby!"

Reuven packed up the rest of his stuff, including a photo of him with Sara and Joshua that he'd long placed in one of his desk drawers. In the photo Reuven smiled goofily while his wife and child forced enthusiasm with tight grins. They didn't look unhappy, just aware of the responsibilities they had in caretaking for a buffoon.

"What an asshole," Reuven said to himself about himself. And he wasn't wrong.

He sealed up his box and walked out of his office, and Pamela turned away when he stopped to say goodbye. Who could blame her? Though she was half Reuven's age, even she recognized how miserably he had failed to act like an adult when the time had come to do so. Reuven's own 15-year-old son had acted less like a child than he. Reuven slumped past embarrassed.

Out on the streets, thousands of other men and women walked towards the trains and subways with their sad work boxes. Reuven had imagined that this day would be a kind of parade where well-wishers, thankful for the Jewish peoples' help in curing a global pandemic would cheer them on, throwing rice and confetti and even panties into men's faces. But this reminded Reuven more of that scene in Schindler's List when all the Jewish people were leaving town for the camps and a little girl repeatedly yelled, "Goodbye, Jews!"

Reuven was halfway to Penn Station when Sam came running down the street. "Reuv! Wow, you've got a fast pace with those long legs," he said, panting.

Reuven hadn't spoken to Sam since the funeral and it felt odd seeing him again, like he was a part of a life that existed before Sara's death and should be left there. Sam read the discomfort on Reuven's face.

"You don't look too happy to see me," he remarked.

"Nah," said Reuven. "Just, you know, late for diner with my kid, so . . . "

"Of course," Sam nodded. "Being a dad is priority. But me and the boys miss hanging out with you. We were just talking about it. And it kills us to think that those neo-Nazi scumbags didn't get the death penalty. We'll get 'em though. The day those bastards walk, maybe it's fifty years from now, a bullet is headed their way—Pow!"

Reuven gave Sam a weary look, so he backed off.

"Anyway, I just wanted to say we'll see you in the Holy Land, okay? What hotel they got you at?"

"Somewhere near the market in Tel Aviv. Seems fine."

"The market? I'll fix that. You're *mishpacha*. You and your son, you're going to be at the best hotel in the city. You can hold me to that."

"Thanks, Sam," Reuven said. "Speaking of Joshua . . . I really better get back."

"You got it, bud," Sam said with a wink. "But don't forget to ring me up as soon as you land. A lot of important people want to meet you. They know about the work you've done and the sacrifice you've made—they have a lot of goodwill towards the Schtinkler name. I mean, look at what we were able to negotiate; the borders, the water pipeline. Amazing! Your wife is a saint to the cause as far as everyone's concerned, and you and Joshua should be welcomed as ambassadors."

After another awkward handshake, Reuven walked off. The interaction made him sick to his stomach. Sam's mention of Reuven's so-called "sacrifice" especially stung since it implied that he'd given Sara up. Sacrificed his wife for the flabby middle-aged men of The Maccabees, which you didn't have to be an expert on sacrifices to know was a pretty shitty one. And Reuven being considered an ambassador in Israel only confirmed that everyone knew it to be true. On the train home he dipped into the box and gazed at the family photo he'd kept in his desk drawer all that time. Maybe Sara always knew he'd screw things up eventually. Joshua too. You could see it in their faces.

"What a mess you've made, ya big schmuck."

When he got home, Reuven went straight to Joshua's room. The door was locked and there was music blaring, which was nothing new, so he knocked.

"We should finish packing tonight," he said to no reply. "I said, we should pack now!" he shouted. Then he immediately regretted raising his voice. He placed his forehead on Joshua's door. "Look, Josh, I know I've lost your trust. And I know you probably hate me right now, and you have every reason to. But I'm going to make good, okay? I don't how. But I swear to God I'm going to find a way to do the right thing by you and Mom." Reuven sobbed a bit, then turned to leave, and when he did, he saw Joshua standing there in the hall holding a can of soda he'd just grabbed from the kitchen. Joshua had grown so tall in the past few months that they were shoulder to shoulder as he walked by his father towards his room.

"Just about finished packing," Joshua said to his dad. Then he unlocked his door with a key and closed it behind him. The music went louder, almost as if the stereo had a setting called, "fuck parents."

Reuven didn't have the courage to repeat what he'd said to Joshua's empty room. Instead he slumped back to his bedroom to pack the rest of his things in the allotted two suitcases they could bring to Israel. He went deep into his closet looking for his favorite belt when one of Sara's brown cardigans fell onto the floor. He picked it up and held it to his face; the smell of goat urine was still pungent. He collapsed right there in the closet and began to cry.

Joshua had heard his father's little speech from down the hall. Did he feel bad for him? Sure, he always felt a little bad for his father. Did he buy what he was saying about "doing the right thing" for him and his mother? Not for a hot second. It took all Joshua had to hold himself back from cutting in on the pitiful soliloquy with, "You want to make good? Leave me the fuck alone!" But Joshua recognized in his father at least an attempt at introspection, and he didn't want to interrupt that miracle.

Now Joshua stood in front of his full-length mirror and picked at the blackheads that had sprouted on his nose. His nostrils had grown wider seemingly out of nowhere, maybe to make room for the slight acne, but also his shoulders had swelled and rounded. He'd been doing push-up and sit-ups, and his muscles reacted as if they'd been waiting all this time to show themselves but never had the chance, like a gaggle of junior debutants at the Steeplechase Ball. Puberty rushed in, doing it's oily, hairy, and smelly work - and it had been a tough hormonal ride- but it had also left Joshua with abs, a defined jawline, and handsome deep-set eyes. Joshua had an instinct to take his first-ever shirtless selfie and send it to Brie, but he fought the instinct. Instead he left his room and wandered into his mother's office. He keyed in the numbers to the safe and fished out his passport, thinking that he'd want to hold it for himself and not depend on his father. That would be kid's stuff.

But when he pulled out the passport, a single folded piece of paper was tucked inside. It was ripped out of a journal like the other pages he'd found and had his mother's neat handwriting on it. This time instead of notes it was only math, a series of numbers and symbols that seemed to create an equation of some kind. Joshua winced that he'd missed this and hadn't texted it to the journalist months before. He took a screenshot of the page and was about to send it to Eric O'Malley with an apology, but then he paused. Since he'd shared the research, O'Malley had become TV famous and even received an esteemed journalism prize for his work. But he hadn't sent Joshua so much as a text in a while. In fact, communication had ebbed completely since the Israel announcement, and that stank of phony to Joshua. So instead of giving the reporter even more fame, Joshua pulled up his contacts and found his mother's number. He attached the screenshot of the ripped-out-page and typed the note, "You're the G.O.A.T." Then he pressed send. Maybe it would send a bleep up to her in heaven?

CHAPTER 16

YOU KNOW WHAT it's like to wake up feeling so rested and happy that you just automatically smile? Some glorious dream of birds gliding across clear blue skies eases you into consciousness and ends so beautifully that it momentarily clouds all worries and responsibilities? You are (for a fleeting second) merely a soul who adores the morning light and the gentle sounds of birds chirping, and the feeling of being rested and calm. Now imagine if that feeling extended for more than just a second—for minutes or even hours—so long that eventually you try to ground yourself in real life? You focus on summoning the lists of annoying tasks and family responsibilities, the personalities who ask of you, the stupid emails and awkward invites. Imagine you attempt that, but those thoughts just won't appear no matter how hard you try? They say that contentment comes when you set a goal for yourself and it comes to fruition, but that true happiness arrives only when you lose your ego entirely and just "be," a soul living on earth surrendered to divine light. Wouldn't a person who achieved that kind of egoless happiness be someone people loved? When it came to Sara Schtinkler, apparently not.

This Sara Schtinkler, the happy egoless one lying in a guest bed in a farmhouse in Tennessee with a bandage wrapped around her head was a total chore to be around. Burt and Molly had been patient. They'd conversed with Sara about how lovely it is to be in nature and how the country air smelled like peach cobbler, and how crazy *Celebrity Cabin Hunter* is this season. But it got old fast. They wanted the old Sara back; the one who was interesting, brilliant, and yes worried about the big things going on in the world like myotonia congenita. But that Sara would not emerge. Instead "Happy" Sara, whose eyes lit up about everything *except* talking about fainting goats and science, and whose face betrayed confusion when you mentioned the global fainting pandemic and her role in a possible cure, was impossibly boring. And nothing they'd tried so far had worked in bringing her back. Not rest, soup, or medications. Molly had once given her a light slap in the face while she slept. A local concussions specialist who Molly made swear an oath to secrecy with a blueberry crumble visited, but that didn't help either. Neither did a local psychiatrist who thought Sara was Molly's cousin Annalee from Calgary. So, Sara just lay there in bed most of the day, a dumb smile on her face, inhaling the wonderful aromas of a distant campfire and fresh flowers that wafted through the window of Burt and Molly's guest bedroom. Once in a while she did a crossword and tapped a pencil against her lower lip to summon the answers. She got some obscure answers right, but when it came to the particulars of her life and work—blank boxes. And she couldn't even look up the answers in the next day's paper.

It hadn't been by chance that Burt and Molly happened to house Dr. Sara Schtinkler in their guest bedroom at their farm in Tennessee. They'd made the long trek to New Jersey months before because they'd discovered something about their fainting goats that was so surprising that they knew they had to deliver the information to Sara face-to-face. Burt loaded up the RV and they drove thirteen hours to Chatham NJ, hardly stopping along the way. They would tell Sara what happened with the fainting goats (who'd stopped fainting again), hand over some more samples, and then maybe vacation for the day in The Big Apple, a place Molly had never been. She always wanted to see the lights on Broadway, and eat at Guy Fieri's American Kitchen and Bar.

The New Jersey freeways had not been kind. Then there's this weird thing in New Jersey where you have to turn left by turning right onto looping sideroads, so they went round and round, and by the time they finally found the town where Sara lived it was dark. Then, just as Burt finally reached Sara's suburban street, they spotted her running out of her house like it was on fire, jumping into a car and racing off. Burt made the quick decision to just follow her, but she didn't make it easy. He tailed Sara's car as it zoomed through red lights and passed stop signs, all the way to the dead-end street where Sara's lab was located, but then Burt lost her and had to drive around several empty parking lots before he spotted her parked car again, and saw the burning barn, which billowed with black smoke and leaping flames. Burt and Molly slowed the RV by the side of the road and watched Sara run from the back barn into the lab building. On the edges of the parking lot, Burt also saw a dark van driving near the exit, and a man lying on the ground with his hands tied behind his back and duct tape over his mouth.

"Stay here and keep the motor running," Burt told Molly. "And call the damn fire department!"

Burt jumped out of the RV and ran low alongside the building where Sara's goats now roamed, bleating out confusion and fear. Burt saw that the side door to the lab had been left open, and he headed that way. But he only made it a few steps before an explosion blasted him onto his back. Burt rolled over, covering his face and shielding himself from the falling debris. He gazed through the haze of smoke and fire and saw that a full hole had been blown through the side of the lab building and through that hole was Sara, splayed out on her back like a rag doll that you'd see in the discount bin at a Goodwill and think some kid's gonna get tetanus if they buy this doll. Flames leapt around her. Burt pushed himself up off the dirt and climbed through the hole in the wall towards her. Sara's head bled profusely and some of her hair was torn out, revealing skull, which was as gross as it sounds. Burt carefully picked her up onto his shoulder as he had with wounded soldiers decades back in a foreign land. He carried her out through the wall and towards the RV. He ducked low, fearing the men in the black van would spot him, but he got past them unnoticed. When he finally got to the RV Molly had already opened up the back.

"Gently," Molly said, opening her first aid kit. Burt lay Sara onto the day bed, and the pillow immediately soaked in blood. "Well, don't just stand there, get us to a hospital!"

Burt got into the driver's seat and did as he was told, but as he drove off the black van in the parking lot screeched out in pursuit. Burt had always fantasized about being in a car chase, but in his fantasy, he was in a red Corvette with a duffle bag of money, and not in an RV with a day-bed full of goat scientist.

"Hold on tight," he told Molly.

Burt didn't know the roads around Livingston, New Jersey, but Molly had already keyed in the address for a local hospital into his phone, so he followed those directions. The black van tailed them as he pulled onto the freeway but then zoomed past at top speed once they got on. Burt squinted in the dark night. He saw a sign for Metuchen and had a flash that an old army buddy lived there, Jerry Goiler, the man he called "The Professor." In wartime, Jerry had worked as a medic in a field hospital and had once dislodged a bullet from Burt's behind. The Professor called Burt once a year on the day of the removal to remind him that he'd literally "saved his ass."

"There. Exit 11A," Molly said.

Burt took the exit towards the hospital and found himself on a dark empty road. He spotted the hospital ahead. But when he pulled into the driveway the black van that had been following him was already there, parked in front of the entrance. Two large men paced around smoking and barking into cellphones. They looked angry. Quietly, Burt turned the RV around. He dialed the number of his old army buddy on his cell phone, and a cranky old voice answered.

"Who's calling me at this hour?"

"Professor, it's Burt Ambler."

"Burt Ambler? It's not even December 5th. To what do I owe the pleasure of your very late-night call?"

"I think I need you to save my ass again," Burt said.

And save Burt's ass he did. Although this time it was not his ass, but Sara's brain.

In the guest bedroom of her farmhouse in Tennessee, Molly took Sara's temperature as she did every morning, and saw a steady 97.8 degrees. She unwrapped the dressing around Sara's head and then per instructions from The Professor, cleaned the wound and re-wrapped it with fresh gauze. The wound had healed up nicely after all this time, and there was no fluid on the gauze from the previous night. As for the healing of her mind, Molly took a wild swing at the bat.

"Do you remember my name?" she asked Sara.

"Of course, you're Molly," Sara replied brightly.

"Good. And do you know your name?"

"Genevieve?" Sara grinned. "I'm hoping it's Genevieve. Sounds exotic."

"It's Sara," Molly said. "Sara, do you know what myotonia congenita is?"

"Of course," Sara said. "That's fainting goat syndrome."

Molly's eyes widened. "You know that?"

"Sure," Sara said. "Burt was just on the phone outside saying it over and over again. I pieced it together."

"Oh," Molly said, disappointed. "Okay dear. You rest now. Maybe some more sleep will bring things back. And later maybe you can finally come to visit the goats."

"Don't they bite?" Sara asked. "I don't want to be bitten."

"I assure you that the goats will be on their best behavior. They've been waiting to meet you all this time, and are starting to get insulted."

Molly left Sara to rest but sighed wearily as she walked out the door. Sara knew that she'd disappointed her host again, that she wasn't giving her something that she desperately wanted. Sara had said that it would be fun to visit the goats not because she was interested in goats per se, but because she thought it would make this darling lady less stressed. Sara wasn't sure if she'd ever spent any time with goats before, but now that she was assured that the goats don't bite she did have a warm feeling when she thought about them. Maybe hanging out with the goats would make Molly and Burt happy? They did seem a little down, even though they were so gracious.

As Sara considered what she would say if she didn't enjoy the goats, she sat up and grabbed a pencil on the side table to write down a few appreciative words that she could repeat to Molly, but the pencil rolled off behind the table. She got off the bed and down on her hands and knees to retrieve the pencil, and when she did, she felt something else lodged under there. It was a cell phone, crusted with specs of blood and covered in dust mites, as if it had been there for a long while. Sara got up off the floor and walked the phone to the kitchen, where she plugged it into a charger. After a moment it booted up. On the screen underneath the date was a "New Text" alert from someone named "Joshua." Sara wondered aloud who that could be and how on earth she could figure out the password so that she could read his text. But nothing came to mind.

CHAPTER 17

THE JEWS ARE a nomadic people built for travel, and yet the mass exodus of the global Jewish community from their homes around the world to the Holy Land was not without incident. Per my new Yiddish dictionary, it was what is often described as a "*verkakte* situation." In Italy, flights were delayed when a group of *meshugenah* passengers toting suitcases filled with bottles of red wine weighed down the plane. Similarly, Russian *schlemiels* with bags stuffed with vodka were forced to either drink or discard their liquids, and an enormous party broke out in the Moscow airport. New York was a whole other brand of *mishigas*. Orthodox men from Crown Heights refused to take seats next to women, causing delays as the airline tried to accommodate. But that insulted the tough New York women who were already up to their *pupik* in stress, and they revolted by changing their meal orders to vegan and celiac-free, so all the pasta and veal parmesan had to be replaced at the last minute with couscous and tofu. The Governor (who was already *shvitzing* in his *schmattas*) got involved, proclaiming an edict that women and children would all be moved to First Class, but that caused *tsuris* in the Orthodox men who refused to get on the plane, causing a standstill that lasted until all New York flights were canceled. They had to try again the next day, eventually separating the Orthodox completely from others in separate planes. *Oy vey,* what a *schlep*!

Per family policy, Joshua and Reuven were given

tickets to the same flight but Joshua secretly went on the El Al app and moved his seat to the back of the plane so that he wouldn't have to spend thirteen hours next to his father, who he was still too angry at to look at in the eyes. Reuven was already aggravated with Joshua because he insisted on wearing a bright yellow hoodie that Brie had given him as a parting gift. The hoodie had the words "Pussy Riot" emblazoned on the back. They were Brie's new favorite rock group, which Reuven felt was too crass to wear in public. Also, it had a ketchup stain on the sleeve, which made it all seem worse.

"What if we see someone from the synagogue?" Reuven complained.

Joshua agreed to turn the hoodie inside out until they boarded the plane, but as soon as they got on, he flipped it and Reuven watched him walk off to a different seat, "Pussy Riot" and ketchup stain on grand display. When Joshua found his seat, he knew immediately that he'd made the right decision. There was a young hip couple, maybe mid-twenties in the seats next to his. Both were dressed in black and wore dark sunglasses and messed up hair. The guy wore an Alabama Shakes t-shirt, the coolest band Joshua knew of other than Pussy Riot, and the woman, who had dyed green hair, played Fortnite Battle Royale on a handheld Sega.

"Are you in the window?" the guy asked Joshua. "Ruby, move over for the kid."

"Aisle's fine. Thanks, though," Joshua said.

The woman with the green hair took off her sunglasses, revealing friendly, almond-shaped eyes. "Aw, you're a sweetheart. If I can't see outside when I take off, I puke. Oh, my gawd is that a Pussy Riot sweatshirt? Sick!"

Joshua smiled as he put down his bag and pulled out a book. Then the guy geeked out about that. "You're reading Saad Z. Hossain?" he asked and pulled out his worn copy of *The Gurkha and The Lord Tuesday*. "We're total freaks. Have you reached the part where—"

"Don't spoil it for him," the woman said.

"Where the Kathmanduites start ripping out their microchips?" Joshua cut in.

"Oh my God! How far are you into the trilogy?"

"This is my third time reading it," Joshua admitted. "The one you're reading has a wild ending too, but I won't spoil it."

The guy threw up his hands. "We struck the lottery, Ruby. On this ridiculous trip to Jewish captivity, we found the coolest dude on the plane. I'm Alex. This is Ruby."

"Joshua."

"Ever listen to Dorian Electra?" Ruby asked, handing Joshua an ear pod.

Joshua put in the pod and heard melodic howling voices and screeching guitars that was the rawest, coolest music he'd ever heard.

"Not one of those musicians are Jewish, FYI. Alex gave Joshua a fist bump, and Joshua laughed.

Forty seats towards the front of the plane, the Father, Reuven Schtinkler, was eating a total shit sandwich when it came to his seatmates. He sat between a religious married couple from San Antonio who refused Reuven's request to sit together so that he wouldn't have to be squeezed between them, but then they passed a smoked fish sandwich back and forth over his head while they ate. And they ate endlessly, spraying fish bits on Reuven's hands and brushing rugelach crumbs on his pants. When they were done eating the couple held hands over the back of his head, and though they didn't touch Reuven's head exactly, it hovered, and he could smell the whitefish, which is an unpleasant sensation. When the plane finally took off and Reuven ordered three small bottles of wine he was informed by the haughty stewardess that the limit was two bottles, and he could feel the married couple judging him. Eventually Reuven couldn't take it anymore, so he went to stand by the bathrooms and just sip ice water in peace. If you've ever stood by an airplane bathroom, you know how awful a situation must be before you choose standing there instead. He tried to refocus himself on the whole point of this trip—yes, to help the world solve the fainting pandemic, sure—but to him, it was to reconnect with his son, and so far he's done a crappy job of that.

Airborne, Joshua was having the time of his life with his new friends Alex and Ruby. They'd broken out the travel version his favorite board game, *Ticket To Ride*, and were deep into an epic match. "Don't you dare block Nashville," Ruby chided Joshua.

"That's my go-to first move. The one place on the board that goes right down to Miami."

"He's a shark this one," Alex said, then laid down three trains, Denver to Oklahoma City. "Suck on that for a while."

"So, why aren't you sitting with your parents?" Ruby asked. "Are they embarrassing?"

"My dad's up at the front," Joshua replied. "We're not talking right now."

"What about your mom?"

"She didn't come."

"Non-fainter, huh?" Alex asked.

"Something like that," Joshua replied.

"Well, guess what? We love half-breeds. It's the gung-ho Jews we're worried about. Like, I don't even believe in God."

"Alex, not here."

"What? He's a friend. Might as well tell him where I stand. I think the whole 'Chosen People' thing is just a fairytale. We Jews are just inbred. So inbred that by some genetic fluke we don't get this one disease that everyone else gets after getting every other disease in history. Like, you ever heard of Tay-Sachs? Jewish disease. The BRCA2 gene?"

"My mother had that," Joshua said.

"I have it too," Ruby said. "They said eventually I'm going to have to get surgery to prevent cancer. Some prize,

I mean, look how nice these are." She held up her chest proudly. Joshua blushed.

"We're just genetic freaks," Alex went on. "Dogs with spots. And because of that we're all on planes heading to some location where thousands of years ago spotted dogs ruled in some half-hearted attempt to cure the globe. Never going to happen. The Jews in power won't let go."

"They say it's supposed to work," Joshua said.

"Even if it does, I guarantee there's probably a Jewish person hidden in every town to make sure this social distancing thing doesn't work. No one knows how to cure myotonia except for one person, Dr. Sara Schtinkler, and she's dead."

Joshua's eyes welled up with tears, and his head dropped.

"See Alex. You're too much. Apologize."

"I was just telling him the truth. Sara Schtinkler was on the road to a vaccine and they fucking assassinated her and blamed it on neo-Nazis—"

"She's my mother," Joshua said, cutting him off. "Sara Schtinkler was my mother. I'm not a half breed. I'm just a guy whose mom died."

Alex gulped. Ruby placed a hand on Joshua's arm. They all took a deep breath as Joshua continued, "Part of the reason I'm not talking to my dad is he cheated on my mom right before she died. He was living in a hotel and I didn't mind it that way, to be honest. Now I'm supposed to mourn with him? Hang out with him like nothing happened? Screw that." Joshua started to cry. "Sorry, I haven't slept."

Alex gave Ruby a look. She opened her bag and held out her hand to reveal several gummy bear candies. "These may help you sleep, or at least relax. They taste like raspberries," she said.

Ruby and Alex both popped one and then Joshua shrugged and took one too. After twenty minutes, when Joshua tried to speak and just said, "Blah-blah-blah, bingo," Alex and Ruby broke out in tearful laughter. Joshua laughed too, in a release of joy he hadn't experienced in many months.

Reuven heard the laughter from his spot next to the bathroom. This was much better than the noise he heard coming from inside the bathroom, though that irked him too. He was glad his son had found some friends but also felt regret that he wasn't with him. Reuven had hoped to spend the flight reading Israeli guidebooks with his son, circling tourist spots and restaurants they could check out. They would have three months together in Israel but that could go by in an eye blink if they didn't plan ahead. Reuven was looking through those guidebooks, circling Tel Aviv markets that looked good when a short man in a crisp white shirt and kippah approached him. He had blotchy red skin and blond eyelashes that were so long they curled.

"Better to stand up here than get sandwiched, right?" the guy asked Reuven in a South African accent. "I'm between two Minnesotans who won't stop talking about their trip to Niagara Falls. Like it's Japan or Mars. Niagara Falls! They say the casino is the best in the world. I'm like, is that so?"

"Mine have been eating a smoked fish sandwich over my head for two hours," Reuven replied, grinning sourly.

"I'm Selwyn," the guy said and looked both ways as if to make sure no one heard. "You won't remember this, but we've actually met. That White Power Rally in Poughkeepsie. I was wearing a hood."

"You were one of the embedded guys?" Reuven forced a smile. He was hoping to avoid anyone associated with The Maccabees during the trip, but he was realizing how hard that might be. He was so done with all of their macho bullshit and just wanted to focus on Joshua. But he also suspected that this guy might report back to the others, and if he was impolite they might accuse him of being disloyal, or worse put him on some kind of enemy's list. He would just have to pretend for a while. "Tell me, how did it feel to finally rip that hood off and show those Nazis that you're a Jew? I bet pretty good, right?"

"Like being the last man in line at a bukkake party. Awfully satisfying, but very messy," Selwyn said, and Reuven had to hold back gagging. "Is there ever a bigger *shanda* than a hero in a middle seat? I tell you, each of us Maccabees should be flying private."

"Nothing but champagne and 5G," Reuven added.

"Ah, it'll be different once we land," Selwyn said. "Sam set up everything so that The Maccabees are VIPs. They have us up at the Norman Hotel and rented out half the place for the duration. We're going to live like Royals. Not to mention when things get split up, you can be sure The Maccabees are getting our share."

"Split what up?"

"You didn't go to the All Hands meeting?" Again, Selwyn looked both ways. "Rabinsky told us this cure isn't going to work for these Goyem. He's sure of that. They're missing a key part of the formula, which involves a vaccine. Mossad confirmed it. Once the three months end we'll be in a position to renegotiate with the powers that be, this time from a place of real power. Twenty-three million of us in one place. A return to glory that's near-Biblical."

"Sounds like someone's got a touch of Jerusalem Syndrome?" Reuven smirked.

"You're skeptical, Reuven, I get it. But the way I see it either you're in or you're out. And if you're in there's going to be a lot of treasure going around. Beyond our wildest dreams. And if you ask me, it's about time. My family was so poor that my eight cousins and I each split a Swatch watch as a *bar mitzvah* present."

Reuven caught a glimpse back at his seat. The San Antonio couple were now feeding each other rice pudding, and he watched as some fell between them onto his seat, and they didn't clean it up.

"Maybe it is time we got out of the middle seat," Reuven mulled.

"Now, you're talking. Private jets. Where we belong."

In the back of the plane Joshua wobbled as he tried to make it to the bathroom way at the back, by the communal magazine rack. He spotted his father yucking it up at the front with some other dad in a kippah. He was glad his dad had found a friend; he was lonely after all. "Maybe I shouldn't be so hard on him?" Joshua found himself asking out loud. The gummy bear had taken hold, giving him a mellow boost of confidence but also a level of empathy for his father that he hadn't had in a while, and wasn't sure he wanted. Joshua laughed to himself thinking they should advertise this as a side effect on the gummy bear package. He entered the bathroom and gazed into the mirror, admiring the hair on his chin, which had been bare only months before. His mother would have said that his quick puberty was a defense mechanism; a realization that he'd better grow up quick since he didn't have anyone to protect him anymore. Not his mother and certainly not his father, so he had to be the man. When Joshua squeezed out of the bathroom Ruby was standing there, eyes glazed and grinning. She had a cup of ice and was crunching cubes in her mouth. She handed Joshua the cup, and when he placed an ice cube between his teeth it was the most refreshing thing he could imagine, which in Joshua's case was riding a slurp machine down a lava flow. He laughed about this image for a while, until some grumpy lady with her hair in a tight bun interrupted him, trying to get into the bathroom.

"Me and Alex aren't going to Tel Aviv after we get off this plane," Ruby whispered.

"Where will you go?" Joshua asked.

"We know a place out in the desert, a kind of *kibbutz*. A bunch of us are going. Get away from all this craziness. Alex and I want you to come," she said. "I mean, we know that you'd have to ask you dad—"

"I'm in," Joshua nearly cut her off.

"Really?"

"I don't need to ask him anything. I'm definitely coming to a desert *kibbutz* with you and Alex. I'm not an idiot."

Ruby smiled. "Good. You're a special guy Joshua. We can't bear to see you flock with the rest of the sheep. You need to run wild with us wolves."

"Aa-oooooo," Joshua howled, and Claire doubled over with laughter. From his seat, Alex turned around and repeated, "Aa-oooooo!"

The grumpy woman with the tight bun who pushed by him to get in, now was trying to push back out, and Joshua had to stop his howling to let her by.

Ruby was right about Joshua. He wasn't one of the sheep. And he shouldn't be herded along with his father, who was the biggest follower Joshua knew. He knew this would hurt his dad deeply, but if he went with him to Tel Aviv they would tear each other apart. Joshua was a man now and needed to go his own way. Plus, he was a wolf, and a wolf has to roam. Aa-oooo!!

CHAPTER 18

SARA SLID OUT of bed feeling lighter and better rested than she had in days. She put on a floral sundress that belonged to Molly's niece Annalee and stepped out of the guestroom and into the glittering morning sunlight. It was her first time being outside on her own, and she marveled at the fragrant green grass and swaying trees, the melody of birds chirping and goats bleating from the barn. It was a fragrant Mozart sonata come to life. Or was it more jazzy, like early Duke Ellington? Regardless, everything felt soft and pleasurable, and the warm wind tickled her skin. What was life before this? Sara couldn't guess but if it was anything like this that would have been amazing.

Burt and Molly had been so kind to her since taking her in. They fed her hearty soups and slices of blueberry pie; kept her company with folk music on the radio and light conversation; Molly had even filled in a book of *Mad Libs* with her, and didn't mind when Sara's only answers were, "What's happening?" Sara walked along the dirt path and found her way to the barn where Molly was parsing out feed for three small goats. They had little goatees and slits as pupils and proud chins.

"As I live and breathe she rises," Molly said, seeing Sara up on her feet at last.

Sara smiled shyly, looking at the goats. "You sure they don't bite?"

"Not if you befriend them," Molly replied.

"How do I do that?"

"Goats are playful. If you're up to it there's a little ball on a rope in the back. Tap it to them and they'll hit it back. Do that for a few minutes and they'll be bonded to you for life."

"You have tetherball?" Sara asked, remembering in a flash some set-up at some summer camp in her youth. Or did she see it on TV? She touched her head, trying to recall.

"Don't overdo it, dear. You're still healing. It takes time."

Sara walked to the back of the barn, where a half-deflated ball hung from a rope resting on a rusty pole. She tapped the ball lightly and it slowly unwound around the pole. The goats noticed. They ambled out of the barn and soon stood around watching.

"You want a piece of this?" she asked the goats.

And then she tapped the ball again and it tethered its way pleasantly around the pole. The biggest of the goats stepped forward, bleating loudly as if to say, "Your advantage of having hands doesn't intimidate me." Sara stepped back, served the ball up, and the goat leaped forward and hit the ball back with its horns. The ball almost hit Sara in the face. She laughed and shook it off, then looked the goat dead in the eye. "Oh, it's on now!" They played several matches. It felt so natural for Sara, and she didn't remember being so exhilarated. And though the exercise was exhausting, it did something to her mind—shook it up a bit. Sara had lovely flashes of other goats and other tetherball games, of three names that kept ringing in her head, and she didn't know why: Spencer, Lillia, and Chewy.

CHAPTER 19

I APOLOGIZE IN advance as this is going to sound playfully anti-Semitic, but why can't Jews be happy? Ever? They were given free airfare to a hot weather climate where the beaches are nice and the hummus is heavenly. They got unlimited Nova lox, discounted online shopping, and the superpower of not fainting every time their Wi-Fi kicked out. And yet when they arrived in Israel, it was nothing but bellyaching. From the plane's bumpy landing to the lack of luggage carts at the airport, to the scarcity of cabs that didn't stink of human sweat, they complained endlessly. The hotel rooms were too cold and had weird shower knobs, and the markets had flies. Dinner at 6 p.m. "So early?" Okay, 7 p.m. then. "So late?" *Gevalt.*

Reuven was no stranger to complaining, but from the moment he landed in Israel he engaged in the other great Jewish pastime: worrying. Joshua had disappeared from his sight at the airport. One minute he was standing next to him at baggage claim, the next he was gone. Reuven looked around the airport for hours, calling out Joshua's name in bathrooms, peeking under stalls until the cops asked him what he was up to and a kinky married couple asked if he'd like to join in. He texted and called his son incessantly to no reply, and then had airport security call Joshua's name over the intercom but they did it with such a thick Israeli accent that who could hear? In desperation Reuven called Nancy back in New Jersey, who was kind enough to talk him down, telling him that Joshua was a smart kid; he knew the hotel in Tel Aviv where they were supposed to stay, he had money and his passport. Maybe his phone died, and he just got in a cab to the hotel? He was probably there waiting in the lobby.

"If he calls me, you'll be the first to know," she said, adding, "you cheating asshat."

Reuven lugged all four of their suitcases to the cab line and called the hotel to see if Joshua had checked in but the woman who answered the phone said sorry, can't help you! Too many Jews checking in. He'd seen Joshua yucking it up with that hipster couple on the plane. They looked high, frankly, and he didn't like how loud they laughed. Maybe the couple brought him out for an illicit night on the town? Joshua was almost sixteen, and when Reuven thought about what he was up to at that age, it was plausible. I mean the kid was mourning his mother. Maybe he just needed to let loose, have a beer or two. He'd be back in a few hours. At the very least he'd need a change of clothes in the morning.

"Mr. Schtinkler, welcome to The Norman Hotel," they said at check-in. It was just like in the photos; a gigantic historic beachfront marvel with an enormous lobby, four glittering pools, and bow-tied waiters racing around with overpriced drinks. The rooms were plain and neat, might as well be an upscale Hyatt, but the place had a high-end charm with its ultra-thick carpets and embroidered drapes. Reuven's room faced the city, not the Sea, but the view of downtown was charming. Reuven opened his windows and marveled that this was Israel, that he was breathing the same air as those in the old stories of the *Torah*. He was sure if he looked hard enough he could see where God had asked Abraham to kill his son! Across the road he thought he spotted Joshua with his ridiculous yellow Pussy Riot hoodie. He leaned out the window and called out his name but when the man turned he was probably twice Joshua's age and heavily bearded and the sweatshirt read "Pussy *Shabbat*," which is an entirely different kind of pussy.

Reuven closed his window and right then, as if by some miracle, his phone dinged with a text, "Sorry I left the airport without saying goodbye. I'm fine. I just need some time. I met some nice people on the plane. Going to hang with them for a few days. Bye, Dad. Love you."

"Call me immediately," Reuven texted back, furious, and then waited, staring down at his phone as if his phone was going to be shamed into shaming Joshua's phone into shaming Joshua into coming to the hotel. "I'm waiting," he added.

A knock came on the door. Reuven kept staring at his phone as he opened it. Selwyn, The Maccabee from the plane, stood before him in a Hawaiian shirt and a cabana hat. Looked like he'd been on a vacation for weeks.

"You get held up at the airport or something, friend?" he asked. "I've already been to the pool. Refreshing with this desert heat."

"My son—we got separated. He just texted me so he's fine, but I'm agitated."

"Teenager, right? Remember being a teenager? You needed some time to spread your wings, chase girls. You seem like a cool dad, Reuven, but who the hell wants to be with their old man for this long?" He smiled, waved around. "We're at the Norman Hotel in Israel, one of the most luxurious spots in the country. He'll find his way back. In the meantime, you've got to check out these waitresses. They're blonde with tanned skin, its bananas."

Reuven grinned despite himself. "I don't feel much like it."

"Hey, snap out of it, buddy," Selwyn said, putting a hand on the doorframe. "Your son will be back. He has a cell phone. Let him breathe a bit. In the meantime, there's going to be work for us to do, and you're going to feel bad if you miss out."

"What do you mean, work?"

"You know . . . Maccabee work. Top Secret."

"But we're in Israel. It's all Jews."

"Yeah, some of whom are lefty assholes crying about Arab rights, saying we're trying to take over the world. It's our job to talk some sense into them. Maybe not so rough as we used to in the States, but we need them to fall in line. After all, there's nothing more dangerous than a self-hating Jew. Except for Woody Allen. He's a legend."

"You're not wrong about that," Reuven said.

"Come to the meeting. Sam told me directly to bring you with. Apparently, there's going to be Montreal bagels."

"And cream cheese?" he asked.

"And cream cheese," Selwyn confided.

Reuven looked down at his phone, which still had not dinged back, and relented. "I'll be down in two."

"I'll wait for you by the bar. Get happy, buddy. This all we ever dreamed of!"

Joshua didn't have many experiences that could be described as "cool." He once took a selfie with Billie Eilish at a mall in Short Hills, NJ, but you could see Sara in the background holding double-thumbs-up and welling with tears of pride that her son had the courage to approach her, which reduced the cool factor by about 200%. But right now, as Joshua sat in the backseat of a topless red Jeep headed into the Negev desert sandwiched between his new friends Alex and Ruby, Bob Dylan himself might have been like, "Whoa, that kid is cool." In the front seat was an Israeli woman, Hannah, with wild black hair and bushy eyebrows, and driving was an older smiley guy (maybe late 30's) with his hair pulled back in a ponytail named Gol. They smoked Israeli cigarettes and blasted Israeli music, which Joshua recognized as both cheesily earnest and kind of funny at the same time. Ruby pointed out strange cactuses and breath-taking rock formations and distant lakes to Joshua out the window. The landscape looked like

Mars or Tatooine from Star Wars, and Joshua wondered if this is where George Lucas had filmed it, and if so how Mark Hamill kept his hair from getting frizzy. Gol lit a joint and Joshua caught whiffs as they drove on, but he passed up offers to take a hit having not fully come down from the raspberry gummy bears he'd consumed on the plane. Instead he looked out at the view and thought about his dad. Ditching him at the airport like that had been cruel, especially since he knew how worried he'd be. He could have just told him what he was doing at the airport, but he knew that his dad would never let him go off alone with strangers to who-knows-where without an embarrassing spectacle. It was the first adult decision he had to make, and like all adult decisions, it involved betraying your father.

"I know what you did was hard," Ruby said, reading his mind. "But you're safe with us. He'll be safe too."

Joshua wasn't sure he agreed that his father would stay safe, but he nodded anyway, deciding to push away the feelings. They drove in silence for a while until they made it to the edge of a cliff that looked out onto an endless expanse of the desert. The sky was ocean blue and the sun was high and bright in the distance. Gol cut the engine and they all got out and stretched. Ruby did a yogic sun salutation at the edge of the cliff. Alex yelled, "*Sababa!*" and it echoed down into the canyons below where jagged rocks jutted up like stalactites. The raven-haired woman, Hannah, took out her cell phone, rushed forward and whipped it off the cliff. "*Sababa!*" she yelled, and her voice echoed along with the sound of her cellphone ricocheting off the rocks. Gol did the same thing, hurling his phone over the edge, then Alex and Ruby did too. Ruby threw hers tomahawk-style, and it flew off towards the sun like a bird.

"All right Joshua, time to be rid of your robot master," Gol said.

Joshua hesitated. Ruby took him aside. "Text your dad," she said. "Tell him you're in good hands. Then let go.

We're going to a place of peace but there are people in power who would rather see us as pawns in their stupid game. Without phones they can't track us. You want to be free, right?"

Joshua nodded. "Okay, just give me a second?"

"Take as long as you want."

Joshua turned around and sent two texts. One to his father, "Sorry I left the airport without saying goodbye. I'm fine. I just need some time. I met some nice people on the plane. Going to hang with them for a few days. Bye, Dad. Love you." Then he sent another to his mother's phone, "You're the G.O.A.T. Greatest of All Time." Finally, he checked his high score on Sugar Rush just to have a mental image of his triumph. Then he ran forward towards the cliff's edge and whipped his cellphone out into the chasm, yelling, "*Sababa*!" He ran so fast that he almost stumbled forward into the canyon itself, but Gol caught him and held him back. Joshua's voice echoed down below as did the clattering of his phone hitting the rocks. Everyone yelled "*Sababa*," until their voices became one. I don't know what the exact translation of "*Sababa*" is, but I think it's something like, "We love throwing electronics into ancient caverns!"

Reuven re-read the text he'd received from Joshua as he rode the elevator down to the lobby of the Norman Hotel. What was chilling to Reuven were the final words, "Love you." Reuven didn't think his son had said, "Love you" to him since he was a little boy, and that was only after prodding from Sara and maybe a promise for ice cream. *Love You.* He wished he could have heard Joshua say those words with his own ears. On text it felt a little ominous, like his son was telling him something that he didn't want to regret not telling him if they didn't see each other for a long time. Reuven was re-reading the text again when he arrived at the hotel bar where Selwyn had asked him to meet up.

"I got us shots!" Selwyn waved Reuven over. He held up two glasses filled to the rim with amber liquid. "They say the whiskey here tastes like taking a bite out of a camel's saddle."

Reuven sipped from the glass and winced. "More like a camel's ass."

Selwyn laughed. "Regardless. You know how hard it is to get good whiskey in this country? The locals drink this licorice flavored thing called Arak. Bloody terrible if you ask me." Selwyn gulped down the contents of his glass. "Hurry up with yours. We don't want to be late."

He put a hand around Reuven's shoulder like they were old buds, and they headed down to the ballroom for the big meeting. It was every grand hotel ballroom; terrible paisley carpet, ornate wall sconces, and an enormous chandelier. There was a long table with coffee, juices, fruits and pastries, and a podium with a microphone set up at the front. Hundreds of men milled around, chewing and slurping and talking loudly. Reuven recognized the same skulking male energy from the club back in New York, almost as if everyone was wearing a cologne called Skulking. Men who recognized each other embraced but squeezed each other's biceps as they did. They spoke English and Hebrew, Russian and Arabic, Spanish, and Amharic, but all had the same bravado in their tone.

"I had this one racist dickhead up against bar, and I just pulled down his pants. Smallest uncircumcised dick anyone had ever seen! Like three balls!" one said, and the group of men around howled with laughter.

Reuven felt a pit in his stomach. He thought about Joshua and how sickened he would be by this macho display, and he didn't blame him. If he hadn't left him at the airport Joshua probably would have abandoned him now.

"Gentlemen let's get going." A man with heavy black eyebrows tapped the mic at the podium. "We lose the room to the Women of Hadassah at noon. And as many of us here know you don't want to mess with Jewish women. They'll castrate you for sport." There was a roar of laughter in the crowd, and Reuven felt his stomach worsen. "I am honored today to welcome our leader, straight from the other Israel, New York City, Dr. Jacob Rabinsky. Dr. Rabinsky will be in Jerusalem with the bigwigs starting tomorrow. But for today he has a moment to give us a few words of encouragement."

And in strut Rabinksy, right up to the podium. Reuven felt a chill down his spine as he watched that phony bleached smile, the helmet of elegant graying hair, the pointing and waving like a politician on TV. He swore that Rabinsky pointed directly at him in the crowd, but it must have been his imagination.

"Gentlemen, we made it back!" Rabinsky said with a chuckle, and the men in the crowd cheered. "For thousands of years our ancestors awaited the return of the Jewish people to their native land, and now we're back and in power. And this time, no bullshit from the Romans." Big applause on that and Rabinsky raised his hands to encourage it, again waving and pointing. "Go on, celebrate that," he said, then suddenly changed tone as he looked down at some notes. "But do not be fooled, my brave warrior friends. Enemies remain at the gate. Most stand 2,000 miles away, gathering, biding their time. My grandfather survived Buchenwald, and he always told me that the one thing that unites people of different walks of life is hatred, and these people hate the Jews, don't be fooled!" The crowd of men grunted and shook their heads, rattling invisible sabers. "We did good work in our home countries. Built up the economies, the arts and sciences; contributed culture beyond their wildest dreams. Where would America be without the movies of Spielberg, the music of Gershwin, the science of Einstein? Nowhere. And yet they still hate. Some say it's envy, but I say who cares why they hate Jews? Hate is hate. And hate turns quickly to violence. Fortunately, there are great warriors amongst us today right here in this room, those who gave those Jew-haters what they deserved when the time was right. From my own hometown of New York I see some of you Maccabees in the crowd. Raise your bruised knuckles proudly."

Fifty or so men did, but Reuven kept his down.

"We have Reuven Schtinkler here today," Rabinsky said calling him out. Reuven flinched upon hearing his name spoken out loud, and Rabinsky looked straight out at him, pointing. For years at TV awards ceremonies Reuven had longed to be publicly acknowledged, but for this event he hated it. "Reuven is one of our bravest soldiers. A real *Sabra*. Let's give him a hand." Rabinsky led the applause for Reuven, and the men around him including Selwyn patted Reuven on the back like he'd caught a home run ball in the stands at Yankees Stadium. "Reuven paid the ultimate price when his wife was taken from him by neo-Nazis in a savage arson of her science lab in New Jersey. Dr. Sara Schtinkler was only trying to help them, but they seem to be beyond help. We pray for Reuven on this day and admire his bravery in the face of such depravity."

There was a moment of silence as the men in the room dropped their heads, now respecting Reuven's extreme sacrifice for the cause.

"We owe Reuven for his strength, and as a tribute to his wife's memory. Thanks to Dr. Sara Schtinkler's research we have returned home." A pause. "And yet, and with the utmost respect to Dr. Schtinkler's research, "The Schtinkler Solution" as they call it, isn't what you think. It's not in fact the Sara Schtinkler Solution, but the Reuven Schtinkler Solution that will save us, that will protect us. It's you men erasing hate, eviscerating thousands of years of anti-Semitism with direct action. We've been waiting for this moment, Boys. Our ancestors have been waiting for this moment!" Rabinsky slapped the podium with both hands and the men in the crowd roared. "We have it on good word that the science behind the Schtinkler Formula is incomplete. It could take many years to solve that missing piece of the formula. That this experiment of social distancing is likely not going to work the way the gentiles hope. So, what do you think they're going to do in three months when they're still fainting? They'll look at this situation and say, 'We've got them all in the one place—let's finish them—finish what Hitler started.' Well, we have to make sure that we're ready for that day. And when that day comes, and it's likely on its way, we will win, because we always win. And then we will lead this world of fainters just as *Hashem* wishes. We are Kings don't forget, and it's time for us to sit on the throne that God bejeweled us. And if these gentiles won't yield, if they won't be led, then we must give them no choice."

Another roar from a crowd of men who suddenly saw themselves as Divine Kings and not a bunch of *schlubs* who'd just eaten too many whitefish sandwiches.

"Maccabees! Maccabees!" the men sang out.

Rabinsky strut offstage amidst cheers and was led out by Security. Some Women of the *Hadassah* had already begun filing into the room, rolling their eyes and trying to avoid the smell of skulk. Reuven was about to head back to his room for a nap when he was approached by a large man in a suit and security earpiece.

"Dr. Rabinsky would like a word," the man said to Reuven.

"Lead the way," Reuven replied. He knew to be affable with the guards. Even after being lauded onstage the slightest frown would not be taken kindly.

Reuven was escorted down the hall and into a private library on a lower floor. The walls were deep green and lined with oak panels; cigar smoke emanated the air. Two massive security guards flanked Rabinksy, who sat at an enormous carved wood desk. He motioned for Reuven to sit.

"Rather stand," Reuven said, tightly. He'd hidden his disdain for Rabinsky thus far, but he could feel it slipping.

"They say standing is better for the sphincter!" Rabinsky grinned. He took a long look at Reuven, sizing him up. "Look, I know what you think of me, Reuven. I can read it all over your face. You think I'm a big phony."

"I never said that."

"But you think it," Rabinsky said, and Reuven realized that all this time he'd been fooling no one. "Look, I meant what I said out there. It's you, not your wife who should be the face of the Schtinkler Formula. Sure, before 'The Return' it was time for science, for discussions, for intellectuals. But now it's time for guts, and yes, even for fists."

"I heard your pep talk," Reuven said. "You really put me on the spot out there."

"And that's exactly where I want you, Reuven. On the spot—in the spotlight. I want you in my inner circle. It's what I intend to tell the brass in Jerusalem tomorrow. But I need to know that you're with me."

Reuven tried to stay calm. The mere mention of Sara's name coming out of Rabinsky's lips made him want to jump over the table and thrash out in rage. But he also understood how dangerous that would be, and also how much harder life in Israel might be made for him and Joshua if Rabinsky was an enemy.

"I so appreciate your words," Reuven begin, as politely as possible. "But I don't think I'm ready for that kind of position. I'm a reality TV producer."

"And a really good one at that. I'm a big fan of *Celebrity Smell-evator*."

Reuven couldn't help but feel proud that Rabinsky knew one of his earliest creations, where Celebrities try to guess the source of foul smells on an elevator.

"And that's why I have spoken to your company

president, Brigit, and she assured me that the production company will be understanding. You and your son can even have time to explore the sights. How is young Joshua, by the way? Have you spoken since the airport?"

At this question Reuven's pulse jumped. "He's with some friends," he replied, reddening.

"Friends, yes." Rabinsky seemed to savor the words. "My men will make sure he's safe with those friends. But at a certain point he may be too far gone."

"You know where he is?" Reuven asked, revealing his angst.

"We do," Rabinsky said. "And in due time he will be brought to Jerusalem to be with you. And he will be kept safe in the meantime. But there are limited resources for that kind of thing. So, I need to know what your commitment is." Rabinsky leaned forward, a glint in his eyes. "We're talking about the seat of power, Reuven. The room where it happens."

"Where what happens exactly?"

"Destiny."

"Then you'll bring Joshua back to me?" Reuven asked.

"You have my word."

Reuven nodded.

"You're a smart man, Reuven," Rabinsky said. "You represent what could be for our people in a future that is emerging at light speed. A future where Jews don't have to be afraid anymore. Certainly, you'd be up for that?"

CHAPTER 20

YOU KNOW WHAT'S FUN? Lying on a barn floor and letting goats dance around your head. Doesn't that sound like a blast? Well, according to Sara Schtinkler, who giggled almost to the point of peeing herself as Burt and Molly's goats pranced around her, there's no better time. Luckily, the goats managed to avoid Sara's head and the massive bandage still tied around it, since had they accidentally bonked her it could have been dangerous. But for Sara the soreness in her head actually seemed to fade away when she was with the goats, no matter how frisky they were. And they were! Such zestful little devils! How they butted heads, waggled their tongues, and bleated when they were excited. How devious they were! They pulled at her pant legs and it tickled, so Sara giggled and giggled even more until she may have peed a little bit indeed. She giggled so hard that she didn't even hear the police car roll up the driveway and park outside the farmhouse.

Molly and Burt noticed however and were scared half out of their wits. They hid in the pantry, hoping to dissuade the officer from venturing any further than the driveway, but when the hefty, mustached officer with his mirrored sunglasses and cowboy hat got out of the car, they quickly set out to greet him.

"Burt," the officer said, tipping his hat. "Molly. Top of the morning to you."

"Vernon," Burt greeted the officer.

"Anything we can help you with, Vern?" Molly asked. "We were just about to head to the store."

"Is that right?"

"Yup," Burt said. "Seeing as it's just the two of us, we like to shop together."

Just as the words escaped Burt's lips the sound of Sara's mad giggling rang out, and Sara burst out of the barn door, chased by goats whose tickling she'd momentarily escaped. "Leave me alone, you zany goats!" Sara said, laughing so hard that she doubled over onto the ground.

The police officer observed Sara with her bulbous curly hair pouring out of the bandage on her head and the pee stain on her jeans, and slowly turned back to Molly and Burt for an explanation. "Just the two of you, huh?"

"Oh, you mean Annalee?" Molly grinned. "That's just my niece from Alberta. She's uh, not all there, bless her heart." They all looked back at Sara, who was pretending she was an orchestra conductor and waving an imaginary baton. The goats all danced and then chased her back into the barn as she cackled wildly. "Poor, girl," Molly continued. "Fell off a horse at a ranch back in Canada. Kind of unwired her brain. Hasn't been the same since."

"I see," the officer said skeptically, though the woman did seem certifiably insane. "You might want to register her as a visitor. The municipality office is doing checks of all residences over the next week to make sure there's no, well . . . "

"Hidden Jews?" Burt let out a chuckle.

"Anyone who might compromise the quarantine," the officer replied with a stern look, and Molly got uneasy.

"Vernon, how'd you like a slice of my famous blueberry pie?" she asked. "I'll wrap it up to go?"

The officer smiled. "Don't mind if I do. Thank you, Molly."

As Molly ran inside, Vernon took a step towards Burt and spoke in low tones.

"Listen, Burt, I've known you and Molly growing on thirty years and I've never heard of a niece from Alberta."

"Guess it never came up," Burt replied.

"I'm going to say this because we go way back. The municipalities aren't playing around. If they catch someone around here that ain't supposed to be here they'll arrest them and you, maybe even take your farm. Now I wouldn't want to see that happen and you wouldn't want that to happen so . . . "

"Like I said, Vern, she's Molly's niece from Calgary. Ain't nothing else to say on that. And if the government needs to steal my farm, then well, I got the right to protect my property, so we'll just have to see about that."

Vernon understood the threat and snarled.

"Here's your pie!" Molly ran out of the farmhouse. "Warm just like you like it."

She placed the warm wrapped pie in the officer's hands. It smelled like buttered heaven. The officer tipped his hat and got back into his cruiser. "Think about what I said, Burt," the officer said. "Afraid I won't be able to help if there's a problem."

Burt nodded, Molly waved, and the police car drove off into the woods. Next to the barn, Sara was now ballroom dancing with one of the goats.

Burt sighed. "We might have ourselves a little problem."

CHAPTER 21

JOSHUA WAS ASLEEP in the backseat of a red Jeep heading into the Negev desert, looking as cool as one can as they drool a puddle of saliva onto a Pussy Riot hoodie. He dreamed of his mom and how they used to trade TV diner trays every few days, in her words to, "Mix it up." In this dream Joshua passed his tray to his mother but couldn't hold his hands steady and the ramen kept spilling. "It's the bumpy road," his mother said, cryptically.

She turned on the TV to watch Joy Reid but instead it was the movie *Ben Hur*, and instead of Charlton Heston playing Moses, it was his father. He wore a long robe and held up the Ten Commandments, "Woe unto thee, Oh Israel!" his nasal voice said.

"Ugh, I hate this actor," Sara said. "Couldn't they at least cast a Jew to play the second most famous Jew of all time?"

Joshua looked at the screen again and then turned to his mother to ask if the number one most famous Jew was Weird Al Yankovic, but now it was Reuven sitting next to him, shirtless with blood on his hairy chest.

"Join me," he said to Joshua. "We're the same, after all." Joshua looked down, and he too had blood on chest.

A bump in the road jutted Joshua forward, hurling him into consciousness. His eyes strained to focus but he saw that he was still in a Jeep driving up a long gravel road, and had drooled half a cup of saliva onto his sweatshirt. Alex and Ruby sat next to him, and the ponytailed Gol drove as

Hannah rested her head on his shoulder. It was a scene only slightly less weird than his dream.

"You're quite a sleep talker," Ruby said to Joshua with a grin.

"What did I say?"

"Something about ramen noodles. The rest was babbling."

It was dusk, and the sky was orange and purple as they approached a gate, which was flimsy and had a little broken-down security hut next to it. A young guy in jean shorts and a bandana walked out. He seemed like the kind of security you might have at Woodstock, after the real security guard was dosed with LSD.

"*Kadima.*" He waved Gol in, smiling.

Inside the gates, Joshua saw a row of modest apartments with low-slung clotheslines and garbage cans painted in rainbow colors. Children played with sticks and balls on the dirt roads; dogs that desperately needed grooming roamed around, panting in the early evening heat. There was a little basketball court with seating carved out of stone.

"Welcome to our dusty little *kibbutz*," Gol said. "My grandparents helped build it in the 1950s. Now my parents, my whole family live here. There's not much to do and the Wi-Fi is terrible but it's safe, and we have bonfires most nights."

The Jeep parked at a small apartment where a little girl in pigtails and pink-framed glasses drove a tricycle in circles, and a tiny Tibetan Spaniel with overgrown fur yelped in excitement.

"She never met any Americans before." Hannah smiled. "She's been waiting to show off for you all day."

The little girl jumped off her tricycle and picked up her dog in her arms, presenting it to the foreign people in the Jeep like a gift. "*Ze* Chumie," she said to Joshua in a thick Israeli accent. Then she giggled and blushed and put down the dog and ran up the stairs to her mother, who was just walking down the stairs. The mother, who was young and had beautiful sharp features, listened to her daughter whisper something into her ear before turning to Joshua.

"She thinks you're very handsome. Like a movie star. Come, we have a bed for you and a hot shower."

While Gol and Hanna peeled off to their place next door, Joshua followed Alex and Ruby inside. The apartment was small and clean, the kitchen taking up most of the space. Joshua was given his own little room right next door to Alex and Ruby. There was a mattress on the floor with crisp sheets and a fan plugged in next to it. In the bathroom there were clean towels, soap, and a sealed toothbrush as well.

"Thank you so much for your hospitality," Joshua said to the woman when she turned to leave.

"You are family now," the woman replied. "Make yourself at home."

Her little girl, Chaya, hid behind her leg giggling. "She's your fangirl, as they say in America. She says you look like The Kid LAROI—it's the only pop star she knows."

Joshua took this as a compliment even though he thought The Kid LAROI had peaked after "Still Chose You" and had been pretty disappointing ever since. He got down on his knees to say thank you, but the little girl just ran away giggling and her mother followed.

Joshua lay down on his mattress and tried to take in the events of the last twenty-four hours. He'd woken up in his bed in suburban New Jersey, and since then he'd abandoned his father halfway around the world and landed with new friends at a *kibbutz* in the Negev desert. Sounded like a Bruce Springsteen song, if his real name had been Bruce Spring-stein.

"The shower pressure is amazing," Ruby said, peeking into Joshua's room. "There's a campfire in an hour or so. Zev is hoping we can all be there."

"Who's Zev?"

"He's like the community leader of the *kibbutz*. Hannah said she'll introduce us."

Joshua got up and showered, and the pressure was incredible, as promised. Joshua had never spent much time thinking about shower pressure, but now that his eyes had been open to it, he couldn't stop thinking about how satisfying this shower was. When he got out there was a change of clothes on his bed; over-sized underwear, jean shorts and a tie-dye tank top. He looked like someone who had danced off forty pounds at a Phish show.

Gol laughed when Joshua joined them in the kitchen. "My clothes fit you well."

"You look like Lisa Bonet." Ruby laughed, and though Joshua was too young to understand the reference, he assumed it must be some Jewish kid who wears tie dye, and he laughed also.

"I appreciate it, Gol. Thank you," he said.

Alex and Hanna lay food on the table along with plastic goblets for wine. There was cucumber and tomato salad with feta, curried lentils, lamb kabobs with tzatziki sauce, and toasted pita. The aroma alone was enough to make Joshua salivate. They poured wine and Hannah said a prayer, and then Joshua dug in. His appetite was catching up with his growing teenage body, so he had to hold himself back from taking seconds of the delicious meal before the others finished taking firsts. He drank wine too, which tasted sweet like dark cherries.

"Apparently the little girl next door is cutting hearts out of pink paper and writing Joshua's name on them," Ruby said with a chuckle. "But because she can't spell in English yet they all say 'Gosh.'"

"Gosh!" Gol laughed.

"This must happen to you all the time at home," Hannah chided. "How many girlfriends do you have in America?"

"I had one once," Joshua admitted. "But it didn't last long."

"We men never do the first time," Gol said with a laugh, but Hannah slapped him.

"You still don't last long, pig!" she said, and everyone laughed, expect for Joshua, who wasn't a fan of family fuck talk, having suffered through his dad being a big fan of family fuck talk for years.

It was dark out when they were done eating but still warm as they walked along a gravel path to the bonfire. The moon was so bright above that it lit their way, and Joshua heard music playing in the distance. When they arrived at the hillside, Joshua entered what might have been his second "cool" moment, if cool had frozen in Berkley in 1969. Dozens of young men and women danced around laughing, drinking beer and smoking rolled cigarettes. Flames crackled from a campfire so big that it seemed to touch the sky, and the sky was like, "Oh, that's my special spot."

Gol handed Joshua a beer, which was cold and delicious to drink. Most of the people gathered were young Israelis but there were visitors from around the world as well. Gol introduced Joshua to people from Yemen, Brazil, France, Argentina, and even New Zealand. Josh didn't even know they made New Zealand Jews. In his life Joshua had only met Jews from New Jersey and California; most were pale and anxious and talked too fast. But these were a different brand. They laughed easily and came in all shades and sizes.

"*Shabbat Shalom* everybody and welcome." A handsome man with tanned skin and a spectacular mop of curly black hair hopped up on a boulder, beer raised. Joshua thought for a second it was the drummer of the Strokes but then thought, would the drummer from the Strokes be at this *kibbutz*? Which then made Joshua wonder if the drummer from the Strokes was even Jewish. Joshua regretted throwing his phone away. For the first time in his life, he really needed to Google something. Then Joshua thought, maybe he was a little drunk.

"I said, *Shabbat Shalom*!" the man repeated, and the music was lowered as everyone turned his way. "Such a beautiful night, no? *Hashem* could not have created anything so beautiful as this moonlight." He smiled easily and looked around the group of people, delighted by what he saw. "I want to welcome our new friends from around the world to our little dusty kibbutz. I am Zev. You will know me because I am the one who never stops talking."

Several of the Israelis laughed, lifted their beers. "Finally, the truth!" one said, and Zev laughed at that.

"What can I say?" he went on. "For all of us from around the globe to come together and drink and relax, this is some kind of wonderful thing. I see before me a mini-UN, and it is how it should be. And yet I wish we'd met under different circumstances," he said and shook his head. "I wish we'd met not because we are Jewish and do not faint but because we are all human beings in search of peace. This, I hope, is what will keep us together. But don't be mistaken. Because for the very reason we are together and feel as one, there are people in power trying to divide us, to make war. As we speak, important men in suits meet at fancy hotels looking for ways to use their guns and bombs. They seek land and they seek money and power. They seek to increase not decrease the pain the world is experiencing right now. It is not a stretch to say that these men want to control the world."

A few of the new people in the crowd chuckled, feeling that the speech was a bit overboard. Joshua was amongst the skeptical.

"You laugh, but you will see," Zev went on. "First they will talk about national security. They will say that the Jewish people are vulnerable being all in the same place, so the enemy might plan to finish us all finally. They will draw on fears. And once those fears have taken root they will speak of striking first. You think I'm crazy, but you will see." He took a pause. "It is our duty on this dusty little *kibbutz* to be a thorn in the side of that plan and to educate ourselves on the truth. We must learn our history and seek paths to peace inspired by those who have triumphed before us. History has proven that peace can be attained without guns, without bombs—only with an uncompromising commitment to goodness. So tomorrow we educate each other. We build a plan for peace, game it out, and design ways to resist." Then he smiled as if thinking of an inside joke to himself. "But not tonight, tonight we party. After all, we cannot let our friends from around the globe think we are all bummers, no?" Zev raised his beer again and hopped off the boulder as music came back on. People crowded around Zev, patting him on the back. One man whispered in Zev's ear and pointed out Joshua in the crowd and Zev nodded.

Joshua, who stood next to Hanna near the fire, noticed that she was shivering a bit, holding her arms. He took off his sweatshirt and handed it to her.

"Ah, a gentleman. At least someone is around here." She looked at Gol.

"I was just going to . . . "

Hannah put on the sweatshirt and looked at the logo. "Pussy Riot? That would be one hell of a riot. You are wild, Joshua. Dance with me." She pulled Joshua's arm and they danced. Joshua noticed Zev watching him from a distance. When the song ended, and Hannah was pulled away, Zev approached, a broad smile on his face.

"I see you are enjoying our little community?"

"Thanks so much for having me," Joshua replied.

"Gol tells me that you had to leave your father behind at the airport to be here. That could not have been an easy thing to do."

"We see things differently," Joshua said. "He'll be fine."

"We already have much in common, Joshua. I see things differently than my parents too." Zev chuckled. "But it's not their fault, I think. When you get older, survival becomes the big concern, and I think it shrinks your vision."

"Is that so?" Joshua asked.

"Mother and fathers become a bit phony to ensure the safety of their families. It will probably happen to us too one day."

"My mother was never phony," Joshua muttered.

"Yes, Gol also told me that. I am sorry for your loss, Joshua. I wanted to tell you that we all have a deep respect for what Dr. Schtinkler was doing. She was certainly an ally to the cause of peace. I hope that if she was alive today that she would feel comfortable to join us."

"My mother wasn't much of a joiner either," Joshua said. "And no offense, but she would have been uncomfortable with your speech. Too many moral platitudes."

Zev laughed, taken aback by Joshua's brashness. "I like you Joshua! You have a fire, and we need fire. I can tell that you're too smart for flowery words. So, let me tell you plainly. We want to stop the men who insist on war and if we must use violence as a last resort to stop the violence then that is what must be."

"Finally, the truth."

"So I need to know, Joshua. If it comes to that, are you with us?"

"My father once asked me the same question," Joshua replied. "Did I want to go beat up some bad guys with him? So, I'll say what I said to him: sounds like a dick measuring contest to me."

Zev laughed again and not just because he thought fondly of a few real dick measuring contests he had once been part of. He clasped his hands. "I underestimated you, Joshua. You are more of a teacher than a student. You have already given me wisdom that no one else had the guts to give." He clinked beers with Joshua and winked. "I will see you in the morning, my new friend."

Joshua watched Zev dance away, and when Zev tripped on a rock and stubbed his toe, Joshua found himself chuckling. The guy was a bit goofy, both self-aware and totally un-self-aware. It was almost charming. But Joshua decided to put aside judgment of Zev for now. If this *kibbutz* was some kind of resistance movement then he would have to leave and find his way back to the city. But for now, he decided to just enjoy the night. The brightly moonlit sky was too beautiful to waste on plans. Alex handed him a fresh beer and Joshua joined Ruby in dancing by the fire.

But what he didn't see as he enjoyed himself with his new friends was Zev walking off with Hannah towards the Jeep. If he had he would have heard Zev instruct her to retrieve Joshua's shattered cell phone from the canyon. "If there is something important on that phone the government cannot find it first," Zev told her. Hanna nodded and started the engine. It was getting chilly out, so she zipped up Joshua's yellow hoodie.

"I will try," she said, then drove off into the night.

CHAPTER 22

AS MANY TOURISTS to Israel quickly discover, Jerusalem is nothing like Tel Aviv. Whereas the sounds and smells of Tel Aviv are of the nightlife (laughter, techno, some drunkard yelling, "Free my falafel balls!" repeatedly), Jerusalem sounds and smells like early morning with its distant bells, shuffling feet, trucks backing up to unload, and the dewy aroma of fresh vegetables and burned incense. Reuven took all this in through the window of an air-conditioned Lincoln Town Car, which had been furnished by Rabinsky himself.

Arriving in Jerusalem, he observed the Hassidim in their black hats and the women in their wigs and the children with their *kippahs* and tallit with the look of, "How come I couldn't have been Reform?" The small shops selling *Kiddish* cups. The big shops selling *Kiddish* cups. The medium sized shops selling *Kiddish* cups. Basically, there are a lot of places to shop for *Kiddish* cups. Inspired to share these sights with his son and worried about his whereabouts, Reuven dialed up Joshua's number incessantly and left messages, but eventually his voicemail was full, so he texted instead, "I'm in Jerusalem. The King David Hotel. Call me now, please. Dad. Love You."

The King David in Jerusalem was not quite as luxurious as The Norman, but the view of the Old City was spectacular; The Dome of The Rock, The Mount of Olives, The Tower Of David, etc. Also, two dogs humping a falafel cart was visible from Reuven's hotel window, but that's much less of an audacious tourist attraction. He unpacked for the second time in as many days. There was a blinking message on his room phone with instructions to meet down by the bar in an hour, and though he thought he was going to collapse if he didn't take a nap, instead he took a long shower and put on some nicer clothes. He'd had a lot of time to think on the drive to Jerusalem. He knew he was being used by Rabinksy, yet again. But this time it was with the goal of keeping Joshua safe. And if Rabinsky needed Reuven to play the brave, bereaved husband or to somehow represent the War Hawk that must swoop in when the Dove of Peace fails, he would do that in exchange for his son's safety. At least that's what he kept telling himself as he rode the elevator to the bar.

He arrived fresh-shaven but far from rested. He was surprised to see Sam there waiting to greet him. Reuven did a full double-take. Sam's shiny bald head had been replaced with dark, lush hair (Was it plugs? A wig?), and his teeth were bleached blindingly white, the way Rabinsky had them.

"One-Punch Schtinkler returns!" Sam said, dodging some fake punches. His new hair bobbed and weaved with him, and Reuven was transfixed. "Plugs," Sam said, pointing up at his mop. "I was told I might have to do more TV while we're here, and I was sick of seeing my cue ball shine under the camera lights. Not everyone can have a full head of hair like you."

"It's looking very natural," Reuven lied.

Sam handed Reuven a beer. "Heard about your kid," Sam said. "Classic teenager stuff. Probably following some girl, and you can hardly blame him with these Israeli women. That said, we have people tracking his movements. There are some real crazies out there, so its best we get him home to Jerusalem quick."

"Thank you so much for that," Reuven said, and he meant it.

Sam walked Reuven over to meet a table of men, most

wearing ridiculous Palm Beach-style attire. One wore a tank top with the Israeli flag that read, "Phew, I'm a Jew!" Reuven thought to himself, I guess they were out of the "Jew-Wish You Were Here!" pins.

"Gentlemen, I give you the one and only Reuven Schtinkler," he said. "Reuven, meet the Palm Beach Chapter."

The men seemed to know precisely who Reuven was, and their eyes widened like they were meeting a celebrity.

"An honor," one of them said, shaking his hand.

"Same here," another said. "My brother-in-law is going to freak out when he heard I met you."

"Let's get a group photo," a third suggested, fumbling for his phone.

They all leaned back into a selfie like it was Ellen DeGeneres and her A-list friends at The Oscars. Reuven smiled but couldn't perceive exactly what was going through their minds. Were they making fun of him or genuinely fanboying? Was he a sucker to them or a hero? Would his pupils go red in the selfie, and could it be photoshopped out?

"We heard about how you lead the Kunkletown raid," one of them said. His voice was shaky, and Reuven recognized that the man was nervous addressing him. "How the leader pissed his pants because of you. Legendary."

"Well, that wasn't exactly me."

"See how humble he is? I told you!" Sam said to the guys. "One-Punch never brags. But I saw it with my own eyes."

"It was a team effort," Reuven found himself saying, surprised that a little drip of pride entered his voice. His voice was even a bit surprised to have pride left inside of it.

Once the photos were taken Sam said it was time to meet up with the others in "The War Room." The men all slurped down the rest of their drinks and got up, leaving only a table full of empty glasses and cocktail umbrellas. Reuven wondered whether the Palm Beach contingent traveled with cocktail umbrellas or if the hotel carried them just for such occasions.

"You're going to love this, Reuv. I set it up just like New York." Sam put an arm around Reuven's shoulder.

They rode the elevator to the top floor of the hotel. Two security guards were stationed in the hall, and about twenty other men were waiting around. When the guards saw Sam, they opened a door. The suite inside was massive, ten times as big as Reuven's room. It sprawled two levels with a bar, floor-to-ceiling windows, and a view of the Old City like in postcards. Next to a grand piano there was an original Chagall painting, but Sam had taped photos over it to match the wall at the bar in New York. There were recognizable anti-Semitic foes at the top: The President of Yemen, The Chancellor of Iran, YouTube's PewDiePie. On a lower line with a question mark next to it was a photo of the Olsen Twins. Below were lesser-known targets, many looked Jewish to Reuven.

"The top part is a moonshot list," Sam said, pointing to the rogues' gallery. "Lifelong anti-Semites all of them. And you better believe one whiff of weakness and they'll try to murder us all wholesale. But we also have domestic threats." Sam moved to the lower part of the board. "Self-hating Jews who've been brainwashed to fight for the other side. Turncoats. Many of them are small fries, but you've got to do your housekeeping to prepare for the keeping you have to do outside your house."

Reuven looked at Sam, who had a distinct look of wishing he could get that metaphor back.

Amongst the photos was of a man with curly black hair and handsome dark eyes. He looked like the singer of an indie rock band.

"Like this guy," Sam pointed. "He's got an anarchist commune in the Negev desert. Goes by the name of Zev."

"A traitor," one of the men said.

"Exactly," Sam said. "We've intercepted emails and texts. Talking about being a thorn in the side of the establishment, and that's us. But some of it is more explicit. Plans for action. Protests. Roadblocks. Bombings too. All against his own people, if you can believe that shit. He wants to put us at a disadvantage if the enemy attacks so that when these three months are over the other side can pick us off like ducks in a barrel. Ducks are kosher, by the way."

"We've got to stop him!" the man in the tank top said.

"Exactly my thinking," Sam said. "Luckily, we have surveillance and found the location. What do you say we pay a visit to his little anarchist enclave and remind these so-called Jews what side they're supposed to be on?"

As the others cheered, Reuven convulsed. "You want us to raid a *kibbutz* filled with Jews? The way we did to neo-Nazis?"

"These are self-hating Jews," Sam said.

"We're all self-hating to a certain extent. Who's next, Larry David?" Reuven asked, and the men in the room listened, seeing his point. They only knew him as One-Punch Schtinkler the brave leader thanks to Sam, and now that ploy was working against Sam. "And what hard evidence do you really have? It might just be a bunch of college kids with stupid ideas. Who among us didn't have wild ideas when we were young?"

One of the guys turned to his friend and said, "Yeah, remember back in college when we were so into butt chugging?"

"See?" Reuven asked. "They'll come around."

"Gotta say I see his point, Sam," one of the other men said. "He looks like a harmless kid who's turned around. Maybe just send the cops to check it out?"

As the others rumbled Sam turned to the security guards at the door and nodded. They dragged in a woman with dark, wavy hair and sat her roughly on a chair next to the photo board. She had on handcuffs and a bandana over her mouth. Reuven lost his breath seeing that she was wearing a yellow "Pussy Riot" sweatshirt, replete with Joshua's ketchup stain.

"Her name is Hannah Galud. She's a member of this group of so-called wayward youths, and lives on the kibbutz with our man Zev." He looked down at the woman pitifully, and he pulled down the bandana covering her mouth. "Tell them what you told me," he ordered the woman. "Or your family in Haifa gets the visit we discussed."

The woman swallowed hard, looked at her hands. "They have plans to—"

"Who?"

"The Vidra El-Shimon *kibbutz*. Has plan to stop the government from destroying the world."

"And what is the direct plan of action to do that, specifically? Don't be shy."

The woman looked up. "We intend to bomb the nuclear launching sites."

The men gasped in horror and Sam threw up his hands. "See? These so-called harmless kids are scheming to commit a series of terrorist acts against Israel's military infrastructure, making it easier for the rest of the world to snuff us out. Did any of you do that in college?"

"No, just butt chugging."

"Is that the general idea, Ms. Galud?" he asked, and he meant the terrorism not the butt chugging, but some of the men were still confused.

"Yes," she said.

"Thank you," Sam said, like a lawyer after a successful cross-examination. He nodded to the security guards, who grabbed Hanna roughly and sat her by the bar. Sam went back to the board. "We managed to hack Zev's phone and found photos and maps of Israeli nuclear facilities. It's been confirmed by Mossad. Is this evidence good enough for you, Reuv?"

Sam looked directly at Reuven, but all Reuven was

thinking about was where in the hell this prisoner with nuclear targets had gotten hold of his son's sweatshirt. Reuven nodded thoughtlessly, and the other men followed his lead.

"Good." Sam was satisfied with the consensus. "We're going to do this quietly, so we only need fifteen men. Who wants to volunteer?"

A handful of them raised their hands, including Reuven.

"Good. We leave in ten minutes. Got to catch them before they miss their comrade here too much. You'll find what you need at the back table."

The men all wandered to the back of the hotel room. There was a table you'd normally see at a convention, but instead of pens and other schwag, it was guns and bullet proof vests. While the men got outfitted, Reuven wandered off to the bar where the woman, Hannah Galud, sat glumly with a cup of water.

"The hell do you want?" she asked Reuven, like he was yet another man who'd come to harass her.

"Where did you get that sweatshirt?" Reuven asked quietly.

"You don't look like a Pussy Riot fan." She glared at Reuven and recognized something familiar in his face. "You're the dad, aren't you? The one Joshua ditched at the airport?"

"If you know what's good for you you'll speak in low tones, got it?" Hannah nodded and Reuven went on. "Is he safe?"

"That depends on what you and your thugs have planned."

"Answer me."

"He's fine," Hannah said. "I mean, maybe a little stoned, but fine. Joshua's a good soul. He won't join you, you know?"

"The hell do you know?" Reuven snarled. "You better not be lying or I'll be back, understand?"

The woman nodded sadly. Reuven walked to the back of the room to join the other men. He grabbed a gun and some body armor. He also picked up a "Phew, I'm a Jew!" t-shirt. This would be just like the raids in New York, Reuven told himself, except this time instead of bloody knuckles he would come out of there with his son.

CHAPTER 23

MOLLY REMOVED THE bandage from around Sara's head and threw it in the laundry bin. "I think it's safe for you to take a shower now," Molly said. "Just be careful when you shampoo. You don't want to scratch the scab."

And so, Sara Schtinkler finally got to take a real shower all by herself. It was long and hot, and she let the steam engulf her as she soaped herself for the first time since she arrived. As Sara cleaned her legs, she saw a tattoo of a goat on her left calf. "Ha, a goat tattoo on my calf!" she said to herself. "Everyone knows a baby goat is a kid not a calf, but lots of people still make that mistake." When the hot water touched her head there was a sting but then a tingle as it rolled over her scalp and onto her face. At once her mind flashed and all she saw was numbers. They whirled and popped and began to affix themselves to specific images. For instance, when she thought of the number 10,246, there was Burt. 60,349 was Molly. Sara's mind wandered to number 112,006, and she thought about the text she had received from the mysterious person named Joshua. The image was of a young, handsome boy that kept morphing into a handsome young man with stubble and big shoulders. But why? The numbers created more questions than answers, but they wouldn't stop appearing in her mind. She had the strange instinct to calculate the numbers into a formula but didn't know why she would do that either. Still, the combination of hot water rolling over her face and the swirling numbers in her mind calmed her. Burt, 10,246. Molly 60,349. Joshua 112,006.

"You're the G.O.A.T.," she found herself saying out loud. She was so excited she nearly slipped. "No, you're the G.O.A.T.! Hahaha!"

"Everything okay in there?" Molly called out from behind the bathroom door.

"You're the G.O.A.T.!" Sara called back to Molly, laughing.

"Whatever you say, dear."

Sara got out of the shower, dried herself off and headed quickly to the kitchen. She grabbed the cell phone that remained plugged in next to the toaster. She tried the password 4628, spelling the word, "GOAT," but the phone didn't open. "No, you're the G.O.A.T.," she repeated, searching her mind. "Joshua. Joshua, Joshua, Joshua . . . Who are you, Joshua?"

"Did you say something, dear?" Molly poked her head in. She had makeup on and a lovely summer dress. "It's a beautiful summer's day. You'd do well to get dressed and come out for some fresh air."

"Molly, you look so beautiful," Sara said in wonder.

"You noticed? Oh well, no use hiding it, but it's my birthday. I like to try on fancy clothes to make sure I can still pull it off. Even a farmer's wife likes to get pretty once in a while."

"What year were you born, Molly?"

"I don't like to tell."

"1949?" Sara said, and Molly was surprised. "And Burt was born on October 2nd, 1946?"

"My dear, how could you ever know that?"

"10,246. It's a date. Burt's number is 10,246 or October 2nd, 1946. And yours is 60,349, 6 is June, 3rd, 1949."

Sara grabbed her phone. "Joshua's birthday. 112,006. That's November 20th, 2006." She keyed in the numbers 112,006. The phone unlocked.

"He's my son!" Sara said triumphantly.

"Well, I'll be damned," Molly said.

"He's a sweet teenage boy who only recently reached puberty. He's a good boy." Sara opened Joshua's text. Above his latest written note, "You're the G.O.A.T.," was an attachment—a photo of a ripped page with a mathematical formula written out on four neat lines. Sara studied the handwriting.

"Do you have a pencil, Molly?"

Molly handed her one and Sara scribbled down the numbers, mirroring the ones she saw in the text. "It's my handwriting. I wrote this," she said.

"I'll get Burt," Molly said and hurried out, not wanting to jinx anything.

Sara walked to her room and scrolled through her phone. She looked at old emails, texts, and then saved photos. There were significant gaps in what she could remember. Mainly, they triggered emotions but not a memory per se. There were lots of photos of her with a tall man with a big square head who she did not have good feelings about but did have sympathy for. Was it Al Gore? Then there was a boy—a doughy, quirky boy with intelligent eyes and a copper afro. Every photo of him made her smile. She was shocked, as with each passing photo the boy went from small and doughy to tall and pubescent. In the last picture in her scroll he had stubble and zits and muscular shoulders and a cynical look in his eyes. He seemed more complex in those photos.

"You're the G.O.A.T.," Sara said to the photo and then laughed in relief. "No, no, no. You're the G.O.A.T."

Burt entered the room tentatively, but Sara was on fire with inspiration.

"I have a home in Chatham, New Jersey. A co-worker named Bruce. A job at The Center for Animal Oddities. A favorite brown cardigan!" she said. "And goats. I have three goats named Spencer, Lillia, and Chewy, but there was a fire in the barn, and an explosion and, and—"

"Don't strain yourself, honey," Burt said.

"—And there's a global fainting pandemic that affects everyone but the Jews, and I'm the only one who can stop it!" she said at last.

Sara fell back onto her bed, the flood of emotions and information too much to keep her on her feet. A weight at once lifted and pressed down on her. She had gotten back some of her memory but in the process realized that she'd been wasting precious time, and that the entire world had been waiting on her to solve a riddle that only she could solve. If you've ever had to solve a riddle, you know how much pressure it can be even without the added pressure of saving humanity. The answer was partially written in a text attachment sent from Joshua. The rest, she hoped, was in her mind.

"I'm going to need clean beakers, tongs, and funnels," she said to Burt, who grabbed a pencil to write all down. "And I'm going to need goats. Lots and lots of goats."

"Let's get bleating!" Burt said, like the best action movie sidekick ever. And he was.

CHAPTER 24

CHUMIE, THE ADORABLE Tibetan Spaniel who desperately needed grooming, licked the bottom of Joshua's feet, waking him from a long night's sleep. It ranked high on the ways to be awoken by Joshua and somewhere in the middle for feet to lick for Chumie. The clock read 1 p.m., and Joshua couldn't believe how late it was. The campfire the night before had been a lot to take in. All those new people, the cold beer in the moonlight, Zev's speech about peace, and then their private conversation about fighting back. It was so much to think about that Joshua almost forgot to miss his mom, which he then spent a while doing until he had to wipe away tears.

He snuggled with Chumie for a while and then got dressed and walked out to the kitchen. Ruby and Alex drank their coffee in somber silence, and Joshua sensed right away that something was wrong.

"Where's Hannah and Gol?" he asked.

Ruby and Alex looked up at him as if just maybe Joshua had the answer to his own question. Then Ruby sighed. "Hannah went out last night during the bonfire and didn't come home. Gol went looking for her."

"Where'd she go?"

Alex looked uneasy at the question. "Zev sent her to the canyon to retrieve our cellphones," he said. "He was worried there might be something on your phone in particular that could be used by the government if they found it. Some old correspondence with your mom, I guess."

"Shit," Joshua said and bowed his head. In a flash he remembered the text and the attachment he'd sent to his mom's phone before he left.

"Shit?"

"There's was a piece of paper tucked in my passport with my mom's handwriting. It had all these numbers. I couldn't make anything of it, so I took a photo of it with my phone."

"The phone you threw down the canyon?"

Joshua nodded sadly.

"You were disoriented. You just woke up."

"Could the photo be in the cloud?" Alex said. "I have a computer. We can retrieve it and then erase it all."

"No cloud. My mom taught me that hackers can get to that easily." Joshua blushed. "I'm an idiot."

"It's okay," Ruby said. "Whatever was on that paper was from your mother to you. You don't owe it to anyone. We have to focus on what's real. Gol thinks Hannah went to visit her cousins in Haifa. She does that sometimes. If she's not back this afternoon then we can worry. But for now we should just go to class. We're already late."

Joshua poured a cup of coffee and followed Alex and Ruby to a portable classroom on the other side of the *kibbutz*. When they entered Zev was up at the front pointing to a map and talking about the peace treaty Israel made with Jordan in 1994.

"Ah, the stragglers arrive!" Zev stopped his presentation when he saw the three of them. "Come in. Sit, sit."

Joshua averted his eyes from Zev but took a seat at the back and then watched him teach. He had to give the guy credit; Zev had a way of explaining history that was passionate and personal. He waved his arms and did voices and told fascinating stories in a way that Joshua only wished his high school teachers had. Instead they had spoken in monotones while probably texting their divorce lawyers about how the presidential stamp and coin collection was non-negotiable! Joshua grabbed a paper and a pen. If he was going to spend the day waiting for Hannah and Gol to return, the least he could do was learn something.

CHAPTER 25

KNOW WHO WASN'T interested in learning Zev's progressive history of the Middle East? The two vans full of armed Jewish men headed towards the *kibbutz*. They were more interested in which self-hating Jewish skull they might get to bash in, and also whether there'd be a restroom break soon since it had been a while, and none of them were packing particularly youthful prostates. For Reuven it felt a lot like the missions he'd been part of in New York, except this time instead of farmhouses and dive bars with Confederate flags out the window there was a dry desert-scape of ancient towns, military checkpoints, and Israeli flags flapping in the wind. This time instead of neo-Nazi skinhead and redneck racists, they were going after Jews.

Reuven had to remind himself over and over that if the prisoner, Hannah Galud, had not by some wild coincidence been wearing his son's yellow hoodie then he would not be in this position. He knew that Pussy Riot sweatshirt was going to cause trouble! She and her hoodie left him with no choice. Reuven by his own admission had been a mediocre husband and a piss-poor father. He'd screwed his family up enough for two lifetimes and didn't expect Joshua to forgive him anytime soon. But if one hair on Joshua's head was so much as tousled by The Maccabees he would never forgive himself, and Sara would likely return from the grave to haunt him for the rest of his miserable life before dragging him down to hell. "Boo!" she might say, and it would be both to scare him and to hiss her disapproval, "Boo, you were a mediocre husband and piss poor father! Boooo!"

So Reuven would try to do what was right for once; he would hide in plain sight, a defender masked as an invader, ready to swoop in and protect and then get the fuck out of there, if only to avoid the terrifying spectacle of Ghost Sara. "Get in and get right the fuck out." Reuven was so focused that he spoke his plan aloud, but the guys were too amped even to notice. They all stroked their guns like kittens they couldn't wait to unleash as full-grown lions.

The sun descended quickly over the hills and darkness enveloped the van. They turned onto a rocky path and Reuven saw a flimsy gate with a little security hut next to it up ahead.

"It's right up there." Sam pointed.

Sitting in the security hut was a teenager in jean shorts and a tank top. He smoked a cigarette and sang along to the radio in Hebrew.

One of the guys chuckled. "If that's the guard this is gonna be child's play."

"Ready?" Sam asked from the front seat. "Get low."

Reuven and the rest of the men in the van crouched down as best they could and the van rolled up. Sam stuck his head out the window, smiling broadly, and the kid in the hut scrambled to his feet.

"Hey, friend. Sorry to bother you. My husband and I are looking for *Z'artez* street?" Sam said, laying on an extra thick American accent. "There's some dance studio place? I have a map, but my Wi-Fi is out. We've been driving in circles." Sam held a crumpled map out the window and let it hang there as if he couldn't make odds or ends of it. The hippie kid stubbed out his cigarette and walked over.

"Ah, you took a wrong turn at *Haviva* Road," he said. "You must go back almost twenty minutes."

He walked to the van and reached for the map, and that's when Sam sprayed him in the face with a small canister of mace, and the guard collapsed to the ground, clawing at his eyes. "Tie him up," Sam said to the men in the van, who weren't ready for any of that to happen so quickly. They fumbled with their seat belts, and then Sam had to un-child proof the child proof doors for them to get out.

Finally, the men, including Reuven, got out and applied duct tape to the kid's flailing legs and wrist, and covered his mouth with a bandana. One of the men went into his pocket and found the gate key.

"We're in," Sam walkied the men in the other van. They rolled up from behind. "Same as usual, Boys, except we're doing an extraction this time. If you see the man they call Zev, don't shoot. He must be taken to Rabinksy alive."

"Yay, we get to beat up some bad guys!" the man next to Reuven said, with the enthusiasm of a Labrador retriever who'd just been given numb chucks.

"There's no need to hurt anyone," Reuven said. "Sam just said so."

"Yeah, but where's the fun in that?" the guy replied, and Reuven winced.

Sam turned off the headlights and drove past the gate and into the kibbutz. It was dark but there were little lights on in small apartments. Reuven saw children's tricycles, clotheslines with pink bathing suits, a basketball court. Looked more like a summer camp than a holdout for domestic terrorists.

"Over there." Sam pointed.

There was a bonfire off in the distance. Young men and women danced around, drinking beer and smoking. A few kids poked sticks into the fire until their parents shooed them away, fingers wagging. Reuven scanned the group but didn't see Joshua anywhere. Maybe he wasn't there after all. Hopefully he wasn't there after all. The vans came to a stop and the men of The Maccabees got out and walked low towards the campfire. They saw a man with curly black hair hop up on a boulder to make a speech.

"Welcome again, my friends!" Zev said.

"That's the target," Sam told the men. "If he comes peacefully we stay steady. But be ready for anything. These are bad people. And bad Jews. They probably say *menorah* instead of *Hanukkiah*."

The Maccabees marched forward out from the darkness until the people gathered around the bonfire saw them: fifteen middle-aged men with body armor, guns, and frowns. They looked like an army of middle school vice principals. A woman screamed and gathered her children, others huddled together, terrified. Gol and Alex, who were amongst the group, turned their beer bottles upside down, ready to fight if need be. Zev saw the intruders and stayed steady like he'd dealt with this type of situation more than once. He even grinned.

"Ah, so we have unexpected visitors. Everyone can relax. Perhaps they just took a wrong turn and need directions." Zev turned to the men. "How can we be of assistance, Gentlemen?"

Sam stepped forward, making himself known as the leader. "We just want a word, Zev. If you come with us there will be no problems."

Zev scoffed. "No problems, eh? Then why the guns? As you can see, we are unarmed. Just a peaceful gathering enjoying the moonlight. Now I'm not sure how you were raised but I have to say it's a bit rude to crash a party armed like this, no?"

"We know about your scheme to destroy government property. We've seen the plans. That concerns us enough to risk being rude."

"What's he talking about, Zev?" a woman next to him asked. "Who are these men?"

"They've come here to intimidate us and spread lies," Zev said. "They want to beat me up and make me confess to some garbage so that the government can start a war. That's your plan, isn't it? Bo-oring!"

Zev was so nonchalant that some of the men in the

group chuckled as if indeed these clubfooted men were too silly to do any harm. "Bo-oring!" one repeated.

Reuven couldn't help but envy Zev's confidence. His inner reality producer imagined Zev might make a great character on a show, maybe as part of an ensemble cast for "The Real Kibbutzniks," which maybe wasn't so niche a pitch as it might have been only a few months ago.

"Just come talk to us, Zev," Sam said, irritated. "We'll bring you and your comrade Ms. Galud back as soon as we can talk."

"You have Hannah?" Gol said, stepping forward. "Bring her back now!"

"She's safe. No harm will be done to her so long as Zev does what he's told," Sam said.

"Son of a bitch!" Gol snarled, his eyes red and glaring. He gripped his beer bottle and then hurled it forward. Sam ducked, and the bottle struck one of The Maccabees on the side of the head with a clank. He collapsed on the ground, but not before tasting a drop of beer that had splattered on his face. "Gross, lager," was the last thing he thought before he lost consciousness.

"Not smart!" Sam yelled, and The Maccabees ran forward to grab Gol.

"Run!" Zev yelled, and everyone scattered.

Women grabbed their children and ran away. Dogs barked and growled. More beer bottles were thrown as Zev jumped off the rock and sprinted off into the darkness.

Sam turned to his men. "Don't let him get away."

Several men ran off in pursuit, guns raised, as the rest of The Maccabees grabbed whoever they could and tackled them to the ground. Reuven watched on in horror when next to the bonfire he saw Alex and Ruby, the couple he remembered Joshua sitting with on the flight from New Jersey. They turned to run, but Reuven tackled Alex, and they tumbled to the ground.

"Get off me," Alex said, struggling beneath Reuven's weight.

"Where's Joshua?" Reuven grunted. "I just want to get him out of here."

Alex looked up and recognized Reuven from the plane. "He went back to the apartment," Alex replied. "Over by the basketball court."

Reuven was about to let Alex go when Ruby appeared above him with a beer bottle held over her head. She was about to slam it down on Reuven when she was pushed by one of The Maccabees and went careening headfirst into a sharp rock. She immediately went unconscious, and blood darkened her green hair and dripped across her face.

"Ruby, no!" Alex yelled.

Joshua heard distant screaming from inside the apartment. He dropped his armful of soda cans and ran out towards the campfire at full speed. What he saw when he arrived was chaos: fighting, screaming, men with guns, glass scattered, and blood. Next to the bonfire Ruby lay on the ground motionless, her face covered in blood. He ran up to her and cradled her head.

"Ruby, wake up. We have to get out of here!" Blood coated Joshua's hands. "Please."

"Joshua, thank God you're safe!" Reuven said.

Through the haze and screaming Joshua heard his father's nasal voice. He looked up and saw him holding Alex to the ground. At first, he couldn't believe his eyes, but as Alex struggled to get away and Reuven stood up, he saw his father in full, replete with a bulletproof vest and his stupid square head.

"You did this?" Joshua asked, stunned.

"I'm trying to save you," Reuven pleaded. "We have to get out of here before you get hurt. These people aren't who you think they are."

"You want me to go with *you*?" He looked down at Ruby and the blood, and then back at his father, disbelief painted on his face. "I never want to see you again."

Several Maccabees dragged Zev out of the darkness, his

face now bloodied and bruised. "We've secured the package," Sam said into his walkie. "Move out."

Reuven stared at Joshua. "Please," he said. "Please come with me. There isn't time."

"Never!" Joshua said, tears streaming down his face.

"Reuven, we got to go," a Maccabee from his van said. "The cops are coming."

"I thought they were on our side?" Reuven said.

"Now!" Sam called out.

Reuven turned back to Joshua. "Joshua, c'mon." But seeing Joshua's glare of red-hot hatred, he instinctively shifted gears. "Can I at least give you some money? I uh, went to the bank."

"Leave me the fuck alone!" Joshua yelled.

Reuven flinched and then did as his son said. He slumped off with the rest of the men with guns, in disbelief that he was leaving alone. "Fuck!" Reuven said to himself as he climbed back into the van. Zev lay across the floor, his wrists bound behind his back. "Fuck, fuck!" Reuven kicked Zev hard in the ribs. After all, if this asshole wasn't to blame for everything, who was? "Son of a bitch!" Reuven barked and kicked him again.

"Relax, Reuv. It's mission accomplished." Sam turned grinning to the other men in the van. "What did I tell you about One-Punch Schtinkler? The guy's an animal."

Zev looked up from the ground, terrorized by this violent man with the square head above him. When Reuven slacked, so did Zev. The van roared forward and past the gates of the kibbutz, past the hippie kid they'd tied up earlier, who still struggled to get free and maybe warn Zev to be careful, these guys might be violent.

At the bonfire, Joshua watched the vans drive off, rage boiling in his veins. Ruby still wasn't moving, and a nurse ran over and checked her pulse, then gave Joshua a sign to let go. Alex and the nurse lifted Ruby onto a stretcher and carried her off. Joshua sat there in the dirt, grinding his teeth. He grabbed a broken beer bottle from the ground and sprinted towards the gate, and then hurled the bottle with all of his might.

"Murderers!" he screamed in the darkness, and he felt a small sliver of satisfaction that his father might have heard him.

CHAPTER 26

SARA TRANSFORMED BURT and Molly's Tennessee barn into a makeshift Center for Animal Oddities. It wasn't the same without the state-of-the-art centrifuges and PCR equipment, not to mention the sloths, but Burt managed to fish out his daughter's Middle School science kit from the attic, and several of the beakers were still in working order. Sara did what she could to create a clean, safe environment to work, and even wore Burt's soldering goggles and dishwashing gloves for protection. When it was all set up Sara pulled up the formula Joshua had texted her and began to follow the steps; melting chemicals, mixing compounds, and adding ingredients.

"Do you have gefilte fish?" Sara asked Molly, who just stared back at her, confused. "Or kippered salmon could work."

"We have canned tuna?" Molly posed.

Sara thought about it. "Okay, but no mayo."

The formula was unorthodox to say the least. A mix of chemical compounds and culturally Jewish ingredients that kept Sara shaking her head and muttering, "This can't be right."

Molly brought her the tuna, the crust from a pumpernickel bagel, and a half pound of chopped liver with onions. "You really think this could work?" she asked, wondering if maybe Sara had just lost her mind instead of healing it.

In addition to the staples of Jewish food the formula

called for plant-based healing compounds like phytosterols, acyl lipids, nucleotides, and CBD oil, all of which (especially, surprisingly, the CBD) Molly and Burt had were able to secure without too much trouble. It all seemed far-fetched, but Sara had to trust this formula that she had once written and that had been sent to her by her own son. She had to trust the former Sara. Really, what choice did she have? She boiled and mixed, added and subtracted, cooled and re-heated a mixture of compounds that made little sense to her but was her only hope.

Eventually, a glowing neon greenish substance settled in her beaker. The color reminded her of the feathers of the Turaco bird of Sub-Saharan Africa; a neon green that turned almost yellow in the sun. She briefly thought about how weird it was for her to remember this obscure bird when she still hadn't fully regained her memory, but that's the brain for you. The substance bubbled and steamed, emanating a smoked fish smell. Sara inserted a syringe, sucked out the neon liquid and held it up to the light. She then turned to the goats in the barn, who looked back at her skeptically, maybe less because of the glowing syringe in her hand than the intense look in her eyes.

"Please God let this work." Sara sighed.

The goats bleated, as if to say, "Why bring God into this?"

Sara tickled each goat gently under the ear and then injected the serum one by one into their hind legs. The goats bleated again, not pleased by the injection, but when Sara said, "Tetherball?" they all followed her out to the court to play, a bit sore, but maybe wanting a revenge win. And the goats played well, though perhaps it was that Sara was more focused on observing their behavior than winning. After less than a minute, one of the goats wobbled off to the side and vomited, and then crouched down to have a bowel movement that was very loose, since it poured down the goat's legs and onto the dirt like a river. If this seems disgusting to you, then I recommend you not read much about science. Most breakthroughs involve a good deal of goat diarrhea. Steve Jobs himself claimed he got the idea for the iPhone from watching goat diarrhea. I don't know that for sure, but it seems right.

Sara observed that the expelled liquid had a green hue like the goat had eaten some spinach amongst its feed. The other goats joined in as well, suddenly all at once relieving themselves. They all looked up at Sara, bleating sadly, wondering just what in the hell had she had done to them? Sara got down behind the goats and took samples of their excretions. It was so sloppy that she got some on her shirt and arms. As they kept excreting, Sara worried that the sickness would not stop and may even kill the goats. But thankfully, after entirely relieving themselves the goats looked better, a bit listless, but recovering. They staggered back to the barn and drank water, which was a good sign, and they kept the water down, which would help them avoid dehydration. Sara carefully placed the vomit and diarrhea samples in the fridge (which is not where most people keep their vomit and diarrhea) and was just about to wash the excrement off her shirt when Molly came running into the barn, pale and sweaty.

"We have company," Molly said, breathless. She smelled Sara's goat samples and held her nose. "What happened in here?"

"I'm hoping a miracle?" Sara replied.

Sara tried to clean the excrement off her shirt but there was so much of it. She rolled up her sleeves and followed Molly out of the barn. There in the driveway Burt spoke with two men in FBI jackets and aviator sunglasses.

"Annalee, there you are," Burt said to Sara, with a wink. "These are FBI Agents Harris and Dales, who see absolutely nothing out of the ordinary here. Say hi, Annalee."

Sara gave a little wave but saw that she still had some diarrhea on her wrist. "Oh, uh, a little mess in the barn . . . " She blushed.

"Canadian, eh?" Agent Harris, the friendlier FBI Agent of the two, said. "I've got friends in Strathmore, 'bout a mile out. What part of Calgary are you from?"

"Uh, midtown?" Sara answered, knowing nothing of the place.

"Hmph," the other Agent, Dales, looked skeptical. "Well, we're on a task force to make sure that all the non-fainters are out of town. You understand how important that might be, ma'am?"

"I do."

"Normally, we would bring some fainting goats over here to see if they're still fainting. But since we know Burt's got stiff-legged goats to spare, just want to see how they do with a little scare. As a precaution, you know?"

"I'm going to say no to that," Molly cut in.

"Now, why would you do that?" Agent Dales asked, frowning.

"Our goats, our land. And I don't see a warrant," Molly said.

Agent Harris pulled out a sheet from his pocket. "This declaration gives us the right as a matter of national security to do as I said. Now please step aside from the goats, ma'am. Unless you want to be hauled in?"

"You wouldn't dare," Burt said.

Agent Dales gave Burt a look that said not only would he dare, but he would double dare with a gun on top. "Guess we're going to have to do what the gentleman says, dear." Burt gave Molly a doleful look.

Harris put away his warrant and both agents walked towards the barn. Molly, Burt, and Sara followed nervously behind. When they entered the barn the smell of the ordure was ripe.

Harris pinched his nose. "What have you been feeding these goats?"

"A vegan mix," Sara lied. "They love it in Alberta."

Agent Dales gave Sara a long, hard look; he settled on her thick, curly hair, the crook of her nose, the vegan admission. It all screamed Jew to him. And he was used to screaming about Jews. "Let's find out what we've got here," he said. The agent turned to the goats, hands outstretched, and screamed, "Hiya!"

The goats were shocked by the stranger's yell and began to teeter in place. Burt covered his face with his hat. Molly bit her lip. Blood drained entirely out of Sara's body as she knew it was all over.

"It's not their fault!" Sara shouted. "Blame me!"

The FBI looked at Sara and then turned back to the goats, who still hadn't fainted. In fact, they bleated at the FBI Agent a bit defiantly as if to say, "You're going to have to do a lot better than that to spook us!"

The agent shouted again, louder this time, "Hiya!" Agent Harris pulled out a little firecracker, lit it, and laid it on the floor. When it popped, the goats jumped. But again, they did not faint. There was zero myotonic reaction.

"Well, I'll be," Molly said under her breath.

Agent Dales looked unsettled. He turned to Sara. "You were saying," he asked. "What isn't their fault?"

"Oh," Sara shrugged. "The uh, puking and diarrhea smell–that was all me. I should never have given them the vegan feed. I came here on my own with it. It's all my fault! Blame me!" Sara began to fake cry when out of the corner of her eye she saw that her beakers, filled with neon green liquid, were poking out from under the tarp. She gave Molly a look, and she quickly covered it up without being noticed.

The FBI agent looked suspiciously at Sara, then at Burt and Molly, then at the goats and back to Sara. All just shrugged innocently. Finally, the agent put back on his mirrored sunglasses and tipped his hat. "You have a good day, Ma'am," he said and stalked out of the barn, followed by Agent Harris. Dales pulled a handkerchief out of his pocket and held it over his nose. "I know these vegans are up to no good," he muttered, disgusted.

Sara, Molly, and Burt stood in the driveway and waved as the FBI cruiser pulled off into the woods.

"Well I'll be," Burt said.

"Did those goats just not do what I think they just didn't do?" Molly asked Sara.

They all ran back to the barn to check. Though the smell did not cease, the goats milled around as usual, chewing feed and bumping into things.

"Time to find out for sure," Sara said. She slipped a mask over her head, which she'd sown with burlap to look like the one in *Texas Chainsaw Massacre*.

"Kraaaa!" She yelled and jumped in the air, fingers outstretched like claws. "Kraaaa!"

The goats skittered but didn't faint. Sara removed the mask and turned to Burt. "May I borrow your rifle?" she asked. "And all of your pots and pans?"

"Let's find out if this thing is for real," Molly said, catching Sara's drift.

Sara, Molly, and Burt raised holy hell in that barn. Gunfire, firecrackers, yelling, thrash metal music. They introduced more visceral fears as well: snakes, spiders, public speaking, getting canceled by Millennials on Twitter for writing something playfully racial ten years ago that is being willfully misunderstood, etc. As each new element failed to make the goats faint, Sara just stood there, shaking her head.

"So, they're cured?" Molly asked finally.

"I think so," Sara replied.

"Now what?" Burt asked.

"Now, more testing," Sara said. "The human kind." She gazed at Burt and Molly like they were a tray of pastries.

Burt looked down at the sloppy piles of excrement on the barn floor and winced. "Oh, hell. I just ate," he said.

CHAPTER 27

"YOU SHOULD GET some sleep," the nurse told Joshua, putting a hand on his shoulder. "You've been up all night."

The *kibbutz's* medical clinic, which was just a portable classroom with single beds, was packed with patients. The Maccabees had beaten a few of them to concussion; others had cuts from flying beer bottles. Among the patients was Gol, who had gotten beaten up pretty good after throwing the first beer bottle, and was nursing a swollen eye. On the final bed in the clinic lay Ruby, her head wrapped in gauze, an IV injected in her arm. The doctor had managed to get a pulse, but it was dangerously weak, so Alex sat bedside monitoring her breathing. Joshua worked with the doctor and nurses through the night; they taught him how to clean wounds, dispense waste safely, ice inflammations, and sigh deeply. And he did so without rest. Now he sat on the floor head bowed, wading in and out of consciousness but refusing to sleep.

"At least take a shower," the nurse pleaded, smelling the musk of Joshua's teenage B.O. "You've certainly earned it."

Joshua got up groggily and walked out of the clinic and towards the apartment. On the way there he saw that the kibbutz was still in shambles—broken beer bottles everywhere, tables overturned, clotheslines ripped down. Like a frat party gone awry, or like a regular frat party. One of Zev's sandals remained by the campfire, a reminder that he'd been taken. Joshua thought about his father, the pathetic look in his eyes, the ridiculous bulletproof vest. Even then Joshua could sense his father's narcissism. His arrival at the *kibbutz* wasn't about saving Joshua at all—it was about the optics of not having his son with him in Jerusalem. He was simply worried that it made him look bad. Well, fuck optics and fuck him, fuck everything his father thought he stood for while he was off cheating and lying.

Joshua entered the apartment. He looked at his bed longingly, but instead of collapsing there he went to Ruby's room and retrieved her toothbrush and a change of clothes for her. He was heading back to the clinic when right out his door blocking his path was a small, black goat. Joshua hadn't seen too many goats while he'd been in Israel and none on the *kibbutz*. But the goat strode right up to Joshua, stared him in the eyes and then bowed his head. Joshua scratched the goat behind the ears, and it nuzzled up. Then the goat turned and trotted away, rounding the corner of the apartment. Joshua followed but when he did the goat disappeared like it all had been a mirage. Joshua rubbed his eyes, wondering if lack of sleep was making him crazy. He walked back to the clinic and heard sobbing from inside. When he entered, Alex had his face in Ruby's lap and Gol and the two nurses and the doctor stood over him wearing sorrowful frowns.

"What happened?" Joshua asked.

Ruby's face was pale white and callow, her mouth slightly opened.

"She woke up," Alex cried. "She just woke up and looked right at me and said she felt better and wanted to take a bath . . . and then . . . and then . . . "

"They tried everything," Gol said.

Joshua thought he might scream. That Ruby, who was so full of life with her big smile and green hair, who had teased him about girls and danced with him barefoot around the fire only hours before was gone was too much to take in. His mind filled with thoughts of revenge. But not normal high school revenge like starting a rumor that your nemesis in the Student Council election has crabs. His mind filled with biblical type revenge, like how Exodus says, "Eye for eye, tooth for tooth," but then just keeps going with weirder things like, "hand for hand, foot for foot, burn for burn, wound for wound . . . " and then gets so violent that most people are like, "Woah, okay buddy, we got the point after the tooth thing, no need for the rest!"

"Zev was right," Joshua found himself saying. "They won't stop until there's war. Zev and Hanna were just a dry run. They'll call Ruby collateral damage. These men who include my own father want to rule the world. They're preparing even now, growing even now, getting their guns and missiles ready. We have to stop them. We have to spread the word of their lies and their murder. We have to fight. For Zev and Hannah, and for Ruby. Who will stop them if not us?"

Later that same day the men and women of the kibbutz gathered on the hillside to lay Ruby's body into the ground. Alex sobbed as he shoveled dirt over the coffin, and a woman sang the Mourner's *Kaddish*. It made Joshua think about his mother's funeral and his fateful meeting with the journalist Eric O'Malley. If Joshua hadn't sent him that text maybe none of this would have happened. He'd still be in New Jersey and Ruby would still be alive. He bit his inner cheek as punishment until he drew blood.

"The way you spoke at the clinic was inspiring." Gol put a hand on Joshua's shoulder.

"I was emotional. I'm sorry," Joshua replied.

"Never apologize for speaking from the heart. We need that here especially with Zev gone now. I'm afraid we're a bit directionless without him. You're right that we have to let the world know what happened here. Like you said, we can't let Ruby's death go unnoticed. And I need Hannah back with me."

"What if I delivered some kind of message? Did a video," Joshua suggested. "I once did a YouTube thing about the top ten Fortnite Hacks, and it got over a three hundred views. Do you think they'd listen to a kid?"

"You're more a man than you know," Gol said approving of the idea. "And like it or not you're a symbol of your mother's dream, a symbol of an end to violence. It's time for you to stand up for that. Like you said, who will stop them if not us?"

Joshua nodded and then just stared at the ground. Gol led him away from the funeral to a portable classroom at the edge of the *kibbutz*. Inside they had a video camera set up in front of a green screen, normally used for classes. Seeing it all ready to go was overwhelming.

"I need a minute," Joshua said, feeling anxiety rise in his chest. He rushed outside to breathe and there again standing before him was the black goat he'd seen that morning. He was relieved that it hadn't been a mirage. The goat bleated, waggled its head, and then trotted off again. "You're literally the goat," Joshua muttered. He took a deep breath and walked back into the classroom and nodded. "I'm ready."

Gol positioned the camera, and Joshua stared directly into the lens as the red light flicked on.

"Hi, my name is Joshua Schtinkler. You probably know me from my other YouTube video, Top Ten Fortnite Hacks. Anyway, my mother was Dr. Sara Schtinkler. And here's my story . . . "

CHAPTER 28

WHAT BETTER WAY to mark a successful Maccabee mission than a party full of middle-aged dudes binging shawarma? Sam hosted the celebration in his luxurious penthouse suite at The King David Hotel in Jerusalem. There was a keg of He-brew Beer, and an abundance of rugelach and yes, a working shawarma spit manned by a grill master named Whalid. He's available for bar mitzvahs, by the way. The men who'd raided the *kibbutz*, including Reuven, gobbled and slurped and told rollicking stories of their victory, and there was much great fanfare. Plus, they got their man: Zev the "self-hating Jew and terrorist betrayer with the ridiculous hair." He was tied to a chair, wrists bound behind his back with a bandana over his mouth. Next to him was Hannah Galud, still in Joshua's sweatshirt and similarly restrained. Beyond the obvious terror that had been caused to them, they also didn't get any of the shawarma, which Whalid thought was a crime onto itself.

Sam adopted his standard showmanship as he swaggered past Zev and Hannah and up to his wall of photographs. He X'd out the *kibbutz* in red, and then hovered his marker over the photo of Zev's face.

"How about we do this one in person?" he asked. He walked up to Zev, grabbed him by the hair and drew the red X on his forehead. The men in the room snickered and cheered. Sam capped the marker and threw it on the ground. "You know what these two miserable traitors were up to?" he asked the room. "Nothing less than treason. Nothing less than trying to destroy our means to defend ourselves against those who want us dead. Shame on you!" Sam grabbed Zev again by his curly hair. "Well we've got you now, hun. And thanks to The Maccabees you're not going to do a damn thing. Isn't that right?" Sam yanked Zev's hair so that he nodded. "Exactly. Glad we agree."

The men in the room hissed at the dejected prisoners, baring their teeth. One threw a rugelach at Hannah. Which, if you ask me is not how you should treat prisoners or pastries.

"Enjoy the refreshment, boys. This is just the beginning," he said and stepped back into the fray.

Pearl Jam's "Vitalogy" came on the stereo and everyone turned from the prisoners and began drinking and noshing and telling wild stories again. "Vitalogy" does that to testosterone fueled middle-aged men. In the bedroom there was a basketball game on TV, and a group of men gathered there to watch. It was a guy party after all. Reuven seemed to be the only one who found all this to be grotesque. He hadn't told anyone that his son was amongst those at the *kibbutz*. He was still too much in shock to see Joshua's face and the seething hatred towards him in his eyes. He was hurt by Joshua's refusal to join him and, yes, embarrassed that he could no longer control his fifteen-year-old son. He wasn't Darth Vader luring Luke to join him on the Dark Side, after all. He had a nice room in a hotel where they could swim in the pool and get room service. All Vader had was the ability to strangle people from afar. If Sam was telling the truth then Joshua was in the company of bad people with violent plans, and his son was surely being used. And though the *kibbutz* they'd raided appeared more like it was being used to plan a group sex romp than the weakening of Israel's military infrastructure, facts are facts. Reuven wondered if his son had already been involved in a group sex orgy, and he felt an odd pride rise up, but that turned quickly to disgust in himself as he remembered the words Joshua had said to him, "I never want to see you again!" Although, maybe that was because he was planning on having an orgy and who wants to see their dad during an orgy?

Reuven grabbed a couple of cans of seltzer from the buffet and walked over to the prisoners, Zev and Hannah. He pulled down the bandanas over their mouths and fed them some liquid.

"Thank you," Zev said.

"Shut up," Reuven replied. "I have no sympathy. You seem to be running some kind of anti-Semitic cult, and I wouldn't give a shit except that I know someone you've abducted."

"Yes. Joshua," Zev said. "Hannah told me, but I couldn't believe it."

"He's just engaging in some teenage rebellion," Reuven said. "But I want him out of trouble."

"He's a good man, your son."

"He's just a kid," Reuven glared at the guy. With his stupid curly hippie hair he looked like a total fuck-up to him, and a bad influence on his son for sure. "What kind of trouble have you gotten him in any way?"

"As long as terrorists like The Maccabees exist your son will not be safe," Zev said.

"We're terrorists?" Reuven snarled. "What about the nuclear facilities you were planning to bomb?"

"Lies," Zev said. "We disagree with what your organization has planned and aren't afraid to say it, so we are tied to chairs. You visited our dusty little *kibbutz*. We don't even have any guns. We barely have Wi-Fi."

"What about the plans he found on your phone?"

"Planted there by your fearless leader Sam Kanter. Google 'Nuclear plans for dummies,' and you'll find the same image. Even use 'I Feel Lucky.' But I see it tricked you all."

"Regardless," Reuven cut him off. Some of The Maccabees had noticed his conversation with the prisoner and were giving him looks. "Things could get pretty rough over here for you. Or they could be easier. But if you help me—"

"You think I can bring Joshua back to you? You're dumber than you look."

One of the men called out to Reuven, "Hey, One-Punch, you buddying up with the enemy?"

Reuven forced a smile. "Just wanting to see what kind of piece of shit we're dealing with. I'm happy to report that he's a real piece of shit." Reuven put the bandana back over Zev's mouth roughly but whispered in his ear. "You help me get my son back and I help get you out of here. Deal?"

Zev nodded. Reuven strolled back to the guys. They handed him a beer. There was a rumble in the bedroom and Reuven assumed the basketball game had gone into overtime.

"Hey, Reuv, get in here," Sam called from his bedroom.

"Let me guess, OT?" Reuven asked.

He walked into the bedroom and all the men turned to him with strange glares. Reuven looked at the TV set, and to his disbelief Joshua was on the news. He looked so much older that Reuven almost didn't recognize him as his own. The newscaster explained that a video had been released on YouTube from the son of Dr. Sara Schtinkler, who was living on a *kibbutz* in Israel. She cued the clip.

"Hi, my name is Joshua Schtinkler. You probably know me from my other YouTube video, Top Ten Fortnite Hacks. Anyway, my mother was Dr. Sara Schtinkler. And here's my story . . . "

The volume was turned up, and the room watched Joshua's full statement as he named The Maccabees as a radical Jewish group bent on violence and power. He accused them of murdering one of the women on the *kibbutz* he was staying at, Ruby Gall, and kidnapping two others, Zev and Hannah. He accused them of preparing for a global war if the cure didn't work at the end of the three months. Joshua said that he knew it was true because his own father was one of them, and he had been since before the move to Israel. Reuven could feel the men around him step away from his side.

One of the men sneered, not shielding his disgust. "You raised a real talker, huh?"

"Those are some pretty serious accusations he's leveling. Whoever these Maccabees are could sue."

"Yeah, he's going to have to learn to shut his trap or someone's gonna teach him," another said.

Reuven turned to the guy who said that and grabbed his shirt. "The only lesson that's going to be taught here is the lesson of you shutting up!" Reuven felt like he was getting better at making dramatic one-liners.

Joshua went on. He pulled out documents that showed The Maccabees' plans to attack specific ports that would collapse the world's food supply. Sam reddened as Joshua went on, and he raced out of the room in a rage. He grabbed Zev by the hair and yanked. "How the fuck did you get hold of those documents? Tell me now or I swear to God!" He threw Zev fell to the floor and he landed on his face. Hannah screamed though her bandana.

"Tell me." Sam pulled back Zev's bandana. "The documents."

"I hacked your email," Zev said, with grin. "What kind of idiot still uses 'password' as their password?"

"Kill him, Sam. He's scum!" the men called out.

Sam kicked Zev in the stomach again and again until Reuven rushed forward to hold him back.

"Enough," Reuven said. "We might need him to rebuke on camera. He can explain that he drugged my son. That he invented all this to get back at me."

"Bullshit," Zev said.

Sam pulled Zev up off the ground, put the bandana back over his mouth.

"You're right," Sam said to Reuven, cooling down. "We need to issue a counter-statement. But it can't be from this dumb fuck. Your kid, your fucking clean-up, Reuven. Hope you're ready for your close-up."

They set it up like a post-game press conference. Three mics on a long table, an Israeli flag set prominently in the background. Reuven sat next to Rabinsky, who looked calm and suave as ever, and Sam, who would ostensibly represent The Maccabees' American contingent. To say that Reuven was nervous for his live television debut would be like saying Noah Ark was in preparation for a light drizzle. The makeup artist complained that he'd sweat off the base she applied twice, and so she had to use a special numbing spray to close his pores. Reuven tried nasal breathing to calm himself, but his pulse raced.

"Ready?" the cameraman asked.

"I was born ready!" But then to himself Reuven thought, "Just not for this."

When the lights came on and the camera pointed his way, Reuven was worried he might faint and then people might think he wasn't even a real Jew, on international television nonetheless. What would his Hebrew School teacher say?! But there was a teleprompter set up so all he had to do was read the words.

"Just focus on your son," Rabinsky said, leaning in. "You want him safe, right?"

"Got it." Reuven understood the veiled threat as well, which is something Reuven had been getting a lot better at understanding. He swallowed hard, focused on an image of his son's quickly maturing face, and gave the thumbs up. A red light appeared atop the camera and it was go-time.

"Hello, my name is Reuven Schtinkler. I am the husband of the late Dr. Sara Schtinkler. We were married for eighteen wonderful years." His voice was squeaky but at least something came out, so he continued. "I am also the proud father of Joshua Schtinkler, who has been taken captive by an anti-Jewish cult located in the Negev desert.

I'm afraid that Joshua has been emotionally vulnerable since his mother's death at the hands of a group of American neo-Nazis, and so provided an easy target for the predators of this cult. But I'm not here to speak of that group or their crimes. I want to talk to you directly, Joshua. Most of all I want to apologize. Since your mother's death I've acted in ways that I'm not proud of. I was stern with you when I should have been caring. I was controlling when I should have given you space. I was very sad after your mom died, Joshua, and I was scared that I might lose you too. So please, if you see this, forgive me, Son. And come home to me. I promise that I will be more understanding, more patient, and that I will give you the space you need. Family should be together. I'm your father. And your father loves you very much."

Reuven hadn't written the words he spoke, but they affected him deeply enough that real tears rolled down his cheeks. Reuven wanted to find out who wrote it. Maybe they could help him with his holiday cards. Rabinsky, impressed by Reuven's show of waterworks, lay a sympathetic hand on Reuven's shoulder.

"You have our best wishes, Reuven, and we all look forward to Joshua coming home to you soon," Rabinsky said, then he turned to the camera. "As an elected representative of the Jewish People here in Jerusalem, I'd like to also directly address some of the allegations that Reuven's son has been made to level against his own people by the anti-Jewish cult that has abducted him. To clear up the first misnomer, there is no such thing as an organization called The Maccabees who go around beating people up. It's actually an old anti-Semitic trope that goes back centuries. The Maccabees don't exist and never existed in the modern world. My people want a healthy world, and we want peace. We've gathered here in Israel in good faith to help heal the world of myotonia congenita, and so we would hope that the world would give us the benefit of the doubt and not pay attention to the outrageous lies being spread on YouTube by a bunch of radicals." Rabinsky smiled broadly, even chuckled a bit, like he was glad he'd finally cleared up that silliness, and now the adults could get back to reality. "If anything, it's us Jews who might be concerned. After all we know our history. Most times we've been gathered up it doesn't end well for us, am I right? My grandfather, who survived Buchenwald, can attest." Rabinsky turned to Reuven and Sam for assurance, and they both understood to return meaningful nods. "So actually, we find ourselves in a defensive posture. In the Bible, the Pharaoh of Egypt released Jewish slaves only after a series of divine plagues tormented them. But let us not forget that the Pharaoh changed his mind and sent his soldiers to enslave the Jews once again even after the agreement was made to free them, and the Jews were only saved by the parting of the Red Sea at God's behest. We Jewish people pray that God will protect us from those who wish to enslave us, but we cannot rely on divine intervention alone. We've uncovered evidence that the very anti-Jewish cult that claims there is a Jewish conspiracy to rule the world, the same one that kidnapped Joshua Schtinkler, is planning a series of malicious attacks within our borders. Their goal is to weaken our military infrastructure in order to help our enemies destroy us. If this turns out to be true then we are entitled to self-defense, and we ask that the world allow us to deal with our own domestic affairs without meddling. God willing, we will remain safe so that you can continue to heal from this terrible fainting plague once and for all. We all want the same thing: an end to myotonia congenita, and a return to normalcy for the entire world. Thank you."

Rabinsky nodded to Sam, who leaned into his microphone.

"Thank you," Sam said. "We will be holding weekly press conferences as things progress. We all pray that it does quickly and peacefully."

The cameraman called cut. Rabinsky and Sam stood

up and shook hands and had a quick word before Rabinsky was escorted out of the room. Reuven was a bit shell-shocked by the whole thing.

"Nicely done." Sam walked over to Reuven and put a hand on his shoulder. "Rabinsky's really happy with how that went."

"Glad to hear it," Reuven said, but then he leaned in close to Sam. "Do you want to tell me why Rabinsky sounded more like a General heading into war than someone interested in correcting some wayward *kibbutz*?"

"I didn't see it that way."

"What exactly is going on here, Sam?" Reuven asked. "I did what was asked of me. I deserve to know."

Sam sighed, then led Reuven to the corner of the room where they couldn't be heard. "I'm going to tell you, but I want you to know that this is top secret stuff," Sam said, and Reuven nodded. "You were right about the *kibbutz*. Most of the people there are just Socialist kids with some stupid ideas. You know, kids who couldn't get into Peace Corps and then were rejected by Teach for America, and then were turned down by Smoke Weed with Exotic Locals Corps. Except for one." Sam unfolded a piece of paper with a photo on it. It was a dopey looking man with a ponytail and scruff. Reuven vaguely remembered that he'd been the idiot who threw the beer bottle during the raid. "Name's Gol Chametz. He's ex-Mossad. He was stationed out in Jordan for four years back in the nineties and rose up through the ranks there. He's one of only a few intelligence officers still alive who knows the location of a secret missile site that went dark decades ago."

"So, he knows of an old military base outside the country. So what?"

"It's a nuclear site, Reuven. And it could be used against us," Sam said. "We intercepted a cell phone call from the *kibbutz* today. He's planning a trip over the border, and we suspect he's headed to the site. We are set to apprehend him immediately."

"You're going back to the *kibbutz*?"

"I know that this is hard for you to hear but there are people at that *kibbutz* who simply don't value Jewish life, and your son has found himself in their company. Sometimes to beat these guys you have to take an offensive posture. I know that you understand that, Reuven. You're one of our great warriors."

CHAPTER 29

THE SON OF one of the Maccabees' "great warriors" stood in a classroom on the *kibbutz* surrounded by wide-eyed children following his every move. Joshua had a puppet on each hand; a frog wearing a crown and a bear with a bowtie and a jester hat. "And that's when Mr. Bear realized that he could help the Frog Queen up the tree to be with her family," Joshua said. "Oh, thank you, Mr. Bear, all the frogs of my family are so happy to see me again—Croak! And everyone wants to—Croak!—know how we can help you.' So, the Bear said, 'Grrrowl! Well if you can reach some of that honey, I am awfully— Grrrowl!—hungry.' So, the Frog Queen said, 'Ribbit-ribbit—Croak!' and all of her frog followers helped Mr. Bear reach the honey, and everyone got fat and lived happily ever after. And now you say—"

"*Ze* End!" the children yelled in their adorable mix of accents. They all jumped around and yelled, "Ribbit! Ribbit—Croak!" and tried to imitate Joshua's American accent.

Gol entered the classroom as the kids ran off for recess. "Who knew you were the Jewish Frank Oz?" he said.

"Frank Oz was Jewish."

"The even more Jewish Frank Oz."

"I'm an only child. You develop certain talents," Joshua replied.

"Maybe in your next video you should use the puppets?" Gol smiled, but then his eyes got serious. "Listen

Joshua, there's someone here to speak with you. He's a friend of the *kibbutz*."

"I've got a few minutes," Joshua said.

Joshua followed Gol outside and a man with curly black hair and big hazel eyes waited. He wore dusty army fatigues and a *kafiya* around his neck as if he'd just made a long trek through the desert, or was a sophomore at Brown.

"I am Elon," the man said, extending his hand to Joshua. "Zev is my brother. He told me about you before he was taken. He said that you are brave. These men have confirmed it."

"Do you know where Zev is? And Hannah?" Joshua asked.

"They're in a place that cannot be infiltrated. But we have friends on the inside. They are safe for now. Zev sent an urgent message. He said that I must get you out of here immediately."

"Me?" Joshua asked. "Why?"

"Your video message made an impact. You have brought up many emotions, opened the world's eyes to what might happen if Jewish power goes unchecked. I worry that the men who came for Zev and Hanna will come for you too."

"Then let them come," Joshua said. "I won't go with them. I won't leave."

The man pulled out his phone and showed Joshua the video of his sweaty father urging Joshua to come to him, and then Rabinsky speaking of snuffing out the enemy and them being slaves chased to the Red Sea by the Egyptians.

"You are dangerous to them now, Joshua. You've sparked a movement, and like it or not you're the symbol of that movement. They already have your father. And Zev says they will stop at nothing to get you too."

"Where would we go?" Joshua asked.

Elon was about to explain when the guard from the front gate came sprinting over the hill. "Vans are coming!" he yelled. "Take cover!"

Parents ran their children back into their apartments, grabbing their dogs along the way too. A shriek came from the gate and then the sound of gunfire as people scattered in every direction. A black van roared onto the dirt road and crashed into a parked car.

"We must go now!" Elon said to Joshua and Gol. The three of them ran towards a dusty military Jeep and jumped in.

The door to the black van swung open and a soldier in SWAT gear jumped out and raised his gun. Joshua crouched down, hands over ears as machine gunfire pinged around him. Elon gunned the Jeep forward.

"He's hit," Elon said, and Joshua saw that Gol slumped forward in his seat, his shirt soaked in blood. In the rearview mirror, the SWAT soldier ran towards them, gun raised. "Hold on!" Elon yelled and slammed on the gas.

The Jeep lurched ahead and cut to the right off the road and down a rocky hill as bullets flew past. Joshua nearly flew out of his seat as they raced down the hillside past where Ruby was buried and towards the back fence. Joshua wondered how they could get out when a man waved the Jeep forward and pulled back a hidden part of the fence under an acacia tree. The Jeep rushed through and the man closed the fence quickly behind them. Joshua could hear gunfire from the kibbutz behind them, but no vehicle followed as far as he could tell. Elon stopped the Jeep and tended to Gol.

"Stay with me," Elon said, ripping his shirt to create a tourniquet for Gol's bleeding stomach.

"Go to Tel Sheva," Gol muttered. "My uncle is a mechanic. He will hide us." Elon handed Joshua a canteen, and Joshua poured water into Gol's mouth, but it mostly dribbled out on his chest. "Go now," Gol said, and then he lost the strength to speak.

Elon pulled onto a dirt road that led deeper into the desert. They drove in silence for a while, and Joshua tried to keep Gol hydrated as he winced in pain. There were Jolly

Ranchers in the glove compartment, and Joshua encouraged Gol to have one.

"Ugh, watermelon? Are you trying to kill me?"

"It's my favorite kind."

Gol's skin turned a shade of jaundice yellow, and Joshua wondered what Jolly Rancher flavor that might be, but feared for the worst, "Sour Apple."

Finally, a small town appeared in the distance with a few dusty buildings and a row of trading posts. Elon found the mechanic's shop at the edge of town and turned the Jeep into the garage. An old man playing sudoku stood up when he saw the Jeep, and quickly closed the garage door behind them. It was dark and cool inside. The old man looked at Gol, with his blood-soaked shirt and clammy skin, and his eyes widened. He rushed off and brought a young woman with sharp features and glasses, along with two other young men.

"When was he shot?" the woman asked.

"It's been over an hour," Joshua said. "I tried to keep him hydrated."

She looked at Gol's wound, annoyed almost by the severity. "Bring him inside," she told the two men. Carefully, they carried Gol away and the woman followed.

"My granddaughter is a doctor," the old man said to Joshua and Elon with a hint of pride. Then he turned away and walked inside with his sudoku, turning off the lights in the garage as he did. Joshua and Elon sat in darkness.

"Now what?" Joshua asked.

"Now we wait," Elon said. "When it's dark we can drive across the border."

"Is that legal?"

"We have friends who will let us through," Elon said. "For now, we rest."

Elon closed his eyes and pulled back his seat. In seconds he was snoring softly. Joshua sat in stunned silence wondering how he'd even gotten into this mess and how he might get out. He also wondered if the old man had an extra sudoku he could do? He'd also need a pencil since he didn't have one of those either.

When it was finally night, Elon opened the garage door and drove the Jeep out into the street and then quickly out of town. Dark roads snaked past other small towns and military checkpoints, which Elon avoided, always seeming to know an alternative route. He was like a Human Jewish GPS. Joshua faded in and out of sleep until a light emerged in the distance. It was a small security checkpoint with an army Jeep parked next to a flagpole with an Israeli flag. Beyond the small portable building was a tall electrified fence with barbed wire. Joshua's pulse pounded when a soldier with a rifle slung over his shoulder walked out of the hut and towards them, but Elon rolled the car forward towards him.

"You have only a few minutes," the soldier spoke to Elon in low tones. "The cameras and alarms are down but you must hurry. Leave the car behind the dumpsters just beyond the gate. There's transportation they cannot detect waiting for you. Hurry. And good luck, brother."

The soldier walked back to his hut, and the gate opened slowly. As the Jeep rolled forward Joshua noticed three other soldiers inside sleeping in chairs, vodka bottles littered at their feet. Joshua had seen this sort of thing in a movie, and he couldn't believe it really worked. Elon drove slowly past the gate, which closed silently behind them. An unlit path led to a series of dumpsters, and next to one of them was a camel wearing a tasseled leather saddle.

"Our undetectable transportation," Elon said to Joshua as he parked the Jeep.

They rode the camel for hours along a windy path through abandoned towns, passing ancient mosques and empty homes. Joshua sat back-saddle, and his groin was punished by the sudden movements until he wished they could be in a slightly more detectable and slightly less groin-punishing mode of transit. In the moonlight he saw rabbits, sand rats, foxes, and even a family of gazelle roaming around. Without human occupants the hunt for food was more challenging for the animals, and screeches and low growls could be heard as predators stalked prey. Elon led the camel off the road and after another hour of riding Joshua spotted a tent next to a hillside lit by a single candle. It was the first flicker of light he'd seen in a while.

"We're here," Elon said.

"Where?" Joshua asked.

The camel rode forward, then Elon jumped off and tied the camel to a wooden pole next to the tent. He helped Joshua down and his legs teetered. Inside, three men in robes and turbans sat on a carpet surrounding a Moroccan lantern. One of the men was older and had a leathery face and kind eyes. He spoke to Elon in Arabic.

"Give them your clothes," Elon said to Joshua, as he started to undress.

"Why exactly?"

"Because they're horny for teenage clothes. Kidding, it's a precaution. If drones followed us here, they will follow the camel back to the border. They will think it was just an excursion gone wrong."

Joshua got undressed and handed over his t-shirt, jeans, and sneakers, and one of the men handed Joshua his robe and sandals. Once switched, the two younger men walked out of the hut, mounted the camel and rode off.

The old man in the turban stood up and rolled back the carpet that he had been sitting on. He felt around on the dirt floor and then dug up a lever, which he pulled, revealing a secret door that led into a dark tunnel below. The man smiled at Joshua.

"Go, go," he said.

Elon climbed down onto a metal ladder and Joshua followed. The ladder descended into cold darkness, and Joshua felt a jolt of panic as the lid closed above his head.

"What is this place?" Joshua asked.

"I will explain everything. For now you'll have to trust me."

They climbed to the bottom where they found themselves in dark pit with walls that were wet and slimy, which is the worst kind of wall. The floor jolted and began to descend below their feet, making Joshua whimper in fear. He thought about how alone he was, how no one even knew where he was or what had happened to him, or how he happened to be wearing a Bedouin robe. He didn't even know Elon. He thought about his mother, how even in her grave she might be worried about his whereabouts. What an idiot he'd been. What a naïve child! He thought about Brie and tried to be strong. He would need her to get through this. When the floor finally settled, a door directly in front of them opened and Joshua was blinded by fluorescent light. When his eyes adjusted what he saw beyond the doors made him question his sanity. It was a massive, brightly lit warehouse with poured concrete floors, white walls, and modern metal staircases. Along the sides of the warehouse a few men in lab coats and clipboards milled around next to a dozen or so school-bus-sized missiles all shiny, sleek, and gray.

"What is this place?" Joshua asked.

"When Jordan made peace with Israel back in 1994, they concocted a plan," Elon said. "If the Arab states attacked Israel's nuclear capabilities, Israel would have the option of a proxy nuclear attack. Jordan agreed to house that proxy for a price. When diplomatic relations collapsed years later, the Jordanians took control of the site and then moved it to a location unknown to the Israelis. This is that proxy."

"We're at a nuclear launch site?"

"Once the fainting pandemic hit, no fainter could be closer than a mile from this place, or they would freeze up. It was too stressful. So a few Jordanian Jews, mostly scientists, have kept it going," Elon said. "Israel has a nuclear option. They can end the world with the turn of a few keys and some coordinates—billions of people dead. This place may be the last stand against that."

“And that last stand means dropping a nuclear bomb on Israel?”

“We must show them that we have no intention of firing, but if they decide to launch missiles at the world, we can retaliate. And that is the reason why I brought you here, Joshua. You need to be the one in front of the launch panel for the world to see, with your hand on the keys.”

“I’m not even old enough to have my hand on car keys,” Joshua said.

“I’m sorry you’ve been put in this position. Your father’s TV speech gave us no choice. But you made yourself a leader. Someone who represents your mother’s work. This is a terrible responsibility, but it must fall into your hands,” Elon said. “In the command center we have a scrambled internet site. You will be able to communicate by video conference with the commander at Israeli’s nuclear site and not be traced. If nothing happens then you will relax here for a while, read books in the air condition. We even have Xbox.”

Joshua had always wanted an Xbox, but he didn’t like that finally getting one came with the responsibility of launching nukes. Wasn’t that always the way?

CHAPTER 30

SARA PACED NERVOUSLY outside the farmhouse while all hell broke loose inside. Burt and Molly had agreed to be the first human test cases of Sara's vaccine because there was literally no one else around. She needed both a male and female specimen to make sure that the vaccine didn't act differently across genders. So now Sara wrung her hands and fretted over what she'd done to her hosts; the very people who'd saved her life! Meanwhile, Burt and Molly took turns vomiting and experiencing explosive diarrhea inside. The noises emanating might be heard in the restroom after a chili eating contest or at a vomitorium in ancient Rome after an ancient Roman chili eating contest. Burt and Molly ran in and out of the bathroom, faces green and clammy, liquid racing out from both ends of their bodies.

"Stay hydrated!" Sara shouted from outside. "Keep drinking water."

"Why drink water if it's just going to shoot out the other side?" Burt asked.

"Just try," Sara said, "Oh, and please don't flush. I need the samples."

The goats had been steady since their injection of Sara's neon green formula. After their initial fits of vomit and diarrhea, they'd been lethargic, but had gained strength and even appetite hour after hour. Even more importantly they'd stopped fainting entirely; a scientific breakthrough that Sara had been working towards for over nine years. Still, the world would all but ignore a vaccine for myotonia congenita unless it could be used on human beings and not just goats. "Not cool," Sara thought.

When Molly and Burt finally emerged from their respective bathrooms, both looking pale and weak, they didn't expect to walk right into the business end of a rifle.

"Die now, SCUM!" Sara yelled through the burlap of her Chainsaw Massacre mask.

She shot the rifle inches above Burt and Molly's heads, and the couple reeled back in fear. Burt shielded Molly and whispered, "I'll see you in heaven, Sweetheart." They crouched together on the ground, shaking and crying. But neither of them fainted. They did lose control of their bowels just a little bit, but no fainting.

"It's okay guys. It's just me!" Sara pulled off her mask, smiling widely.

Burt and Molly looked up in horror, wondering if this woman had truly gone insane or was just a terrifying sadist. Sara put the mask back on and pointed the gun again and shot, this time even closer to the nice couple's heads. They flinched again but showed no myotonic reaction.

"Oh my God," Molly said, finally realizing what was happening.

"Well I'll be," Burt repeated. "I definitely just soiled myself again, but it may have been worth it."

And with that, and for the first time in many months, Molly and Burt peeled off their soft helmets and tossed them onto the ground.

"You're the G.O.A.T.," Molly said to Sara.

"Nope," replied Sara. "You're the G.O.A.T.."

Sara spent the rest of the day in her makeshift lab tweaking the chemical composition in her formula. She dialed back a few unnecessary components, added others, experimented on whether she could remove the diuretic to make that side effect less unpleasant (she could not). She wondered how well she could preserve and ship this strange neon green liquid and then mass-produce it for billions of people around the world. She kept her eyes peeled on Burt and Molly and the goats, whose vomiting and diarrhea had ebbed completely, and whose appetites returned quickly to normal. Sara stayed up all night breaking down the compounds again and again, distilling and refining the vaccine until it was scientifically bulletproof. When dawn broke, Sara heard Molly and Burt making coffee. The fact that they could even think of drinking coffee was a good sign onto itself.

"Meet your maker!" she yelled, a rifle leveled at their heads.

"Stop it, Sara, stop!" Molly pleaded. "I need this coffee."

"We're healed," Burt said. "I even cut my finger peeling an apple this morning and I didn't even feel woozy."

Sara pulled out a notepad and marked down the time and "No myotonic reaction." Not for Burt and Molly and not for the goats who Sara had tortured with firecrackers and yelling.

"Let's have breakfast and talk," Molly said. "I put on flapjacks."

And so, the three of them sat down for breakfast. Sara, who was just as ravenous as Molly and Burt, ate a full mini-stack and a heap of bacon fit for a trucker. Molly complained that she's never consumed so much food, and wandered off to the den to lie down. "Why did I have that extra pancake?"

"Because you made 'em so delicious, and you expelled the entire content of your stomach lining?"

Burt kept eating. "So, what now?" he asked Sara.

Sara thought for a moment. "Well, if I can observe you both for say three to four weeks then I think we can go to the government with an initial report," Sara said, dipping her bacon into the maple syrup. "Then the government will start four stages of clinical trials, which takes ten months to a year at the very minimum."

"A year?" Burt said. "Can't go any faster than that?"

"Too many variables," Sara said. "The FDA requires testing on at least twelve hundred people before you move to vaccine development. Science doesn't like to be rushed."

"Well, then I guess the world will have to wait then."

"Shhhh!" Molly said from the den. "Quick, better get in here."

Burt and Sara entered the den as Molly raised the volume on the TV. There was an urgent update from Israel, and Sara was stunned to see footage of her son, Joshua, on screen. He sat calmly looking at the camera, as handsome a young man as she'd ever seen. "Hi, my name is Joshua Schtinkler. You probably know me from my other YouTube video, Top Ten Fortnite Hacks. Anyway, my mother was Dr. Sara Schtinkler. And here's my story . . . "

"My Joshua!" Sara gasped, eyes welling with tears.

She watched spellbound as Joshua spoke of her death, of his father's connection to a violent Jewish organization called The Maccabees, and of their nefarious plan to take over the world. When Joshua was done the newscaster cut in to say that a counter-statement had been made by the Jewish representative Dr. Jacob Rabinsky, and Joshua's own father, Reuven Schtinkler. Sara winced at the sight of Reuven with his sweaty face and square head.

"That's my knucklehead husband if you can believe that," Sara said.

"That man is in serious need of a beta blocker," Molly commented.

Reuven's quavering voice spoke directly to the camera as he urged his son to come back to him. "Family should be together. I'm your father. And your father loves you very much."

"You lost him already, you fool!" Sara yelled at the television.

When Reuven was done, and the camera panned to Rabinsky, Sara felt a chill down her spine, which intensified as she listened to the man's veiled threats and references to ancient Egypt and the parting of the Red Sea.

"I know fascism when I hear it," Burt commented. "All that talk of self-defense and national security and Bible talk. That's what someone says before they're about to stab you in the balls."

"Burt!" Molly gave him a slap for language.

The newscaster shuffled her papers and looked thoughtfully at the camera. "Given Israel's full nuclear arsenal, Global Leaders worry what Israel might do if they deem the threat of an attack. It could mean global annihilation," she said. "And now with local sports, it's our own Scottie Dugout!"

Molly flipped off the TV. "Maybe you can find a way to speed up that clinical testing you were jabbering on about?"

CHAPTER 31

WHAT KIND OF callous buffoon could sleep at a time like this? Sara's callous buffoon. In his Jerusalem hotel room Reuven snored loudly, submerged in an erotic dream involving Natalie Portman, when there was a knock at the door. It was pitch black outside so Reuven just put a pillow over his head, but the knocking persisted. He looked at the clock— not even three in the morning.

"You better be Natalie Portman," Reuven grumbled as he stumbled out of bed towards the door. He squinted through the peephole and saw Sam and two guards in the hallway.

"Jesus Sam," Reuven groaned as he opened the door. "Couldn't it wait?"

"Afraid, not, Bud," Sam said. "Seems we have a real problem on our hands."

Sam entered, leaving the guards outside the room. Reuven turned the light on in the kitchenette and Sam spilled a file out of black and white photos onto the table. One was the face of a man with curly black hair, army fatigues and a *kafiya*.

"A Brown graduate?" Reuven asked.

"This is Elon Chamle," Sam replied. "He's the brother of Zev Chamle, our prisoner number two. He's connected to all sorts of bad shit. Like really bad."

Reuven rolled his eyes. If Sam wanted to pitch another Maccabee infiltration couldn't it wait until morning? Then

Sam flipped to the next photo. Three men, one of them the ponytailed guy named Gol, the other Elon, drove along a desert road in a Jeep. It took Reuven rubbing his eyes repeatedly to see that the third man in the photo was Joshua.

"This was just outside the Tel Sheva, a little town near the *kibbutz*. We sent vans last night, but they escaped. Arial footage suggests Gol was dropped off, and the other two, Elon Chamle and your son Joshua, got across the Jordanian border."

"They left Israel? How is that even possible?" Reuven asked, surprised to learn that Jordan bordered Israel.

"A border guard flipped. We've apprehended him but he's not talking yet."

"Well, where the hell are they going?" Reuven asked.

Sam walked to the windows and looked suspiciously through the blinds before tightening them. "Our theory is they're headed to the proxy nuclear launching site."

"Jesus Christ."

"We think they brought Joshua as a kind of symbol for the resistance. The world will be more sympathetic if it's the son of Sara Schtinkler with his hands on the nuclear launch keys."

"He's not even old enough to have his hands on car keys," Reuven said in disbelief.

"A teenager whose father is a voice for Jewish strength and whose mother is a symbol for the end of myotonia congenita. It checks out."

"You think my son Joshua is going to drop a nuclear bomb on the Jews? He loves Jews, especially his 8th grade religious school teacher. We kept getting notes that he had boners in her class."

"How mad at you is he, do you think? Scale from one to ten."

"Uh . . . eight?"

"We must act now," Sam said.

"And what exactly does that look like?" Reuven asked.

"We're hoping you can talk him back down to earth. Get him to reveal his location."

"And if I can't?"

"That wouldn't be ideal," Sam said, and in his head imagined that "ideal" was the world not exploding in a ball of flames.

"You're talking about the end of the world?" Reuven asked.

"Only if you fail."

CHAPTER 32

TEARS STREAMED DOWN Sara's face as she hugged the goats goodbye. Burt and Molly were already in the RV, antsy to get going.

"Time is not on our side," Burt called out the window, honking for emphasis.

"I said I'm coming!" Sara called back, sniffling.

She laid out some extra food for the goats and then lifted her tray filled with neon green-hued beakers along with stool and vomit samples from Burt, Molly, and the goats. A full two days after her subjects had been vaccinated not one had experienced a myotonic spell or any other physical symptoms that she could observe. Sara did notice that Molly had been a bit vocal, playfully nagging Burt more than usual, and in uncharacteristic ways. For instance, Molly wondered aloud why Burt never finished his college degree and when he was finally going to finally fix the showerhead like he said he would ages ago. "My mother always told me to either marry a man who can fix it or who can pay for it to get fixed." Molly grinned.

"Your mother never said anything like that!" Burt responded. "*Gevalt* with you, woman," he muttered.

"What did you just say, Burt?" Sara had asked.

"I said her mother never said such a thing."

"No, after that. You said, '*Gevalt*.'"

"Did I?"

Sara continued to observe small changes in behavior, nothing dramatic, but little things. Burt, who could eat a horse and not even burp said he felt queasy after drinking a single glass of milk. "Dairy doesn't agree with me," he said in a voice that was more nasal than usual. Sara might have diagnosed a deviated septum. "You know what I'm craving?" Burt added. "Seltzer!"

"Ooh, and a tuna salad sandwich on toasted rye!" Molly added.

"Sour pickle and brown mustard. No mayo."

"Never mayo!" Molly gasped like it was anathema even to mention, and yet she had used mayo in almost every meal that Sara had eaten at their farmhouse up to that point.

Sara marked down the unusual behavior as merely the effects of dehydration from all of the vomiting. They simply craved seltzer because they needed water. And tuna had so many vitamins that could rebuild strength. But lactose intolerance? The goats also acted a little off, more scholarly, which is not easy for a goat to do. It was all behavior that Sara would have to account for in her write up, but now as she loaded into the RV with her tray of samples and vaccines, she had to file it away for later.

"Did you remember to kiss the goats goodbye for the umpteenth time?" Burt asked, oozing sarcasm. "I mean what's the deal with that?"

"Ha! Burt, you're such a kidder!" Molly laughed. "My sides hurt."

Back on the road Burt put on the radio but flipped it away from the country station. When he found 90's Hip-Hop, he left it there.

"Tribe Called Quest, now there's a band I can listen to. They say Fife Dawg had a Jewish uncle. Shame about his diabetes."

Burt and Molly bopped to "Buggin' Out," and turned the volume to ten. But just as they made it onto a stretch of open road a police car trailed the RV and flashed its lights on.

"Oh, for heaven's sakes," Molly said, putting back on her soft helmet. "It's the po-po."

"Fuck da police," Burt chuckled.

Sara covered her samples with a jacket as Burt pulled to the side of the road. He lowered the music but not all the way. The officer got out of his cruiser and strode up to the RV at the very moment KRS-1's, "Sound of da Police" played on the radio. Molly quickly shut it off.

"There a problem, Officer?" Burt asked the cop.

"License and registration," the officer said.

"Don't shoot, it's just a wallet," Burt joked and handed over the documents.

The officer looked over his license skeptically, then peeked into the RV, first at Molly and then at Sara in the back, who smiled and waved.

"Where you folks headed today?" the officer asked.

"Oh, just to get some plywood. The gate's rotted through, I'm afraid."

"You drove the RV just to make a hardware trip?"

"Truck's on the fritz," Burt explained.

But just as Burt spoke the officer caught a whiff of the stool samples Sara was hiding in the back. When the officer gagged, Burt shrugged. "Wish I hadn't had that bean burrito for breakfast." He winked.

"I'm going to need you all to step out of the vehicle," the officer said.

Burt and Molly pulled off their seatbelts. Sara covered the tray of samples, but as she exited the RV, she slid a syringe full of vaccine into her pocket. Molly caught a glimpse of what Sara was up to and her eyes nearly popped out of her head. "Are you crazy?" she whispered. Sara just put a finger to her lips.

Molly, Burt, and Sara stood outside the van, arms crossed as the officer paced before them. "Reason I stopped you is there've been some reports of non-fainters around here. Hiding in the woods. Y'all haven't seen any of 'em have you?"

"What on earth do you mean, Officer?"

"Jews? You seen any Jews lately?" he stopped in front

of Sara, looked her up and down, settling on her mass of curly copper hair. “ID, ma’am?”

“That’s Annalee. Our niece from Calgary,” Molly said.

“I didn’t bring my purse,” Sara said.

“That’s a violation right there,” the officer said, annoyed. He turned to Burt. “Don’t mind if I take a quick look inside the RV, do you?”

“No thanks?” Burt replied.

The officer ignored him. He stepped into the RV, sniffed the foul smell and traced it to the jacket that covered Sara’s samples and the beakers filled with vaccine. One of the bad parts of being a cop is smelling out gross stuff. He grabbed his walkie talkie. “Precinct, this is Officer D. McCoy. You know that scientist you’ve been looking for? I might have stumbled on her. Over.”

The officer was placing his walkie back into the holster when he heard Molly yell, “Now!” and something sharp entered his buttock. The officer turned and saw Sara standing there with an empty needle in her hand. He looked at her like she was insane and went for his gun, but a wave of fluids exited his body before he could. The officer stumbled out of the RV and vomited onto the road. Then an even more vile look came on his face as he lost control of his bowels. “You put a Jew curse on me!?” he asked Sara.

“I’m really sorry,” Sara said, hands raised.

As the officer continued to vomit, Burt unclipped his holster and relieved the cop of his gun, walkie, and car keys. “Relax,” he said to the cop. “You’ll never faint again.”

“You won’t get away with this!” the officer yelled between heaves.

“Probably right about that,” Molly said. “But gosh darn if we’re not going to try.”

Burt hurled the officers’ walkie talkie and car keys deep into the forest by the side of the road and pocketed the gun as he jumped back into the RV. Sara and Molly hopped into their seats too.

“How long do we have?” Molly asked.

"He'll be nursing the side effects for a while before he can do any police work. Twenty minutes, easy."

"I'll take it," Burt said, driving off. "It's going to take every second we got to get out of this verkakte situation."

CHAPTER 33

REUVEN TRIED EVERY method he knew to contact Joshua. When texts didn't work he signed on to his dormant social media accounts and sent DMs that ranged from, "Call me please. Love you," to "Are you fucking crazy leave that fucking place! Come to Jerusalem now!" to finally, "If you start a nuclear war, you're grounded for life!" He even tried writing it in emoji, but he didn't know how to communicate, "Don't kill all the Jews" with emojis.

No response.

He sat in an air-conditioned black van with plush leather seats and bottles of sparkling water, though he really craved coffee. Sam made calls next to him, most of which consisted of oblique messages like, "Plan Z is on," and "The package will be delivered," and "Don't eat the kugel, the kugel is from Costco."

Reuven gazed out the window and wondered how things had gone so very wrong. Joshua was smart but also stubborn just like his mother, and Reuven always had a hard time controlling him. Even when he was a baby, Reuven's attempts to potty train Joshua failed miserably and had to be passed over to Sara. So how was he going to talk his teenage son down from launching a nuclear missile? How might he appeal to his sense of familial loyalty -his sanity- and in the process possibly save the world from total destruction? Seriously, how? I'm now asking you.

The van drove to the outskirts of the city and then

turned onto a heavily guarded private road. Or at least what seemed like a heavily guarded private road. Reuven hadn't been on too many private roads, but this definitely seemed like overkill. The road was smoothly paved and didn't seem to have any tire marks on it, as if it had been built that morning for this van alone to traverse, which was at once cool and creepy. The sun descended in a glittering orange orb on the horizon, and Reuven tried to focus on that beauty and push out of his mind that it was exactly how he would describe a nuclear sunset. Eventually it got dark and they arrived at a military checkpoint. Instead of waving the van forward, the armed soldiers waved them off the road, so the driver simply turned off onto the dry, rocky dirt and continued driving. Reuven tried to identify landmarks in case he had to make his way back on his own, but all he saw was dark rolling hills as far as the eye could see.

Eventually they arrived at the base of a mountain, where a man on a camel appeared out of nowhere. The van approached him, and the driver rolled down his window. Reuven half expected the camel to roll down its window, but then remembered that's not how camels work.

"Mordechai Richler was not only a strong Canadian equivalent to Philip Roth, but his later novels surpassed Roth in their surprising narrative forms," the driver said to the man on the camel.

"Many of the Brooklyn gangsters who surrounded Al Capone were Jewish, including Tick-Tock Tannenbaum and the great Bugsy Seigel," the man on the camel replied. "And everyone knows there'd be no Vegas without Bugsy."

Both men nodded, then the man on the camel rode off into the distance, dismounted his camel and sat on a bolder. A few minutes later the ground in front of the van rose up to reveal a secret entryway into a dark tunnel. The van rolled forward into it, and for a while was enveloped in total darkness, provoking a fit of claustrophobic anxiety in Reuven's stomach.

"I once went to a hidden coffee shop in the Lower East

Side where you had to walk through a phone booth," Reuven said to Sam, trying to calm himself. "Yup, pretty, pretty cool, and the coffee was delicious. Hey, you think they'll have coffee where we're going?"

"Quiet," Sam said, annoyed.

Eventually the tunnel came to an end and the van stopped. A man in SWAT gear approached, shinning his flashlight in the driver's face and pointing a machine gun. Slowly, the driver lowered the window.

"Bernie Madoff's behavior was morally reprehensible," the driver said to the man with a gun pointed in his face. "To steal money not only from his wealthy clients but from the Shoah Foundation? Terrible. And not so good for the Jews."

"When it comes to the biggest OGs in the rap game no one talks about MC Search of 3rd Bass. Why do you think that is?" the man in SWAT gear asked.

There was a buzz and the wall in front of the van rose up, flooding them with light. The driver rolled forward into what looked to Reuven like a futuristic docking site out of Star Wars. A tall woman with a Bride of Frankenstein-like streak of white in her long black hair waited for the men in the van to emerge.

"So glad you could make it," she said to Reuven. "I'm Farnaz. I'll be getting you situated."

"Appreciate that," Reuven said. "Is there coffee where I am to be situated?"

Farnaz chuckled, thinking he was kidding, but Sam shot her a look that made her understand just what kind of moron she was dealing with. As you've read this book, you know exactly what kind of moron. "Just follow me," she said.

Farnaz walked Reuven and Sam out of the parking dock and down a series of long florescent-lit hallways until they reached a heavily guarded elevator. One of the officers stepped forward and took photos, then fingerprints, then temperatures from Reuven, Sam, and Farnaz.

"No messing around," Reuven smirked, trying to fight his anxiety.

The elevator opened and five floors down they were re-admitted by a team of security who confirmed their identities again. When the final door buzzed open, Reuven followed Farnaz and Sam into a massive darkly-lit office space with monitors everywhere and an enormous digital map of the world glowing and beeping on the wall above.

"Welcome to the War Room," Farnaz said. "This is where it all goes down."

"But hopefully not, right?" Reuven asked.

"Right . . . "

A tall bald man with dead eyes and a black suit joined them. "This is the man?" he asked, looking Reuven over, deeply unimpressed. "I thought you'd be more impressive."

"Reuven, this is Levy," Farnaz said. "He'll be your companion in the launch room."

"Hey there, roomie," Reuven smiled, and Levy rolled his eyes.

As they walked to a private room beyond the map of the world, Farnaz explained everything. Mostly, it was what Sam had told Reuven before they'd left Jerusalem. There was an Israeli nuclear launch site in Jordan at a location that had been lost years before. There was speculation that Reuven's son Joshua was there helming the panel, and was therefore in charge of a nuclear arsenal that if aimed directly at Israel, could mean the end of the Jewish People. Reuven's mission, whether he chose to accept it or not, was to use the direct communication system established between the two sites to talk his son down to sanity again, and oh, if he could find out his location, that would be really swell too.

"Should be no problem," Reuven said.

"Our protocols require that only two people can be in the launch room at once. Until Dr. Rabinsky arrives, that will mean you and Levy."

"Sounds fine. Any chance I could get that cup of coffee I was asking for earlier?"

"No hot liquids allowed in the launch room. You

understand." Farnaz keyed a code into a thick safe-like door, which opened with a slow swoosh into the launch room. "Good luck, Gentlemen."

The room was cold and dark with an extra-large TV screen and a single seat placed before a panel of nobs and pulleys, like in the cockpit of an airplane. Under a glass case were four keys standing upright in their keyholes.

"Is that for the nukes?" Reuven asked.

"I will stand here by the door as is protocol," Levy said, as the massive door shut behind him. "Press the green button to your right and the video feed will transfer directly to the launch room in Jordan. If the man sitting before you is your son, proceed. If not, quickly press the button again, which will hang up the feed. Do you understand?"

"I think so."

"And yes, the keys under the glass are for launching the nuclear bomb. But let's try to avoid that, shall we?"

"Of course."

"What happens next will have a lasting impact on the entire human race," Levy warned. "Try not to shit the bed."

"No pressure," Reuven said.

Reuven sat down and looked up at the giant screen in front of him. "I'm ready to speak to my son," he said to no one in particular. He pressed the green button and the screen blipped on for a second, turned to fuzz, and then Reuven found himself staring up at a man in a dark room like his own, wearing a Bedouin robe and sipping from a Turkish coffee glass. Reuven was about to press the green button again as instructed when he realized that this was indeed his son, just less the smooth-faced child from mere months ago, and more a full-grown young adult in a Bedouin robe.

Reuven looked at Joshua, and then back at Levy and said, "Hey, how come he gets to have coffee?"

Joshua just rolled his eyes.

CHAPTER 34

AT HIS HOME in Metuchen, New Jersey, Burt's old army buddy Dr. Jerry Goiler (aka "The Professor,") opened his front door to three fugitives from the law.

"How come every time you come to visit there's some kind of problem?" he asked.

"Get out of my way, you old sea biscuit. I need to use the bathroom," Burt said pushing forward, and Molly followed quickly behind him.

Sara stood there with her tray of vaccine and excrement samples, and the smell quickly wafted into the doctor's nostrils. "Is that? . . . "

"Human and goat samples. Oh, and a possible vaccine to myotonia congenita."

The Professor looked at Sara like she was insane, then he peeked over her shoulder to make sure no one was watching before ushering her in and closing the door.

When Molly and Burt returned from the bathroom there was a fresh pot of coffee, and they all sat around the kitchen table together. They talked The Professor through everything. How Sara finally regained her memory, how a text from her son included a written formula that led to a vaccine that worked on the goats and then also Burt and Molly to cure myotonia congenita. How the only physical side effects had been explosive diarrhea and vomiting for about twenty minutes, which is a big price to pay, because dry cleaning is expensive. And then, of course, how they had assaulted a police officer in Tennessee and injected him with the vaccine since the officer seemed to be in cahoots with a powerful cabal of police officers who knew that Sara was alive and was looking to capture her and possibly kill her all over again. The Professor listened to the story with a severe expression on his face. He then turned to Sara and her tray of samples and neon green liquid.

"Bring those samples to my lab immediately," The Professor said. "We have work to do."

It took hours for Sara to convince The Professor that the chemical compounds that led to the neon green liquid she'd created were safe. In scientific fashion, he questioned her process, the purity of the elements, criticized the tiny sample of people she'd used to base her research on. When Sara acknowledged all of those shortcomings, The Professor closed his eyes and shook his head.

"This can never work," he said. "I'm sorry but the answer is a final no. There simply aren't enough test cases."

With his eyes closed, the Professor didn't see Sara slip on her burlap Chainsaw Massacre mask, but when he opened them again he witnessed the terrifying spectacle of her jumping in the air, fingers outstretched like claws, yelling at the top of her lungs.

"Why?" the Professor gasped as he froze in a myotonic spell.

Sara knew he could still hear her. She removed her mask. "How would you like to widen the amount of test cases right now?" she asked him, and The Professor managed to roll his eyes.

When the Professor regained control of his muscles, he became the third human test case of Sara's vaccine. Sara was surprised at how queasy The Professor was around needles, and then after she injected him how much more vomit and diarrhea he exhumed than even Burt and Molly. She wasn't sure if she should tell him this, because who wants to know they're the best at shitting and vomiting?

"I'm *schvitzing*," The Professor said, emerging from the bathroom with his samples. "And *plotzing*."

Sara already had a butcher's knife leveled at The Professor's face when he emerged. To be sure that he was healed she threw the blade, and it careened over the Professor's shoulder and hit a vase, which fell to the floor and broke.

"Mother's ashes!" The Professor gasped, looking down at the broken vase. But he did not faint. He shook his head, looked at his hands, and then very seriously at Sara. "We still need more test cases," he said. "Clinical testing must be elaborate and that will take months. Maybe even years."

"Agreed," Sara said. "At least a few hundred more test subjects before Stage Two."

Sara was making a note when Molly ran into the lab looking pale. "It's the damned TV again," she said. "Better come quick."

Sara and the Professor followed Molly into the den, where Burt was rubbing his hands together in worry. On the TV screen were photos of Joshua and Reuven on a split screen.

"This can't be good," Sara said. Split screens are rarely good.

A reporter's voice spoke over the images, "Sources have confirmed that Joshua and Reuven Schtinkler are each seated at the helm of different nuclear launching sites that are pointed at each other in a stand-off. If one pushes the button to launch a nuclear attack then it might trigger an all-out nuclear shoot out and that could mean . . . the end of humanity as we know it." And with that, the reporter fainted. Another nervous-looking reporter took over. "We will continue reporting on this important issue in a moment, but first, local sports." In the background of the newsroom, you could see people fainting all over the place.

The Professor turned to Sara, who was trying to ward off a panic attack by manifesting the soothing smell of goat urine. "Perhaps under the circumstances we could speed up testing a tad," he said, and Sara nodded vigorously in agreement.

CHAPTER 35

"HEY, HOW COME he gets to have coffee?" Reuven asked, and Joshua rolled his eyes.

"Hello to you too, Dad," he replied.

Reuven looked up at the screen where his son's face stared back at him. He was immediately struck by what a handsome young man he was, so much like Sara with that crazy curly hair. A flush of pride came over Reuven, so much so that he almost forgot that he and Joshua were locked in an existential battle that could mean the end of the human race.

What Joshua saw on the screen reminded right away of the terrible situation they were in and the planet-altering stakes attached. This sweaty, squared-faced man sitting in a futuristic bunker was never one to calm him, especially now. Joshua noticed how worn his dad looked; the dark circles under his eyes, the graying hairs on his temples. He didn't look any wiser, just worn.

"Are they feeding you okay?" Reuven asked his son. "You look thin."

"There's a Michelin Star chef on staff," Joshua replied, wryly. "It's lobster Thermidor for lunch, thanks for your concern."

"They haven't hurt you, have they?"

Joshua scoffed. "Dad, enough with the kidnapping narrative. It may play on TV but you and I both know I'm here on my own."

"Right, of course." Reuven raised his hands to keep

things peaceful. "That's good to hear. I'm glad you're okay, is all."

A moment passed where Reuven didn't know what to say and Joshua rolled his eyes again. "Well it's been nice catching up, Dad. Really. But I need to get back to monitoring if you and your buddies are going to destroy the world. So . . . "

"I'm sorry about your friend," Reuven found himself saying. "The one who got hurt—"

"You mean the woman who got killed?" Joshua retorted.

"Yeah, her," Reuven said. "I want you to know that I had nothing to do with that. I was only there to bring you home."

"Funny story," Joshua said. "But I saw you with a gun and bulletproof vest."

"That was just—"

"Are they aware you're a reality TV producer, not Rambo?"

"Oh, they know," Reuven said, aware that his son was making fun of him and that he deserved it. "That why I've been so easy to manipulate." Reuven searched his son's face for a shred of sympathy and found none. "I don't suppose you'll tell me where you are? Then this can all be over."

"And I can join your army of Jewish thugs? Hard pass, Dad."

"Nothing like that," said Reuven. "We'll just . . . hang out. Go see the markets and wait for this thing to end."

"It's not going to end," Joshua said. "If this experiment fails, the men in power are going to attack innocent people, all in the name of self-defense."

"Is that what they've told you?"

"It's what I believe. The Jewish Leadership are going to use this situation. They're going to try to control the world."

"And what would so bad about that?" Reuven threw up

his hands. "So, the Jews rule for a bit. Wouldn't it be about time?"

"You can't be serious."

"Why not? Every few hundred years since the dawn of time someone has tried to kill us. Every few hundred years an attempted mass murder where our allies turn the other cheek. So, we ensure our survival for a while by making the rules? Would that be so bad?"

"Ah, the Jewish victim narrative. Yawn."

"We have trauma. It's in our DNA."

"So, you're a victim of your DNA?"

"We all are."

"Whatever," Joshua said. "You and your Maccabees aren't even real Jews. That's the crazy thing."

"Don't be ridiculous."

"Jews are supposed to abide by a moral code. That's the whole point of religion. That's what the Torah is—a bunch of stories meant to influence people to be nicer to each other. You think morality is some kind of birthright? That you're automatically moral because you had a *bar mitzvah* party at Powerhouse Studios? A person should only be considered Jewish if they at least try to be good."

"It's more complicated than that—"

"Mom was good," Joshua cut in. "She lived by a moral code. She tried to help people. She tried to save the whole world."

"I agree with that."

"And yet you cheated on her. Adultery. That's a bad one in the Torah, right? I think it made it into the top ten list."

Reuven sighed, both because he regretted his adultery and because he couldn't remember if it was in the Ten Commandments. "I know you won't understand this, but I loved your mother very much. We had a lot of good years together. But our marriage had been fading for a while."

"Victim mentality again. Do you ever take responsibility for anything, Dad? Or is everything someone else's fault in your mind?"

"I had a different upbringing. I've experienced different things than you."

"Oh no, not your traumatic three years at a private school where some rich kid drew a swastika on your geography textbook again. Am I allowed to nap?"

"That's not fair."

"Why?"

"Because that was a real thing for me!"

The door to Reuven's room buzzed and then opened with a swish. Levy exited the room, and in his place Rabinsky entered with his perfect hair and expensive suit.

"One-Punch Schtinkler," Rabinsky said. "Hello, Joshua."

"Enter the puppet master." Joshua sighed.

"Joshua, don't be disrespectful," Reuven said. He turned to Rabinsky. "Would you mind if I get this time alone with my son? I think we're uh, getting somewhere."

"Of course," Rabinsky said with a smile. "I'll just stand here where I'm supposed to, per protocol. But I've been listening in. And honestly, Reuven, it doesn't sound like you're getting anywhere at all."

"Yeah, well."

"Must feel strange knowing that your fifteen-year-old is more of a man than you."

"Excuse me?" Reuven asked.

"Well, listen to him and listen to you," Rabinsky went on. "He's talking about Judaism at its core. Values, morals, tradition. You're sitting there crying about Junior High School like it was anything more than a test of manhood that you failed." Rabinsky took a step towards the screen and looked directly up at Joshua. "What do you say we cut your dad out of this and talk just between us? Bring it back to religion and morals?"

"Fat chance," Joshua replied.

"I want to hear what it is that you want, Joshua. I'm in a position to give it for you. To begin with, I can offer you a seat at the table in the new government. To air your grievances, change people's minds about policy towards peace. You will have an official position in the Jewish Leadership where you can make change from the inside. You can even bring some of the people from the *kibbutz*. So, what do you say to that?"

"Nice pitch," Joshua said. "I'm going to think about it."

"Oh, good!"

"Thought about it," Joshua cut in. "You can shove it back up your ass now."

Rabinsky reddened.

"Joshua!" Reuven said, aghast.

"You're in way over your head, kid," Rabinsky snapped, no longer able to hold in his rage. "Do you even understand what's at stake here? Do you know that the people you're helping are murderers and anti-Semites?"

"You mean Gentiles?" Joshua yawned.

"Yes!" Rabinsky said. "Tell us your location and we'll get you out of there. You have my word. Where are you? Where are you, you fucking twit?!"

"Was this the plan, Dad? Good cop dumb cop?" Joshua asked.

"Hey," Reuven turned to Rabinsky. "Watch how you speak to my son, all right?"

"Oh, shut up, Reuven," Rabinsky snapped back. "You're nothing but a mark. We groomed you all the way through this. And now your own son is outsmarting you, and he's right. You're not even a real Jew. You're just a schmuck who's obsessed with a Middle School bully. Do you even know where Robert Thurston III is today? He's a recovering heroin addict in Vancouver. Had surgery and now he has to shit into a colostomy bag. His dad lost all his money in the recession."

"Really?" Reuven marveled.

"No, you idiot. He's a hedge fund manager living in the Bay Area. Plays squash on the weekends with Elon Musk. His wife is a tantric yoga instructor who runs a charity for abused children. His three kids are all at Winsor Academy, and Harvard is a lock. Don't you see? The anti-Semites always win. And you always lose."

"Oh."

Rabinsky pulled a gun from his jacket and pointed it at Reuven's head. "We tried to do this the easy way, Joshua. A conversation with Daddy. But it's too annoying, and you've already wasted too much time," Rabinsky sneered as he looked directly into the camera. "Now it's time for my way. You tell me your location immediately or your only living parent gets shot in the head. Understand me, son?"

"I do," Joshua said. "And I have to say I'm impressed. Must have taken some digging to find that info on my dad's middle school bully. But guess what? I've also done some homework on you over the months, or should I say that my friend hacked into your ancestry.com profile, which she said was surprisingly easy. Who's makes their password 'password' anymore? Anyway, you talk a lot about your grandfather being a Holocaust survivor, but I found out who he really was. Haim Schneider, not Rabinsky. He worked with the Nazis, helped them round up his own people, didn't he? That's why you changed your name. He was a coward of the worst kind and you've got his coward blood surging through your coward veins."

"Lies!" Rabinsky yelled, pushing the gun deeper into Reuven's head.

"Is this photo a lie?" Joshua said, holding up a black and white. "Your granddaddy with Eichmann himself? He's smiling in that photo. I wonder why? Maybe Eichmann told a joke about kikes? You know, I can really see the resemblance too. Especially the hair."

"Joshua, I'm not certain this is helping," Reuven said, feeling the gun at his head shake.

"Apple didn't fall far from the tree, huh?" Joshua pushed on. "Helping to eradicate your own people for power. A coward makes a coward makes a coward."

"Son of a bitch!" Rabinsky reddened, rage coiling and

pulsing in his neck. "I should have finished you off when I did your mother!"

Reuven cranked his head. "You said it was neo-Nazis."

"Who cares who it was? She had to be stopped," Rabinsky seethed. "And I paid a pretty penny for those scum bag Nazis to go jail for the rest of their lives to do it. Funded a whole new KKK chapter in Alabama."

"So you did kill her?" Joshua said.

"And what if I did? What the hell are you going to do about it?"

Eyes welling, Joshua flipped open the glass case on the nuclear panel and put his hand on the keys. An alarm went off in both rooms, a red alert.

"What are you doing?" Rabinksy said, suddenly aware of his mistake. "Take your hand off that thing. You're just a kid."

"A kid whose mom you killed."

"You don't have the balls," Rabinsky said. "You're not like your father. You have no idea what it's like to spill real blood!"

Reuven looked up at Joshua and then down at his hands and watched them curl into fists. A flash of red rage surged through his veins, and he pulled back and elbowed Rabinsky so hard in the gut that his gun flew across the room and Rabinsky collapsed on the floor gasping. Reuven got up and retrieved the weapon. He tucked it in his pants, walked over to Rabinsky and yanked him up by his thick graying hair. Over his shoulder through the small window in the door, Reuven saw soldiers lining up to get in. Reuven pulled out the gun again and held it to Rabinsky's temple.

"You kill me and you're dead," Rabinsky yelled. "Your son is dead! Your whole family is dead!"

"Oh, I'm not going to kill you, Rabinsky. That wouldn't be any fun." Reuven put the safety on the gun and put it back in his pocket. Then, legs spread wide like he'd learned in boxing class, he reeled back and punched Rabinsky right in the jaw. Rabinsky fell back onto the floor, his teeth scattering in every direction like Chiclets.

"Dad, look out!"

The door busted open and security came rushing into the room, machine guns leveled at Reuven. Reuven jumped back to the panel and raised the glass enclosure. He held his hands on the launch keys.

"Back off or I do it!" Reuven shouted at the soldiers.

"And if he launches, I launch!" Joshua said on the screen above.

Rabinsky yelled from the ground through a mouth full of blood. "Shoot him, goddamn it!"

The soldiers looked unsure. Both the Schtinkler men had their hands on the nuclear keys, and one false move would mean global, mutual destruction.

"Hey, Josh," Reuven said. "What do you say we go see mom?"

"Let's go see mom," Joshua said.

And they both closed their eyes.

CHAPTER 36

"WILL THIS THING even fly?" Sara asked, skeptically.

Sara and The Professor stood in a field in Lamington, New Jersey, along with Burt and Molly who watched on. Cows mooed in the distance, so completely obsessed with their own cow concerns that they were totally unaware of what was happening with the humans nearby. There was a big dilapidated barn, dried up cornfields, and a long dirt landing strip that cut off at the woods. The Professor oiled the hinges of a rusty yellow propeller plane.

"Ol' Nelly used to top corn with the best of 'em," replied the Professor. "I'll bet my life she's got at least one more run in her."

"You may have to," Molly said, and that made Sara even more uneasy.

Sara and The Professor had spent all night and well into the morning refining the formula for a vaccine to human myotonia congenita. They used enthalpy formation to determine the expansion of properties for safe mass production; fractional distillation and latent heat to create a chelate carbon chain; and an endocrine disruptor with a triple bond to trigger an ionic reaction that exhibited isomerism without leachate; they'd even added rugelach crumbs. In the end they produced four enormous vats of the vaccine; enough to fill up three kid's swimming pools or fill the tank of a crop duster plane to capacity. Based on

Sara's calculations it was enough vaccine to inoculate a small town in a concentrated population, if injected. But it was The Professor who'd figured out that the vaccine could be turned into a mist, ingestible thought inhalation and ocular reception—through the mouth and the eyes. If they could simply get a group of people to open their eyes and/or mouths wide enough at the same time, then the mist would work like a simultaneous injection, and provide more test cases, or at least that's what The Professor hypothesized.

"Time to meet our maker," The Professor said, again making Sara very worried at the poor choice of words. The Professor climbed into the plane's cockpit and turned on the propellers— sounded like a box of nails caught in a turbine. "You coming?" he asked Sara.

Sara looked at Molly and Burt. They'd been so wonderful to her. She gave them each a big hug. "Wish me luck," she said, tearing up.

"Since we met you, Sara, you've been making your own luck. Someone up there is watching you. I just swear it to be true."

Sara climbed onto the plane and into the seat behind the Professor. The propeller turned freely now, and the aircraft thrust forward on the dirt landing strip with a jolt.

"The flying ban is still on," The Professor said. "So, if we get up we'll need to fly low to avoid being detected."

"What do you mean 'if we get up'?"

The plane picked up speed and then unsteadily took flight above the runway and over the trees. Sara didn't know that she was afraid of heights until that very moment, which is an appropriate but inconvenient time to realize it. She used deep nasal breathing to calm herself.

"Well I'll be damned, she got up!" The Professor laughed. He seemed surprised.

Sara fought off queasiness as they flew over forests and farms and elevated water tanks and green fields. If she weren't so nauseous it would have been a real sight to see.

Eventually, The Professor spotted a sign down below for a new town.

"There it is. Summit, New Jersey," he said.

Sara had assured The Professor that Summit was the least Jewish, WASPiest town in the region, and that their Sunday Farmer's Market was the shiniest example of that WASP culture. Instead of hummus the vendors sold crab dip; instead of babka it was bunt cake. The lobster rolls were mostly mayonnaise and the people of Summit liked it that way. Sara watched as the farms of New Jersey receded beneath her and a large town with more than one William Sonoma materialized. When they arrived near the Farmer's Market, the crowd was more robust than usual. They were having their annual Kid's Talent Show, and a local camera crew was there filming as a little blonde girl in equestrian apparel sang the theme song to *My Little Pony* on stage. The little girl was unaware that her parents were part of Reuven's *Wet, Hot American Bronies* presentation tape. Throngs of parents in soft helmets, Vineyard Vines shorts, and tennis shirts pointed iPhones and cheered the girl on. Others shopped for chicken pot pie, club sandwiches, and onion dip for later. When the crowd of market patrons heard a rumble in the sky, they worried it might be a sudden thunderstorm that could rain them out. Many turned their phones from the stage to the clouds. And then they saw it—something they'd rarely seen in this area in months—a low flying propeller plane.

"Someone's flying!" a mom shouted. "Be careful!"

The camera person, who'd been lazily covering this quaint community event titled her lens up to the sky, hoping she might catch a newsworthy emergency landing helmed by some over-confident fainter.

"When I get directly above them, I need you to pull the red lever to your left," The Professor called out to Sara. "That will release the vaccine. And careful, Sara. We only have one shot at this!"

Sara eyed the Farmer's Market in the distance. There

was a good population of people looking up; some had their mouths open in surprise. The Professor veered the plane towards them and with all of Sara's might, she pulled the lever.

"It's stuck!" Sara yelled to the Professor. "It won't budge it!"

"I've got some oil!" The Professor said, and passed back a small canister. "Let's hope that's enough!"

The plane flew past the farmer's market and the Professor made a wide turn to take another shot. The camerawoman managed to zoom in close enough to get an image of the pilot and the passenger on the plane. She couldn't believe her eyes when he saw Sara's unmistakable mane of copper curls flowing in the wind.

"Unless my eyes are fooling me, that's Dr. Sara Schtinkler on that plane," she said.

Someone in the crowd overheard her. "It's Sara Schtinkler! She's alive!"

All of the cellphones now turned up to the sky to capture footage and confirm this miracle. The reporter grabbed a microphone and pulled the camera towards him.

"This is Rory Charles reporting live from the Summit Farmer's Market in Summit, New Jersey, where a propeller plane is circling that seems to have, among its two passengers, the recently deceased scientist, Dr. Sara Schtinkler! That's something you don't see every day." The camera tilted up to the sky as the plane made another low flying loop around the market. "The question everyone's asking here is how did Dr. Schtinkler survive the explosion at The Center for Animal Oddities? Why on earth is she in a propeller plane flying above the Summit Farmer's Market? And what's better with olive martinis, Strawberry Shortcake or Fondue?"

Up in the sky Sara emptied the canister of oil onto the lever but it still wouldn't budge. "It's not working!" she yelled to The Professor.

"Pull it harder!"

A military drone fitted with missiles appeared on the horizon. On the ground, an army van filled with soldiers in full SWAT gear controlled the deadly machine.

"The order is shoot to kill," the Commanding Sergeant in the van said, and then he fainted, so another Sergeant took his seat. "Uh, shoot to kill."

The Professor spotted the drone in the distance and knew that time was not on their side. "I'm pulling back around!" he yelled back at Sara. "But this is our last chance!"

The plane made a loop. As the drone followed close behind, the Professor made his descent over the crowd.

"Now!"

Sara grabbed the lever and screamed. She thought about Joshua and Spencer, Lilia, and Chewy, and summoned all the power left in her body when at last she felt the lever give with a satisfying click. A lot of clicks are satisfying, but this was possibly the most satisfying click of all time.

"Shoot him, goddamnit!" Rabinsky yelled at the soldiers. "They don't have the balls to turn those keys!" He lay on the ground with his mouth filled with blood, his broken teeth jutting out like misshapen stalactites. "I said shoot, you idiots!"

Reuven's hands held firm on the launch keys as did Joshua's on the massive screen above. The soldiers hesitated, guns raised but confused by a situation that seemed way above their paygrade. At least they should be bribed for this.

One soldier cocked his gun and pointed it at Reuven when Farnaz, with her Bride of Frankenstein hair a shade whiter than before, ran in, eyes bulging and red.

"Stop!" she yelled as if the world depended on it, and it did. "There's something on the news you need to see."

Farnaz pointed a remote control at the screen, and at once a local newsfeed from America was patched in.

"This is Rory Charles reporting live from Summit, New Jersey, where I can now confirm that the passenger on the propeller plane flying above the local farmer's market is Dr. Sara Schtinkler. It's not clear what she's doing on the plane at this point. It has circled twice and seems to be turning back around. If you look up at this shot, you can see her glorious hair flying in the wind." The camera zoomed in, and on a rusty dust cropper, was a man in goggles and in the seat behind him, Sara.

"Mom!" Joshua shouted.

"Sara?" Reuven said, stunned.

"She's alive?!" Rabinsky snarled. "Somebody owes me a refund."

The camera panned from the yellow propeller plane to an ominous black drone that followed close behind, its sharp missiles pointing.

"It seems that the military has come in with a drone," the reporter said breathlessly. "Hopefully just to urge the plane to land safely so that we can thank Dr. Schtinkler for her service. But it looks aggressive. Oh, don't hurt her, you mean drone!"

Rabinsky smiled through the blood. "Go ahead, Joshua, launch the missiles. Then you'll never get to see your dear sweet mother again."

"This is what you wanted all along, isn't it?" Reuven said, cutting him off. "If a missile is launched from Jordan you'll claim Israel is under attack. That will give you the right to counter-attack. You've wanted war all along."

"Wow, what a genius you are," Rabinsky said. He shot up and grabbed a gun from the holster of one of the soldiers. Reuven saw a flicker of light and felt a searing pain enter his body.

"Dad, no!" Joshua shouted.

Reuven looked down at his stomach and saw that it was soaked in dark blood. He thought blood was a lighter color. It is blood, isn't it? He's not leaking motor oil? No, he remembered a CSI where the blood was dark red. Never mind. The room went fuzzy and his ears buzzed. He knew that he was going to pass out, but before he did, he pulled the keys out from the nuclear launching panel, placed them on his tongue, and right before the world turned upside down the last thing he remembered doing was swallowing.

"Open fire!" the Commanding Sergeant in a military van in Summit, New Jersey said before fainting.

"But there are civilians below, Sarge," the soldier manning the drone said, as he fainted on top of him.

"I said, open fire, soldier!" the next Commanding Sergeant yelled to the next soldier in line.

He fired off both of its missiles before collapsing in the heap of bodies. And as the world watched on live TV the drone's missiles blasted forth through the air towards the plane, which veered at the last second, barely evading the strike, and the rockets careened past and into a parking lot full of Teslas.

"Pull the damn lever, Sara!" the Professor shouted.

"I got it!" Sara yelled back, as the lever finally gave.

Down below the attendees of the Farmer's Market looked up in awe as the propeller plane swooped above and a sheet of neon green mist fell onto their open-mouthed faces. The Commanding Sergeant in charge of the drone stepped out of the van to watch and caught a healthy mouthful of the mist as well. You could hear the collective groan on live TV as everyone (including the reporters and camera people, the parents, and even the little girl in her equestrian costume) all began to experience the explosive side-effects of Sara's vaccine.

"Sorry!" Sara said as the plane flew past.

Around the world people were glued to their TV sets

watching the Professor's propeller plane fly off into the sunset as down below crowds suffered from an outbreak of diarrhea and vomiting that could best be described as yucky and at worst described as not appropriate for TV. The reporter Rory Charles, heroically reported through his own spell, wincing into the shaking camera, "Dr. Sara Schtinkler's plane seems to have escaped missile fire and has sprayed us locals with some kind of green mist."

"It's a vaccine!" a woman shouted from the background. "I'm not fainting! Look!" The woman, who was covered in her own vomit and feces, slapped her husband's face hard, a sure trigger for a myotonic reaction. "He's staying awake!"

Other wives followed suit, slapping their spouses in the face only to watch in wonder as they did not faint, but did have violent fits of vomiting and diarrhea.

"We're cured!" a man with a bloody lip and soiled pants screamed out in bliss.

"Dr. Sara Schtinkler saved us!" another exclaimed between dry heaves.

Joshua and all of the people of Israel, Jordan, and the world watched it play out in real time.

"You're the G.O.A.T.," Joshua said to the screen. "Greatest of All Time."

And just like his father had, Joshua pulled the keys out of the nuclear launch panel, placed them in his mouth and swallowed.

CHAPTER 37

THEY SAY THAT history is written by the victors. In the case of the end of human myotonia congenita it was all of humanity who won, and therefore all of humanity who agreed that their future ancestors might be better off not hearing the particulars of the fit of explosive vomiting and diarrhea that sent the entire world racing to the bathroom, always a few seconds too late.

When the U.N. came together to ask Sara to sign an NDA and to promise not to talk about the grotesque side-effects of her vaccine she vehemently refused, citing scientific ethics and the need to inform and protect future generations. As a result of her non-compliance it is was agreed by World Leaders to simply write Sara out of history. In the revised version The Professor (Dr. Jerry Goiler), who had passed away peacefully in his sleep two months after he released the first batch of vaccine from his propeller plane, would henceforth be known as the architect of the vaccine to human myotonia congenita. Sara would merely be a local farmhand who happened to board his plane when The Professor went to disseminate the vaccine over the Summit Farmer's Market. In exchange for her agreement to abide by the new narrative, Sara was offered her very own goat farm, along with a fully-funded, state-of-the-art laboratory for the rest of her life. Also, she would avoid the dozens of lawsuits aimed at her by attendees of the Summit Farmer's Market who were suing for dry cleaning costs.

The idea of spending the rest of her days reunited with Spencer, Lillia, and Chewy, and doing her work in peace, along with Bruce who she immediately hired on as her Chief Lab Technician, all appealed to Sara, and in the end she signed the agreement. Who needed the attention anyways?

Similarly, both Reuven and Joshua were asked to sign NDAs to bury their involvement in a father-son nuclear showdown that almost ended in global annihilation. For their troubles, Reuven, who recovered from a bullet wound that had missed his major arteries, was given a small cash settlement and also a signed talent deal with CAA for his as-yet-unwritten screenplay. Joshua was offered fully paid tuition to the university of his choice, but he turned that down to volunteer at a local arts organization for kids, along with Brie. Joshua's "History of The World" puppet show remains a big hit. Reuven friended Joshua on 247backgammon.org, and the two went from playing aggressive wordless games to sometimes texting while they played. Reuven even suggested they play in person sometime soon, and when Joshua didn't say no, Reuven wept with joy.

And so, with that messy bit of history tucked away The Schtinklers became anonymous again. Just a regular Jewish family from New Jersey who returned from Israel after the pandemic ended and watched the world deal with the aftermath.

Front and center in the news, Dr. Jacob Rabinsky was arrested for conspiracy to commit mass murder, and was given many life sentences along with an itchy orange prison suit that made his ass look fat. Sam too, and many other of The Maccabees were brought to justice for their violent crimes, though many of the neo-Nazis they'd beaten up refused to press charges. Which is pretty cool of neo-Nazis.

Those not entangled in legal battles commenced healing. A global commitment to health and stress reduction weaved into popular culture (making the yoga app GloFit the highest traded IPO in history), and the planet became healthier overall. Still, there were little-known side-effects to being cured that didn't seem to go away. Communities across the world craved strange foods like tabbouleh and baba ganoush. Zabar's expanded globally, opening more locations than Starbucks and in places as remote as Papa New Guinea. The Beastie Boys, Leonard Cohen, and The Grateful Dead all shot up the Pop Music charts, and Larry David was showered with Emmys and a Nobel Prize for a record 19th season of *Curb Your Enthusiasm*.

At dinner tables around the world debating flourished, but also complaining about small things that bothered you. "Giving lip" thrived even in cultures where peace and tranquility were sacrosanct. The Dalai Lama himself wondered aloud why United Airlines had to charge extra for luggage only to squeeze you into seats so small you had to eat your knees?

As for me, the writer of this unknown history, 23andMe.com claims that I'm a full 11% Jewish despite my ancestors arriving directly from a small village in Northern Ireland. Perhaps my slice of Jewish DNA is why I'm currently writing this stationed in a gastroenterologist's office, who worries that an ulcer will form if I don't stop it with the chicken-liver sandwiches already. On the plus side, my family, who were never much for exhibiting emotion are deeply worried about my health and have been over-supportive as I experiment with magnesium supplements and steel cut oatmeal. My mother calls me at least twice a day to check-in and to remind me that I can always go to law school if this "book thing" doesn't pan out. Sometimes we talk for hours.

In sum, the world is a bit different now. A little more careful, a lot more vocal, and more prone to bagel and schmear brunch. Word is that Sara Schtinkler called it quits with Reuven, and after submitting to a full beauty makeover from Mitch The Makeup Maven, has been spotted attending lectures with a friendly blue-eyed llama scientist named Scottie Prewitt, who Joshua met and approves of.

"He's kind of like Tom Hanks, if he wasn't Jewish," Joshua told his mom.

"But Tom Hanks isn't Jewish," Sara replied.

"I mean post-vaccine."

Scottie likes to cook and even hosted a Passover Seder at Sara's house last Spring. His matzoh ball soup was raved over by the guests, though behind closed doors everyone agreed that the dryness of his kugel was a *shanda* on the whole tribe.

ACKNOWLEDGEMENTS

I would like to thank John Baltisberger, Publisher at *Aggadah Try It* and *Madness Heart Press*. Perusing Twitter I thought I was having a fever dream when I read that you were looking specifically for Jewish speculative fiction. Glad it was real, and that you liked my book enough to publish it. Would also like to thank Editor Maxwell Bauman for your brilliant suggestions, edits and overall (big) contribution to the manuscript. Such a pleasure working with you!

Special thanks to Ethan T. Berlin—genius comedy writer, inspired teacher and friend. Your feedback and jokes made this book far better (and funnier) than it ever would have been without you. Eternally grateful!

Finally, to my darling wife Liz and son Evan for dealing with me while I wrote this book, and to my parents and brother David for reading early drafts and always encouraging me to write.

ABOUT THE AUTHOR

Jeff Oliver is the author of the novels *Failure To Thrive*, and *The Two-Plate Solution*, which earned a Starred review in Publishers Weekly: "Fully human characters make this hilarious send up a standout." A veteran TV producer, Jeff developed the hit series *Cutthroat Kitchen*, and has worked on reality classics like *Big Brother*, *Last Comic Standing*, and *Watch What Happens Live with Andy Cohen*. Jeff lives in Maplewood, New Jersey with his family and a clingy dog named Luna. You can find him at jeffoliver.tv.